Off Pitch

New York Stars Book 1

Ashley Bow

Contents

Author's Note

Off Pitch is a romantic comedy full of spice and laughter. There is some content to be aware of, though.

- Explicit language

- Explicit sex scenes

- Alcohol-consumption

- Misogyny (not between the two main characters)

- Image-based sexual abuse (not between the two main characters)

These may be difficult for some readers, so please consider yourself first—you are your number one priority, and your mental health matters.

For readers unfamiliar with baseball, there is a **glossary** in the back with every baseball term used in the story! It's there for your reference whenever you need it.

<u>A special thank you to:</u>

Larry
Hannah
Lauren
Emy
Alina
Natalia
Lizan
Emaan
Maria

This book wouldn't be here without you. Words cannot express how much I love and appreciate each of you.

To the ones that can take care of themselves but still dream of finding love... and a man with a dirty mouth.

New York Stars Roster

Pitchers
Damian Anderson (#38) – SP
Fernando Arevalo (#20) – RP
Monte Calderon (#10) – RP
Su-jin Choi (#41) – SP
Evan Fowler (#45) – SP
Miguel Gutierrez (#23) – RP
Jessie Lutz (#29) – RP
Byron Morrow (#43) – SP
Koji Okada (#11) – RP
Chris Rockman (#18) – RP/CP
Grant Shaffer (#31) – RP
Knox Spencer (#49) – SP
Collin Ware (#32) – RP

Catchers
Arturo Rivas (#6) – C
Martin Scholl (#8) – C

<u>Infielders</u>

Jay Bonner (#24) – 1B/3B

Tyler Dailey (#17) – 2B/SS

Josh Garro (#34) – 3B

Alejandro Pena (#35) – 2B

Cole Pierce (#27) – SS

Eric Waller (#19) – 1B

<u>Outfielders</u>

Rafael Ayala (#26) – LF

Lane Brooks (#15) – CF

Neil Mansfield (#12) – RF/DH

Jeff Novak (#28) – RF/CF

Andrew Pelton (#13) – LF/DH

Prologue

Seven years earlier...

"WHAT THE..." I SAY, stepping into my apartment hallway after my shower.

I adjust the towel wrapped around my hips as I start to follow the trail of discarded clothing leading to my bedroom door.

Skirt.

Blouse.

Bra.

Panties.

And I can feel the excitement stir below my waist when I know I'm going to find my favorite brunette beauty on the other side of the door.

"Emily," I say, pushing my door open. "What are you doing?"

"Waiting for you," I hear her voice reply in the dark. When she flips on the bedside lamp, I can finally take her in.

Completely bare, save for a pair of red high heels.

"Fuck, Em." I'm across the room in seconds, my towel dropping as soon as I start climbing on the bed to descend on her. "What the fuck did I do to deserve this?"

She runs her finger up my throat before resting it under my chin, turning me to face her. "We still need to celebrate you, Knox."

"All it took was getting drafted first overall to earn this, huh?"

Emily leans up to kiss me as she slowly lets her legs drift open. "Let me show you how proud I am of you, baby."

With my last coherent thought, I grab the box of condoms I keep in my nightstand.

There's no way in hell I'm letting her leave my bed tonight.

One

Harlow

I DON'T KNOW HOW Ella doesn't break her finger with that rock sitting atop it. Mine hurts just looking at it.

"Josh can't do simple, can he?" Lucia laughs as Ella waves her hand around, finally showing off the engagement ring we've been dying to see.

"You know him, right?" Ella replies. "There was no way that man didn't go for the biggest diamond he could find."

"He's the epitome of go big or go home," Rory says as she tucks her dark, curly hair behind her ear.

I take Ella's hand and inspect the ring for myself. "And he's absolutely mad about you." I let go of her hand, and she rests it on the table. "How's his leg feeling now?"

"So much better," Ella replies happily. "He's so excited to be back on the field for Opening Day tomorrow."

"We're glad he's going to be back, too," I reply. "The Stars couldn't even survive the first round of the playoffs last year without him."

Lucia swishes the glass of red wine in her hand. "Blame him for not stretching enough during training. If he did, he might not have torn his ACL."

Rory eyes her mischievously. "Shouldn't we blame the trainers for not making him stretch enough?"

"The players are grown men," Lucia chides, crossing her arms. "I can't make them do shit. I can advise them, but it's on them to actually do it."

"There's no way my dad doesn't get on their asses to listen to you and the other trainers, Luc," Rory replies back.

"Well," I say, steering the conversation back, "let's get back to why we're even at dinner tonight." I turn to Ella now. "We're so excited for you and Josh." Lucia, Rory, and I raise our wine glasses in a toast. "To the future Mrs. Garro."

Ella smiles happily as we all clink our glasses together before sipping and setting them back on the table.

Lucia faces me now, pushing her silky black hair behind her shoulder. "You know, Lo, talking about that story would really help out your blog. A player engagement would bring in viewers."

"I write about their stats, Luc, not their damn personal lives. That has nothing to do with how they're performing."

"Writing about their personal lives would probably help you reach a larger audience, though," she says, popping a cherry tomato off her fork.

She's right—that would help me significantly. *Starred and Fast* does well enough, but I've struggled to get it out there. I have some very loyal followers, but I need more. Rent isn't cheap in NYC. My ad revenue is enough to keep me afloat, but I don't want to "float" forever—I want to expand and be seen. My brother, Cole, is a great shortstop for the Stars but keeps a relatively low profile, enjoying a quiet life rather than trying to become a household name. And not that I want to ride on my brother's coattails, but his desire for privacy is not doing me any favors in getting myself noticed.

"I honestly don't know how I feel about that, Luc. I don't want to become a tabloid reporting on everything they do. I want to keep my focus on the game's workings and how the players perform."

"I think you could find a balance, Harlow," Rory adds. "Your readers can get the game and player stats on any sports website, so you need to do something to stand out."

"I know," I respond with a sigh. "That's what I'm hoping I can do with the interviews. I'll finally be able to give an in-depth look at the people themselves. The players never really get a chance to control the narrative surrounding them, and the personnel is all but forgotten amid the team's performance. I want to give them a voice, too. They're just as much a part of the success as the players themselves."

"I seriously love that idea!" Ella exclaims. "It shouldn't be too hard for you to get interviews with anyone because of your brother. I'm assuming you'll start with Cole?"

I shake my head. "You would think so, but considering my brother tries to live in obscurity, he doesn't want extra attention on him right now." I use my thumb to point at Rory sitting next to me. "I have Rory set up for my first interview tomorrow. Since she's Skipper's daughter and Lane's nanny, I figure she'll be a good start to get this side of the blog off the ground."

I've always found it odd that the Field Manager—essentially the head coach—is called Skipper in baseball. Since it wouldn't be right to call him Coach Fisher, everyone just calls him Skip.

"You're interviewing personnel, and you're not interviewing me, your best friend?" Lucia places her hand on her chest in mock offense. "I can't believe you, Pierce." She dabs away a tear that isn't there. "I thought we were closer than that."

"I'm interviewing one of our *other* best friends, Luc," I reply, playfully shoving her shoulder as she laughs. "You're on my list, though. I just think Rory and her *take-no-shit-and-give-no-apologies* attitude will be the perfect starting point. Plus, Paul was a hall-of-fame player—everyone knows who she is because of her dad."

"Ooh, you know who else you should interview? Knox Spencer!"

"Seriously, Luc? Knox might entice people with how he looks in baseball pants, but the man is known for hating interviews. I don't think I've ever even seen him smile."

"He looks good in baseball pants, huh?" Rory smirks.

"Hey, I just call it like I see it. But even if he was blessed with such a perky backside, it doesn't make up for his shitty attitude. There's no way the man would ever agree to an interview."

"He's friends with Cole, Josh, and Lane, though," Ella adds.

"And I think he's spoken a total of ten words to me in the three years that I've known him. He never talks when we're all together."

"So wear him down then. Mr. Grumpy Pants could use some of your sunshine to brighten up his rainy parade." Lucia shrugs her shoulders.

Knox Spencer is known across the league for his terrible attitude and the lack of enthusiasm he gives in interviews. The guy can throw a hell of a fastball, and he's one of the only pitchers in the league who can successfully throw a knuckleball. He's damn good at what he does, and he knows it. The media circus around him knows it, too, and they try their damnedest to question him about it. But Knox doesn't care. He shows up for his post-game interviews because he is contractually required to do so. He gives short replies and peels out the moment he's able to.

Getting a guy like that to interview with *Starred and Fast* would be massive for me. Fans love watching him on the mound, but that's the extent to which anyone knows him. He's a mystery, an enigma. So maybe Lucia is right—perhaps he just needs some sunshine to warm him up.

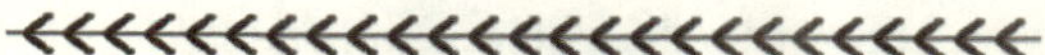

Water cascades around me as I wash away the day, rinsing all my stress down the drain. Dinner with the girls helped, but I can't sate my worry.

Worry about my blog and how I can increase traffic.

Worry about my brother as he starts a new season with the Stars and how he will perform.

Worry about getting friendly enough with the players and having them agree to do interviews with me.

I know it's going to be hard to break through to Knox. But I can't help but feel that there's more to him beneath the surface. Under that gruff exterior could be a heart of gold, someone sympathetic and charming. Knox is one of Cole's closest friends, and Cole is like me—bright and optimistic. He wouldn't keep the company of someone who doesn't have any redeeming qualities. Hopefully, I can learn more about him through the season as I try to become more friendly with the players.

When the hot water runs out, I step out of the shower and into the steamy bathroom, wrapping myself up in one of my favorite plush towels. Standing in front of the mirror, I take a look and see all my freckles prominently displayed across my nose, cheeks, and chest. I never used to mind them, but my ex-boyfriend Derek was not a fan. He always said they made me less attractive. Since then, I've kept them covered with copious amounts of foundation and concealer, rendering them virtually unnoticeable. That's just the way I prefer it now.

I reach for my hair dryer, plug it in, and set it to medium heat. The air blows my hair out as I finger comb my sandy blonde tresses. I'm not a natural blonde. I have to get mine from a salon. For that reason, I've always been jealous of Cole—he has the blonde hair I always dreamed of from years spent outside in the sun. He has the beachy, surfer look that you would expect on somebody out of San Diego, not somebody from freaking Brooklyn.

But I digress.

Once my hair is dry, I switch the dryer off, set it down, and then fan it out over my shoulders. It falls a few inches past my collarbone and has a slight waviness to it. I may hide my freckles, but at least I've always loved my hair.

I head into the main area of my studio apartment and grab a set of flannel pajamas for the night. They aren't cute or anything, but even though it's baseball season, New York City is still cold as shit in April. These will help me stay warm with the dodgy heater that my landlord is dragging his feet on fixing.

Padding my way into the kitchen, I grab myself a glass of wine and head over to my desk, setting the glass down and flipping my laptop open. With tomorrow being Opening Day, I need to make sure this post is ready to go before the game starts just after noon. The rest of my night will be spent right here, editing and perfecting the entry.

Might as well make myself comfortable.

Lucia

What time are you all getting to the stadium today?

Ella

I'm already on my way

Harlow

I'm getting dressed to head out the door as we speak

Rory

Running a bit behind today

Sage had some strawberries for her snack this morning and mashed them all through her hair, so I had to give her a bath

I'm still packing up her bag before I can get her out

Lucia

Are you bringing Sage out to watch the game today?

Rory

I'm going to try to, at least for a bit

The wind is chilly today, so I'll bundle her up and try to catch a couple of innings before we probably end up back in my dad's office, where it's warm

Ella

Good

I can always use some company back there

Lucia

You'll have some company if you come to watch the game with us, Ell

Ella

I could, but I could also watch the game on TV and not have to worry about getting hit with a foul ball

Harlow

Anyway…

Do you think Sage will recognize Lane out there this year, Rory?

Rory

I have no doubt. I've been playing some old games for her throughout the day lately, and every time Lane was up at bat, she would point at the screen and say, "Dada! Dada!"

Lucia

That is so fucking cute!

Harlow

Ugh, Sage gives me such terrible baby fever

Lucia

You need a man again before you can have a baby

Harlow

I don't need a man

Ella

You do if you want a baby

Harlow

I could always adopt, you know

Lucia

Lo, you're twenty-five and single

I hate to be the bearer of bad news, but it's doubtful any adoption agency would accept you

Rory

Which means Harlow needs to get herself some dick

Harlow

Jesus, Rory

Does your dad know you talk like that?

Rory

Hell no

And I would prefer to keep it that way

He still acts like I'm a kid sometimes

I'm twenty-five, for fuck's sake!

Lucia

This is getting off-topic

You coming or what, Harlow?

Harlow

<<<<<<<<<<<<<<<<<<<<<<<<<<<<<<

Beers in hand, I find my way down to our seats. Cole made sure he got our parents and me a set of four season tickets so we could catch as many games as we wanted with an extra ticket to share with whoever we chose. And since the seats are in the front row on the first baseline, we're always right in on the action. Our parents don't make it to many games so that usually leaves me with three tickets I can share with my friends.

When Lucia and Rory join me for any games, they'll sit with me here. It works out well for Lucia since she's an athletic trainer for the team. She needs to be able to get to the field if there's an injury—these are the perfect seats for her to do that. Ella usually stays back during the games, but she'll join us out here sometimes.

I originally started going to games because Cole wanted to. He had started playing Little League and wanted to see what the professionals looked like. The first game we watched saw the Stars beat the Atlanta Thunderbirds in a walk-off grand slam. I've been hooked ever since. I eat, sleep, and breathe baseball now.

That's why I started *Starred and Fast*. I don't have any athletic ability, but I'm a voracious enjoyer. Why not use my knowledge of the sport and help fellow baseball enthusiasts who may not understand all the ins and outs learn about it? I have a number of male followers, but most of my readers are women—ones who started enjoying the sport later in life because of boyfriends, husbands, and friends. Through me, they obtain a better understanding of what's happening.

But that's why I need to expand. I'm currently appealing to a very niche market, which won't be sustainable long term. I want to start these interviews to bring in more people. That's why I have to lay the charm on Knox Spencer. I need to crack open the mystery of the man with the lowest ERA of starting pitchers in the entire league.

"Want one?" I ask Lucia, offering her one of the beers in my hand as I take my seat.

"Can't drink, Lo. You know I'm working during games," she replies, tossing a blanket over my legs. It's barely above freezing today. We're both bundled up in puffy jackets and gloves right now to keep ourselves warm. "Now, let's stop pretending you didn't know that and admit you bought two beers, knowing you'd be drinking both."

I smile in response. "You know me too well."

"You're an open book, Lo," Lucia laughs.

Bringing the ale to my lips, I take a sip and let the hoppy flavor consume me. "Yeah, but the alcohol will help keep me warm today." Lucia just shakes her head at me before we turn our attention to the game.

Lane is today's leadoff batter, followed by Josh and Cole. Lane bats it up the center, but the second baseman nabs it and tosses it to first, tagging him out. Josh strikes out with his at-bat, and then Cole cracks the ball into the outfield, where it's then caught by the left fielder. No runs for the Stars in the first inning, but there are still eight more to go.

Knox Spencer takes the mound at the bottom of the first, pitching a 1-2-3 inning. This is why Knox is so well-known—he's a damn good pitcher. And he keeps up that momentum until the bottom of the sixth when the batter hits a two-run home run. That's when Paul Fisher, the Team Manager and Rory's dad, relieves him for the rest of the game. Knox waves to the crowd as he walks toward the dugout, and relief pitcher Miguel Gutierrez sprints across the infield to take his place on the mound.

Through the next two innings, the Stars bat in a total of three runs, taking the win over the Detroit Hawks 3-2. Fans start pouring out of the stadium as Lucia and I approach the tunnels, joining the players as they head toward the clubhouse. And since I'm now two beers deep with liquid courage flowing through me, now is as good a time as any to start getting to know the players better.

Two

Knox

"Is there anything you would have done differently today?" the reporter asks.

"Not thrown a changeup," I say. The media is always so invasive, especially after a game. Even when we win, they're still scrutinizing my performance, wondering why I pitched a two-run homer in the sixth inning. Because perfection is apparently all I'm allowed. It's fucking irritating.

"Do you think a knuckleball would've been more successful on that pitch?" asks a different reporter, a woman in the back of the room.

"I guess we'll never know."

This here is why I've earned the nickname of Fort Knox. Like the home of the US gold supply, the namesake of this damn nickname, you can't break me, mainly because I don't give a shit about what they think. Why do they need all the details of my life? I'm playing a game; I'm not a goddamn celebrity.

Well, I guess that's not entirely true.

I'm well-known as one of the best starting pitchers in the league. Every baseball fan knows who I am, but it goes beyond that, too. As of the past couple of years, I'm also known off the field.

That's partially because of the Fort Knox persona but mainly related to some stupid internet poll. Some tabloid put together a list of attractive male athletes, and for some reason, I made the list.

That damn poll has become the bane of my existence. I just want to play baseball and go home to the solitude of my penthouse. I don't have that luxury anymore, though. I always see cameras and reporters when I'm out. Just gives me even more of a reason to always stay inside.

That's a large part of the reason Cole and I get on so well. Neither of us wants the fame surrounding us. We just want to live our lives. Lucky for Cole, he manages to go unnoticed. How? No damn clue considering he's one of the better bats on the team. Not to mention that he's the hometown hero, having grown up in Brooklyn. As for me, everywhere I turn, there's a reporter trying to talk to me or a photographer snapping a picture to submit to some tabloid, all wondering about the unnavigable "Fort Knox."

"Do you think resting for the next four days will have you ready to start Sunday's game?" yet another reporter asks.

"Hope so," I say, standing up and waving my goodbyes as I leave the media room.

Most teams just do post-game interviews on the field. You only deal with one reporter and then head back to the clubhouse. However, Skip says we should foster a better relationship with the media. So, every game I pitch, I'm stuffed into the small media room we have at the stadium, smelling terribly of sweat and body odor before I can get to the clubhouse to take a damn shower.

Lane catches up with me in the hall after he finishes with his line of questioning. "Hey, Spence," he says, wrapping his arm around my shoulders. "Great game today, huh?"

"Don't call me Spence," I say as I shrug his arm off me. "I fucking hate that."

"Which is exactly why I do it, Spence. Gotta get you riled up somehow."

I just roll my eyes as I follow Lane into the clubhouse.

Freshly showered with only a terrycloth towel wrapped low on my waist, I walk over to my space in the clubhouse. My jersey is hung up and ready to be cleaned, and I'm ready to head home, binge-watch some Netflix, and order some takeout so I don't have to cook tonight. Might as well give my arm a rest after throwing out ninety-four pitches today.

As I'm about to drop the towel and get ready to get my ass out of here, I hear a voice behind me. "There you are, Knox. I've been looking for you."

Simon Helbin, my agent.

I turn to face him. "Where else did you think you'd find me right now, Simon? I just got out of the damn shower."

"We'll circle back to your attitude in just a moment. But I figure you'll want to hear from me, seeing as I just got off the phone with one of the execs at Axis."

"Yeah?" I say, a rare bit of optimism to my tone. "What did they say?"

Axis Athletic Co. is one of the largest global sports apparel companies. Signing an endorsement deal with them is a huge career boost for athletes. They're currently considering me for a future campaign.

"They said that the grumpy asshole persona has to go before they'll offer a contract."

"There's no fucking way they actually said that, Simon."

"Not in as many words, but the sentiment was the same." He takes a seat on the sofa across from my space. I join him now, just the two of us currently in the clubhouse. "They love what you do on the field, you know that, but Axis is a very famous brand. They don't sign endorsement deals with players they believe could be a liability."

"How the hell am I a liability?" I reply, the irritation in my voice evident. "I come for practice, play the game, and then go home. I don't do a damn thing that should worry them."

"That right there is what they're worried about."

I sigh, scrubbing my hand over my face. "Fort Knox is the problem, isn't it?"

"Yes," Simon responds, letting out a breath. "All of Axis's clients are role models on and off the field. They want somebody people admire to represent their brand and the company's integrity."

"Axis is a goddamn corporation. How much integrity can they actually have?"

Simon pinches his fingers over the bridge of his nose, no doubt questioning his life choices that led to him signing me as a client, though I'll forever be grateful for him. My career almost ended before it began—I wouldn't be here without him. "This is part of the problem, Knox. You can't say things like that if you want people to like you."

"I don't care if people like me, Simon. You should know that by now."

"If you want to get this endorsement, you need Axis to like you. They're holding off on offering the contract for now. They've said they want to see a major improvement from you over the season before they make their final determination on whether to extend the offer or rescind the contract altogether."

"Fuck me."

How do I become someone approachable and likable when the media is the bane of my existence? I don't let people in, especially nosy reporters.

"I'm brainstorming ways to help you through the season. We're not giving up on this; we just need a solid approach to handling it. You need this endorsement deal."

"I know," I say, sighing again as I lean against the sofa.

Once Simon finally left the clubhouse, I threw on a pair of black joggers and a gray T-shirt. Thank fuck the MLB doesn't make us wear suits to and from a game like the NHL does. Having to wear a suit at least six days a week is something straight out of a nightmare to me.

I grab my jacket from the hanger, throwing it over my shoulder as I step into the hall. Cole is standing right outside chatting to a couple of women—Lucia, one of our trainers, and a blonde in a baseball cap. Even with her back to me, I know who she is—Harlow Pierce, Cole's sister.

I'd be remiss to say that she's never crossed my mind during some ... alone time when I'm home. She's fucking stunning. Her wavy hair falls down past her shoulders. She has the brightest blue eyes I've ever seen. And her other... assets... are more than enough to continually attract my gaze.

Attractive as she is, though, she's not my type. She's way too fucking *happy*. Like, all the time. She's the female version of Cole. I could never manage that without going out of my mind.

There's that, as well as the fact that she runs a blog about the Stars. She's trying to be seen, while I'm someone who wants to stay in the shadows. Incompatible, if you ask me.

Cole spots me as I shut the clubhouse door behind me. "Hey, man. How are you feeling after our first win?"

I reluctantly make my way over to join them. I might be considered an asshole across the league for my unwillingness to speak to the media, but I do still try to show my friends and teammates some respect.

"Not bad. Good to get a win," I say, sidling up next to Cole.

"You pitched a great game tonight, Knox," Harlow says, peering up at me. I forgot how small she is—I'm six-four and easily have a foot on her.

"Uh, thanks," I reply, running a hand through my hair. "Media doesn't think so," I add. If I have to pretend to be approachable, it'll be easier to do that around people I already know. I don't know Harlow or Lucia well, but I'm familiar with them since we have the same circle of friends. I might as well get a start on all of this now. Simon will be happy, at least.

"The media is full of dicks looking for a story," Harlow replies. I actually laugh at that, earning a side eye from Cole since that's unlike me. "They just wanted to get you worked up so you'd say something they could run with."

"Yeah, I guess so." Why is Harlow trying to talk me up right now? I've known her for years because of Cole, but we've exchanged maybe five sentences with each other in that time. So that's weird. Changing the subject, I turn to Cole. "Lane already leave?"

"Oh, yeah," he says, rubbing his neck. "Sage was tired, and he wanted to get her home. Rory went to help get her down."

Lane Brooks is our center fielder and the third member of our friend group with Josh Garro. He's like a damn golden retriever, lapping up the attention and giving the fans everything they crave. He always has women falling at his feet... which is how he ended up a single dad from a one-night stand. But the guy's a damn good father. And his daughter Sage could melt even the coldest of hearts, including mine.

Skip's daughter, Rory, is actually Lane's nanny. Rory was always around the team because of her father, and she has a background in childcare. When Lane unexpectedly became a dad, she jumped right in to help, traveling with Sage and the team around the country for games.

"Oh!" Lucia chimes in. "I need to find Josh before he leaves the stadium. I have to see how his leg held up today to get an idea of what stretches he needs to work on ahead of tomorrow's game."

"I'll come with," Harlow adds. "I'll see you for breakfast tomorrow, Cole, and I'll see you at the game tomorrow, Knox."

With a wave, they both turn on their heels and head back down the hallway. And I get a view of Harlow's hips swaying side to side as she struts away. Adding that to my memory bank for later.

"Dude," Cole says, shoving my shoulder. "Since when does my sister actually talk to you?"

"I have no fucking idea, man."

"Weird." He pulls a hoodie over his head—navy with yellow accents and the Stars logo front and center. "Well, I'm heading out. Catch you tomorrow, Fort."

Cole takes off down the hall and heads the way Harlow and Lucia left. I turn around to head in the opposite direction to find Simon standing right behind me.

"Christ, Simon. What the hell are you doing?"

"You seem friendly with Cole's sister," he says, completely ignoring my question.

"That's the most we've ever spoken," I reply honestly. "She seems nice and all, but I'd hardly say I know her."

I can see Simon working through something in his head. The gears are turning. I have no idea what he's thinking, but I'm sure that I won't like it.

"I've got some things to work out tonight, but meet me in Conference Room A before the game tomorrow. I've got an idea..."

Three

Harlow

"So, what was with you chatting up Fort yesterday?" Cole asks as he stuffs his face with a bite of his spinach omelet. Cole and I have a scheduled weekly breakfast together since we don't see each other as often during baseball season. At least, that's what we told ourselves when we started it. I've since started joining the Stars on the road as I work on my blog, so we see each other nearly daily. We decided to keep the tradition going, so we still meet up every Wednesday morning and alternate between whose apartment we meet at.

"I'm trying to be more friendly with all the guys on the team this year," I reply, taking a bite of my French toast that Cole grabbed from our favorite diner. "With me wanting to start interviewing players and personnel for *Starred and Fast*, I want them to all be comfortable around me. To understand that I'm not a reporter, and I'm not going to include anything in a post that they don't want me to."

"Most of the guys already know that, Lo. You're practically friends with everyone on the damn team."

I take a sip of my coffee—two creams, one sugar. "Everyone except Knox," I say, shrugging. "Knox is a mystery to me still."

"Knox is a mystery to everyone," Cole replies, letting out a breath. "Hell, I've been friends with him for three years, and sometimes I feel like *I* barely know him."

"Which is why I'm going to use my charm and bright personality to win him over."

Cole's hand flies up to his mouth to prevent him from spitting out the coffee he's sipping, several drops of dark brown liquid falling through. "That's fucking hilarious, Lo. Fort Knox will certainly be swayed by your cheerfulness and positive attitude."

"Fuck off, Cole," I retort, stabbing my fork in the air at him. "I'm a delight—he'd be lucky to know me."

Cole grabs his empty plate and mug, carrying them over to the sink and rinsing them off before placing them inside. "You're something else, Lo. Gotta admire your confidence, though."

Does he mean my faux confidence? I've been getting my confidence back, but Derek did such a number on me mentally. I didn't let him shake me completely, but I wouldn't consider myself confident again. Not yet, at least.

A knock at the door takes me out of my thoughts. "I'll get that," I say, jumping off my stool and heading toward the door. Before my visitor can knock again, I swing the door open. "You're early, you know."

"Yeah, yeah," Rory replies, stepping into my apartment. "I just didn't want to be late."

"Who was at the door, Lo?" Cole asks, stepping into view. "Oh, uh... hey Rory. I didn't know you were coming over."

"She's my first interview for the blog," I state, leading Rory to the small couch in my tiny living room.

Cole rubs his neck. "Skip's daughter. Seems like a good place to start."

"Oh, please," Rory fires back. "The followers would much rather hear about you than they would about me."

"Maybe..." he says, looking uncomfortable. Weird. "I just don't like interviews, that's all." Cole takes a breath before continuing. "I'm actually gonna head out now, Lo. I need to get ready for strength training."

"It's nine-thirty, Cole. You don't need to be there until noon."

"I want to get some extra batting practice in beforehand. I'll see you at the game later, Harlow. Good seeing you as well, Rory." With that, Cole picks up his bag and heads out the door.

"What the fuck was that?" I ask no one in particular. "Cole was acting weird, right?" I add as I turn toward Rory.

"You're asking me if the man who all but sprinted out of your apartment the moment I got here was acting weird? No, not at all." Rory laughs, and I roll my eyes. "Probably just tired of seeing me, is all. I'm sure I see him more than he wants since I'm always with you."

"You're literally friends with him," I say. "You've been friends for three years."

"Yeah, but he's always been awkward, Lo."

"Yeah, maybe," I respond. "Cole's my damn brother, and it sometimes feels like I know him as well as I know Knox."

"And how well do you know Knox?" Rory asks, cocking an eyebrow suggestively.

"You're unbelievable, you know that, right?" She just smiles brightly at me. "How did we go from talking about my brother to you now insinuating I have some kind of sex life with Knox Spencer, of all people?"

"I'm not insinuating that you currently have one, dear Harlow. But I am suggesting you have some fun again. You tell me, Luc, and Ell everything, so I know you haven't had any action since you broke up with Derek. I'm willing to bet the league's favorite grumpy pitcher knows *exactly* what to do in the bedroom."

"Jesus, Rory. I hardly even know him; I'm not trying to jump into his bed. Or anyone's bed, for that matter."

"Too bad," Rory retorts. "I bet a good lay would finally put a smile on Fort Knox's face."

"You're fucking shameless, Ror. Now, quit distracting me. You're supposed to be doing an interview."

"Aren't you glad I came early then?" I just lightly shake my head while breathing out a laugh rather than reply. "So, what questions have you got for me, Pierce?"

"They're all important to have people get to know you, but we'll start off with the easy ones like favorite color, favorite food, favorite Taylor Swift song..."

"That's an important question?"

"Very important." I smile. "Your favorite could define who you are as a person. It's essential for getting to know you."

"You're insane, Lo, but I love you." Rory thinks for a moment. "Let's see... my favorite color is maroon, my favorite food is chicken parmesan, and my favorite Taylor Swift song would have to be *Dress*, I'd say."

"Of course, that's your favorite. I shouldn't expect anything less from you, Ror." We both dissolve into laughter as my phone vibrates. I pick it up and glance at the screen.

"Who's that?" Rory asks.

"I actually have no idea. It's a text from a number I don't have saved."

Unknown

Hey, before the game tonight, my agent wants to meet with us

Think you could stop by early for that?

This is Knox, by the way

"It's from Knox. How the hell did he even get my number?"

"The team directory, probably."

"I'm not part of the team—why would I be in the directory?"

"Lo, we both are. We're unofficial members of the team because we travel with them and do things for the team. We're both listed in the team directory."

"Oh."

Unhappy with my lack of communication, Rory prods me. "So... what did Fort Knox have to say?"

"He's asking me to come by early for the game today. Says his agent wants a meeting with both of us."

"Did he say why? That's kinda weird."

"Let me ask."

I'd hardly call yesterday a conversation or anything

I tried to talk to you, but you weren't very responsive

Hell, this chat here is more than you've ever spoken to me

Knox

I can already tell this is going to be a bad idea

Harlow

But you just told me you don't know what this is about

Knox

I don't

But you're already giving me shit, so whatever Simon has up his sleeve is giving me pause

Harlow

Well, I guess we'll find out together then, won't we?

I'll see you before the game, Fort

Knox

You're just like your goddamn brother

"So apparently," I say to Rory, "he also has no idea what this meeting is about."

"Maybe this is some ploy to get you alone so he can tell you how much he wants you."

"Your imagination knows no limits, Rory Fisher," I say, playfully shoving her shoulder. "Now, let's finish this damn interview."

‹‹‹‹‹‹‹‹‹‹‹‹‹‹‹‹‹‹‹‹‹‹‹‹‹‹‹‹‹‹

Once Rory leaves to grab Sage before today's game, I hop right into the shower, curiosity plaguing my mind. I wish I had any inkling of what this meeting could be about and why his agent wants me there. I barely know Knox, and I've never even met his agent.

Before leaving my apartment, I throw on my favorite pair of jeans and my *Pierce* Stars jersey (number twenty-seven for Cole), pull my hair into a high ponytail, and grab the same hat I wore to the game yesterday. Once I have my Chucks on and grab a light jacket, I'm ready to head out. Yesterday's game was frigid, but tonight is going to be much warmer. The weather here is fucking weird.

Security lets me into the stadium early, thanks to the team pass I have, so I'm currently trudging the halls trying to find the damn conference room. I'm wandering around aimlessly when I hear a familiar voice behind me. "You lost?"

I turn around to find Knox a few steps behind me, ready for the game in his white home uniform with the Stars logo on the chest.

God, I love baseball uniforms.

"Yeah," I reply sheepishly. I'm not usually nervous around people, even if I don't know them. Still, the mystery of this meeting is giving me a bit of unease. "I have no idea where the damn conference room is."

"Follow me," he says, stepping in front of me. I guess we're back to short responses. But watching him walk with those baseball pants hugging his backside? I sure as hell won't complain about that.

Knox leads me down a few hallways, up a flight of stairs, and down several more hallways. I was never going to find this damn room on my own.

He finally stops us outside a large oak door emblazoned with the words Conference Room A in bold letters. Knox pushes the door open, gesturing me inside. "After you."

"At least you're a gentleman," I say as I slide past him, hoping to mask the nerves in my voice.

The room has a sizable wooden conference table with leather chairs surrounding it. Across from us is a man with salt-and-pepper hair, hands folded on the table as he watches us take our seats. This must be Knox's agent.

"I'm thrilled you could both make it for this. I know the meeting was short notice," the man says before turning his attention to me and extending his hand. "Hello, Harlow. I'm Simon Helbin, Mr. Spencer's agent."

I accept his hand and shake. "Nice to meet you, Simon."

I glance over to Knox to find a blank expression on his face. Typical for him. "Are you going to tell us why we're here now, Simon?"

Simon brings his hand to his face in exasperation. This must be how their conversations usually go. "This is why, Knox. You're unapproachable. Being dubbed Fort Knox isn't something to be happy about."

"Seems fine to me," Knox retorts, leaning back against the leather of his chair and resting his hands behind his head. "Now everyone knows they can't get anything out of me."

"That's literally the damn problem! You're not supposed to be so closed off that any tidbit of information the media can find becomes tabloid fodder. If you want that contract, you have no choice but to work on your public image."

This feels like a conversation I have no place in. Awkward...

Scrubbing his hand over his face, Knox relents. "I know…" He sighs. "I know I do."

"I assure you that it will be worth it. All we have to do is get rid of your gruff exterior. You'll need to be more gracious with the media. You should be seen more and become more involved with the team. And you'll need to do something to show everyone that the man who refuses to let anyone into his life can do just that."

"And how the hell do you suppose I do all of that? That's a long list there, Simon. Maybe this deal isn't worth it."

"Sorry to interrupt," I interject, "but this doesn't seem to involve me at all. Why am I here?" I hope that didn't come off as rude but I'm very confused right now.

"Right, of course, Ms. Pierce. We got sidetracked for a moment. But you are involved in this process."

"So, what's going on here then? All I'm gathering is that Knox is up for some kind of contract and needs a better image. I don't understand where I'm coming into play here."

"Let me start with the details," Simon responds. "Knox has been in talks with Axis Athletic Co. to sign an endorsement deal. Axis is interested based on how he performs on the field, but his demeanor off the field is the issue. They want somebody respectful and likable to represent them. He needs to improve his public image, and I think a great place to start is by proving he can let somebody into his life."

"What the hell does Harlow have to do with any of this, Simon?" Knox fires off, clearly annoyed. "I told you yesterday that I barely know her."

"I'm aware that you two know of each other but don't associate much. But from what I know of Ms. Pierce, she has a sunny personality and could make friends with anyone. She's also Cole Pierce's sister. He may not give much about his personal life either, but from his media interviews, they clearly have the same attitudes. *That* is what you need, Knox. You need some cheer to brighten you up in the eyes of the fans, media, and Axis."

Fear creeps across Knox's face as I sit there stunned. I read romance novels—I know where this is heading.

"What are you saying, Simon?" Knox asks apprehensively.

Simon looks on, smiling widely at his brilliant idea. "I'm proposing that you two fake a relationship."

I sit there silently, speechless for one of the first times in my life. I always have something to say—not this time, though.

"Why the fuck would we fake a relationship, Simon? What the hell?" Anger is evident in his voice. He does *not* like this idea. And it's kind of hard to blame him. This is something that happens in books. The idea of it occurring in real life seems ludicrous.

"Because if you want this deal," Simon intercedes, stabbing his finger in the air toward Knox, "then you have no choice but to improve your image. You're one of the most well-known players in the league with a piss-poor attitude to show for it. If you want the Knox Spencer legacy to extend beyond your playing career, you need this contract with Axis. If you don't, no one will remember who you are. I know you hate the fame that comes with this, but I also know how much you love the sport. You want to be remembered for your achievements on the field. You 'date' Harlow for the season and get the deal with Axis, the media and fans will soften to you. You'll be remembered as one of baseball's greats."

Knox is silent for a while. He's lost in his mind right now, trying to make sense of what Simon is suggesting. Finally, he sighs and says, "What does she even get out of this? I'm not doing something that benefits only myself. That's shitty, Simon."

Is he seriously considering this?

"That I'd need to talk to Ms. Pierce about. We wouldn't want to put her in a position where she would not benefit from an approximately six-month arrangement. If nothing else, we can offer her payment for agreeing and her silence on the matter."

"I don't want money," I say, my voice barely above a whisper. Louder now, I continue, "That's not what I'd want out of this. But there is something else..." They both turn to me, Simon, with hope in his eyes, while Knox remains stoic and unreadable. "You know of my blog *Starred and Fast*. That's why I'm always with the team. The blog is doing well enough, but I've been struggling to get a better reach. I may be Cole's sister, but since he keeps a low profile off the field, it doesn't drive any traffic to me. But faking a relationship with arguably the best pitcher in the league could really help me reach new followers and teach more people about the sport."

Wait—am *I* seriously considering this now?!

"Look at that," Simon says, looking at Knox. "Harlow does benefit from this arrangement as well. We can still work out the details, but if you're both on board, I think this could work really well for both of you." Simon turns his attention back toward me. "What do you think, Ms. Pierce?"

I take a deep breath. This situation is unexpected, to say the least. But if I want to expand *Starred and Fast*, this might just be the way to do it. Before I can change my mind, I firmly reply, "I'm in."

We both turn our attention to Knox and wait for his response. He's leaning forward, his elbows on the table and his hands tucked under his chin, probably wondering how he found himself in this position. After another minute of silence from the most mysterious man in the league, he finally speaks.

"*Fuck it*... I'll do it."

Four

Knox

IF IT WASN'T FOR this fucking Axis contract hanging over my head, I'd have never found myself in this situation. Now, I have to pretend to date one of my closest friend's sisters. No chance that'll come back to bite me in the ass, I'm sure.

But Simon was right, just like usual. I want to leave a legacy for how I played on the field, pitched on the mound, and was one of less than one hundred players in MLB *history* to regularly throw a knuckleball. That's what I want to be remembered for. And nobody will remember the asshole that refuses to ever let anybody in. So, as much as I don't want to, it's time for a change.

Harlow is spirited and happy—the antithesis of myself. But maybe that's exactly what I need. Perhaps I need my complete and total opposite to help me open up, at least a bit. I'm too fucked up to let anyone all the way in, but allowing everyone to see past some of the walls I put up around myself would go a long way.

"So..." Harlow says, reminding me that we're both awkwardly standing in the hall outside of the conference room after our meeting with Simon. "That was... unexpected."

I breathe out a sigh. "To say the fucking least."

"Are you okay with this, Knox? I can't imagine this will be easy for you." Her concern is unexpected, but it is nice. It says a lot about who she is when one of the first things she does is check on how the dickhead pitcher is feeling.

I give her a small smile, tilting up one corner of my mouth. "I think I have to be," I reply honestly. "But if I have to do this, at least it's with you. You're tolerable."

"I'm tolerable?" Harlow brings a hand up to her chest. "Knox Spencer, that might be the nicest thing you've ever said to *anyone*."

"Keep that shit up, and I'll take it back."

"Too late. The moment you told me I'm tolerable will play on repeat in my head for the rest of the day." She's so much like Cole. That dick will probably revel in this weird as fuck situation, even if it is with his sister. "Well, I'm going to grab a beer and then head to my seat. I'd wish you a good game, but you're a starting pitcher. One game, and then you have to rest your ass for four days."

"Kick me in the dick, why don't you? You go out and pitch one hundred mph fastballs and tell me you don't need four days of rest."

"Lucky for me, I don't need to. You also don't need to—you can pitch knuckleballs." She turns on her heel and heads now in the opposite direction. "Have fun in the dugout tonight, Spencer."

As she struts down the hall, seeming to be at ease with this awkward situation, I allow myself to watch her as she goes. A man can check out his fake girlfriend, right?

⫷⫷⫷⫷⫷⫷⫷⫷⫷⫷⫷⫷⫷⫷⫷⫷⫷⫷⫷⫷⫷⫷⫷⫷

I make my way back to the clubhouse after Harlow walks off. I've been ready for the game, but I need a quiet moment to collect myself. The past half hour has thrown me for a goddamn loop.

I lay back on one of the clubhouse sofas, pinching my brow, trying to decide if I think this is a good thing or if it will blow up catastrophically in the end. Right now, I have no fucking idea.

The door to the clubhouse swings open, so I quickly sit up, trying to look like I'm not going out of my mind. But it's Cole who walks in. And he's already side-eyeing me, so he knows something is up. Did Harlow talk to him already?

"What are you doing back in the clubhouse, Fort?" he asks, raising an eyebrow. "You got ready before everyone else today."

"Oh, I, uh... just forgot something in my bag. That's all."

"Then why are you lying on the sofa and not grabbing something in your bag?"

"Of all the people to walk in here right now, it had to be you, didn't it?"

"And that's why you're the asshole of the league."

I sigh. "Yeah. Sorry about that, man."

Cole stops and slowly turns to face me. "Did you just... apologize?"

"Shut up," I say. "The league thinks I'm an asshole, but you know damn well that I'm not."

"Yeah, but I don't think I've ever heard you apologize like that. What's going on? Am I being pranked right now? Are there hidden cameras?" Cole looks around the room, searching for any hint of a device recording his every move.

"Why the fuck would I be pranking you?" I have to ignore the pit forming in my stomach at the thought of hidden cameras.

"I don't know!" he replies, throwing his hands up in the air. "But you don't apologize for your attitude, so something is up." He takes a seat next to me on the sofa. "Is everything okay, Knox?"

"Yeah, everything is fine. Life is just crazy." I take a deep breath and turn to face him. "It's that Axis deal."

"What's going on with that?"

I give Cole the rundown on what Axis and Simon said about what I need to do now to get this endorsement deal.

"You need to be approachable? *You?*" he laughs. "And you need a better image. How the hell are you going to do that?"

"Well, Simon thought a good way to do that is…" I sigh, dreading the need to admit out loud that my image is so bad I need a fake girlfriend to improve it. "Simon wants me to fake a relationship with someone for the season. It'll help show that the guy who doesn't let anyone in isn't as cold as he appears. He says that should help jumpstart my public perception and help me land the contract."

"Wait, you're going to have a fake girlfriend?" He pauses to laugh like this is the funniest thing he's ever heard. "Who's the unlucky lady having to spend the next six months 'dating' you?"

"It's, uh… um…"

Cole's eyes narrow in on me. "Who is it, Knox? You're stumbling, so it must be someone I know."

I take the cap off my head, covering my face. He might find this whole situation funny. Still, there's always the possibility that he won't like the idea of me fake dating his sister. I'd rather not see his face if that's what it will be.

"It's Harlow."

Cole is silent, unmoving. I remove the hat from my face, trying to gauge his reaction. He's stoic right now, not giving me any indication of what he's thinking.

Finally, he fills the silence. "You're going to fake date my sister?"

Resting my head in my open palms, I reply, "Yeah. She already agreed to the idea."

When the silence becomes deafening, he doubles over in laughter. "Oh my God, Harlow is going to be your girlfriend? *Happy-as-a-clam, every-day-is-a-good-day, smiling-is-my-favorite* Harlow? You're so fucked, man."

"You're going to fucking enjoy this, aren't you?"

"Oh yes. By the end of this season, grumpy Knox will be gone. She's going to break you down. We might even start seeing you smile."

"This is fake, Cole. She's not going to break me down. We're putting on a show."

"Keep telling yourself that."

I groan. "I know you didn't come in here to rib me, so why are you here?"

"Ah, almost forgot." He reaches into his bag for something. "Hair tie."

"You wouldn't need a hair tie if you got a goddamn haircut."

"Fuck off, man."

Five

Knox

WE WON LAST NIGHT'S game against the Hawks 4-1, taking a 2-0 series lead to start off our season. Cole tried to discretely fuck with me the entire game. He's already enjoying this far too much, and we've not even launched this fake relationship. At least he stopped when Lane kept glancing over. The fewer people know about this, the better.

After the game, Harlow texted me and told me we should meet up this morning to go over everything. Get our story straight, essentially. That's how I find myself on a rickety ass elevator inside a shabby building in the heart of Kips Bay.

Once the elevator door dings and I'm sure I won't plummet to my death, I step off onto the seventh floor. She apparently lives in apartment 7B. I find my way to her door and knock. When she answers, I take in the sight in front of me.

Harlow is dressed in a pair of tight black leggings and a low-cut long-sleeved white top. Her hair falls over her shoulders in blonde waves. She's a goddamn vision, even dressed casually. This fake dating thing will be much more difficult if she keeps looking like *that*.

"Come on in, Knox," she says, gesturing me inside. "Welcome to my humble abode."

"This is a shoebox, Harlow," I state as I step into what might possibly be the tiniest studio apartment I've ever seen. The main area has a tiny couch, a small table, a bed tucked into the corner, and a kitchenette. There appears to be a free-standing closet on the far wall as well. "You live in this?"

She crosses her arms, and her eyes narrow in on me. "Not all of us have multi-million dollar contracts that can buy us a penthouse. I run a blog—this is the best I can do."

Good job, Knox. This is the first time you've met up since you started this, and you're already coming across like an entitled prick. "I wasn't trying to make it sound like that," I say before quickly adding, "Sorry."

"It's fine." She lets out a sigh. "Cole's offered to help me with rent on a better place, but I won't let him. I want to be able to make it on my own. It's hard to be taken seriously as a woman so heavily involved in a male-dominated sport, and I want to prove that I can do it without help."

"That's admirable," I admit, earning me a soft smile in return. "But isn't your benefit from this arrangement essentially having me help you?"

"You're just going to bring me attention. People will wonder all about Knox Spencer's girlfriend, the woman who could warm his icy heart. They'll look me up, find the blog, and hopefully stick around after this is over."

"I do not have an icy heart," I reply indignantly.

"You'll have to show me that then. So far, you're cold and distant. But I'll warm you up through the season."

In an effort to keep my mind from going somewhere it *really* shouldn't with talk of warming me up, I bring attention to the two coffees in my hand. "I, uh... I brought coffee."

"Now you're speaking my language, Spencer. Maybe you can be sweet after all."

"I didn't bring them to be sweet," I admit. "I brought them because I'm a colossal dick early in the morning, and I thought I should probably be more welcoming today."

Harlow brings her hand up to cover her mouth, hiding her laugh. "I appreciate the honesty. Now, are these black coffees?" I nod. She walks over to the fridge, pulling out a bottle of coffee creamer and then a container of sugar from the counter. "I've got cream and sugar here then. How do you take your coffee?"

"Two creams, one sugar," I answer. "Black has always been too bitter for me."

"Ooh, something we have in common!" she says excitedly. "That's the exact way I drink my coffee. We can bond over coffee."

"You want us to bond over coffee?" I say, cocking an eyebrow.

"We have to bond over something, don't we?" she responds, shrugging her shoulders. "Might be a good starting point."

She starts walking over to the tiny couch, and I follow, taking a seat right next to her—literally right next to her. Harlow is much smaller than I am, but we're still basically on top of each other right now. "So, uh... how should we start this?"

Harlow brings her coffee to her lips, takes a sip, and moans in enjoyment. "Mmm, this is good coffee." Let's forget that sound. Let's not imagine her making similar sounds in a very different situation that involves far less clothing. "I thought we should learn a bit about each other to help us get everything straight. I know nothing about you."

"No one knows anything about me."

"Because you're so damn closed off. That's what we need to work on."

I sigh. "I know. You'll just have to give me some time to start opening up. I don't know you well, and I need to know if I can trust you before that happens."

"Do you think I'm going to take anything you tell me and air it on my blog?" she asks dejectedly.

"No, of course not," I admit. "Cole's a good guy, I imagine you're a good girl." Harlow raises her eyebrow and smirks at me. "Oh fuck! Not like that!" I'm stumbling over my words, trying to talk my way out of this. "I mean, maybe you are, I don't know. I don't need to know!"

She snorts from laughing so hard at my stupidity. "Damn," she says, wiping a tear from her cheek. "I thought it would take more than ten minutes for me to make you that uncomfortable."

"I panicked," I say, scrubbing my hand over my face. "This is fake. I don't want you to think I'm suggesting something."

"Note to self then," she replies. "Knox Spencer isn't interested in a physical relationship with me. Good to know." Harlow smirks at me again as she takes another sip of coffee.

I sigh. "Let's not tell Cole about me sounding like a bumbling idiot, please."

"Promise," she says. "Now, knowing how hard it is for you to open up and how awkward you can get trying to avoid that, let's just get our story straight. How did we meet?"

"Through your brother. How else would we meet?"

"True. I imagine you don't give yourself much opportunity to meet women who live in shoeboxes."

I groan, bringing my hand to my face. "I swear that's not what I meant. They consider me the league asshole, but I'm not that bad. I just keep to myself."

"I figured," she replies honestly. "Cole wouldn't be friends with you if you were some horrible, unredeemable person. I know there's going to be more below the surface. That's the Knox I'm looking forward to getting to know."

Despite how I've come across today, Harlow isn't giving up. If I were her, I might've called the whole thing off. But she's instead just going to ease herself into my life. Maybe that'll be a good thing.

I smile at her. "Oh, he does smile!"

"Fucking hell. I can't smile without someone pointing it out."

"Sorry," she says, throwing her hands up in surrender. "Won't happen again. We can get back to details in a minute, but when do you think we should launch this fake relationship?"

"My next start is Sunday night's game. That would probably be a good time to do it."

"Do you know how you want to announce it?"

"Yeah," I say, running a hand through my hair. "I've got an idea about that. But keeping it vague for now might be better so we don't overthink this."

She eyes me curiously. "What do you have up your sleeve, Spencer?"

"I guess you'll see on Sunday."

Six

Harlow

AFTER THURSDAY NIGHT'S LOSS to the Hawks, I came home and started working more on my blog post for Rory. If Saturday is going to be the day I post interviews, I need to finish this article by tomorrow.

I'm almost three-quarters of the way through my first draft when my phone rings. Who is calling me at nearly midnight?

I grab my phone and take a look at the screen.

Lucia.

I haven't spoken to her much today because I'm trying not to spill the beans around a bunch of people, but I need to be able to talk to someone about this situation that isn't Knox or Cole. Apparently, Knox told him yesterday, and he's spent the entire day messing with me about it.

I answer the call and bring the phone to my ear. Before I can even greet her, Lucia says, "Why the fuck were you acting so weird tonight, Lo?"

"Well, hello to you, too, dear friend. I'm doing great, thanks for asking."

"Don't give me that. You barely spoke to me tonight. I asked Cole if he knew why, and he said I should speak with you."

"Of course he did," I say, sighing. "I wasn't trying to be weird earlier, but this wasn't something I could talk about at the game since people could hear. That's why I didn't really talk to you yesterday either."

"Ooh, something secret! That sounds juicy."

"It'll definitely be something you're not expecting." I let out a light laugh before launching into my explanation of the meeting with Knox and Simon and his idea to help us both.

"Harlow!" she says excitedly. "Are you saying what I think you're saying?!"

"That Knox Spencer is my fake boyfriend?" I let out a breath. "Yeah…"

"Oh my God!" she shrieks. "How perfect is this?!"

"How is this perfect, Luc? It's a fake relationship."

"For now. Fake dating never works; the couple always develops feelings. Plus, he's got this whole broody thing going on while you're so bright and happy. Perfect combo."

"You read too many romance novels, Luc," I reply, shaking my head even though she can't see. "We're not going to develop feelings for each other. We barely even know each other."

"But you will. You'll have to spend time together to make this seem realistic. I'd bet money Knox Spencer falls in love with you by the end of the season."

"I don't want him to fall in love with me," I say, exasperated. "This isn't a fairy tale, Lucia. This is real life. That's not how this works."

"We'll see." I can hear the smugness in her tone. And I know this means Lucia will be prodding me through the season to see how this whole situation is going.

She won't be happy with the outcome, though. Knox Spencer is so far out of my goddamn league. With that shaggy brown hair, those vibrant green eyes, and that well-suited scruffy beard, he could have any woman of his choosing. He's not going for his friend's little sister, that's for sure.

Which is fine by me. I don't want anything right now anyway. I'm still fixing the pieces of me that Derek broke. I need to be whole before I can really move on. But I can still play the image of him in a tight gray T-shirt clinging to his muscular biceps in my head when I'm alone. That'll work for me.

❮❮❮❮❮❮❮❮❮❮❮❮❮❮❮❮❮❮❮❮❮❮❮❮❮❮❮❮❮❮❮❮

"So, how are you feeling about tonight?" Lucia asks. "You ready?"

It's now Sunday, the day Knox told me we'd announce our "relationship." I still don't know what he's planning, and it's starting to give me anxiety. I get uncomfortable with the unknown.

"As ready as I'm going to be, I think," I reply. "Knox and I have only been talking to each other for a few days now. We don't know each other well, and I'm afraid that will come across."

"You're not going to be giving media interviews. I'm sure they'll ask him some questions during postgame press, but I doubt Paul will let the reporters get too invasive. I think you'll mainly just need to be seen together in public and pretend you like each other. Shouldn't be too hard for you when you're staring at Knox Spencer."

"Yeah, I guess," I respond, sighing. "I think I'm just nervous about all of it. It feels kinda wrong to be doing this, at least for me. I can help Knox with his image and help him become less of a pessimist. He could actually change through this. But I almost feel like I'm using him."

"Lo, he's probably thinking the same thing about you. Just remember that you guys are doing this for *both* of your benefits. And then you can fall in love along the way."

"Lucia..."

"I know, I know. You don't want him to fall in love with you. Just let me live in a fantasy world where my best friend is finally happy."

I cross my arms. "I don't need a man to be happy, Luc."

She sighs. "I know you don't, Lo. But you're a hopeless romantic. I know the idea of finding your person one day keeps you going."

I wish she was wrong. I'm independent and can care for myself, but I do so badly want to share my life with somebody again. I thought Derek was going to be that person. I know now that he never would have been. Our relationship wasn't healthy; I just didn't see it at the time.

But as much as I want that again, I don't think I'm ready. Derek almost broke me. I'm not whole again, but I'm getting there. I'm just going to focus on myself. Love and romance can come later.

Before Lucia can mention it again, there's a knock at my door. "Are you expecting somebody else, Lo?"

"No," I say, stepping off my stool by the kitchen counter and making my way to the door. "I've been avoiding Rory and Ella, too, so I don't let the cat out of the bag. I'm not sure who this would be."

As I open the door, I find an unknown man standing before me. "Uh, can I help you?"

"Just here to drop off a package, ma'am." He picks up a brown box from the floor and hands it to me. "Here you are."

"Oh, thanks," I say, confused. I wasn't expecting a package. The man nods his head before turning around and heading back down the hallway.

Once I close the door behind me, I walk back into the kitchen and set the package down on the counter.

"What's that?" Lucia asks, sizing up the box in front of us.

"No idea," I reply honestly. "I wasn't expecting anything."

"Do you think it could be from Knox?"

"I don't know why he'd send me something, but maybe. There's no return address on the box, though."

"So then open it so we can find out!" Lucia nudges me to get me moving.

I take a pair of scissors and slice through the tape on the box. The first thing I see when I open it is a letter.

Harlow,

Figured you could use something for the game tonight. Wear whatever you're comfortable with, but as much as I hate it, I know there will be pictures taken of us. I'm sure you'll look great no matter what, though.

-Knox

"Yeah, this is from Knox," I say to Lucia, handing her the letter as two tickets I didn't notice before fall from inside the folded paper.

"What are those?" she asks before turning her attention to the letter.

I grab the tickets from the counter and look them over. "Two front-row tickets for the section next to the Stars dugout."

"Ooh, he wants you right next to him during the game." Lucia fake swoons, holding her arm to her head. I roll my eyes and shake my head at her dramatics. When I don't give her the reaction she wants, she moves on. "Now, what do you think is in the box? Also, I'm not going to allow you to gloss over the fact that he says in the letter that you'll look great." She moves her eyebrows suggestively.

"Jesus, Luc. That's not gonna happen." I carefully unwrap the tissue paper to reveal... a jersey. "It's a Stars jersey. I already have one of those."

"You have a Pierce jersey for your brother, Lo. That's not going to be a Pierce jersey."

"Oh," I say, realization washing over me. I lift the jersey and turn it around, finding *Spencer* stitched across the top with the number forty-nine stitched below. "He... he wants me to wear his jersey tonight?"

"You're announcing your relationship."

"Fake relationship," I remind her.

"Semantics," she replies, waving me off. "If there are going to be pictures of you two like he thinks, it would make more sense for you to wear his jersey instead of your brother's."

"Yeah, that makes sense," I admit. "I feel like it's just now sinking in that this is really happening. How did I find myself in such a weird situation?"

"The how doesn't matter," Lucia says. "What matters is that you are, and after tonight, whatever Knox has planned will show the world that you're dating."

"Fake dating."

"It won't be fake for long. A man seeing a woman in his jersey always makes him feral for her."

"In books, Luc! Life is not a romance novel."

Lucia laughs as she steps off her stool and grabs her purse from the counter. "I have to head in now for their training. I'll catch you at the game tonight."

With a wave, Lucia walks out the door. And I'm left alone with my swirling thoughts.

Seven

Harlow

"This is just so weird, Cole. Don't you think?"

"Nah, I'm loving this."

Lucia is still working with a few of the athletes, so I found Cole while waiting for her. I figured he could help me feel better about all of this. Of course, that's not what's happening.

"Come on, Cole. This is weird. This *feels* weird. It's one of your best friends and your little sister."

"Okay, first, you're two years younger than me, Lo. It's not like you're eighteen or something. Second, the only weird thing is you wearing a jersey that doesn't say *Pierce* on the back."

"You really don't find this situation weird?" I ask earnestly. "Your friend and your sister?"

"Lo, you know I'm not the overprotective brother. You're your own person—I won't try to control what you do. You're both adults anyway. And as much as I've been giving Knox shit over this, I think it'll be a good thing. Even if it isn't real, I think your positivity might just rub off on him. He needs that."

I let out a deep breath as Lucia found us in the hall, sidling up beside me. "Did you come to Cole for a pep talk, Lo?" she asks, elbowing me in the ribs. Well, she went for the ribs but hit my boob instead since she's about six inches taller than me.

"I thought he might be nice about something for once. Instead, he's giving me shit."

Cole crosses his arms defiantly. "I do believe that last thing I said was nice, Harlow. But quit overthinking this. You guys are going to be fine."

"Says the man that won't have to endure the media storm when this all comes out."

"You really think I won't have to deal with the media about this? My sister is dating my teammate. My life won't be nearly as quiet as I like it. I've already accepted that, Lo."

"Shit, I didn't even think about that," I say as I bring my palm up to my forehead. "We should've talked to you about this first. I'm sor-"

Cole holds up his hand to silence me. "Don't apologize. I can try to hide all I want, but the reality is that I'm a professional athlete. I'll never be completely under the radar. I can manage this."

"What are you still doing out here, Pierce?" Paul's voice bellows down the hall. "Get your ass out there for warmups."

"Gotta go," Cole says before taking off down the hall. "Good luck!"

‹‹‹‹‹‹‹‹‹‹‹‹‹‹‹‹‹‹‹‹‹‹‹‹‹‹‹‹‹‹‹‹

Lucia and I catch up with Rory and Ella for a few minutes before we grab drinks and find our seats. I'll be sticking with one beer tonight, no matter how nervous I am. Tomorrow is a travel day, so we'll be on the plane on our way down to Atlanta for another three-game series starting on Tuesday. Plane rides and hangovers don't mix.

"These are some great seats," Lucia says. "Good job, Knox."

The guys are out on the field prepping for the game. Knox is on the mound throwing out some practice pitches to the Stars catcher Martin Scholl.

Knox's knuckleballs are on point tonight. Knuckleballs are hard to hit because the ball moves so erratically, but that makes them hard to throw as well. The pitcher and catcher both need to be in complete sync to make it work. Lucky for the Stars, Knox and Martin are very in tune with each other on the field.

That bodes well for tonight's game. The Stars are going for the sweep of the San Francisco Bulldogs. If they win tonight, they'll take that adrenaline with them all the way to Atlanta.

After Knox throws out his latest practice pitch, he scans the crowd to find Lucia and me. And he smirks at us. At least, I think he smirked. The pitcher's mound is pretty far away from us. It's hard to tell.

"Did he just smile at you, Lo?" Lucia asks happily. "I think he smiled at you!"

"If anything, it was a smirk. Knox doesn't smile."

"You can tell yourself whatever you want, Harlow Pierce, but that man just smiled at you."

"It's just for show then. This isn't real," I whisper to her.

"Mhmm," is all she says in response.

<<<<<<<<<<<<<<<<<<<<<<<<<<<<<<<<<<<<

Once the game starts, the guys are nonstop—hit after hit, run after run. The score is 12-0 at the bottom of the eighth inning.

Knox has given up two walks and no hits in the game so far. His pitch count is pretty good as well—ninety-eight—so he's still in the game. If he can make it through the ninth inning without giving up a hit, Knox will have the first no-hitter in the league this season and the second no-hitter of his career.

Josh strikes out to end the bottom of the eighth. Now, only three outs stand between the Stars and a no-hitter. The crowd watches with bated breath as Knox makes his way back out to the mound. If he's nervous, you'd never be able to tell because he looks as collected as he usually does, even though the viewership for this game will be much higher now. No-hitters are rare. Every baseball fan will be tuning in to this game now to watch how this inning unfolds.

The first at-bat of this inning is San Fran's designated hitter. Knox throws a fastball straight down the middle. Strike one. The next pitch is a changeup, coming in at the corner of the strike zone. The batter swings and misses. Strike two. He throws a knuckleball for the third pitch, the batter again swinging and only hitting air. *Strike three.*

Only two more outs to go now. The Bulldogs' first baseman comes up to bat, and Knox attempts another knuckleball.

Like I said before, knuckleballs can be erratic and hard to throw and catch. The volatility of this one means it slams right into the batter's arm.

Hit by pitch, automatic walk.

Shit.

Since it doesn't count as a hit, Knox's no-hitter is still up for grabs. But he may be rattled. There's a baserunner now, so if the next batter, the Bulldogs shortstop, gets a good hit, he could give up a couple of runs in addition to a hit.

I can see him take a deep breath before raring up again, throwing another fastball right down the middle. The next sound is the crack of the wooden bat as it makes contact with the ball it sends soaring into the outfield. Lane is positioning himself in center field, ready to catch the pop-out. When his glove closes around the ball, the crowd exhales a sigh of relief.

But Lane doesn't pay attention to us. He sees the baserunner turning on his heel from second base to run back to first. The batter didn't get the hit, so he can't advance. Lane guns the ball to Eric Waller at first base, where he is waiting and ready. The runner is just feet away from the base as Waller makes the catch, reaching down for the tag.

The umpire makes the call.

Out.

The crowd erupts into cheers, and Knox's face is filled with shock. He just pitched the second no-hitter of his career, and he's only twenty-eight.

As his teammates rush toward him to celebrate, he points at me. Like a *this is for you* kind of point. That must be what he planned for launching this, *us*. The man who shows no emotion on the field will create a frenzy by pointing at a woman in the stands. That's a nice, subtle way to do it.

Lucia's arms wrap around my shoulders. "Lo, he pointed at you!"

I laugh, unable to contain my excitement about this game. "It's a good soft launch, don't you think?" Lucia smiles, and we go back to celebrating with the crowd.

With my back to the field now, I don't see Knox walking over. It isn't until the fans around us start going wild that I realize something is happening. I turn around... and find Knox's eyes focused right on me.

And then realization washes over me. These seats were explicitly picked for us. We're next to the dugout, but we're also *not behind the netting*. He probably doesn't realize my season ticket seats are open like this, and he wanted to make sure he could reach me.

Knox walks up to me, eye to eye since I'm in the raised seating, and wraps an arm around my waist. He leans forward, giving me a gentle hug.

As he pulls away, he whispers, "Ready for this, Pierce?" and without a moment's hesitation, his lips meet mine.

Knox is *kissing me*. In front of tens of thousands of fans. In front of millions of viewers watching at home, having tuned in to see the completion of a no-hitter.

The surprise washes away, and I quickly return the kiss, throwing my arms around his shoulders and bringing him closer.

At that moment, the outside world ceases to exist. It's just us. It's just this moment. And I have only one thought.

Knox Spencer is a damn good kisser.

Eight

Knox

TIME STANDS STILL. THE roar of the crowd must be deafening, but I don't hear a thing.

I knew we needed a way to launch this "relationship" that left no doubt. Something that wasn't ambiguous where people could try to say Harlow is just a friend. A kiss on the field after an unexpected no-hitter certainly conveys that message.

What I wasn't expecting, though, was for Harlow to *kiss me back*. I thought I'd peck her lips, and that would be that. But as soon as our lips meet, she throws her arms around my neck, pulling me in closer as she molds her body against mine.

But the most unexpected part of this kiss is how good it feels, how *right* it feels. I don't know if it's the adrenaline pumping after a game or how soft her lips feel, but this kiss with Harlow is electric. I can feel the sparks blazing between us, and I've no doubt that everyone around us can see them, too.

One more kiss, and we part, her arms still draped around my shoulders. Her forehead is pressed against mine, and those deep blue eyes bore right into me. "Hi," she says.

"Hi," I reply back. "You good?"

"Yeah." She smiles brightly. "I'm good."

"Good."

"You looked incredible out there tonight. You pitched a fantastic game." She gazes at me for a few more seconds before saying, "Go celebrate with your team, Knox. I'll find you outside of the clubhouse later."

She removes her arms from me, and I slowly walk away, dazed and confused, wondering what the hell just happened.

After we leave the field, Skipper asks Lane, Cole, and me to head into the media room for the post-game press conference. Lane hit a three-run homer tonight, and Cole had a two-run double and a couple of other runs. The three of us had great games tonight.

This will be my first press conference since we started this whole fake dating thing. And since that's only part of rebranding my image, I need to handle the media here more gracefully than usual. That won't be difficult, not tonight. The high of my second career no-hitter combined with the electricity coursing through my body after that kiss will probably make this my best media appearance yet.

In front of the media room is a long table with four chairs and four microphones. Skipper takes the far seat, followed by Lane, me, and Cole, who rounds us out.

After clearing his throat, Skip addresses the small crowd before us. "Thank you for coming here tonight. We had a big win today, and I think the three men up here beside me played a large part in why. We're open to questions now."

A female reporter in the second row raises her hand to speak. "Spencer, how are you feeling right now?"

The corner of my mouth pulls up into a smile. It's hardly a surprise that the no-hitter is the first thing on their minds right now. "I'm feeling pretty good. This is all a little surreal, but it feels good." Cole knows about my need to improve my relationship with the media. Lane doesn't. And he's already giving me side-eye because I never speak this much. I'm sure part of that is also me kissing Harlow in front of everyone when he's entirely in the dark about the situation.

"Pierce," a male reporter in the front row says, "You had one of the best games of your career tonight, five hits in six at-bats. Four runs batted in. What was going through your head on the field tonight?"

"Honestly," Cole starts, "during a game, I only focus on the current moment, the current at-bat, the current defensive play. My only concern is making the most out of every play. Most of that worked in my favor tonight."

"Brooks," another male reporter in the back of the room says. "You hit a three-run home run in the first inning tonight. Do you think the game would have had such a high score if you hadn't provided the momentum at the start?"

"Oh man," Lane says, raking a hand through his light brown hair. "I'd love to take all of the credit. That would really feed into my ego." The room laughs. Like I said before, Lane always gives the media what they want. "But tonight wasn't my doing. We're a team. We play together. If it wasn't me who started the game off that strong, it would've been another one of these guys. I don't think I had any hand in how the game played out."

Lane may be the media darling, but he's a real team player. He jokes about having an ego, but he's probably one of the most grounded people on the team. We're not alike in many ways, but his attitude is why he's become one of my closest friends.

"We have time for a few more questions," Fisher pipes in.

A female reporter in the front speaks up. "Spencer, what did your girlfriend have to say about your no-hitter tonight?"

Ah, there it is. I knew it would come up soon.

Trying to mask the nerves about publicly addressing this for the first time, I speak confidently—or I try to, at least. "She said I pitched a great game tonight. She may be just as excited as I am about it." Cole stifles a laugh while Lane shoots me a *you're-telling-me-all-about-this-later* look.

"Spencer again," a reporter I can't see says. "You're well-known for not sharing any bit of your personal life. Who is the woman that has you willing to kiss her in front of the cameras tonight?"

I can't hide my discomfort this time. I was hoping I could keep it somewhat vague tonight, but with a question that direct, I can't really avoid it. "Her name is, uh," I start, rubbing my neck before taking a breath. "Her name is Harlow Pierce."

"Pierce?" someone in the audience says. "As in..."

"Cole Pierce?" Cole responds with a giant smirk. He's enjoying this too much. "Yeah, Harlow is my sister."

I hear a few *ohh's* from the crowd before somebody speaks up.

"And what do you think of that, Mr. Pierce?"

Cole leans back in his chair, resting his folded hands behind his head. "I think it's a great thing. My sister is a very bright and friendly person. Should help Fort Knox over here become a little less grumpy finally."

The audience laughs as Skipper closes out the questioning, releasing us to the clubhouse.

❮❮❮❮❮❮❮❮❮❮❮❮❮❮❮❮❮❮❮❮❮❮❮❮❮❮❮❮❮❮❮❮❮❮

Once we exit the media room, Lane steps behind me and grasps my shoulders, steering me toward the clubhouse. "You've got a lot to talk about, Spence." I sigh as Cole laughs. Lane glances over at him. "You didn't say anything either, Pierce. I'm adding you to my shit list." Cole goes silent as we finish the walk to the clubhouse.

When we get to the clubhouse and step inside, I find Josh sitting in a chair by my things, three other empty chairs around him. I should've expected that I wouldn't be let off easy tonight.

"You're not even going to let me shower first?" I grumble as Lane leads me to one of the empty chairs.

"Don't pretend to act all grumpy now, Spencer," Lane says. "You just played it up for the media out there."

"I'm just in a good mood," I reply sheepishly.

"And why is that?" Cole prods, shooting me a knowing look.

"Fuck off, Cole. Can't I just be happy I pitched a no-hitter tonight?"

"Not when you ditch us on the field and run over to kiss Cole's sister," Josh adds. "So, you're dating Harlow?"

I sigh. Now it's time to really play this off. Cole is the only one here who knows this is fake. I need to keep it that way. "Yes, I'm dating Harlow."

"When did that happen?" Lane asks. "Outside of checking her out when Pierce isn't looking, you've never shown any interest in her." Cole shoots me a curious look.

"Shut the fuck up, man," I say, shoving Lane's shoulder.

"So, you have been checking my sister out then, huh?" Cole asks, amusement clear in the inflection of his voice.

I really fucking hate this interrogation.

Head in my hand, I reply, "Look, your sister is hot. I have eyes. And I evidently wasn't looking at her discreetly if fucking Brooks noticed."

"Interesting," Cole muses. And I don't like it. I have no idea what he's imagining, and if he's thinking it means something it doesn't.

Josh pipes in. "When did you start dating her?"

Sighing, I respond, "It's new. It's only been a couple of weeks."

"And you feel good enough about the relationship to broadcast it on national television already?" Lane asks in disbelief. Hard to blame him. I wouldn't believe it if I were him, either.

Cole slaps a hand on my shoulder. "When you know, you know, eh, Spencer?" What I wouldn't give to wipe that smug ass smirk off his face.

"Can I please just shower? I pitched a fucking no-hitter, and you're more interested in my damn relationship."

Josh just looks at me, confused. "It's just a little hard to believe Fort Knox has a girlfriend, and he's shown her to the entire world now."

Yeah. Fucking tell me about it.

Nine

Harlow

AFTER REMAINING IN THE stands, awestruck, for another minute after Knox kissed me, Lucia steers me out of the crowd and directly into her office at the stadium. From here, we watch the press conference where Knox tells everyone that we're together. And Cole makes sure to mention that, yes, I am his sister, smirking the entire time.

Fucking brothers.

Lucia already interrogated me about the kiss.

Did I know he was going to do it? No.

How do I feel now? I have no idea.

How was it? Good...

But that's an understatement. It was the most electric kiss of my life. It gave me *butterflies*. It wasn't even some deep, passionate kiss. It was more than a peck but not much more than that. And still, it worked its way into my memory, already knowing I might never feel that during a kiss again. I don't know how the hell Knox did that, but he ruined every other kiss I'll have in my life.

When the press conference ends, Lucia turns to ESPN to see what they're saying. And the only thing they're talking about right now is the no-hitter leading right into a kiss where Knox Spencer shows his girlfriend to the world. I knew this would happen, but I'm still sick to my stomach.

Lucia's office door swings open, and Rory marches inside on a warpath with a sleeping Sage on her shoulder. "Harlow Louise Pierce." She points right at me. "What the fuck?"

"Hey, Rory... enjoy the game tonight?" I say in a dismal attempt to steer the conversation.

It didn't work.

"Harlow. You're dating *Knox Spencer*? How and when did that happen?"

"It's, uh... new. Just a couple weeks."

She's not buying it.

"I was with you on Wednesday when Knox texted you saying he wanted you to meet with him and his agent. You didn't ever have his goddamn number in your phone, Lo. Try again."

I sigh, realizing there's no way I can spin this so Rory will believe me. She was there when this all started, and she knew we weren't together.

"The meeting with Knox and his agent was about this. He needs to improve his image to get an endorsement deal with Axis, and his agent thinks the best way to change his public perception is to... fake a relationship with me." I sink into the chair I'm sitting in, bringing my hands up to my face. "I'm living in a fucking romance book right now."

"Then you should know that fake dating never works, Lo," Rory smirks.

"That's exactly what I told her!" Lucia chimes in. "The couple always ends up with feelings before it ends."

"Yeah, and you also said you bet Knox is in love with me by the end of the season. That's not going to happen."

Rory sits in a chair across from me, putting her hand on Sage's back to keep her from falling. "I'm not so sure about that, Lo. Knox *smiled* tonight during the press conference. He fucking smiled. He does *not* smile for no reason."

"He pitched a no-hitter, Ror. His good mood and happiness had nothing to do with kissing me."

Lucia turns from the TV and swivels her office chair around to face us. "Lo, you didn't see the kiss. I could *see* the damn chemistry you two had."

"I've seen the kiss," I retort. "ESPN has played it fifty damn times now."

"Not from my vantage point. You could practically see the sparks flying."

I just sigh. "Can we just... not tell Ella, please? You two and Cole know. I really don't want this to get to everyone, or it won't be believable."

"We can manage that," Rory replies. "Ella's busy planning a wedding anyway, so she probably won't notice anything weird." Rory's look turns more mischievous now. "Shouldn't you be going to find your boyfriend, Lo? WAGs always leave with their man."

"Those are the real wives and girlfriends, Ror. This is fake."

"Not according to the media."

I groan, realizing that I need it to look real to sell this. "I'm going to go find Knox. I told him I'd find him after the game anyway."

≪≪≪≪≪≪≪≪≪≪≪≪≪≪≪≪≪≪≪≪≪≪≪≪≪

"Ready to get out of here?" Knox asks me when I find him outside of the clubhouse.

"Yeah, let's get out of here. Lucia and Rory interrogated me, so I'm exhausted now."

He lets out a breath. "Yeah, I got into the clubhouse after the press conference, and Josh was there waiting for us to get back so he could interrogate me with Lane and your brother. Fucking night-mare, honestly."

I laugh. "Well, at least we're in this nightmare together then, right?"

Knox peers down at me, a small smile pulling at the corners of his lips. "Yeah, you're not too bad."

"Ooh, I went from tolerable to not too bad. I'm already moving on up."

That earns an honest chuckle from him. "You're something, Harlow."

"Is that a good thing or a bad thing?"

"I'm not sure yet," he says, pushing open the exit door and gesturing me through it. "Come on, I can walk you to your car. It's pretty late now."

"Oh, I don't drive. I don't even have a car. I took the subway. I'm just going to walk to the subway station and catch the line that goes to Kips Bay. The station's only a couple blocks from my apartment."

Knox stops walking and just stares at me. "You usually catch the subway at night and walk alone to your apartment?"

"Yeah," I shrug. "I've been doing it for years."

"Not anymore," he says, shaking his head. "My car's in the lot over here. I'll drive you home."

"I don't need you to drive me home, Knox. The subway is fine."

"Harlow, as far as the city is concerned, you're my girlfriend. I don't trust what kind of creeps will be out for you once they realize it's you. You're far safer with me."

"Am I?" I ask, cocking my eyebrow. "I barely know you. You're practically a stranger to me, Spencer."

He sighs. "Are you really going to fight me on this?"

"And what if I am?" I look at him in defiance.

Knox brings a finger up to my chin to keep it in place as he speaks. "Then I will throw you over my goddamn shoulder and put you in the car myself, Pierce. You're not taking the subway."

That shouldn't turn me on, right? Because it totally just turned me on. A controlling attitude should be a red flag. I don't think Knox meant it to be controlling, though. I think he's genuinely worried something could happen to me because of my new association with him.

I'm thrown off of my game now, unsteady. That might be because I have somebody concerned about my well-being for the first time since I left Derek. And Derek was hardly ever concerned. Knox is showing more concern for a woman he hardly knows than a man I dated for more than a year.

"Okay," I relent. "Where's your car?"

"Follow me," he says, turning and walking off in the other direction.

‹‹‹‹‹‹‹‹‹‹‹‹‹‹‹‹‹‹‹‹‹‹‹‹‹‹‹‹‹‹‹‹‹

"Thanks for the ride, Knox," I say as he pulls up in front of my building. In a black fucking *Maserati*. "I appreciate it."

"It's not a problem." He runs a hand through his hair, letting it fall around his head. The messy look suits him.

"I should probably get inside."

"Just a minute," he says, taking a moment to gather himself. "Thank you for doing this. I owe you a lot. Faking a relationship with the asshole of the league probably isn't your idea of a good time."

I laugh before responding. "I don't know, you don't seem much like an asshole to me, Spencer. You're just mysterious." I lean forward on the center console, bringing myself closer to him, inhaling the musky scent of the body wash he must have used during his postgame shower. "And I'm going to learn all about you; just wait."

"Am I going to get to learn about you in the process?" he asks.

"That depends on whether or not you believe I'm worth knowing, I think," I reply shyly.

"Harlow," he says thoughtfully, placing his finger under my chin again like he did outside the stadium. "You're worth knowing, I'm certain of that. Whatever man made you feel like you aren't was dead wrong."

Breathless.

I'm breathless right now, absorbing the words and trying to take them to heart. Knox doesn't know me well, but he must be able to read me.

I just nod at him, unable to speak, before he glances at something out the window. "Fuck," he mutters under his breath.

"What's wrong?" I ask with concern in my voice.

"There's a man down the street with a camera pointed right at us."

My eyes widen. "How did they find out where I live already?"

"Paparazzi are some shady motherfuckers." He sighs. "Do you want to really sell this?"

I nod, giving him the permission he's looking for. He leans forward, and his lips find mine again. This time, Knox kisses me deeper than he did at the game. He snakes an arm around my waist and angles his head, bringing his tongue to glide against mine.

If I thought the kiss earlier was good, this one is *mind-blowing*. I'm losing myself in this. I know we're putting on a show, but that doesn't mean I can't enjoy myself while we are.

He slowly pulls away, his face flushed and looking as flustered as I feel. I awkwardly sit back, grabbing my bag from the floor. "I'll, uh... I'll see you on the plane tomorrow, Knox."

"Have a good night, Harlow," he says as I step out of the car and close the door behind me. I glance back before I step into my building, finding Knox scrubbing a hand over his face as if trying to calm his racing thoughts.

His thoughts probably aren't racing, but mine sure as hell are. How do I act normally after a kiss like *that*? I don't think I can.

I throw open my apartment door and toss my bag on the floor before heading to my bathroom. I'm in desperate need of a release right now. I've got a waterproof vibrator and a mind full of naughty thoughts, so a shower is what I need before I can fall asleep tonight.

Ten

Harlow

I OVERSLEPT THIS MORNING, so I have to get ready quickly to avoid missing the flight. I throw on the first pair of leggings I see and a baggy Stars T-shirt. Once I pull my hair up into a ponytail and apply a quick layer of foundation, I'm out the door, thankful I packed my suitcase last night instead of waiting until this morning.

Lucia finds me as soon as I arrive at the airport. "Good morning, Harlow," she says, all chipper. "Have a good night after you left the game?" She gives me a knowing look.

I groan. "Those pictures are online already, aren't they?"

"They sure are. So not only did Knox drive you home, you also made out with him."

"He saw the guy with the camera, Luc. We agreed to kiss because we knew it would be better to make this believable."

"Hell of a convincing kiss then." She turns toward me now. "Was it good?"

"Ooh, I want to know, too!" Rory says, coming up from behind me.

Letting out a sigh, I say, "It was a really damn good kiss. I had to take a shower after."

"What kind of shower?" Rory asks, raising her brow.

"*That* kind of shower," I reply, laughing lightly.

"I'm telling you," Rory says, stabbing a finger into my chest, "a man like that knows what he's doing in bed. You need to find out."

"I'm not going to do that. I don't need that in my life. I can take care of myself."

"You know you'd have more fun if Knox was taking care of you," Lucia says as she winks.

I can't decide if I love or hate my friends. Maybe it's both.

Would I have more fun with Knox? Oh, I know I would. If the man is as good in bed as he is at kissing, I know it would be an incredible night. But I'm not about to blur any lines in this fake relationship. Kissing is putting on a show for anyone who sees us. Sleeping together would serve no purpose because nobody would know. That would be just for us, which doesn't fit into this arrangement.

Thankfully, it's time to board the plane before Lucia and Rory can continue this conversation. When everyone is boarded, I find Knox sitting alone, so I slide in right beside him.

He takes an earbud out, surprised since Knox usually sits alone when we travel. "Uh, hey. Why are you sitting with me?"

"Well, we need to make this believable, don't we?"

"Don't you usually sit with Lucia and Rory?"

I smirk. "You've been paying attention to where I sit, huh?"

Worry crosses his face, realizing what he's revealed. But he plays it off. "I pay attention to where everyone sits, Harlow. But I can also see Lucia and Rory looking over at us while they think I can't see. Even if I didn't know, it wouldn't be hard to put together that you usually sit with them."

Damn. That shouldn't really matter, but I think I like the idea of him finding me to look. A confidence boost is always a good thing.

"Right, that makes sense." I peer over at his phone, trying to see what's playing. "Whatcha listening to, Spencer?"

He hands me an earbud. "It's a random playlist. Mostly rock and alternative."

"So, you're telling me you're not a secret Swiftie?"

"Fuck no," he replies emphatically, causing me to crack up. "I'm going to assume you are."

"For sure. Have been since her debut."

He hands me his phone. "Put her on."

I stare at him questioningly. "You want to listen to Taylor Swift?"

He shrugs. "I'm supposed to be getting to know you better, right? I should probably know what music you like."

Stunned, I take the phone from him. "Okay then. I'll play my favorite album."

We relax into the seats as the plane takes off. Knox is at ease with his hands behind his head and eyes closed. And I can't help but smile. Though the gesture to listen to my favorite artist is small, it's still very sweet.

I'm already starting to learn more about Knox than I thought I would.

⫷⫷⫷⫷⫷⫷⫷⫷⫷⫷⫷⫷⫷⫷⫷⫷⫷⫷⫷⫷⫷⫷⫷⫷

Once we land in Atlanta, Rory and I make our way to the hotel room we're sharing for our stay. She keeps eyeing me, and I know she wants to garner more information about anything that happened on the plane. Nothing happened, but I'm sure she and Lucia will both start pestering me once she gets here.

I unpack my suitcase and fill up my side of the dresser while Rory takes care of her side. When that's finished, I flop onto my bed and pull out my phone. I haven't checked *Starred and Fast* since yesterday afternoon—before the entire world knew me as Knox Spencer's girlfriend.

I pull up the page and find the creator dashboard, clicking that to see my stats, such as views, email subscribers, and so on. And I'm dumbfounded.

"Holy fuck!" I shriek, startling Rory. "Holy fucking fuck, Rory!"

"What is going on?! What's happening? Why are we fucking fucks?"

"Rory, the blog. Come look at the numbers." She walks over, and I show her the phone. When she reads through everything, her mouth falls open.

Doubled. Everything has *doubled* since yesterday. Twice as many views. Two times as many email subscribers. This all happened in the less than twenty-four hours since we announced this fake relationship.

"Lo, this is amazing!"

There's a knock at the door. "I hear excitement, and I need to be involved!" Lucia demands, voice muffled through the wooden door. Rory lets her in, and I show her everything.

"Harlow! That's incredible! Your fake relationship is already paying off."

"I can't believe this honestly. It's not even been a day yet. My ad revenue for this month will be much higher than usual."

Lucia and Rory join me on the bed, sitting on either side of me. They lean in for a group hug as Lucia says, "I'm so happy for you, Lo."

"*Starred and Fast* is finally taking off," Rory adds.

The heartwarming moment is broken by the ringing of my phone. I look at the screen, and my stomach drops: *Ella*.

Well, I guess it's time for another interrogation.

"Hey, Ella," I say as I answer the phone. "What's going on?"

"Harlow, you know exactly why I'm calling," Ella replies from the other line.

I let out a breath. "Yeah, I kinda figured."

"Lo, when were you going to tell me you're dating Knox?!"

"It's still new, Ell. I wasn't intentionally keeping it from you."

Technically, it is new.

And technically, I also didn't know we were dating until a few days ago.

"I can't believe you didn't tell me! We just had dinner earlier this week."

"In my defense," I lie, "we were celebrating your engagement that night. I wasn't going to bring up my new relationship at that point."

"And all that talk about not being sure you can talk Knox into an interview? What was that?"

I sigh. "That was me trying to play it off. I didn't want to steal your thunder, Ell. I was going to tell you soon, though."

"Well," Ella says, and I can hear her smile through the phone. "I'm so happy for you! It's so nice to see you getting back out there after Derek."

"Yeah," I reply uneasily. "It's nice to finally be moving past him."

That part's true, at least. Even if this relationship isn't real, I can still feel myself finally moving on after Derek. Maybe this is exactly what I need to do for that.

I continue the call by spinning the web of lies and deceit Knox and I agreed to when we started this whole arrangement. I don't like lying to one of my best friends, but I don't think I have any other choice. We can't have more people knowing than necessary. I know she'll understand when I tell her one day.

Once Ella is satisfied with the details I provide—all fake, of course—she lets me go, and I decide to peruse the internet and see what's happening. There are a lot of articles out right now, and I wonder what people are saying...

Eleven

Knox

Thirty-seven, thirty-eight, thirty-nine, forty. Yup, still forty tiles on the ceiling of my hotel room. Just like there were the last time I counted them. And the time before that.

Even mindlessly counting the goddamn ceiling tiles can't quell my mind from all the insanity of the last twenty-four hours. I can say with absolute certainty this is a situation I never thought I'd find myself in. Yet here I am, pretending to date my buddy's sister, all so I can get a fucking endorsement deal.

Honestly, if this was anyone but Cole, they'd be telling me that I'm a shitty friend and a shitty person. Cole is unbothered, though, constantly ribbing me over this ordeal. I can't say I blame him. I'd be doing the same if it were him.

A knock at the door brings me out of my trance. As soon as I open it, Lane bursts inside. "Hello to you, too, man."

Lane takes a seat on Cole's bed and waits for me to sit down as well before speaking. "Talk, Spencer. What the hell is going on with you and Harlow?"

"We're dating. I think that's pretty clear." Lane just looks at me, telling me he's not buying the story.

"You have never expressed interest in her more than just ogling her when she's around."

"Yeah, well, then I got to know her."

"How? You don't talk, Knox."

"I'm talking to you right now, asshole."

Lane sighs, resting his head against his palm. "Fine. Tell me this, then. How long are you together?"

I let out a breath. "Just through the season."

And then I realize what he just did.

"I fucking knew it!" Lane shouts.

"Fucking hell, Lane. You were just waiting for me to trip up, weren't you?"

"Pretty much, yeah," he says, laying back on the bed with a proud smile. "I knew there was no way it was real. You wouldn't keep that from me."

"Just... don't tell anyone, please," I sigh. "Even Josh. I don't need this getting out."

"Dude, I'm not going to tell anyone. But what's the point of this? Why do you need to fake a relationship with somebody, and why is that somebody Cole's sister?"

"Axis," I sigh. And for the umpteenth time this week, I explain everything that happened with Axis, Simon, and now Harlow.

"Shit, man. Does Harlow get anything from this?"

"Traffic for her blog. She said that's all she wants. Said that once this was public, people would search for the woman who could warm my icy heart. Her words, not mine."

Just then, the bathroom door opens, and Cole emerges to join us. "Ah, she's going to warm your icy heart, huh?"

"What the fuck were you doing in there, Cole?" Lane asks. "I've been here for like ten minutes already."

"I was on the phone, dick. Apparently, my mother is not happy that I didn't tell her my sister is dating Knox here. I just got an earful. Also, you literally just got here, Lane. I heard you come in."

Lane rolls his eyes. "And how long have you known about this, Cole?"

He shrugs. "Wednesday. I needed a hair tie before the game and found Knox in the clubhouse, seemingly contemplating all of his life choices. He told me then."

"And you didn't tell me?" Lane asks, offended.

"Not my news to share, man. I think he had to figure out how to deal with this on his own before everyone else found out."

The sound of vibration fills the air, and I turn to see my phone on the nightstand with a text message notification. I grab it to find several messages from a number I don't have saved.

Unknown

Knox, this is Lucia

I grabbed your number from the team directory

You may need to come help Harlow

She's pretty distraught because she made the mistake of looking at the comments on the articles about you two, and they're not very pretty...

"Guys, do we know what the media and fans are saying? Lucia just messaged me saying Harlow is upset after reading some comments."

"Shit," Cole says, grabbing his phone. "What are they saying?"

The three of us scroll through our phones, looking through articles and comments to discover what's happening. And the comment sections are all the same. Some commentary says we make a cute couple, and they like seeing Fort Knox smile.

But then there are others. Others that ask why I would go for a girl like her and call her a bat bunny.

"Fuck, this is bad," I say, scrubbing my hand over my face. "I need to go check on her."

I stand up, grab my room key, and head out the door after asking Lucia which room I'm going to while Cole shouts something I don't hear as I walk away.

⫷⫷⫷⫷⫷⫷⫷⫷⫷⫷⫷⫷⫷⫷⫷⫷⫷⫷⫷⫷

"Thanks for coming over, Knox," Lucia says as she answers the door. "She's all torn up right now."

"The guys and I looked up the comments after you messaged me. I hadn't thought about the nasty things people might say."

Rory pops into the little hall leading into the room with Sage on her hip. "Neither of you predicted this. It'll get better, but it's bad right now. She just needs comfort."

"Yeah, I can do that," I say as I pinch my brow. "I'm the reason she's in this mess in the first place."

"Rory and I are going to grab coffee. We'll let you two be."

Rory and Lucia exit the room, and I make my way inside. Harlow is currently lying on her bed in the fetal position with a vacant stare on her face. I take a deep breath and sit on the side. "You okay, Harlow?"

"No. People are awful," she says as she wipes tears from her eyes.

"Yeah," I say, letting out a sigh. "You gotta make sure you don't let their words get to you."

Harlow sits up now, sliding in right next to me. "They're calling me a bat bunny, Knox. They think we're together because I wanted to get with a baseball player."

"They must be the ones who don't realize you're a rabid baseball fan then."

She lets out a deep breath. "I think it's because of the blog that they're thinking it. That I love baseball so much that I'd do anything to bed one of the players."

"They don't know you," I say as I put an arm around her shoulder. "*Starred and Fast* exists because you want to help more people understand the sport and the team you root for, not because you want to fuck a baseball player."

She's silent for a moment. Then she turns to face me and says, "You read my blog, Knox?"

"Oh, uh... yeah," I reply awkwardly. "I read through it after the game on Wednesday. Figured I should know about the blog I'm helping drive traffic to."

She gives me a soft smile. "Thank you. I appreciate that."

"You don't need to thank me, Harlow," I state honestly. "The blog is good. You put so much good information there and broke it down in a way that's easier to understand for people unfamiliar with the sport. I think it's awesome."

Her eyes are still glassy, but her smile is brighter now. "You know, I'm really starting to think you might be a good guy, Spencer."

"Ah, you're upset, so your judgment is off, Pierce. You can't trust your mind right now."

She laughs earnestly, and I find myself enjoying the melodic sound. Her happiness is almost contagious. I have a hard time not smiling around her.

"Tell you what," I say. "Why don't you order us some room service, and you tell me more about yourself. We can forget all about what the shitty people online are saying."

Harlow's smile is gentle. "I'd like that."

Twelve

Knox

"You did not. No fucking way, Pierce."

"Swear on my life," Harlow says, hands in the air.

"You wore colored contacts for six months in college to convince the guy you were seeing that you actually had purple eyes?"

"I scrubbed all the evidence from my phone, but I can guarantee my parents still have some pictures somewhere." She laughs as she pops a bite of an onion ring into her mouth. Her excitement over finding those on the room service menu seems to have distracted her from what people are saying.

"What made you stop then? How did you have purple eyes for six months and then suddenly have bright blue eyes?"

"I got an eye infection and couldn't wear my contacts. The guy thought I was an idiot and broke it off with me." She covers her mouth as she laughs, hiding the food from view. "I was a dumbass at eighteen."

"Sounds like it," I reply, taking a bite of one of the onion rings.

She shoves my shoulder. "Is my pain amusing you, Spencer?"

"Very much so."

She rolls her eyes and huffs out a laugh. "Okay, your turn then. I need an embarrassing story from you, sir."

"Sir?" I raise an eyebrow at her.

"Don't get hung up on that," she says as she waves me off. "Tell me a story about you."

I groan. "I was hoping I could steer you away from that."

"Not a chance, Fort. Talk."

"Fine," I say in exasperation. "I've got one from my freshman year of college, too. I met a girl at one of the parties off-campus. She lived in one of the coed dorms. Flirting led to both of us going back to her room. And, well, I'm sure you can guess what was happening. What she hadn't told me, though, is that she had a boyfriend, and when he came knocking on her door, I had to jump out of the fucking window. Thankfully, she lived on the first floor, but I had to hide in the bushes buck naked until my friends brought me some clothes."

Harlow has to bring her hand up to cover her mouth and prevent spitting her food everywhere. "Oh my God, that's fucking hysterical!" She wipes the tears from her ears, happy ones this time. "The blue balls must've been so painful for you afterward."

I snort in reaction to her unexpected concern. "Fucking hell, Harlow. If you really must know, there were no blue balls. The fear of being caught naked outside of a girl's dorm was enough to tame me." She smiles as she softly chuckles. "Now come on. Tell me something random. I need to know more about my fake girlfriend."

"Hmm... random," she says, a look of concentration on her face. "Oh! Here's something random. I don't like flowers."

"What?" I respond in surprise. "Who doesn't like flowers?"

Harlow shrugs. "Me. Flowers die. I always get fake flowers if I want any."

"Yeah, you're definitely something. I've learned today that you don't have purple eyes, you hate flowers, and you have freckles."

Her hands shoot up to her face. "You can see them?!" She looks uncomfortable now.

"You must've removed your makeup when you rubbed the tears from your eyes earlier."

"Oh," is all she says in response.

"Why do you hide them? Today is the first time I even realized you had freckles."

"I just don't like them," she replies quickly, looking away from me. There's more to this, but I won't press her. But I will make sure she gets comfortable with the fact that she has them.

"You shouldn't hide them," I say, taking another bite of an onion ring. "You look good with freckles. They suit you."

She glances at me in disbelief. Before she can ask me more about it, the hotel room door opens, and Rory and Lucia walk into view. "Oh, sorry," Rory says. "We didn't realize you'd still be here."

"Oh, uh... yeah. But she's much happier now." I stand from the bed, brushing a few crumbs from my shirt. "I should get going, though. The game's at four tomorrow, so we have an early practice." I turn to wave at Harlow. "I'll catch you tomorrow, Freckles."

Her mouth falls open. "You think you're slick, don't you, Knox?"

"I know I am." She shakes her head as I wink at her. "Don't look at any more comments, okay?"

"Promise. Never doing that again."

"Good. Have a good night, Freckles."

"Have fun at practice tomorrow, Slick."

I laugh as I make my way to the door and walk out with an actual smile on my face.

⋘⋘⋘⋘⋘⋘⋘⋘⋘⋘⋘⋘

"Why the fuck are you two in my bed?" I ask Lane and Josh as I walk back into my room.

"Cole doesn't want to cuddle, and Josh and I want to see how Harlow is doing."

"How is she?" Cole asks as he sits up on his own bed. "There's some really awful shit out there right now."

"She's doing better now," I say as I sit on the edge of my bed. "She was pretty rough when I first got there, but then she ordered some onion rings, and we just talked. It seemed to help keep her mind off of what people are saying."

"I would've come with you if you didn't take off like a bat outta hell, but thanks for cheering her up, man. My sister's an emotional person—I should've known something like this could happen."

"It's the least I could do, honestly. She's going through this shit because of me. Helping her feel better is at the bottom of the barrel regarding what I could do. But I'm glad it seemed to work."

"I think she'll be okay," Lane chimes in. "She's emotional, yes, but she's tough. She'll find a way to adjust to all this attention."

"She's come a long way after her fucking ex," Cole adds. "I think she's in the right headspace now to handle it. It'll just be hard at first while she's getting used to it."

"She has a shitty ex?" I ask.

Cole takes a deep breath. "Yeah, but it's not my story to tell. I'm sure Harlow will open up about that in the future. She's spent a lot of the past year healing and getting back to the person she was."

"Damn," is all I can say. The Harlow I know now is outgoing, happy, and fucking confident. It's hard to believe there was a time when she may not have been that way. I wonder what that asshole did. And I wonder if he's the reason she hides those pretty freckles...

"So, what did you talk about?" Josh asks, cocking an eyebrow. "Anything fun?"

"Dude," Cole says, throwing a pillow that smacks Josh across the face. "Shut the fuck up, will you?"

"We didn't talk about anything like that, asshole. We just hung out and spent more time getting to know each other." Since Josh doesn't know this isn't real, I add, "I need to know more about her if this is going to last."

"So, what did you talk about then?" Lane asks.

"We shared some embarrassing stories."

"Like?" Cole says, lifting his brow.

I sigh and tell them our stories. They weren't nearly as interested in Harlow's story as they were in mine, of course. In fact, the volume of the laughter in the room right now can probably be heard in the entire damn hotel. Cole, Lane, and Josh are dabbing tears from their eyes and trying to catch their breath.

"Fucking naked outside in the bushes. That's fucking gold, man," Cole says.

"It was fucking mortifying, prick," I reply, using the pillow Cole tossed at Josh to throw right back at him. "I didn't know she had a boyfriend."

"Okay, okay," Lane says, trying to compose himself. "Let's not rag on Spence here. We can just enjoy the fact that he has now admitted he's sharing things with Harlow. A big step from the man who doesn't even talk to his friends."

"I hate you all," I say, shaking my head. "We're getting to know each other. She's my... girlfriend. I'm supposed to be sharing things with her."

I know that's the main reason I shared that with her today, but I can't say it's the only reason. I wanted to cheer her up, and if telling her an embarrassing story about myself did that, that was fine with me. I like her smile—I needed to put it back on her face.

It's kind of scary how easy it is to talk to Harlow. I don't know her well, but I can already find myself wanting to share things with her.

She has such an inviting personality. And that personality seems to have already roped in the man they call Fort Knox.

Thirteen

Knox

I spent a lot of time getting to know Harlow during our series against the Thunderbirds in Atlanta. After that first night, she's been in much better spirits, choosing to ignore anything she sees about herself online.

I still feel like a dick, though, even putting her in this situation in the first place. She's an adult and can make her own decisions, I get that, but I feel like I should have done *more* to prepare her for the onslaught of attention, positive and negative, she'd be met with. But she's taking it in stride now, focusing solely on her blog and what she can do with the traffic that should be coming her way.

We all landed in Houston Thursday night after our game to prep for a three-game series against the Comets. Last night's game was a blowout, unfortunately. Su-jin Choi, one of the other starting pitchers in our rotation, wasn't in his best form. He only lasted three innings before Skip pulled him. Every pitcher has been there before, and it fucking sucks. We couldn't squeak out a win since we never could overcome the Comets' lead on us. I've got tonight's start, and we're all hoping for a better outcome.

Josh finds me in the clubhouse as we're all suiting up to take the field for our early afternoon game. "Hey, man. How's this week been for you?"

"Crazy," I say with a light laugh. "Media isn't leaving me the fuck alone."

"Did you honestly expect them to? You kissed a girl—Cole's sister, no less—on national TV. You're all anyone wants to talk about."

I sigh. "I know. That doesn't mean I have to like it, though."

"Well, tonight's your first start since you went public. You ready?"

"I'm always ready for a game," I say with a sly smile. "Remember, nothing breaks Fort Knox."

"Nothing except Cole's sister."

"Fuck off, Garro." I slide past him as he laughs enthusiastically. I exit the clubhouse and head toward the field since it's almost time for the away team warmups. Josh follows behind me, and we walk to the rest of our team in the dugout.

But I spot Harlow on the third baseline, so I jog over to her instead. She's wearing my jersey again and that glittery Stars hat I saw her in after our first game. It suits her really fucking well.

"Hey there, Freckles," I say as I stand before her. "You by yourself today?"

"Hey, Slick," she says with a bright smile. "Yup, it's just me today. Lucia, Rory, and Sage are all hanging back with the team."

"So, it's only you that I have to impress then?" I ask, raising my eyebrow at her.

"You trying to impress me?" Harlow stands up in front of me now.

"According to everyone, you're my girlfriend. Seems like I should seek to impress you, don't you think?"

"I guess so," she replies with a shrug. "But your last game was a no-hitter, Fort. Gonna take a hell of a lot to impress me after that."

I smile and laugh. "You're never going to go easy on me, are you?"

"Never," Harlow says, her smile reaching her eyes. "Gotta keep you on your toes."

"What do you think about going out after the game today? It should be over around four, so we can grab something to eat or whatever with our friends. Kind of like a buffer when we're still getting used to each other."

"Sounds like fun, Knox." She glances over at the dugout. "Skip keeps glancing at you, and he looks kinda pissed. Might wanna get back to your team."

"You might be right," I say with a smirk. "Catch you after the game, Pierce."

"Good luck on the mound, Spencer."

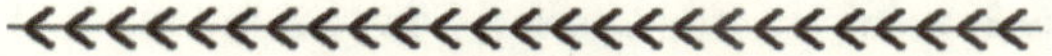

"Well, tonight fucking sucked," Cole says, stabbing his spoon into his froyo. We lost tonight on a blown save by our closer, Chris Rockman. The atmosphere in the clubhouse was pretty tense after two straight losses. I'm grateful that I didn't get the loss for today, but it still sucks when the team doesn't do well.

When we all returned to the hotel, Harlow suggested we get some frozen yogurt. Lane and Rory decided to stay with Sage, but Cole and Lucia joined us. I found a place called *FroYo-A-GoGo* that Harlow seemed really excited about. I think her bowl cost ten dollars alone, with all the strawberries, blueberries, and kiwis she piled into it.

"There's always tomorrow," she says with a smile. She's always so optimistic. I don't know how she does it.

"Yeah," I reply, rubbing my neck. "Anderson's got the start tomorrow, so I think we've got a good chance."

"Damian's good, so that's a real possibility," Harlow replies. "I'll just be rooting from the sidelines for you to avoid the sweep."

Lucia interjects, "How did we end up here with froyo instead of ice cream? Who goes for froyo?"

"That would be your best friend," I laugh. "But I'm not complaining. Froyo is so much better than ice cream."

"Excuse me?" Lucia says, pretending to look offended. "Lo, I'm sorry, but this won't do. You need to break up with him immediately."

"Well, Harlow," I say, turning my attention to her across the table from me. "We had a good run, short as it may have been."

"You're both completely fucking ridiculous," she says, trying so hard not to laugh. "Lucia, I will not be breaking up with him over froyo because your best friend *also* prefers froyo to ice cream."

"It's like I don't even know who you are, Harlow Pierce," Lucia says, hand to her chest. She's serious for a moment before both she and Harlow burst out laughing.

"Get used to it, Fort," Cole chimes. "This is how they always are. Add Rory and Ella, and they're an insane quartet."

"Hey," Harlow says, shoving Cole's shoulder. "My friends are more fun than yours. Your friend group has Knox, and he never talks to anyone."

"What the fuck?" I say. "I thought we all agreed I'm socializing more now."

"Like you said earlier, I'll never take it easy on you." She laughs and winks.

"What did I get myself into?" I grumble, scrubbing my hands over my face.

"The best relationship of your life." Harlow bats her eyelashes at me this time before dissolving into laughter.

She's going to be good at giving me hell; I can feel it. But that should make things more interesting. It'll be more fun to do this with someone who isn't afraid to take jabs in the name of a good time.

I welcome that.

Fourteen

Harlow

"Hey," I hear Rory say as she opens the door to our hotel room after I jump out of the shower.

"Hey, Rory," I hear from a familiar voice.

Knox.

What's he doing here at eight in the morning?

"You can come on in," she says as I hear footsteps from two people in the small entryway outside the bathroom. "Lo should be done with her shower in a minute. I was just heading out to help Lane with Sage, but you're welcome to wait here for her."

"Thanks. I appreciate that." The next sound I hear is the click of the hotel room door as Rory heads out into the main hallway, padding off toward Lane's room.

I hurriedly put on my clothes—dark gray leggings and a navy blue Stars crop top—and brush out my wet hair. I curse internally that I haven't gotten a chance to put on my makeup yet so you can see every one of my freckles, but this will have to do for now.

I exit the bathroom and find Knox sitting on my bed, leaning back against the wall as he waits. He looks so damn handsome when he's at ease, unworried. I hope that I can help him feel that way more often.

"Hey," I say as I step toward the bed, and his eyes shoot open. "I wasn't expecting you this morning."

"I know," Knox replies, rubbing his hand over his neck. "But we've spent a lot of time together this week, and you're not bad to be around. I thought you might want to have some breakfast before I head in for practice shortly." He gestures to the bag beside him, showing me breakfast has already arrived. I didn't notice it before.

"That's very kind, Knox," I say as I move to sit beside him on the bed. "Thank you."

"It's no problem, Harlow." He gives me a slight smile. "Cole told me you like French toast, so that's what I grabbed for you."

"And just like that, you've found the way to my heart," I joke, causing Knox to fully smile.

"Now I know that whenever I piss you off, I can just grab you some French toast to make everything better."

"I hate to say that would work," I reply, placing the French toast in front of me and handing the spinach omelet off to Knox, "but it probably would. I'm such a sucker for French toast. But don't go pissing me off often."

"I'll do my best to avoid that," Knox says, laughing. "I enjoy seeing you happy, and I don't want to know what you look like when you're angry."

"Good choice," I say as I stuff a piece of French toast into my mouth.

"By the way," he adds, "I'm glad I get to see the freckles again."

I can't help but smile as my cheeks flush.

Over the next half hour, we eat breakfast, talk, and laugh before he heads off for practice. This week has really shown me a new side of him, and it's a side I really like. Knox is so much more than a closed-off pitcher. He's actually very kind and attentive.

This fake relationship thing is going to be a breeze.

The Stars win the game against the Comets and avoid the sweep. They have tomorrow off before their next game on Tuesday, so they get a day of rest. We all jump on the plane once today's early afternoon game is finished so we can return to NYC as soon as possible. We've been on the road almost an entire week, so we're all just ready to be home.

I doze off during the plane ride, exhausted from such a busy week, and I don't wake up until we hit the ground back in New York.

I rub my eyes as I see Knox smirking next to me. I turn to him. "What are you smirking at, Spencer?"

"Nothing at all. I'm just glad you're awake—I couldn't take much more of your snoring."

"I do not snore!" I shout.

"How would you know that, Freckles?" He cocks his eyebrow at me.

"Because, Slick," I say as I poke him in the chest, "Cole is my brother. You think he wouldn't have held that over my head while we were growing up?"

Knox laughs. "Yeah, that does sound like something he'd do. You're right, you don't snore."

"So why were you smirking when I woke up then?"

"Did you ever consider the possibility that maybe you look adorable when you sleep, Harlow?"

"Is that so, Knox? Be careful there, or I might just think you're trying to flirt with me."

"Oh, I'd never do that," he responds, the tone in his voice telling me that that isn't exactly truthful. "What are you up to tonight, Pierce?"

"Probably getting some takeout, eating a tub of frozen yogurt, and binging something on TV."

"Interesting. I've got the same plans, minus the froyo." Knox looks me in the eyes. "Care to join me then?"

"Ooh, I've warmed you up enough to be invited over now? I must be doing something right."

Instead of shaking his head like he might have done when this first started, he just smiles. He looks so lovely when he smiles. I think he is actually warming up to me, and I really like that.

"Maybe I thought you could use a little company for your lonely night. Consider that?"

"Nope. I think you like me, Knox Spencer. You want to spend time with me just for fun."

The flight attendants tell us it's time to disembark, so we both stand up and step into the aisle. Knox grabs my bag from the overhead compartment and hands it to me before grabbing his own. He sets his suitcase on the ground before extending the handle and leaning his lips down to my ear. "You know what? I think you're right. I do want to spend time with you—just for fun."

I can't help but smile. This whole arrangement started less than two weeks ago. In that time, we've gone from never speaking to each other to actually beginning to enjoy each other's presence.

Neither of us expected what we're going through to happen, but it seems to be working so far. The traffic to my blog has skyrocketed. The media is ablaze with talk of how Fort Knox is finally opening up. And the more he opens up, the more I like the person he is underneath the mysterious persona. He's easy to talk to and actually a lot of fun to be around.

For the first time, I can admit that I'm glad we're doing this.

Fifteen

Harlow

Once we leave the airport, Knox quickly stops at my apartment. I want to drop off my suitcase and change out of what I wore on the plane. While he's waiting in the car, I throw on a pair of cropped black leggings and a white crop top, one tight enough that it puts my chest on display—I've never been shy about showing myself off. And considering Knox doesn't say a word to me after I get back in the car, I think it's also enough to thoroughly distract my fake boyfriend. He keeps a tight grip on the steering wheel and won't take his eyes off the road in front of him.

When we pull into the parking garage of Knox's building, he leads me through the back entrance to avoid the media out front. In the elevator, he taps the button for the top floor, and we slowly ascend.

"Holy shit," I say as Knox and I step off the elevator and through the front door into his penthouse. "So, this is how the other half lives, huh?"

"I'm just a person, Harlow. No different than you."

I turn to him in disbelief. "You live in a multi-million-dollar penthouse and drive a Maserati. You're not just a person."

He sighs. "I try to be as normal as possible. I'm not some pretentious asshole, but I do allow myself to indulge in nice things if I feel they're worth it."

"That's fair," I say. "Sorry if that just made you uncomfortable."

"I appreciate that, but you're okay. I know it can be a bit of a shock to step in here when it's not something you're used to seeing."

"Yeah, Cole's apartment is nice, but it's not as nice as this. He's not big on extravagance."

"You realize I've been to your brother's place before, right?" he says with a smile.

"Right, that would make sense. Sorry, I'm being a little weird right now, and I don't know why."

He chuckles. "Don't worry about it, Freckles. I'm going to drop my bag off in my room and change. Feel free to take a look around while you wait."

Knox pads off down the hall. When I hear his door shut, I allow myself to roam around and explore the place.

I walk around the kitchen, which I think is the size of my entire apartment, appreciating the luxury appliances I'll never be able to afford. His place is different than I thought it would be. I expected a bachelor pad, but this penthouse is so well put together. There are decorations on the walls, books on the coffee table, and fruit displayed in the kitchen.

I make my way across the living room to the dark navy curtains, which are drawn closed. I swing them open, and I'm stunned by the sight.

Knox lives in Battery Park City. From here, you can see the entirety of Lower Manhattan. The view is stunning. I don't think I'd ever have these curtains closed if I were the one who lived here.

"Enjoying the view?" Knox says from behind me, causing me to jump.

"Shit," I say, hand to my chest, "you can't sneak up on me like that."

I take a deep breath to calm my racing heart, only to find myself taking in a very different, incredible view—Knox in a tight black T-shirt and gray sweatpants.

Fuck me...

"You're looking a little flustered? Everything okay?" he says with a smirk.

"You're in gray sweatpants. It's not my fault that I'm flustered right now."

"Yeah?" he replies, cocking an eyebrow. "What's special about gray sweatpants?"

"You know," I respond, getting even more flustered. "Don't make me tell you what you already know, Spencer."

Knox walks backward, eyes on me with a giant smile on his face, as he moves to sit on the couch across from the window. "I have no idea what you mean, Harlow Pierce."

"So, you have no idea that gray sweatpants show off the bulge of your dick then?" I challenge as I walk to sit on the couch beside him.

"Are you checking out my dick bulge, Harlow?"

"What? No, of course not!" is what I say. But what I meant was *Yes, I am, and I'm impressed by what I see.*

"Thank goodness," he says, pretending to sigh in relief. "I don't think we're close enough for you to be thinking about my dick yet, Pierce."

"Yet?" I ask. "I shouldn't be thinking about your dick at all, Mr. Fake Boyfriend."

He leans back against the couch, chuckling. "I think that's enough about my dick for one day. Let's order some food. How's Thai sound?"

≪≪≪≪≪≪≪≪≪≪≪≪≪≪≪≪≪≪≪≪≪≪≪≪

"Oh my God," I say, sinking down into the back of the plush sofa. "That's the best pad see ew I've ever had!"

"It's my favorite Thai place," Knox says, leaning back and turning to face me. "They have the best food."

"I'm coming to you for recommendations from now on then."

"Have at it, Pierce. I'm not much of a cook, so I know all the best takeout on this side of Manhattan."

"Good to know."

"Happy to be of service, Freckles." We both laugh. "You know, I think I still need to know more about you."

"You need to know, or you want to know?" I ask. "Seems like you *want* to know more about me, Spencer."

He smiles lightly. "You got me all figured out, don't you?" Knox laughs before continuing. "Turns out you're fun to be around. I'd consider you a friend at this point, and I like to learn about my friends, Harlow."

"Lo."

"What?"

"My friends usually call me Lo."

"Okay then," he says, smiling brighter. "Tell me something I don't know about you yet, Lo."

I can't help but smile when he says Lo. Everyone calls me that, so it's nothing new, but it sounds so much better coming from Knox. We're very different people, but I think it's safe to say we hit it off. We're going to be great friends when this is all over.

"Let's see... what don't you know about me yet?" I say aloud as I wrack my brain. "Oh, I'm an ESFJ-A."

"What the fuck does that mean?"

"My personality type," I reply. "I'm considered a Consul—I'm very attentive and social. I'm also very extroverted and take dating and relationships very seriously."

"How do you even figure that out?"

"You take a test and answer questions on a sliding scale; your responses will tell you your personality type."

"Why do you need a test to tell you that?" he asks. "I could have told you that you were extroverted without you having to take a test."

"And I can tell you're cynical without you having to take a test." I smile. "Why don't we figure out your personality type? It could be kind of fun."

He scrubs a hand over his face. "Fuck it. Why not?"

Knox grabs his laptop, and I help him find the testing page. Ten minutes later, he stares at the screen, confused.

"What the hell does ISTJ-T mean?" he asks, confounded by the string of letters staring back at him from his computer.

"Ah, you're a Logistician. That makes sense."

"Doesn't make sense to me."

I turn his laptop and point at different parts of the screen. "It says here that you say what you mean, always follow through with something, and are not attention-seeking. That all seems spot-on for you, Spencer."

"Yeah, I guess," Knox says, running a hand through his hair, letting it fall messily on his head in a way that shouldn't be distracting yet distracts me anyway. He looks good in a way that's so *effortless*.

"It's not bad to be that way, you know."

"Yeah. It does show that I'm completely opposite of you, though, even if we already knew that."

"Well, they do say opposites attract," I say, giving him a soft smile.

Knox scoots closer to me on the couch. "You saying you're attracted to me?"

"Oh, I just mean for our fake relationship," I say with a faux smile. "I would never insinuate that I'm actually attracted to you. I'm not even sure how I could be."

"And yet," he says, leaning in closer and nearly brushing his lips against my cheek. "You are."

Yes, I am, I think to myself. I've always been attracted to Knox, but it was in a physical way. Now that I'm getting to know him, I'm unsure where that's leaving me. I really enjoy being around him. And as surprising as it is, he's easy to talk to. We're very different, but it's undeniable that we have some sort of chemistry between us, even if it is just platonic.

"It's getting late," I say, eager to change the subject. "I should probably head to the subway station so I can get home."

Knox grabs his phone to look at it. "Lo, it's almost midnight. You know I can't let you take the damn subway right now."

"What do you suggest I do then?"

He smiles. "Stay here tonight. I have a guest bedroom with clothing in the closet you can use to wear to sleep. I'll drive you to your apartment in the morning."

I like the idea of seeing how Knox looks first thing in the morning, so my answer is easy. "Okay," I say.

<<<<<<<<<<<<<<<<<<<<<<<<<<<<<<<<<<<<<<

The sun peeks in through the curtains of Knox's guest bedroom. Last night was the best night's sleep I've had in months. The plush mattress and soft sheets were impossible not to sink into. And the Huntington Devils—the Stars triple-A team—T-shirt of his I wore to sleep in is worn out enough to be almost threadbare in spots but the perfect softness in others.

With my messy hair pulled into a bun, I tiptoe into the kitchen in case Knox is still sleeping. But he isn't. No, when I get to the kitchen, I find an unexpected but *very* welcome sight—Knox shirtless while fixing a cup of coffee.

He's turned away from me so he can't watch me as I check out every muscle and ridge on his back leading down to the athletic shorts hanging low on his hips. Beneath that is the ass I've been staring at for three years now. Goddamn, he looks even better than I imagined.

"I know you're there, Lo," Knox says, back still turned as he breaks me out of my trance. "You checking me out?"

"What? No!" I stammer as he turns to face me, chuckling and bringing his coffee cup to his lips. And now that he's turned toward me, I can see all of the definition in his chest and abs that he's earned from years of lifting weights and pitching on the baseball field.

"You're still staring, you know."

I quickly avert my eyes, trying to play it off and failing miserably. "I-I just wasn't expecting to find you shirtless, that's all," I mumble as I slide past him, reaching for a mug to grab a cup of coffee for myself. "You think too highly of yourself, Slick."

I fix my coffee while Knox remains eerily silent. Afraid that I may have offended him, I turn to apologize only to find him slack-jawed. "You okay, Knox?" I ask, slightly concerned.

"Oh, um… yeah. All good." He runs a hand through that luscious, deep brown hair. "I just didn't think I'd be seeing you in my old shirt, that's all."

Ah. Looks like I can fluster him as much as he flusters me.

Sixteen

Knox

My shirt. Harlow's wearing *my fucking shirt*. It hits her almost at her knees and doesn't give anything about her body away... except that she's not wearing a bra. *In my shirt.* Her nipples are peaked in my goddamn shirt.

God help me. The more I get to know Harlow, the harder it is to resist her. Her freckles are on display, and her hair is still messed up from sleep. The sleek legs under the fabric of the tee are tempting me to run a hand up her thigh and find out if she wants me like I want her because seeing her in my shirt was enough to make all the blood rush straight to my dick. I had to tuck it into the fucking waistband of my boxers while her back was still turned to me.

But as tempting as this beauty in front of me is, I have to remember that this is all fake. I can't blur lines by telling her what I'm thinking right now. Especially when doing something about it would be a terrible fucking idea.

"So, uh... I don't have practice today," I say, trying to turn this into a normal conversation.

"Yes, that's usually what an off day means." She fucking smirks as she sips her coffee. I had fun when she was flustered over me being shirtless. Now, she seems to be having fun with me being flustered over her wearing my shirt.

I sigh. "It would be a good day to get out around the city. You know, to really sell this whole relationship thing."

"That sounds fun, Knox. I just want to go to my apartment first and get a change of clothes. Am I allowed to take the subway this time, Mr. Overprotective?"

Groaning, I reply, "I'm not being overprotective. People are insane, especially late at night. You're tied to me now, and I don't want something to happen to you because of it. But it's morning now. You should be fine on the subway."

"Great. I'll head to my apartment and meet you back here in a couple hours."

⋘⋘⋘⋘⋘⋘⋘⋘⋘⋘⋘⋘⋘⋘

With one hand firmly planted against the shower wall and the other tightly gripping my cock, I pump myself until I release, my cum mixing into the water and flowing down the drain. This is what I've come to, apparently—jacking off in the shower while thinking about my buddy's sister... who just also happens to be the woman the world believes I'm dating.

But *fuck me*. How she looked in my shirt this morning will forever be etched into my brain. It's been a long ass time since I've seen a woman wear my shirt like that. I forgot how fucking sexy it is.

Once I'm showered and physically satisfied, I step out into the bathroom and wrap a towel around my waist. I look down at my phone to see some missed texts from Lane and Cole.

Cole

So, how's it going fake dating my sister?

Lane

I bet he's having quite a bit of fun

wink wink nudge nudge

Cole

Fuck off, Lane

I know he checks my sister out, but I don't want to hear if he's fucking her

Lane

Oh, it's going to happen, Pierce

Just a matter of when

Knox

Fucking hell, guys

I'm not sleeping with Harlow

Cole

Thank God

Knox

Thought you weren't bothered by all of this, Cole?

Cole

I'm not, but you not having sex with my sister means I don't need to avoid this group chat

Lane

I thought you'd have caved by now, Spence

Knox

Why the hell do I talk to you guys?

Lane

Because you're grumpy and can't make any other friends

Knox

Thank God I have a new friend now, so I can finally replace you two and Josh

Cole

So, you're friends with my sister, huh?

Lane

Friends with benefits, maybe?

Knox

Christ, my life doesn't revolve around sex

Lane

I just want my friends to have fun because I haven't been laid since I found out about Sage

Knox

Fine, I'll give you all the dirty details next time I get laid. Happy now?

Lane

Very

I set my phone down and hear a knock at my door. Harlow must be back now. How long was I in the shower?

Rather than make her wait while I get dressed, I decide to answer the door as is, so I pad through the hallway before I make it to my door. Standing on the other side is a very stunned Harlow.

"You- you're not wearing clothes!" she says, shielding her eyes. "Why aren't you wearing clothes?!"

I chuckle. "I wasn't expecting you back yet. I just got out of the shower when you knocked."

"Well, go get dressed then! This-" she removes her hands from her eyes and gestures to my body, "is distracting."

"Good to know that I distract you, Freckles." She steps into my penthouse as I walk to my bedroom for something to put on.

The plan today is for this to be a casual outing. Harlow is wearing jeans, a tight-as-sin pink floral top, and brown booties. The perfect amount of casual to work with. After putting on my boxer briefs, I throw on a pair of jeans and grab a long-sleeved gray knit henley from my closet. Once I'm dressed, I head back out to find her in my living room.

"It's safe to look now," I say, the smirk on my face evident. "I won't be distracting you anymore."

Harlow turns around and groans. "You're wearing a shirt tight enough to show off every muscle in your chest."

I walk closer. "You told me yesterday that you're not attracted to me. I didn't think this would be distracting for you." I cock an eyebrow. "Unless you lied, that is." She mumbles under her breath, and I believe I can make out that she doesn't like how quickly I figured that out. I place an arm around the front of her waist and lean my lips to her ear. "Just so you know, your shirt is every bit as distracting to me as mine is to you. Call us even."

She stares at me, breathless, with a racing heart. Well, I imagine her heart is racing because mine sure as hell is. Our banter from the beginning has always been fun, but it's starting to feel more... *flirty*. And I'm not sure that's a good thing.

"We should head out," she says, breaking our eye contact. "Let's go give those tabloids something to talk about."

❮❮❮❮❮❮❮❮❮❮❮❮❮❮❮❮❮❮❮❮❮❮❮❮❮❮❮❮❮❮❮

We start our outing by walking through The Battery, the large city park near my place. On the rare occasions I get out of my house, I like to come here. It's relaxing to stroll through a patch of nature amidst the bustling city.

As we make our way through the tree-covered park, I take Harlow's hand in mine. She looks at me, surprised. "Just in case there are any people with cameras," I reassure her.

"We can do one better, then." With her hand still in mine, she leans her head against my arm as we continue down the trail step by step.

This shouldn't feel so easy, should it? It shouldn't be so easy for us to fall into step with such a romantic position when we're not really dating. Regardless of whether it shouldn't be, it is. It's *easy*. Everything with Harlow is effortless. It all just feels *right*. And I don't really know what to make of that right now.

We continue down the trail and come across one of my favorite places in the entire park. "What is this?" she asks.

"This is Castle Clinton. It was built as a fort between 1808 and 1811, but it was never used in war. It was actually the first US immigration station, years before Ellis Island."

Harlow looks at me with amusement. "You some kind of history buff, Spencer?"

I slide my hands in the pockets of my jeans. "Yeah, I guess. I've always loved history, especially learning about any of the American wars."

"Tell me more about this then, Knox. What war would this have been used in?"

I lead her over to the plaque explaining the fort's history. "If it was ever used in a war, it would've been during the War of 1812. The peace treaty for that war was signed in 1815, and the army gave up use of the fort in 1821, so it never did see battle."

"And you said this was also used for immigration?"

"It was," I confirm. "It was used for immigration until 1890, two years before Ellis Island. Some seven and a half million people came into the US through Castle Clinton."

"Fascinating," she replies.

"You don't have to pretend to enjoy it, Lo. I know history is boring for a lot of people."

"No," she says, turning to face me. "I like hearing you talk about the things you enjoy. Besides, a history lesson could probably do me some good." I can't help but smile. "Now, tell me everything you know, Professor Spencer."

Seventeen

Knox

HARLOW LISTENS TO EVERY word I say with undivided attention. She genuinely enjoys hearing me talk about something I like. And I actually find it nice to be open about myself with someone. It's been so long since I've done that, but she seems to ease my worries and insecurities.

When we continue past the fort, we come upon the SeaGlass Carousel. She somehow talks me into going on with her. I see people taking pictures, so I'm sure images of us sitting inside a giant fish, Harlow on my lap as I hold her close, will end up plastered all over the internet by tonight. And since we both smile the entire time, the pictures will look *real*. That's really what we're both hoping for.

Now, we find ourselves on a bench overlooking New York Harbor as Harlow continues to listen to me ramble on about history. "What would you say is your favorite historical fact?" she asks, glancing up from the spot where she's taken residence on my shoulder.

"In all of history? That's a lot of time, Lo."

She laughs. "Fine. What's your favorite random fact in American history, then?"

"Okay, did you know that Abraham Lincoln's son, Robert, was present for three presidential assassinations?"

"What? He saw three of them?!"

"He did," I reply. "He was in Washington when his father was assassinated in 1863. He was on the scene when President James Garfield was shot in 1881. Garfield didn't die directly from the gunshot but developed sepsis from it, and that's what ultimately killed him. Robert was then also present when President William McKinley was assassinated in 1901."

"Apparently, that man needed to stay away from sitting presidents," she laughs. "That's insane."

"And probably a bit morbid," I reply, rubbing the back of my neck.

"Then I guess it's a good thing I don't shy away from a little morbidness." She smiles at me again, and I think my heart skips a beat. I've been so closed off from everyone for so long that sitting with Harlow and having a conversation is just refreshing. I'm finding that I like her presence more and more.

"So, tell me this, Lo," I say. "Why do you keep asking me about history? It doesn't seem to be something you're interested in."

"I don't dislike history or anything," she replies, "but it was never my favorite subject. I've known you for years, though, Knox, and I've never seen you smile more than you have today. You've been lighting up with every story you tell me."

I feel a smile tug at the corner of my lips as I pull her closer. "Maybe that's because I like that you're so interested in hearing about it. You're trying to learn about what I like, and that's pretty damn cool."

"Well, I like getting to know you. You're a fascinating person."

I smile and press a kiss on her forehead. Harlow has been the biggest surprise of my life. It's not just the whole fake relationship thing. She's surprising me by wanting to actually learn about me. She could've learned just enough to fake this successfully, but she's gone beyond that. She wants to know everything about me.

And in time, I just might let her.

Once Harlow had enough of her history lesson, I suggested we go grab a couple milkshakes. There's a diner not far from my penthouse that makes the best ones I've found in all of Manhattan. Now we're sat on the patio, two milkshakes in front of us as she nuzzles into my side. She claims it's because anyone could see us. I'm starting to think, though, that she's just comfortable around me now. I also think I really like that.

"So, you haven't really talked to me much about how the blog is doing right now," I say, sipping my double chocolate milkshake. It's not really in my diet during the season, but I can make the occasional exception. "How has *Starred and Fast* been performing?"

"Oh!" she says excitedly. "I can't believe I forgot to tell you about that. My numbers have skyrocketed. My ad revenue for April will be much better than it's been. Maybe I'll be able to afford something that's not a shoebox," she says as she playfully elbows me in the side.

"Well, I'm glad it's doing well. You deserve that—the blog is excellent, Lo."

Harlow looks at me with a sweet smile. "Thank you. I've had people in my life before who didn't support me, so that means more than you know."

"I'm sorry that they were too blind to see what you're capable of. You're amazing at what you do." And I hope she knows that I genuinely mean that. Harlow has the right kind of attitude to do anything she wants and be great at it. I'm finding that I really enjoy her spirit.

"You know," she says, locking her eyes onto mine, "when you brought coffee over that day, you told me you weren't sweet, that you were just a colossal dick in the morning. Your words, not mine." I laugh heartily. "But you were wrong."

I eye her suspiciously. "Am I not a colossal dick in the mornings?"

"Not that I've noticed. You were quite pleasant this morning. But that's not what I meant. You're actually really sweet, Knox. More so than I expected you to be."

"I'm usually not," I admit. "That seems to be the case only with you, Harlow."

"I must be pretty special then."

I rest my elbow on the table and prop my head up with my knuckles. "Maybe you are," I say.

We stay like this for a few moments, staring at each other with smiles etched onto our faces. And then we hear the click of a camera. We're broken out of our reverie but remain in the same positions.

"Well, I'm betting that picture will really sell this whole thing," Harlow says as she breaks the silence.

"Oh?"

"Oh yeah. You staring all lovingly into my eyes like that? The tabloids are all going to talk about how Knox Spencer is down bad for Cole Pierce's little sister."

"That would definitely help with this whole charade," I say. "But I know of something else that would help, too."

"Mmm," she replies amusingly. "Now, what could that possibly be?"

"I think you know, Freckles," I say before leaning down and pressing my lips to hers—her soft, luscious lips—the lips I haven't been able to forget since I first kissed her after my no-hitter.

Do I really believe kissing her now will sell this relationship?

Yes.

Is that why I suggested it?

Not entirely.

Today has been nice. Harlow and I have been getting closer since the away trip started in Atlanta, but today is the first time we've really been able to spend time together without a game or travel interrupting us. And all this time spent together today had me *aching* to kiss her again. Why? I'm not entirely sure. But I do know that she is quickly becoming very important to me.

We part after a few more soft kisses. "That, uh... that should convince them," she says, uncertainty in her tone. She seems to be affected by the kiss the same way I am.

"Yeah, that should do it," I say hesitantly. "You're not a terrible kisser, so we should be able to sell it."

Harlow pushes me teasingly. "Not terrible? I'm appalled, Spencer. I'm much better than not terrible."

"Hmm," I say, pretending to think. "I guess I could take it a step up and say you're a decent kisser."

"You fucking suck," she says, laughing and taking a sip of her strawberry milkshake.

"And you fake love me anyway," I reply with a wink, earning a head shake from Harlow.

"Are you gonna eat that cherry, Slick?" she asks, pointing directly at my milkshake. "It's just sitting there, tempting me."

"Nah, I'm not big on cherries. You want it?" She nods. Instead of sliding my glass over to her so she can grab the cherry, I pluck it from the whipped cream myself and bring it over to her lips. And she bites it from the stem.

I feel my dick stiffen against my jeans as she makes an O with her lips when she takes the cherry, leaving me wondering how those lips would look wrapped around my cock. Wondering if Harlow would moan like she did as she sipped that coffee if she was underneath me.

I should *not* be thinking about her like this. This isn't a real relationship, and she's my friend's sister. Even thinking about crossing that line is a bad idea. But I can play the thought in my head as I take another goddamn shower when I get back to my place later.

I won't deny that I'm attracted to Harlow. God, I have been since I first saw her. Now that she's a friend, that attraction isn't just physical—she's incredible. But that doesn't mean I don't physically want her because I *really* fucking want her. Doesn't mean I get her, though. I'll just keep doing what I'm doing now, pushing all those thoughts down.

Even if she smiles at me the way she does, teases me the way she does, *ogles me the way she does.*

...

I'm so fucked.

Eighteen

Harlow

"Fuck...," I BREATHE OUT as my bullet vibrator works its magic against my clit. My waterproof companion has taken up permanent residence in my shower as of late. Knox has my hormones going wild like I'm a goddamn teenager again.

Knox spends his mornings shirtless, so when I see him before practice, I'm always left with an image to think of when I'm doing what I'm doing right now. That first full day we spent together—the day we walked around The Battery a month ago—sparked something in me. He was always good-looking, but now he's so fucking *alluring.* So, in order to not cross a line into a territory we had best not visit, I take care of myself in the shower, imagining it's him.

God, I sound pathetic. Especially when there's no way in hell he's thinking of me the way I've been thinking of him. He's opened up so much more over the past month, and we've actually gotten very close now, but I'm not the type of girl he'd ever be interested in. He could have his pick of any actual bat bunnies or even celebrities. He'd never want someone like me. And that's okay. I'm fine with that.

That's what I'm telling myself, at least.

I lean back against the cold tile of my shower as my breathing intensifies, waiting for my release. And the orgasm that rips through me shortly after leaves me almost completely sated. I say almost because outside of actual sex with Knox, I don't think I'll ever be fully satisfied. But since that's a line I don't want to cross, this has to be enough.

I don't have time to worry about that right now, though. Lane has agreed to do an interview with me for *Starred and Fast* before tonight's game. Rory's interview was well-received, and I've done several more staff members. Still, Lane will be the first player I'm interviewing, and I know my followers will love it.

After I hop out of the shower and dry my hair, I throw on my *Spencer* Stars jersey with a white tank underneath, leaving the jersey open, a pair of jeans, and my favorite Chucks. I opt for some light makeup today, and then I'm on my way to Lane's.

After a twenty-five-minute subway ride into Soho, I find myself at Lane's building. Like Knox, Lane lives in a penthouse, so after the door attendant lets me inside, I start the slow ascent to the top floor. A few minutes later, the doors open into his penthouse, and I'm greeted by Lane, who is evidently waiting for my arrival.

"Hey, Lo," Lane says, gesturing me inside. "Welcome back to La Casa de Brooks. Rory has Sage in her room, so we'll have some quiet for a bit."

"Perfect. Thanks for doing this, Lane. I know my readers are really going to enjoy it."

"Anything for Knox's girlfriend," he says with amusement as we both find our places on his couch.

"Fake girlfriend," I correct.

"We'll see about that," Lane replies with a smirk. I just roll my eyes.

"Between you and everyone else, Knox and I will be miserable for the rest of the season."

"Hey, we just like what we see. Knox is actually fucking happy. I've never seen him like that, Lo. He's happy and smiling. None of that happened until you two started this charade."

"I'm glad he is. He's honestly not all that bad. He's just closed off."

"And you've been opening him up."

"Bit by bit," I reply with a smile. "Now, enough about that. Let's get this interview going."

⫷⫷⫷⫷⫷⫷⫷⫷⫷⫷⫷⫷⫷⫷⫷⫷⫷⫷⫷⫷⫷⫷⫷⫷⫷

"Yeah, there's no denying that Sage was a surprise for me, but my God, I adore that little girl. She's the best part of my life now," Lane says with the biggest smile on his face.

"I think I can speak for everyone when I say we all adore Sage. She's the absolute sweetest. Did you have difficulty adjusting to being a single dad and a professional baseball player?"

"For sure," Lane replies honestly. "I had no idea how to take care of a baby. My biggest saving grace was that she was born in January, not in the middle of the season. I had a chance to learn how to be a dad before I had to get back out on the field. And Rory becoming Sage's nanny has been an absolute godsend. I'm not sure how I could do this without her."

"What would you say is your favorite part of having Rory as Sage's nanny?"

"That she travels with us, hands down. Having Sage in every city with me and every game with me is a dream. Single dads don't get the opportunities I've been given, so I try to just soak it all in and not take it for granted. I know how lucky I am. And then all of my friends around me have become Sage's surrogate family. I appreciate everything I've been given and all the love I've received. I'm very blessed."

"Damn, Lane. You're gonna make me cry," I say as I reach up to brush away a stray tear.

"You're a crier, Lo. That's not hard to do."

"Shut up," I say, playfully shoving his shoulder. "You're getting all sappy on me. I can't help it. Now, let's finish this interview, shall we? I've just got some fun questions left now. What's your favorite color?"

"Green. I've always liked green."

"Favorite food?"

"Oh, anything Mexican. The spicier, the better."

"And last but not least," I say. "Favorite Taylor Swift song."

"*The Very First Night*. That one is just so fun."

"Oh my God," I exclaim. "Are you a secret Swiftie, Lane?"

"I don't think it's much of a secret," Lane replies, rubbing his jaw. "I'd have given my right arm to get tickets when she was in NY last year. But we were in San Diego, unfortunately."

"You're the perfect Girl Dad," I laugh. "Sage is very lucky."

"I'm luckier to have her," he admits. "She rocked my world in the best way possible. But you know who else is lucky?" Lane gives me a mischievous look. "Knox."

I groan. "We're friends, Lane. Friends in a fake relationship."

"I know that's what you both keep saying, but Knox is different, Lo. He's not the guy I've known since he came up to the majors. And that's a really good thing."

"I think I've just helped him see that good things are out there if you look for them. A positive attitude will take you far."

"I don't think that's what it is."

"What do you mean?" I question.

"It's not the attitude, Lo. It's *you*."

"What do you mean it's me?"

"I mean he lights up around you. You radiate so much positivity, and Knox is thriving in it. Even if everything is platonic like you both claim, it's still you doing that to him. I think you've truly changed his life. I just hope it sticks when you guys end this... if you do, of course."

"Lane…" I groan. "It's going to be over at the end of the season. We've already established an end date."

"Not if you fall in love first," Rory says, walking into the room with Sage on her hip. "Sorry to intrude, but Sage wants Daddy."

"Ah, hey there, Lovebug. I missed you." Sage smiles brightly as Lane positions her on his lap. Rory sits down on my other side so I'm sandwiched between them.

"So, we're talking about Knox, are we?" Rory interjects.

"Oh, we are," Lane replies as Sage nuzzles into him, resting her head on his shoulder. "We're talking about how much better he's been lately."

"That's an understatement," Rory says. "I've known Knox since he was brought up to the team, and he's always been grumpy. Seeing him smile was a rarity." She turns her attention right to me. "But not anymore. Now it's a daily occurrence."

"Well, I'm happy about that. Like I was telling Lane, he's not all that bad. He was just closed off. But he's starting to open up, and his light is shining brighter."

"Because of you," she says.

"Maybe," I reply. "I don't think I can take all the credit for it. If anything, I've just helped him see what he didn't before."

"I can agree to that," Lane says. "As long as you mean that what he didn't see before was you."

"You are both absolutely relentless, you know that?"

"We mean well," Lane replies with a smile.

"But don't worry," Rory states. "You guys will see it on your own one day."

As adamant as our friends are, they will be sorely disappointed if this doesn't happen.

When this doesn't happen.

Definitely when. Knox and I are friends now, and that's all we'll be. And once this fake relationship ends, we'll continue being friends because that's all we want, regardless of what our other friends think.

Nineteen

Harlow

"THERE SHE IS," KNOX says as he walks up behind me as I chat with Lucia in the hallway outside the clubhouse.

"Ah, hey there, Slick," I say, turning to face him. "You played a great game in the dugout tonight."

"Such a goddamn tease," he replies, sliding up next to me. I turn back around to find Lucia smirking right at us.

"What?" I ask her.

"Nothing," she says, throwing her hands up. "Nothing at all." I don't believe her, but I'm not pressing the issue. I know what she'll say, and I really don't want to hear it.

The clubhouse door opens, and a few of the Stars players walk out into the hallway. Since these guys don't know about the fake relationship, Knox puts his arm around my shoulder and plants a soft kiss on the top of my head. And even though it's just for show, I can't help but smile at the show of affection.

It makes me wonder what things would be like if this were real. Would he hold me close like this because he could? Would he kiss me around his teammates? Would he take me to bed and ravish me? I'll never find out, but there's no harm in imagining it, right?

As more of the team leaves the clubhouse, Lucia chimes in with a bright-ass smile, "You guys are such a sweet couple." She's doing it to make us feel awkward, but Knox and I have been playing this game for more than a month now—we're used to it.

So, in response, I simply say, "Thank you, Luc," returning the bright smile she gave me. And Knox just pulls me closer.

"What are your plans tonight, baby?" he asks me, and I almost snort in laughter. *Baby?* I never took Knox for someone who would be interested in using pet names, so that catches me by surprise, but I can roll with it.

"Not too much, *babe*," I say as I jokingly push my shoulder into his ribs, earning me a low chuckle. "I'm going to make a frozen pizza, have a glass of wine, and write my blog post for Lane's interview."

"Sounds like a wild Tuesday night. Count me in."

"You want to come over and eat frozen pizza?" I ask him incredulously.

"Yeah, why not?" Knox replies. "I can switch it up from the takeout leftovers in my fridge."

"Alright, Knox. You can come over." I point at him now. "But do *not* distract me. I need to work on my post."

"I wouldn't dream of distracting you, Lo. Never." The tone in his voice tells me I won't be getting much done tonight. And the way Lucia tries to subtly laugh tells me she knows it, too.

<<<<<<<<<<<<<<<<<<<<<<<<<<<<<<<<<

"You know, I do love burnt pizza," Knox says as he takes a slice from the pan.

"Shut up," I reply. "My shitty oven doesn't always heat evenly."

"I'm just pushing your buttons, Freckles." He looks at me and smiles softly. "This is fine, I promise."

That tiny bit of reassurance is all I need to remind myself that Knox isn't Derek. He's not going to lose his shit over some burnt pizza. "You okay, Lo? You seem a little lost in your head right now."

"Hm? Oh, I'm fine!" I say a little too quickly. "Let's go sit down on the couch. You can put something on the TV while I work on my blog post."

"Of course," Knox replies before grabbing my plate from my hand, carrying it across the room, and setting it down on the coffee table.

We both take a seat on the tiny couch, legs brushing up against each other since there's not much room. "You didn't need to carry my plate, but thank you."

"I did tell you I'm not actually an asshole," he replies, smiling as he chuckles to himself. Knox turns the TV to ESPN, watching the highlights of the games across the league as I open my laptop.

He looks at the screen before I can open a new document to start Lane's article. "What were you looking at there, Lo?" he asks, noting the beautiful gowns displayed.

"Ah," I reply. "That was just me daydreaming. I love Rana Dagon's designs, so I like to see the new styles she releases. I'll never afford them, but window shopping is always free."

"I'm used to seeing you in a jersey and jeans," Knox says back to me. "I don't know if I can even picture you in a gown."

"Well, it's not like I ever really get an opportunity for that," I laugh. "Jersey and jeans work for me, though. I like being comfortable."

Knox just smiles at me before returning his attention to the TV so I can start on this post.

When I reach for my slice of burnt pizza, I catch a glimpse of Knox, his eyes staring intently at the screen across the room. And I *really* look at him. He's not who I expected him to be, and I've grown very fond of the person I know now.

I feel something swell in my chest and try to push it down. Whatever that feeling is isn't worth exploring.

"What are you looking at, Lo?" Knox asks, raising an eyebrow as I jump, slightly startled by the sudden disruption of the silence. "You alright?"

"Yep! Totally good." I speak with faux confidence to mask the shakiness in my voice.

"Uh... huh..." he replies, eyeing me.

"You, uh..." I stammer, "You're just distracting me!"

"What?" he says, laughing. "How am I distracting you?"

Well, how is he distracting me? I'm not going to tell him that I don't actually know why I'm so unfocused right now. That when I looked at him, I started to see him differently. So instead, I say, "Your shirt! Your shirt is too damn tight, Knox."

"It's a white T-shirt, Harlow," he says, looking at me curiously.

"A white T-shirt that's clinging to every damn muscle in your arms and chest," I reply, crossing my arms, trying to make it look like this was the problem the entire time.

Knox thinks for a moment before shooting me a mischievous smile. "Would you prefer I take it off, Lo?" He says it in such a husky tone. A tone I know I'll be replaying in my head over and over during my morning shower, imagining it's the one he'd use if we were in bed together.

"No!" I all but shout. "No," I say, quieter this time. "Keep your shirt on. That would be even more distracting."

He leans in closer to me. "It's kinda fun getting you all flustered. You look adorable as you're flailing around over there."

"You're not supposed to be enjoying this," I state, a hint of exasperation in my voice.

"I probably shouldn't," he says before positioning his lips by my ear. "But your goddamn freckles have had me sidetracked all day," he whispers lowly as the stubble from his facial hair brushes my face. He repositions himself, now looking right into my eyes and running his thumb across my cheek. "I like that, though. You look so much better when you show them off."

My breath hitches in my throat, fighting for release. That's an honest admission from a man notorious for not sharing anything. I know by now that he's comfortable around me, but his sincerity still surprises me. And it warms me to know he's secure enough with me to share that.

"So, uh..." I sputter, trying to diffuse what feels like awkward tension. "I-I don't think I'm getting much of my post written tonight." I yawn genuinely. "I'm too tired to focus on it."

"Yeah, uh... I'm pretty tired, too," Knox says, turning his attention back to the TV in front of us.

The silence remains thick in the air as we try to forget what charged between us. But did something actually charge, or is that all in my mind? It doesn't matter either way, so there's no point in dwelling on the thought. And as the exhaustion from today finally catches up with me, I hope I don't dwell on it in my dreams.

❮❮❮❮❮❮❮❮❮❮❮❮❮❮❮❮❮❮❮❮❮❮❮❮❮❮

I rub my eyes, confused for a moment, before figuring out where I am. I'm still sitting on my sofa, wearing what I wore last night.

I must have fallen asleep while Knox was still here.

As I sit up to stretch myself out, I realize that I'm leaning against something, *someone*, very muscular.

My six-four fake boyfriend fell asleep on my couch beside me, leaning over and resting his head on the arm. And I apparently used his chest as a pillow.

It's sort of cute... until I remember that it's Wednesday morning.

"Knox!" I yell, trying to get his attention. "Knox!" I say louder, shaking his arm to wake him up.

He abruptly wakes, confused. "Huh- Lo? What's going on?"

"What's going on is you fell asleep on my couch last night, which wouldn't normally be a problem, but today is Wednesday!"

"Why is Wednesday so special?" he asks as he stands to stretch himself out and relieve his cramped muscles.

Before I can answer, I hear the padding of feet outside my door before the sound of knocking echoes across the room. Realization finally crosses Knox's face.

"Fuck, that's when you meet up with your brother," he says, running a hand through his hair in exasperation. "He's going to make a big deal of me being here."

"That's... probably not the biggest of your concerns right now." My gaze falls, and his follows... right to the morning wood he's proudly displaying.

"Fuck me," he murmurs, adjusting himself as I avert my eyes. "I was asleep—I can't help that!"

"I know," I say quickly. "Just... take care of that and fix your goddamn shirt."

Cole knocks on the door again, and I jog across the room to open it. "Hey, Cole. It's a lovely day, isn't it? How are you on this fine morning?"

He eyes me curiously. "Fine..." he says before stepping into my apartment. When he spots Knox across the room brushing the wrinkles out of his shirt, he breaks out in a wide, teasing smile. "What's going on here?"

"Nothing!" I say too quickly. "It's really nothing. We both just ended up falling asleep on the couch last night."

"You really think sleeping on a couch half your size the night before a game was a good idea?" Cole asks, lifting his brow to him.

"It wasn't intentional," Knox says, exasperated. "But I'm not pitching today, so I'll be alright."

"What an interesting morning this is turning out to be," Cole says, delighted.

"I'm, uh... gonna head out. I'll see you before the game, Lo." As quickly as he can, Knox grabs his things and all but runs out the door, leaving me alone with Cole.

Cole leans back against my kitchen counter. "So, Knox stayed here last night, huh?"

"I didn't know he was going to stay," I reply, hands scrubbing down my face. "I was just as surprised as you were when I woke this morning."

"A month and a half into this whole fake relationship, and Knox is already sleeping on your couch." He smiles playfully. "Interesting."

"Why is that interesting?" I ask. "It's not like we did anything. Hell, we haven't even kissed outside of when there are cameras on us."

Cole watches me curiously. "Do you *want* him to kiss you, Lo?"

"What? No! Of course not!" I shout, trying to sound convincing. Cole passes by me to set out our food, laughing as he does, confirming that he's not buying what I'm saying.

He should believe me, though. Why would I want Knox to kiss me? This is a show. We're putting on a *show*. I don't need him to kiss me outside of when it's necessary.

And yet, after seeing him last night, I secretly wish he would kiss me just because he could. Not because of cameras, not because anyone's around. Just because he wants to. Just because he wants *me*.

A thought like that will take me down a very dangerous road...

Twenty

Harlow

"I'm so glad we're going out for your birthday tonight, Luc," I say, leaning back on the sofa at Josh and Ella's. "I desperately need a night out."

"Why is that?" Lucia asks, a curious look on her face.

"Because life has been fucking crazy lately."

That's kind of the truth. Everything since the start of this season has been an absolute whirlwind. But I don't think that's the biggest reason I need this right now.

It's mainly because I'm so goddamn *confused*.

It's been six days since that night in my apartment. Six days since something came over me, and I started seeing Knox in a new way. It's also the night he made it a point to tell me how good I look with my freckles and how they keep distracting him.

I've been more confused lately as it is, and that did absolutely nothing to help me. I shouldn't be looking at Knox differently. He's still my friend, my fake boyfriend.

The problem with that is we're so good at faking it that it's starting to seem genuine.

"I bet life is crazy for you," Ella says, sitting in the chair across from us. "You're dating Knox, and your face is plastered on the front of every tabloid."

"I'm still not used to that," I admit. "I don't know if I'll ever get used to that."

"They'll ease up soon," Rory says from the other side of me on the sofa. "When my dad was still playing, I'd end up with pictures on covers, too. I was a literal child then, and I'd still see my face whenever I went to the grocery store. But eventually, they eased up, and I haven't had a problem really since."

"That's good to know," I say, letting out a breath. "I'm just worried because Knox is at the height of his fame right now, and the media seems to *love* the story of Fort Knox and the woman who got through to him."

"Tabloids suck, let me start with that," Ella says. "But I do kinda get it. Knox is so closed off and has been the entire time he's been in the league. Him opening up with somebody and sharing her with the world is a big fucking deal."

"I know. I try to let all that roll off me and enjoy my time with him."

"And how have you been enjoying your time with Knox, hm?" Lucia asks with mischief in her eyes.

"Not like that, bitch," I say with a laugh. "We hang out and talk, but that's really it. You know we haven't slept together."

"Poor Knox," Rory adds while stifling a laugh. These two just have to egg me on, don't they? They know damn well that this isn't real, so we're not going to sleep together.

"Wait," Ella says loudly, light brown hair fanning over her shoulders, "you're not sleeping together? I'm not judging you, but we've been friends for years, Lo. It's a bit surprising."

"Oh," I say uneasily. "We're just taking things slow, that's all."

Yes, we're moving so slowly. We went from setting up a fake dating arrangement with Knox's agent to kissing on national fucking television four days later.

Moving so slowly.

Glacial even.

"Fair enough," Ella says back. "To each their own. Me? I don't think I could do that if I wanted to. Josh is just-"

"Did I just hear my name?" Josh says, walking into the room.

"Such an ego, Garro," Lucia fires off. "Not everything is about you."

Ella just laughs. "You heading out now, babe?"

Josh walks up behind Ella and wraps his arms around her. "Yeah, heading over to Fort's now." He looks up at me now. "I'll tell your man you say hi."

"Why, thank you, Josh," I say while laughing.

"I'll see you tonight, Ella." He leans down and kisses her. "I love you."

"I love you, too, Josh. Have fun." Josh waves at the rest of us before walking across the room and out the front door.

Josh and Ella are a very sweet couple, so madly in love with each other. I love getting to see two friends as happy as they are.

But it also gives me a pang of jealousy.

I'm jealous because I realize I've never had somebody look at me like I'm their entire world. Like I'm the most important person to them.

I'm twenty-five; I have plenty of time to find my person.

But I do so look forward to the day that I can find what they have.

And a very small part of me wonders if I might find a particular broody pitcher waiting for me on the other end.

Hey there, Slick

How's the day off treating you?

Knox

Not too bad

Been nice and quiet without you around today

Harlow

Ass

You know you miss me

Knox

Maybe I do, maybe I don't

I guess we'll never know, will we?

Harlow

Play coy all you want

You enjoy my presence, and you know it

Knox

Yeah, maybe I do

In all honesty, today is a little too quiet

Harlow

Ha! I knew you missed me

Knox

You think mighty highly of yourself, Freckles

Harlow

I'm just confident, Spencer

Give that a try sometime

Knox

Maybe I will

You getting ready for your night out?

Harlow

Yeah, we're getting ready now

You asking for a picture or something?

Knox

Oh, God no

I don't need to see you at all

Harlow

You're such a dick

Knox

Go enjoy your night out

We'll talk in the morning, Lo

Harlow

See ya, Fort

⫷⫷⫷⫷⫷⫷⫷⫷⫷⫷⫷⫷⫷⫷⫷⫷⫷⫷⫷⫷⫷⫷⫷⫷⫷

"Ouch!" I say as I fall over while trying to shimmy myself into my damn dress. I just had to go for the strapless black dress that's a bitch to put on. "Fuck, that hurt."

"You're that clumsy already, and you haven't put on heels yet. You haven't even had anything to drink," Lucia says as she laughs.

"The only reason I'm not snapping back at you, Luc, is because it's your birthday. You're fair game tomorrow, though."

Rory flops herself down on the floor beside me in black leather pants and a corseted top. "How's it feel to be in the last year of your twenties, Lucia?"

"It makes me feel like I'm too old for my friends," Lucia laughs. "I've got no one over here with me."

"Hey," Ella says. "I'm twenty-seven. I'm basically right there with you."

"I'm also turning twenty-six in August," I add. "The only baby here is Rory."

"You're literally four months older than me, Lo," Rory says, crossing her arms and narrowing her eyes at me.

"What I'm hearing here," Lucia chimes, "is that I'm still older than all of you." Lucia applies a shade of red to her lips that matches her dress perfectly. "Here, Lo," she says, tossing me the tube. "This will go great with your heels."

"You don't think the red is too much?" I ask. "I'm not sure I can pull it off."

"Harlow," she says with a pointed look, "you can pull off anything. The blonde waves, smoky eyes, and red lips? You're a total bombshell."

"I don't know about bombshell," I say with a dismissive laugh while I turn to the mirror and apply the red lipstick. "Ooh, I think I actually like that."

"Like Lucia said," Rory adds from her position at my feet. "Total fucking bombshell."

"Just wait until Knox gets a look at you in that," Ella says with a bright smile. "Man's not going to want to take it slow anymore, that's for damn sure."

Oh.

If only she knew the real situation. Then she'd understand that literally nothing can happen between us.

As if sensing my thoughts, Lucia walks up behind me and whispers in my ear. "You really should just go for it, Lo. You *know* it would be good."

Shut up, Lucia! I say in my head. *Do not tempt Horny Harlow.*

Horny Harlow is the one that wants to jump on his dick and ride him until we're both out of breath.

Horny Harlow is the one that wants to get on her knees and have him mouthfuck me with his cock.

Horny Harlow needs to sit her ass down.

I can want him more than anything right now, but I'm sure as hell not making any type of move on him. I've been feeling more confused around him this week, and sex would only complicate things. We'll just keep this arrangement to business.

Ugh.

"Alright, ladies," Ella says, spreading her hands over the blush pink jumpsuit she's donned for tonight. "How does this look?"

"Fucking amazing," I say enthusiastically. "Josh is going to lose his damn mind when he sees you tonight."

"Oh, he loses his mind *every* time he sees me. The damn man's insatiable."

"Insatiable only for *you*," Lucia says with a smile. "He did put a ring on it after all."

"He did," Ella smiles. "God, I can't wait to marry that man."

I walk over and throw my arms around Ella's shoulders. "Just seven more months, and you get to do just that."

"Alright, ladies," Lucia chimes. "Let's hit the town!"

I slide on my strappy red heels before we make our way down to the street and hail a cab. My feet are already killing me, so I'm ready to drink enough to forget they even hurt.

Twenty-One

Knox

"Cheaters. Every last fucking one of you," Lane says, pointing at each of us around the table. Because what do four professional baseball players do when they have two nights off? They play Monopoly, apparently...

"You landed on a property with hotels, man," Josh says to Lane. "That's how the game goes."

"The hotels are on fucking Boardwalk. You're robbing me blind, Garro."

"Damn," Cole says. "I forgot how much of a sore loser Brooks is."

"Reminds me of why we never play fucking board games with him," I grumble.

"Hey, there's the grumpy Knox I've always known," Josh says, slapping a hand on my shoulder. "Been a while since we've seen you."

"Yeah," Cole says. "Ever since he started dating my sister, he's a completely different person, isn't he?" He smiles widely, clearly amused.

Lane smirks. "Completely different. Had he ever smiled before Harlow?"

I groan, mostly at Cole and Lane, seeing as they know we aren't actually dating. But Josh has no idea, so they're milking the hell out of this since I can't deny it with him here. "Fuck off. I smiled before Harlow."

"Not nearly as much," Cole replies, pleased with himself.

"I mean, regular sex certainly puts a smile on my face," Josh says.

"That's still my sister, man," Cole replies as he kicks Josh under the table.

"Who just so happens to be dating this guy over here. Don't be naive, Cole."

"We're, uh…" I rub my neck awkwardly. "We've not actually… slept together."

With Josh's look of surprise, he misses the smirks on both Lane and Cole's faces. "That's… surprising," he finally says. "Wouldn't have pegged you for the holding out type, man."

I sigh. "It's complicated," I reply, running a hand over my face. "Definitely not a discussion I want to get into, though."

Why don't I want to get into it? Because I can't say that Harlow is constantly on my mind now. That I jack off fucking daily in the shower to the thought of her. That I so desperately want to know how she moans as I sink my cock into her. I want to know how she tastes, the sounds she makes, the look on her face as she comes.

I don't know if I've ever wanted somebody as bad as I want her right now. My fantasies about her aren't new, but the way I feel around her is. And whatever that is could surely only complicate things.

We need to keep this arrangement professional. Kisses and affection when people are around and nothing more.

Pure fucking torture.

"So," Lane says to Josh, breaking the silence that filled the room. "How's the wedding planning going?"

"Really well," Josh says with a smile. "We've already set a date in December of this year."

"That's awesome," Cole states. "You'll even have some time for the honeymoon before next season starts," he adds with a wink.

I stand from the table, walk to the fridge, and pull out four beers. "I say we properly celebrate. We haven't had a chance to do that yet."

The men all agree, so I walk back to the table and spread the beers around. We toast and sip before diving back into meaningless conversation. And thank fuck we did because I *really* need to get my mind off Harlow tonight.

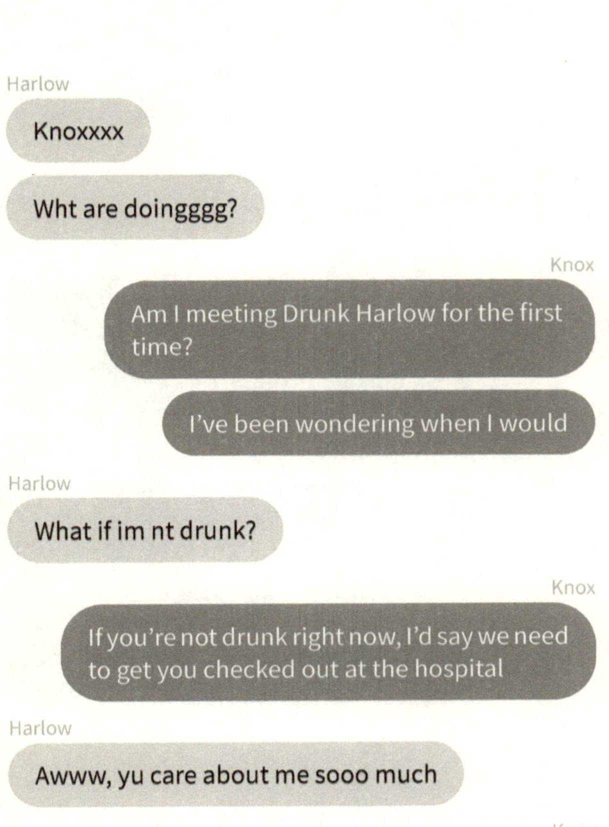

Can you even stand right now, Freckles?

Harlow

Duh

I cn't danceee if Im sittin down

Knox

I don't think there's anything I can say to that

You good, though?

Harlow

I feel grateeeee

Knox

At least you feel good

Because you can't spell for shit right now

Harlow

Ella sys to spot talking to u and dnce

Knox

Then go dance, Lo

Then get your ass home to sober up

<<<<<<<<<<<<<<<<<<<<<<<<<<<<<<<<<<<<<<

"How the fuck do you go from bitching about landing on Board-walk to kicking the rest of our asses, Lane? How the hell is that possible?" Cole yells, tossing the rest of his Monopoly money onto the table.

"And you call me a sore loser," Lane replies, chuckling and fanning his cash out before him.

"Guys, it's fucking Monopoly," I cut in. "Chill the fuck out."

"I seem to recall you grumbling a while ago, Fort," Josh pipes in.

"I fucking hate this game," I mutter under my breath.

Lane's laughter is silenced by the vibration of four phones. We all reach for our phones in tandem, seeing a group message with a video from Rory on our screens.

"Why did Rory send us a video?" Cole asks.

"Let's find out," Lane replies as we all press play. What we're greeted with is loud cheers from what sounds like Rory and Ella as Harlow is grinding on Lucia. So much for getting her off my mind tonight because I'm sure as hell not forgetting a video that hot.

"Ah," Josh says. "Just Fort's girlfriend dancing on our favorite trainer."

"I could have gone my entire life without seeing Lo dance like that," Cole gripes.

"Oh, but I bet Knox loved it," Lane smirks.

Bastard.

"Can we not go there?" I ask, trying miserably to forget the video. What I wouldn't give to see Harlow move like that on me...

The awkward silence that comes as Cole eyes me suspiciously is broken by a knock at the door. Curious as to who would be here at nearly ten, I go to answer only to find four *very* drunk women standing in my doorway: Lucia, Rory, Ella, and Harlow... in *tight as hell* black minidress.

God help me...

"I told you guys he would answer!" she shouts as the other girls dissolve into laughter.

"He's your boyfriend!" Ella slurs. "Of course, he answered!"

I stand there awkwardly, not quite sure what to do. "Uh, hi? What are you doing here? Didn't we just get a video of you all still out?"

"That's no way to greet your girlfriend, Fort!" Rory says, poking me in the chest. "And I forgot to send the video until we got here." The rest of the guys come to the door now to see what the commotion is.

"Joshy!" Ella says excitedly, running inside and wrapping Garro up in a hug. He's stunned for a moment before he hugs his fiancée back.

"Rory? Lucia? Harlow?" Cole says. "What are you guys doing here?"

"Cole!" Rory replies loudly. "Lucia said we should visit you guys, so Harlow brought us here! Isn't that fun?"

"Is that okay, Knox?" Harlow asks, worry in her voice.

"Oh, uh... yeah. That's fine, Lo. Lane just finished kicking our asses in Monopoly, so you have good timing."

"Thank God we didn't get here earlier then." She comes closer, placing her palm on my chest. How drunk is she? "I don't want to see my boyfriend lose."

"Not in front of everybody else, Lo!" Lucia teases from the kitchen where the rest of the group has gathered. "Save something for the bedroom."

"Fuck off, Luc," Harlow fires back.

Rory laughs from her place around my kitchen island before she settles on a look of panic. "Lane!" she shouts. "Where's Sage?!"

Lane chuckles before replying. "She's hanging with Grandpa Fisher tonight, Rory. We didn't abandon her."

Rory sighs a deep breath of relief. What a night this is turning into...

The group that gathered only stayed around an hour before everyone dispersed back to their own places, with the exception of Harlow. Because as much as I wanted time away to think today, I didn't want her to leave once I saw her here. I'm also sure as hell not letting her take the subway when it's getting close to midnight and she's too drunk to walk in a straight line.

After I close my front door, I walk back into my living room to find Harlow sprawled across my couch, head resting on the arm and legs splayed out in front of her. Her dress is riding up dangerously high, making it *really* difficult to focus.

"There he is," she slurs as I sit down beside her. "There's my fake boyfriend."

I can't stop the laugh that escapes me. "Just how much did you have to drink tonight, Freckles?"

"Mmm... not sure," she replies. "A lot."

"Yeah, I kinda figured." I smile at her as she decides to sit herself up, almost tumbling off the couch in the process.

"What does that mean, Mr. Slick?" she asks, poking me right in the chest. Hard.

"That means that you're clearly shitfaced right now, Lo. You almost fell off the couch as you sat up."

Harlow sighs. "I know," she says as she leans her head on my shoulder. "But it was fun."

"Yeah, we saw the video."

"Mmm... bet you liked that, huh?" she asks in a knowing tone. Because, of course, I fucking liked it.

"Not bad," I say, smirking down at her as she picks her head up and glares at me. "You've got some decent moves, it seems."

"Well, you and your sexy ass will never get to see them."

"My... sexy ass?" I ask, raising my brow.

"Don't act like you don't know that!" She pokes me in the chest again. "You have like the best ass in the entire damn league."

The smile that crosses my face is unavoidable. "Is that so?"

"Yes!" she replies, exasperated. "If your ass didn't look so good, maybe I wouldn't need to take care of myself in the damn shower every day."

Did she just say that?

Did that just happen?

"Okay, Lo," I say. "I think you need to get in bed before the room starts spinning."

She lays back across the couch. "It started spinning like two hours ago."

I bark out a laugh and then stand up from the couch, reaching my hand out for her. "Come on, Lo. Let's get you set up in the guest bedroom."

We stumble to the bedroom, and I sit Harlow down on the edge of the bed. "Wait," she says. "I need to take my makeup off."

"I don't have anything for that. Do you?"

"I have some makeup wipes in my clutch, but I left it in the kitchen," she pouts.

I shake my head. "Stay here. I'll go grab it."

I quickly make my way to the kitchen, grabbing her clutch from the island before joining her back in the guest bedroom... where she is now lying on the bed, looking confused. "The ceiling is moving, Knox," she whispers. "Why is your ceiling moving?"

"What am I going to do with you tonight, Lo?" I laugh, crossing the room and sitting down next to her. "Can you even sit up again?"

"Don't think-" *hiccup* "-so."

Seeing as she's too incoherent to do it herself, I carefully reach into her clutch, pulling out a package that I assume is makeup wipes. At least, I hope it is. I don't really want to have to rummage through her shit to find them.

To my delight, the package says makeup remover.

I pull one of the sheets from the package and bring it up to her face, starting with her cheeks. "First things first, we have to bring those freckles back out," I say as she smiles softly. I gently rub it across the rest of her face and eyes, removing every trace of makeup I can see. When her skin is clear, I say, "All set, Lo."

"Thank you." She smiles a little wider. "You're so nice to me."

I chuckle. "Don't let it go to your head. There's clothing in the closet like last time. Are you okay to get yourself ready for bed?"

"Yeah," she replies. "I'll take the dress off and pass out like that."

"Okay," I say, voice wavering. "Good night, Lo."

"Night, Knox," I hear as I shut the door to the bedroom. I then make a beeline straight to my fucking shower.

That dress was tight enough to throw me into a tailspin with how it framed her perfect body. But then she had to tell me she likes my ass and that she touches herself in her own shower to the thought of it.

Fucking hell. How do I keep myself away from her?

I doubted that Harlow had any thoughts of me like I do of her, but her drunken confessions proved me completely wrong. Nothing can happen between us, though—this whole arrangement is fake. But that won't stop me from taking hold of my cock under the running water and pumping myself into delirium.

And when her name slips past my lips as I release, I'm hoping like hell that she didn't hear.

Twenty-Two

Harlow

Tuesday morning, I woke up mortified. I remembered *everything* I said to Knox the night before, regardless of how drunk I was. I told him he has a sexy ass and that I think of him in the shower. The ground could've swallowed me whole right then, and it would've been a welcome reprieve.

My only saving grace was that he didn't acknowledge it the next day. He could have tormented me about it, how his friend's little sister, his fake girlfriend, thinks of him when she gets herself off. He could have laughed in my face, and I would have understood. But he didn't, thank God.

We've still seen each other every day, and I've had to pretend that I don't feel awkward so we can continue to not acknowledge what I said. It's been easy enough to avoid, though, when the Stars had a two-game home series they split with the LA Suns. Once Thursday's game finished, we all jumped on the plane to head off to Pittsburgh to start a ten-game away trip. And since we slept on the plane, Knox and I didn't need to acknowledge it then, either.

When I wake up Friday morning, I know I need to talk to *somebody* about it. Ignoring it completely is driving me crazy, and since I don't want to talk to him about it, I figure Lucia and Rory will be good, even if they tease me about it like I know they will.

Since Rory and I always share a room, Lucia comes to meet us. "Okay, what's up with a nine a.m. meeting, ladies?" Lucia asks as Rory lets her into the room.

"Your guess is as good as mine, Luc," Rory replies. "This is Lo's doing."

I smile sheepishly from my bed. "What's going on, Lo?" Lucia asks, eyeing me curiously as she and Rory sit on Rory's bed across from me.

"I, uh…" I start awkwardly before falling back on my bed, hands over my face. "I massively embarrassed myself, guys, and I don't even know what Knox is thinking."

"Oh, we gotta know what you did then," Rory says. "Where's the popcorn?"

"I hate you," I say, but she just laughs. I take a deep breath before I blurt out, "I told him that he has a sexy ass!"

"You actually told him that?" Lucia pries.

"Yes," I reply, sitting myself back up again. "After you drunkenly decided we needed to visit the guys Monday night, I slept in Knox's guest bedroom, and I told him he has a sexy ass."

Rory smirks. "I mean, you're not wrong."

"That's not helpful, Ror." I sigh. "But it gets worse."

"You did more than tell him his ass is sexy?" Lucia prods, trying not to smile. She's clearly amused.

"Sure fucking did," I say as I try to compose myself. "I may have also told him that I think about his ass… when… I'm in the shower." I wince when I say it aloud.

Lucia and Rory can't contain themselves and double over in laughter, gasping for breath. "Lo, you did not tell him you masturbate while thinking of him," Lucia says as she wipes a tear from her eye.

"This isn't funny!" I shout. "I'm fucking mortified."

"So," Rory says, "what I'm gathering is that you like touching yourself to the thought of Fort Knox."

"Rory!" I shout. "Please seek therapy. You should not always be thinking about sex."

She roars with laughter. "I don't always think about sex, Lo. But it is *so* fun to mess with you."

I groan. "What the hell do I do?"

Lucia asks, "Well, are you going to keep being awkward around him if you don't talk about it?"

"I think I'm going to be awkward no matter what," I reply honestly. "How the hell can I be normal around him again?"

"Try not to think about it when you're around him," Rory says. "Eventually, you'll stop thinking about it altogether, and you can forget it even happened."

"I have no idea if I can do that."

"Don't let it faze you, Lo," Lucia adds. "You're a woman who likes sex—own it."

That I'm going to have to try to do.

⬅⬅⬅⬅⬅⬅⬅⬅⬅⬅⬅⬅⬅⬅⬅⬅⬅⬅⬅⬅⬅⬅⬅⬅

The Stars played a damn good game tonight. They didn't get the win, but Cole was part of a great 6-4-3 double play.

And all through the game, Knox kept looking at me, smiling every time he did. I couldn't help but smile brightly in return.

We've been getting so much closer, to the point where I look forward to seeing him each day. And I think he does, too.

And I think I really, *really* like that.

Now that the game is over, I'm sitting on the floor outside of the away team clubhouse, Sage sitting right in front of me. Rory needs to talk to her dad, so I'm watching Sage while we wait for Lane.

"There we go," I say, fixing the small ponytail atop her head. "All set, Sagie." She claps before she turns around and gives me a slobbery kiss on my cheek. "Aww, thank you, Lovebug."

The clubhouse door opens, and Lane, Knox, Cole, and Josh step out. "Ah, there's my baby girl," Lane says as he leans down and scoops Sage off the ground.

"Dada!"

"Why are you still up, Sagie? You're usually asleep by now."

I stand up to join them. "Rory said she ended up taking a late nap today. We haven't been able to get her back to sleep yet."

"Well, that means we're in for a long night, aren't we, Sagie?" She giggles as Lane tickles her. "I'm heading back then. I gotta try to get Sage down for the night."

"I'll head back with you," Josh says. "I want to talk to Ella before she falls asleep."

"We'll see the rest of you tomorrow, then," Lane states as he, Sage, and Josh take off down the hall.

I look to Knox and Cole. "You had a good game today."

"We lost, Lo," Knox replies. "Not what I'd call a good game."

I shrug. "You can't win 'em all. But it's not like you got the loss either, Knox. Stars were still in the lead when you came off."

"There's always tomorrow," Cole adds. "We can still win the series." He thinks for a moment. "Where's Rory, Lo?"

"She had to talk to Skip about something. She's probably still with him."

"Ah, okay," he replies, rubbing his neck. "Makes sense."

I eye him. "Why are you being weird, Cole?"

"It's weird to ask where my friends are now, is it? I don't think that's very weird." He crosses his arms.

"That's not weird," I reply. "But you're acting weird as hell."

"She's got a point, man," Knox adds.

"I should've known this whole—" he gestures between Knox and me, "—*thing* would've had you two ganging up on me."

"Ooh, he's getting testy now, Knox," I say as I look at him. "What do we think he's hiding?"

"I'm not sure," he says with a smirk, "but I bet we can find out."

Cole throws his bag over his shoulder and grumbles, "I'm getting out of here before either of you keep talking," before he takes off down the hall away from us.

Knox and I both laugh. "He can dish it, but he's never been able to take it," I say.

"That's not surprising in the least," Knox says.

"What are you up to tonight, Slick?"

"Ah, I will just be enjoying the freedom of having my own room for this series."

"Ooh, how'd you swing a solo room, Fort?"

"Not a fucking clue, but I'm not going to complain." He pauses for a moment. "Why don't you come over? We can watch something or just talk."

I smile at him slyly. "Are you just trying to get me all alone, Knox?"

He leans to my ear. "I'm constantly alone with you, Harlow. But if you're worried about me trying to come on to you tonight, I promise you're safe."

I laugh it off, but it's still kind of... disappointing? It's not like I expected him to go for something. And if he did, I'm not even sure what I'd do.

...

Yeah, that's a lie. I think I can admit to myself that I clearly want Knox. But wanting is one thing; giving in is another. We're friends now—friends who just happen to be in a fake relationship. We don't need any complications or strings.

At least, that's what I'll keep telling myself...

Twenty-Three

Harlow

KNOX AND I PART briefly when we get back to the hotel. I want a shower after sweating at the game all night. Once I'm cleaned off, I throw on a black tank top and a pair of gray shorts before I meet him in his room.

He greets me at the door in nothing but a pair of blue athletic shorts. Tonight is going to be fucking torture if I have to look at him like *that*. "Come on in, Lo," Knox says as I walk into the room.

I sniff the air as I walk in. "Knox, does it smell like... onion rings?"

He rubs his neck. "Uh, yeah... I ordered some onion rings from room service. I remember how much you liked them before."

I take him by surprise and wrap him in a hug. "Thank you. That's sweet."

"Do we hug now, Freckles?" he asks with a laugh as he wraps his arms around my shoulders.

"You've had your tongue down my throat, Knox. I think you can handle a hug."

"Well, I do know I can handle your kisses," he says as he pulls me in a little tighter.

I lean my head back. "Knox Spencer, are you flirting with me?"

"Have I not been doing that already?" he replies with a smirk as he breaks the hug and walks over to his bed. "So much missed opportunity then."

"Why you wanna flirt with me?" I ask as I sit on the bed beside him, inhaling the heavenly scent of onion rings.

Knox smirks at me before grabbing an onion ring and taking a bite. "Why wouldn't I wanna flirt with you, Lo?"

"Answering a question with a question is a terrible deflection, you know."

"Deflections are easier than the truth, though," he says lowly.

What exactly does that mean? If that's not the truth, what is?

Maybe this desire does indeed go both ways. Maybe he *does* want me like I want him.

That is highly enticing... and very dangerous.

"So, uh..." I stammer, trying to break what feels like awkward tension. "Do you want to watch something?"

"Is it weird if I say I actually just want to talk tonight?"

"From the man who used to not utter more than two words to me, it's a little odd, but I'm getting used to this new version of you."

He laughs and shakes his head. "You really are something, Lo."

"You keep telling me that. I don't know if that's supposed to be good or bad, though."

"It's good." He smiles at me softly. "It's definitely good."

"Now, that is some high praise from you."

Knox leans in closer, his lips brushing my ear. "You like praise, Harlow?" A shiver runs down my body, and my breath catches in my throat.

"I, uh... I don't know," I admit. "I've never actually been... praised before."

He places a finger under my chin, and his eyes meet mine. "Then you've been with some shitty men, haven't you?"

"Something like that," I reply softly, hands instinctively rising up to cover my cheeks.

Knox reaches for my hands and lowers them. "You covering those pretty freckles has to do with one of those shitty men, doesn't it?"

I take a deep breath and cross my legs as I turn to face him, Knox doing the same. "Yeah," I admit. "My ex-boyfriend Derek wasn't a fan of my freckles."

"What does that mean, Lo?"

"It means that he told me they made me..." I sigh, "Less attractive." I turn my head down and look at the bed. It's hard to admit something like that. I'm ashamed of letting Derek get into my head like he did, but I've been fighting like hell to get myself back.

"Harlow," he says, taking hold of my hands. "Look at me, please." I slowly lift my head up to face him. "He couldn't have been more wrong." Knox lightly runs his thumb across my cheek. "You're stunning. You always have been. But the freckles help you stand out even more."

"You don't need to talk me up. I've been getting better about not letting his words affect me anymore, but you don't need to just say things to make me feel better."

"Come on, Lo," he says with a slight smile. "We both know I wouldn't do something like that. Too much of an asshole, remember?"

That actually makes me smile. "You're not an asshole, Knox. I don't think you ever have been."

"Ooh, that's where you're wrong, Freckles. I bet if you keep getting to know me, you'll figure that out."

"So, tell me more about you then. I've been learning a lot, but I want to know more."

Knox sighs. "Okay," he relents. "But tell me more about what this jackass Derek did first so I can tell you just how wrong he was."

I snag an onion ring and take a bite. "Oh, he was just your run-of-the-mill misogynistic prick."

"Ah, the kind of man who's intimidated by a woman's success," he says, taking the onion ring from my hand and popping the rest into his mouth. He smiles as I laugh.

"He was the kind of man that would put me down. My freckles made me less attractive. Running my blog was a ridiculous idea because 'girls don't care about sports.' I needed to keep in shape so he'd still want me. Things like that."

"Well, I already covered the freckles. As far as the blog, it's a fucking fantastic idea. Saying that girls don't like sports is one of the most absurd comments I've heard because there are entire leagues of women's sports, and the stands for our games are always filled with female fans." He hands me another onion ring to replace the one he stole. "As for that last one, that's the most incorrect thing you listed. Fuck what shape you're in. Anybody would want you, Harlow."

"Anybody, huh?" I say, flirting with him like he did with me earlier.

Knox looks me right in the eyes as he says, "Anybody."

Oh, there's that charge between us again. This time, it's unmistakable, though. The heat pooling between my legs proves that.

Knox wants *me*. And I know I want him. But we can't do a goddamn thing about it. This is fake. He's my brother's friend, I'm his friend's little sister. He's Fort Knox, I'm an open book. We're incompatible in so many ways.

Tell that to my body, though, since it didn't get the memo. My entire body is on fire right now, and if Knox touches me, I might actually combust. It's a bad idea, but *fuck*, do I not care about that right now.

"So," he says, severing the tension and electricity between us. "How long were you with him?"

"Oh," I say awkwardly. "Just over a year."

"That's a long time for someone to put you down that much. Must've been hard to get over."

"I'm still getting over it," I reply honestly. "I'm much better now than when I left him about a year ago. I struggle occasionally, especially with the freckles, but I've really improved."

"They didn't tell me the details, but the guys all talked about how you're more like your old self again."

"Yeah." I sigh. "The year I was with him had me at my absolute lowest. It took a lot of encouragement from my friends and family to leave him since he had me believing nobody would ever want me if he didn't. But I left, and I've gotten a little bit better each day since."

Knox rubs his hand up and down my arm. "I can't imagine knowing you without the spark in your eye."

"Technically, you did. We just didn't talk much then, so you wouldn't have noticed."

"A terrible mistake on my part," he says shyly. "But I'm happy I know you now."

"I'm happy you do, too." We share genuine smiles as I note the sparkle in Knox's beautiful green eyes. Butterflies erupt in my stomach, and I have no control over them. My breathing quickens as I try to grapple with my mind, telling myself it doesn't mean anything because I couldn't be developing feelings for the mysterious man in front of me right now. That just wasn't possible.

Right?

"I, uh... promised you that I'd tell you more about me as well," Knox says, breaking eye contact.

"Yeah," I reply clumsily. "You did say that."

"Well," he says, gulping, "how much do you wanna know?"

"Just whatever you're comfortable telling me." I place a hand on his arm to reassure him. "I know it's hard for you to trust someone, so I don't want you to do anything you're uncomfortable with."

"That's the weird thing about this arrangement, Lo." He smiles at me. "It might be fake, but I trust you completely. That's hard for me to do, yes, but there's something about you that puts me completely at ease."

I smile widely. "I'm really glad you can trust me then, Knox. I'd never do anything to break that trust."

"I know you wouldn't. That's the only reason I'm considering telling you this."

"Telling me what?" I ask curiously.

He sighs as he lays back on the bed. "About what happened that made me become who I am. The guy known as an asshole who won't ever let anyone in."

I lay down on the bed beside him, and we both turned to face each other. "You weren't always like that?"

"No," he admits. "I honestly used to be pretty optimistic. But one situation took all the optimism out of me, and I've kept most everyone at arm's length since."

I reach out my hand and lightly rub his arm. "Don't say anything you don't want to, but whatever you do say, I promise it's safe with me."

He softly smiles at me and says, "I know, Lo. *I trust you.*" That admission is all I need to relaunch the butterflies, but I fight them harder this time. Knox deserves my undivided attention, so I don't want to rummage through my own mind right now.

He takes a deep breath before starting. "Okay, the first thing I need is for you to promise you won't judge me. I was a naive young adult at the time."

I eye him curiously. "I'm not going to judge you, Knox. Whatever happened won't change how I look at you."

"Thank you, Harlow." He lets out a deep breath. "This happened right after my junior year of college. Cole obviously plays baseball, so I'm sure you're familiar with how the draft works, but I turned twenty-one the previous September. The draft was held in early June that year, and the Stars took me with the first overall pick.

"I know it will sound conceited, but I was one of the most sought-after prospects in that draft. I honestly had teams interested in drafting me when I was eighteen, but I opted to play a few years of college ball before heading to the majors. All that to say, my name was well-known already, and once I made my debut with the Stars, it was likely to only get bigger. Everyone would know who I was.

"Well, I had a girlfriend at the time—Emily. We'd been together for maybe six months at that point. When I was drafted, Emily planned a night for us to celebrate my achievement. I was a horny twenty-one-year-old, so I'm sure you can guess what that entailed."

"I'm going to guess you spent that entire night in your bedroom," I say with a snicker.

"Yeah," Knox says quietly. "Really wish I hadn't, though. Because what Emily didn't tell me was that she had set up cameras around my room when I was in the shower. Every part of that night, the sweet, sensual, and very X-rated parts, were recorded in HD."

"She recorded you!" I say, gasping at the audacity of this woman I've never met. "I can't imagine what it was like when you found out."

He runs a hand through his hair. I've started to notice he does that when he's nervous. "I wish I could say that's the worst of it, but that's really just the beginning. It doesn't get better from here." He sighs, clearly uncomfortable.

"Knox," I say, cupping his cheek in my hand. "You don't need to tell me anything more."

"No," he replies. "I actually want to. I've never told anyone about this because my life could've been ruined, but I want to get it off my chest. I *want* to tell you." Knox takes a few more deep breaths before continuing the story. "From the recordings Emily took, she made several... sex tapes," he says as if in physical pain. "But the tapes weren't for her or for me. She planned to sell them."

"Oh my God!" I shriek, completely dumbfounded. How could somebody do that to such a sweet man like Knox?

"She had left her computer open once and had an email on her screen. I didn't have a reason to suspect anything, but I couldn't shake the feeling that I needed to see that email. So, I peeked... and found that she had been communicating with a certain tabloid. They'd formed a plan. Once I made my debut for the Stars, they would distribute the videos. They were going to be plastered *everywhere*. When everyone knew who I was, they were going to put that out."

"Why would she do that?" I ask, fighting back tears. I can hear the hurt in Knox's voice as he tells me this, and it breaks me to see him that way.

"When I confronted her about what I found, she told me it was because she wanted to be famous. Evidently, there are reality TV stars who were propelled into stardom after their sex tapes leaked. For hers to matter, it needed to be with someone with a name people recognized. Once I hit the majors, I was going to be that person. She was going to launch herself and become a household name. I was just collateral damage on her quest for fame."

Tears spill from my eyes as I can't hold them back any longer. "Knox, I'm so sorry. What happened after that?"

"I broke it off immediately. I couldn't stand the sight of her. I was thoroughly embarrassed by what happened, but I knew I needed to talk to somebody about it... so I spilled everything to the agent I had just signed with—Simon. It was hard to admit all of it, but without talking to him, I never would've known to contact a lawyer. That her releasing the tapes could be seen as revenge porn since we weren't together anymore. A strongly worded letter from an attorney to both Emily and the tabloid she was working with that threatened legal action with possible jail time if they released the video was enough to get them to back down. The attorney ensured Emily erased all the footage so there was no more threat. Since then, I haven't trusted people or the media. I don't open up because I don't want anybody to find ammunition to use against me again. I can probably count on one hand the amount of hookups I've had since, but they've all been in my hotel room. It's the only way I can make sure there aren't cameras around."

"Knox," I say as I all but launch myself at him, wrapping him tight. "I'm so sorry you had to go through that. You never deserved that."

"I wasn't the greatest guy or anything, Lo," he says as he returns the hug, bringing me in close with my face flush against his bare chest. "Maybe I did deserve it."

"Never, Knox. You *never* deserved that. You're not the man everyone thinks."

"Do you actually think that, Harlow?" he asks, lifting my face up by my chin. His eyes are glassy and full of worry and sorrow. I've never seen him like this before.

"I *know* that. I think you're a great person, and I think my life is better having you in it. She never deserved you, and she also doesn't deserve to still have an effect on you."

Knox smiles softly. "Thank you," he says as he brushes a stray tear from my eye. "You know, you're not supposed to be the one crying."

"Your fake girlfriend is an emotional mess." He laughs before lightly kissing my forehead.

"Did you, uh... want to stay here tonight? Just to sleep. It might be nice to have someone beside me tonight. That's the first time I've told that story in almost seven years."

I give him a reassuring smile. "Of course I will. I feel like that's the least I can do after you just poured your heart out."

Knox chuckles softly. "I really didn't think I'd enjoy your presence so much when we started this whole thing. But you're not at all what I expected."

We both sit up on the bed to finish off the onion rings we've been neglecting. Knox grabs one and holds it up for me to take a bite. "Look at you being all cutesy, Spencer."

He barks out a laugh. "I'm not fucking 'cutesy,' that's for sure. But that does remind me of something. You know how the Stars' Charity holds an annual dinner, right?"

"Of course I do," I tell him. "My brother does play for your team."

"I'm ignoring the sass," he says while laughing. "But the dinner is next month on one of our off days. Significant others are all invited to attend. Do you want to go with me?"

"Seeing as everyone thinks I'm your girlfriend, I probably should." I smile at him. "That sounds like fun. I guess you'll get to see me in a gown, after all."

"I think I like the idea of that." He grins. "Do you have a gown you could wear?"

I sigh. "Well, running a blog doesn't really send me to anything where I need formalwear, so I do not."

"We'll get you a dress then. But we can talk about that tomorrow." He brings a hand to his mouth to cover a yawn. "I'm pretty tired right now."

"Yeah, sleep sounds like a good idea." I stand to move the now-empty container of onion rings off the bed and to the small table. Knox meets me as I stand up and wraps me up in another hug.

"Thank you again, Lo." He lets out a contented sigh. "It's surprisingly kind of nice to have someone else who knows."

I bring my head back and look right at Knox. "We're friends now, Slick. You can lean on me when you need it."

He rests his forehead against mine and smiles. And the goddamn butterflies retake flight. And the electricity sparks. And the heat flows through my body.

It's undeniable now that there's something between Knox and me. That's worrying because we're supposed to keep things light and easy. No complications, no strings. A fake relationship that ends when the season is over.

But when Knox's mouth captures mine, kissing me for the first time without an audience, things start to seem heavier. As he parts my lips to stroke his tongue against mine, things begin to feel more complicated. And as he rests his hand on the back of my head to deepen the kiss, things start to feel a lot stringier.

My heart is happy, and my brain is scared. What do I do from here?

Twenty-Four

Knox

AFTER OUR TEN-GAME ROAD trip between Pittsburgh, Boston, and Miami, we finally returned to New York. And now that we're home, I have got to clear my goddamn head.

I kissed Harlow that first night in Pittsburgh.

It's not like we haven't kissed before, but it was the first time without watchful eyes, and it was so much *better*. It was just us, caught up in a moment and surrendering ourselves to it.

Things have felt a bit awkward since the kiss, though. We still see each other daily, but it feels like we're both afraid of acknowledging the kiss because we know it was different. And we don't know if it actually means something.

But it did teach me one thing. It taught me that resisting Harlow is going to be fucking impossible. If I gave in so easily to a kiss, how much longer can I keep myself from trying to get her into my bed? I'm a weak man. It's only a matter of time before the temptation wins...

"You got something on your mind there, Fort?" Lucia asks. She happens to be the trainer working with me at practice today on stretches for my shoulder before my start tomorrow night.

Lucky me, having to work with Harlow's best friend for the next hour.

"Nope," I lie. "Just thinking about tomorrow's game."

She snickers. "You're not a good liar, Knox."

I scoff. "I'm not that bad."

"Well, you're lying now, and I'm not buying it," she says as she takes my right arm and extends it, stretching it out and then up.

"I'm not talking about it," I reply, wincing as she moves my shoulder around again. I had a high pitch count during my last start, and my arm is evidently still feeling the effects.

She leans closer, lowering her voice to a whisper as she says, "It's about the kiss, isn't it?"

I groan. "Of course, she fucking told you about that."

"Not willingly," Lucia retorts. "But she's been acting weird since that first night in Pittsburgh, too, and I eventually got it out of her." She releases my arm and lets it rest at my side. "You guys don't need to be weird about this. It was just a kiss." She eyes me now, raising her brow. "Right?"

"Right," I mutter. Because even if I wanted to kiss her again, kissing can easily lead to more, and I still need to do my damnedest to avoid that.

"Well then," Lucia starts. "it's lucky for you that Rory and I are coming along to pick out dresses later." She looks at me and smirks. "We'll be there to stop you in case of temptation."

I roll my eyes as she gets back to work on my shoulder, manipulating it every which way.

My mind drifts to this afternoon when I agreed to take Harlow dress shopping for the charity dinner in a few weeks. Lucia and Rory are coming along as buffers; Ella apparently already bought a dress with Josh. But if two of her best friends are with us, I'm much less likely to do something I could regret. And seeing Harlow in a nice dress sets it up for me to do something monumentally stupid.

But she's excited about this afternoon. She told me the last time she wore a formal dress was prom. Her excitement excites me as well. I like seeing her happy. And I want to show her that not all men are like her ex. She deserves to be celebrated in every way possible.

As long as we're faking this relationship, I'll be the one to do that for her.

❮❮❮❮❮❮❮❮❮❮❮❮❮❮❮❮❮❮❮❮❮❮❮❮❮❮❮❮

After practice, I go back to my penthouse to find something more presentable to wear. Athletic clothing probably isn't the correct attire for where we're heading. I throw on a short-sleeved black Henley top and a pair of dark jeans and then head to the garage to grab my car before texting Harlow that I'm coming to pick her up.

When I pull up in front of her building, I find her waiting out front for me... and several people with cameras waiting in the bushes across the street. Fucking ridiculous. But I'm not about to be seen as less than chivalrous.

I hop out of my Maserati and walk over to greet her. "Hey there, Lo," I say before leaning down and kissing her softly. So fucking dangerous because now I want more.

Harlow's lips still brushing against mine, she asks, "Cameras?"

"There's always cameras," I tell her as I wrap my arm around her shoulder and lead her to my car. I open up the passenger door and help her into her seat as she just smiles at me.

Once I walk around and jump into the driver seat again, she looks at me and says, "You know, for a fake boyfriend, I think you're better than any of the actual boyfriends I've had."

"Like I said before, you were with shitty men."

"Are you not a shitty man then, Knox?" she asks with a smile.

"I have my moments," I reply honestly, returning her smile. "But I like to think I'm not so shitty with you."

"You're not," she says as I pull out onto the street before she adds in a lower voice, "You're so much better."

My heart swells. Or it feels like it did. Regardless, such a small comment like that shouldn't do this to me, right?

But she just told me I'm so much better than anyone she's been with. It's hard not to take that for truth when Harlow doesn't say anything she doesn't mean. I'm a lucky son of a bitch because I'm pretty sure I hit the fake girlfriend jackpot.

"So," she says, taking me out of my thoughts. "You never did tell me where we're going today."

"All you need to know is that you're shopping for your dress for the charity dinner. You'll find out where we're going when we get there," I reply coyly.

She rolls her eyes and laughs. "You're so damn lucky I like surprises, Slick."

"I do consider myself lucky," I say honestly, and I hear her breath catch in her throat. She caught on to my double meaning there, just like I thought she would. She makes it difficult to not be completely honest, though, so I just spill what I'm thinking. That'll probably bite me in the ass at some point, but so far, it's going well.

She's quiet as I weave in and out of traffic on our way to midtown Manhattan. Maybe my honesty was a bit too much. Or maybe she's mulling it over, figuring out what she thinks about it.

Either way, her train of thought is broken as we finally reach our destination. Lucia and Rory are both waiting for us outside of the building.

"Knox," she says with excitement. "You did not!"

I smile. "I did."

"This is Rana Dagon's studio."

"It is," I say with a light laugh.

"I love Rana Dagon's designs."

"Lo, that's exactly why we're here. You mentioned how much you like her designs, so I figured this would be the perfect place to find your dress."

"How did you even get an appointment?" she asks, turning to me. "Her waitlist is years long."

"Harlow, I'm arguably the best pitcher in the league. And if you were unaware, Rana happens to be a massive Stars fan. I pulled a few strings, and here we are. She's waiting inside to help you three find your dresses for the dinner."

Before I can process what's happening, Harlow leans across the seat and pecks my lips. "Thank you, Knox," she says, smiling sweetly as she exits the car to meet Lucia and Rory.

I'm left in my thoughts for a moment, running my thumb over my bottom lip, where the feel of her kiss still lingers.

<<<<<<<<<<<<<<<<<<<<<<<<<<<<<<

"Ah, please come in!" Rana says as she ushers us inside. "I'm thrilled to finally have a Stars player here, though I never expected the first one to be Fort Knox."

"Yeah," I say, rubbing my neck. "Surprised me, too."

Rana laughs as she takes note of Harlow. "Ah, here's the one to thank for the demeanor change. You must be Harlow Pierce."

Harlow slowly reaches her hand out to take the one Rana is extending and shakes. "Uh, yeah. I'm Harlow." Her voice is shaky. The ever-confident Harlow is starstruck and nervous right now.

"Your blog is phenomenal," Rana says. "You've done a wonderful job."

"You- you've read my blog?" She asks with stars in her eyes.

"Yes, dear," Rana says with a light laugh. "Now, why don't you all follow me so we can discuss and find the perfect gowns for you."

Rana throws an arm around Harlow's shoulder, leading her, Lucia, and Rory away.

Lo looks back at me and mouths *Oh my God,* causing me to laugh as I start after them.

Rana leads us all into what looks to be a consultation area, fitted with two blue velvet sofas and a dark wood table across from a matching blue velvet chair. Harlow and I take our seats on one sofa, Lucia and Rory take the other, and Rana takes the chair.

"Okay, ladies. Let's talk about styles, colors, everything. I'll start at the end here. You're Paul Fisher's daughter, Rory, right?" Rana asks as she turns to face Rory.

"Yes," she replies, tucking her hair behind her ear. "Not quite the same fitness as my dad, though."

Rana waves her off. "Not to worry, darling. I'm confident I have something here that will complement you well. You have quite a beautiful complexion."

"Perks of being biracial, I guess," Rory says.

Rana says, "An olive green would suit you beautifully, Rory. How do you plan to wear your hair for this event? Your curls are absolutely stunning, but the best neckline for you will depend on how you style your hair."

"I usually pull it up."

"A V-neckline then. I have the perfect dress for you." Rana turns her attention now to Lucia. "You are Lucia? I believe that's what Knox told me when he set this up." Lucia nods. "What olive complexion do you have, if you don't mind my asking?"

"Spanish," Lucia replies. "My parents are from Spain, along the Mediterranean."

"I think a cherry red would be perfect for you, Lucia. Something strapless. I have something I think you'll love." Rana now turns to Harlow. "Now for Harlow. Your skin is relatively fair."

"Oh yes," she laughs. "I always need to go heavy on the SPF if I don't want to burn."

"A pastel blue for you. It will complement your skin and bring out the blue of your eyes. I have a few necklines that might suit you, but I love the idea of you in a plunging neckline."

Yeah, I think I like the idea of that, too.

"I can't wait to see what you pick then."

Rana stands up. "Okay, ladies," she says, clapping her hands together. "Why don't you head to the fitting area, and I'll pull some options for you?"

We make our way to the fitting area as Rana spends a few minutes grabbing dresses from her stock. When she comes over, she disperses the gowns amongst Harlow, Lucia, and Rory, and they disappear to try them on.

Is it wrong that I'm not paying attention at all to what Lucia and Rory are wearing because I'm so focused on Harlow? The three women all come out to see what the others are wearing and comment on how it looks and fits, but whenever they're in front of me, I only look at Harlow. She's tried on two gowns so far, both light blue. I thought they looked great and told her so, but Lucia, Rory, and Rana seemed to have differing opinions.

As she goes back in to try on her third option, Rana's favorite, Rana sits beside me on the sofa outside the changing area. "She's lovely."

I smile. "She really is." And I mean that. Harlow has such a beautiful soul that shines through to everyone she meets. How anyone could find it in themselves to dull that sparkle is unfathomable to me.

"As a Stars fan," Rana says, "I fully support this pairing. Your pitching has only gotten better since you two went public."

"Yeah, I guess it has," I admit. And that's something I never really thought of, but she's right. I've always been able to maintain a low ERA and a high number of wins, but we're almost two months into the season now, and I don't have a single loss. My numbers this year are better than they've ever been. Does that actually have anything to do with Harlow, though?

"I can see how much you care about her." I give her a questioning look. "Hey, you might be Fort Knox to everyone else, but I can read people. And you have hearts in your eyes every time you look at her."

"Oh," is all I can manage to say.

Rana chuckles. "She's looking at you the same way. You make a very sweet couple."

Couple.

Of course, she thinks we're a couple. The entire world thinks we're a couple. Even if we actually aren't. But that word doesn't sound as bad as I expected when hearing it from a stranger.

It's actually sort of... nice.

I hear the curtains in the changing area open. As Harlow steps out, all coherent thought leaves my body.

She stands across from me in a pale blue gown, long enough to touch the ground, with a thigh-high slit and a plunging neckline that hits below her chest.

She is downright *stunning*.

"What do you think, Knox?" she asks softly with a nervous smile. Does she think she needs my approval for this? I'd give it to her if I could speak right now, but she doesn't need my approval for anything.

After a few more moments of silence, Rana pipes in, "He's completely speechless, darling." She laughs. "This dress was *made* for you, Harlow!"

"Really?" she asks, her face slightly brighter.

"Yeah," I manage. "You look incredible, Harlow. Blue is definitely your color." The blush that spreads across her cheeks is adorable, and I can't help but smile.

As I hear a few snickers from the side, I'm reminded that Lucia and Rory are indeed still here. And thank God for that because the desire to march Harlow back into that fitting room with me is strong, and I can't act on that.

"So," Rana says, severing the silence. "Is this your dress, Harlow?"

"Yeah," she replies with a smile. "This is the one I want."

"Perfect!" Rana claps her hands together. "Why don't you three get changed back and bring your dresses out. We'll get everything squared away."

As Harlow, Lucia, and Rory disappear back into their changing areas, I grab my wallet and pull out a black card. "Here," I say to Rana. "This is all on me."

Twenty-Five

Knox

"I STILL CAN'T BELIEVE you bought all three of our dresses, Knox," Harlow says from her perch on my kitchen island, sipping from her mug of coffee. She's expressed the same sentiment at least a dozen times since we returned to my penthouse last night.

"I still can't believe that you can't believe it," I say with a smirk. "Rana Dagon is an expensive designer, Lo. I had no intention of letting any of you pay for your own dresses yesterday." I take a sip of coffee from my own mug. "You really struggle to let people help you with things, don't you?"

Harlow sighs as I set my mug down and lift myself up to join her on the island. "Yeah. Part of trying to be all self-sufficient, I guess."

"You can still be self-sufficient if you let people help you sometimes, Lo."

"Big talk from the man that only recently let someone into his life."

I chuckle. "Those aren't even comparable, Freckles. They're not nearly the same thing." She shrugs and takes another sip of coffee.

"I should head out," she says, jumping off the counter. "You have practice soon anyway."

I hate the idea of her leaving. I've grown so accustomed to spending time with her that I think I'd prefer she's always around. It doesn't make sense since none of this is real, but I'll just shrug that off for now. "I'll see you at the game tonight then, Lo," is what I say in response.

Harlow grabs her bag and heads out the door. I let out a breath as I scrub a hand over my face. Why am I starting to feel like this? Why do I suddenly care when she's not around? Why can't I get the image of her in that dress yesterday out of my mind no matter how many times I take a damn shower?

I'm brought out of my thoughts by my phone vibrating on the counter next to me. Simon's calling.

I grab the phone and bring it up to my ear. "Hey, Simon. What's up?"

"I think that's the nicest greeting I've ever gotten from you, Knox," he says from the other line, and I just roll my eyes. As irritating as it is, though, I owe Simon my entire career. I wouldn't be where I am if he weren't there for me with Emily.

"Yeah, according to the media, I'm evidently a nice guy now."

"Which is precisely why I'm calling. In just two months, your public perception has massively increased—more than we could have expected, truthfully. You and Harlow are working together well—everyone is talking about you two."

"I know," I say with a slight sigh. "I constantly see cameras when we're out."

"And everything looks believable. I assume her blog is doing well?" Simon asks.

"Yeah, it's really great, actually," I reply enthusiastically. "The traffic to *Starred and Fast* has taken off. She's bringing in more from ad revenue than ever before."

"Wonderful," he says, not quite dismissively but in a way that suggests he was only asking about her because he felt somewhat obligated to do so. "Now for Axis."

I let out a breath. "Have you heard from them?" I ask hesitantly.

"I spoke to one of the execs last night. Axis *loves* what they're seeing. Your image is improving, and if you keep it up, Axis has every intention of extending that contract at the end of the season."

"That's great!" I reply happily. The contract is technically the reason we're doing this whole fake relationship. But I'd be remiss to admit that I all but forgot about that entirely.

"Keep up the show, Knox. Everything is going according to plan," Simon says before saying his goodbyes and disconnecting the call.

Keep up the show.

The more time I spend with Harlow, the more this *doesn't* feel like a show. I genuinely enjoy her company. I like having her around.

In what kind of way?

Well, that I'm not entirely sure of yet...

Strength training this morning could have been better. I'm so unfocused right now; my mind is racing with thoughts of Harlow and what I should and shouldn't be doing. I need to clear my fucking head before I pitch a god-awful game tonight.

When the rest of the guys leave the clubhouse for practice, I stay behind for a moment to calm my mind.

It's not going well.

The clubhouse door swings open, and Lane walks in. "Thought I'd find you here," he says. "Skip wanted me to find you so you can get your ass to practice."

I let out a deep breath. "Yeah, I'll be out soon. Just need a minute to myself."

"Everything okay?" Lane asks, crossing the room to join me on the sofa.

"I have no fucking idea," I admit.

"Things still going well with Harlow?"

"Yeah, that's all going exactly to plan," I say. "Her blog is doing great, and according to Simon, Axis is pleased with my image right now. It's just…" I start but trail off, unsure of where that sentence is leading.

"It's not going the way you thought it would."

I sigh. "Yeah," I confess. "Everything feels so… different."

"In what way?" Lane asks, cocking an eyebrow. I shove his shoulder before I groan, giving in to the temptation to talk about it. Maybe that'll help me clear my head.

"I like having her around," I start. "I feel like I'm actually getting close to her, which is something I never expected. But…" I take a deep breath and run a hand through my hair as Lane continues eyeing me, waiting for me to admit what he knows I'm going to say. "But I want her, man."

"About fucking time you admit it," Lane says with a laugh. "I've been telling you all season that you would."

"I shouldn't want her, though," I say. "This is all fake. Sleeping with Harlow would probably fuck everything up."

"But maybe it won't," he says with a shrug. "If she wants it too, then I don't see a problem with it."

"Well, she's Cole's little sister, for starters."

Lane rolls his eyes. "She's fucking twenty-five, man. Don't act like she's a child. She's Cole's *younger* sister, not little." I rest my head against the back of the sofa. "You're both adults. Cole won't want details, but he's not going to give you shit if you sleep with her. He's never been that kind of guy."

"I know," I sigh. "But how can I even be sure *she* wants it? It's not like I can just point to my room and say, 'Wanna fuck?'"

"Jesus, it's not been that long since you've had sex, man. You know how to tell if she wants it." I eye him. "Body language. It's all in her body language. Read that, and you'll know what to do."

"It still could be a terrible idea," I sigh.

"Maybe. But it's just sex, dude. As long as things are as fake as you two say they are, that shouldn't complicate anything."

He's right. If that's all true, it shouldn't cause any issues or rifts. But is everything as fake as we say? It doesn't seem like more, but I also know that I don't like it when she's not around.

I'm just going to hold on to the hope that we're correct in how fake all of this is. Every day is a battle with myself to not go for Harlow, no matter how badly I want her. And from what she admitted when she was drunk, I'm pretty sure she wants me, too.

<<<<<<<<<<<<<<<<<<<<<<<<<<<<<<<<<<<<

I stayed on the field to practice longer today to make up for the time I missed while talking to Lane. Because of that, I don't see Harlow outside the clubhouse like usual. Instead, as soon as we take to the field to prep for the game, I find her right where she told me she'd be tonight—front row, right off the first baseline where her season tickets are, with Lucia and Rory holding Sage on either side of her.

I jog over to meet them before I throw some warm-up pitches with Scholl. "Hey, you," I say as I approach her. I like that she sits here because the seats are just above field level—when she stands, she's eye to eye with me.

"Hey, Fort," she says. "Ready for your game tonight?"

"I am now," I reply, snaking an arm around her waist and pulling her closer. "Media seems to think you're a good luck charm."

Harlow laughs. "You were already the best pitcher in the league. You don't need a good luck charm."

"Maybe not." I lower my voice to a whisper. "But I certainly don't mind looking at this good luck charm all night."

"You flirting with me again, Knox?" she says slyly.

"I thought I was being more obvious about it this time. But if you need me to tell you explicitly," I reply, leaning my lips to her ear. "I flirt with you every chance I get, Lo."

I feel the shiver run down her body, reacting to my breath on her ear. "Then I guess it's a good thing I've been trying to get your attention, huh?"

I lean back now and look at her, leaving my arm around her waist. "You've had my attention longer than you realize then," I admit.

"So, it's not the jersey that does it for you?" she asks with a smile.

"Oh, that doesn't hurt at all. You look fucking good with my name on your back, Lo."

"I don't know," she teases. "I'm a Pierce. I always thought that one looked good."

"You look better with Spencer," I say, putting a finger to her chin and finding her eyes with mine. "I like it. A lot."

Harlow's breath is uneven now... just like mine. This became more intense than I expected. Now I hear Scholl calling for me, so I know I need to head over.

"I'm being called upon," I say.

"You are," she replies before adding, "But there's still cameras all around us."

"If you want a kiss, you can just ask." We both smile before I lean in, capturing her lips with mine. I'm enjoying myself a bit too much, but I have to break away so this doesn't go too far.

Once we part, I notice the blush across Harlow's cheeks. I really like the effect I seem to have on her. "Good luck," she says finally.

"Good luck to you, too," I reply as she gives me a curious look. "Lucia and Rory have been watching this entire interaction. You're fucked."

She groans. "I hate you."

"No, you don't," I laugh, jogging backward to meet up with Scholl and get ready for the game. Once I see Harlow take her seat, I turn around and head to the mound, a smile on my face. I don't need a good luck charm, but I sure as fuck like having one anyway.

≪≪≪≪≪≪≪≪≪≪≪≪≪≪≪≪≪≪≪≪≪≪≪≪≪≪≪≪≪

"Cheers!" Harlow says, clinking her beer against Lucia's, Rory's, and Ella's, and the glasses of water Cole, Josh, and I have. I only gave up one run tonight, and Cole hit a three-run homer, so the girls talked us into going out tonight. None of us guys are drinking because we have a game tomorrow, and Lane didn't join us since he needed to get Sage home. I'm only slightly jealous of him at the moment.

"How are you guys feeling right now?" Rory asks, looking at Cole and me. But I don't need to respond when Cole quickly jumps in.

"Pretty good. Tonight was a great game," he replies.

"I bet you do think so," Rory says. "You batted in three runs yourself, Cole."

"You keeping track, Fisher?" Cole asks, raising a brow.

"Don't flatter yourself," she says, waving him off. "The scoreboard kept track for me." Cole laughs that off, but it almost seems... forced?

"Knox had a damn good game, too," Harlow pipes in. "Only gave up one run."

"All that flirting before the game was good for him, it seems," Lucia says with a smirk.

That grabbed Cole's attention. "You were flirting with my sister?"

"Dude, he's dating your sister," Josh remarks. "Of course, he flirts with her."

"I always see them flirting," Ella adds.

"Sold out by our own friends," I say, looking right at Harlow.

"Can't hide anything," she smiles.

This whole arrangement is fake, but our flirting is very real.

"I don't want to hear about them flirting," Cole grumbles as our friends turn their attention to him now, leaving Harlow and me to ourselves.

"You know," she says, a sly look on her face. A look that I've learned means she's about to give me shit about something. "You did have a great game, but that slider in the fifth. What were you thinking?"

"You criticizing my performance, Freckles?"

"I run a blog, Slick," she replies with a smirk. "Writing about the games is a large part of my job. Interviews, too, but I still haven't been able to sell you or Cole on the idea yet."

"I don't think my performance was all that bad," I say, smirking back.

"I'll be the judge of that," she fires back, tension filling the air.

I don't think we're talking about the game anymore.

"Fucking hell," Cole says in exasperation. "Stop making eyes at each other, will you?"

That seems to snap Harlow out of... whatever this was. "I, uh... I'm going to run to the restroom really quick. I'll be right back." She scurries away from the table, moving faster than I realized she could.

Lucia and Rory are both giving me knowing looks. I need to escape this, too. "I'm gonna... go grab another water," I say as I stand up from the table, heading off in the opposite direction of the bar.

"Your water is practically full," Josh shouts, and I just ignore it. Because I need to talk to Harlow.

Should I be waiting for her in the hallway outside of the bathroom door? No, I'm sure I shouldn't, but here I am anyway.

After a couple of minutes, she walks into the hall, stopping when she sees me leaning against the wall. "Oh... hey, Knox," she says, voice wavering.

"You really think my performance was bad?" I ask, inviting her to come closer.

She closes the gap. "I don't know," she says. "I don't think I know much about your performance."

I flip her around, pinning her against the wall with hands planted on either side of her head. "You've been watching me pitch for years, Lo." I smirk and press my forehead against hers. "You should know all about my performance, shouldn't you?"

"Maybe I need to learn more," she challenges, shaking off any unease or nervousness she's feeling.

"I'm not sure there is anything more for you to learn." I instinctively grind my hips into hers, searching for any friction. Harlow gasps when she feels how fucking hard I am in the middle of the damn bar, wearing those gray sweatpants she likes so much.

"I'm sure there are things you could teach me," she says in a low tone.

So fucking *seductive*.

"Harlow..." My lips brush against hers.

"Knox..." she says, pressing her body tight against mine.

Body language. This is what Lane was saying earlier. I can *see* how much she wants me right now. I could lead her out of here, take her back to my penthouse, and fuck her all night, and she wouldn't protest. She *wants* me to do that.

But I'm still not sure that's a good idea. I don't want to fuck things up between us. We're getting along well. Really well. I want to ensure

I keep her in my life when we end this whole arrangement. Sex could ruin all of that. We could lose all the progress we've made.

I can't risk it...

"We, uh..." I stammer, peeling my body off of hers. "We should head back to the table before they start wondering where we are."

"Right," she says, looking dejected and a bit embarrassed. She removes herself from under my arms and pads off down the hallway.

I scrub a hand over myself, wondering what the fuck I was thinking coming over here in the first place. I all but invited her to tell me how much she wants me... and then I fucking stopped it from going further. Now I'm left with a goddamn hard-on in the middle of a busy bar.

I need to get a grip on myself. She's just a woman. An insanely attractive woman whose company I happen to thoroughly enjoy. But still, just a woman.

But she's not just a woman, is she?

No, she's the one woman I never thought would be able to get through to me. Now, I seek her out at every game. I see her every day. I go to fucking dive bars just because she wants to go.

So no, she's not just a woman. She's *Harlow*. The woman whose attention I crave more than anything.

Fuck me.

Twenty-Six

Harlow

It has been just over three weeks since that night in the bar.

Three weeks since it seemed like Knox was ready to make a move.

Three weeks since he pressed his fucking dick against my hip and then left me standing there.

Of course, I've told myself we shouldn't do anything anyway. So, I should be fine with nothing happening. But also, don't rile me up in the middle of a bar if you're not going to take care of me, you know? I think I almost broke my vibrator that night.

Knox and I have continued flirting with each other, but we haven't taken things that far again. We've been very close in public, with plenty of new photos showing up in the tabloids, but when it's just us, he usually tries not to be right next to me.

If we're on the couch, he sits on the other end. If we're in the kitchen, he'll lean on the cabinet opposite me.

It's kind of frustrating. He goes from acting like he was ready to bend me over and fuck me in the middle of the damn bar to holding himself back from me. So, have I been misreading the situation? Was he just caught up at the bar? Maybe he doesn't actually want me, and he's trying to back off so I don't get the wrong idea. Bit of a confidence blow if that's what it is, but I've bounced back from worse.

Tonight is all about confidence, though. Tonight is the Stars' Charity fundraising dinner. We'll have to be close to each other all night to play the part we've agreed to. The players interact with the donors for much of the night since it helps bring in donations. Knowing Knox, he's dreading even the thought of having to schmooze with people he doesn't know, but at least I'll be there to help and encourage him.

I find myself in front of Lucia's building now since she, Rory, Ella, and I are getting ready together for tonight. I grab my dress bag from the back of the taxi I took to Chelsea and walk inside, heading straight to the elevator and taking it up to the fourteenth floor.

"She finally made it," Lucia says, opening the door and gesturing me inside.

"So fucking dramatic, Luc," I reply. "I'm not late. Ella's not even here yet."

"No," Rory says from her place on the sofa in the living room. "But I've been here for half an hour already." Lucia takes my dress bag from me and hangs it on a hook by the door.

I sit beside Rory on the couch, and Lucia takes the plush chair beside us. "You ready to play the doting girlfriend tonight, Lo?" Lucia asks.

"Yeah," I reply. "I can manage that. I feel like we've gotten pretty good at this fake relationship thing." Rory tries and fails to stifle a laugh. "What's that for, Ror?"

"Lo, how fake is it actually?"

"Very fake," I say, my voice wavering.

"Very convincing," Lucia says with a smile. I throw my hands over my face and sink into the back of the couch as I groan.

"Ooh, she realizes that, Luc," Rory adds. "But it might be kind of hard to ignore that scene before the game a few weeks ago."

"That day has me so fucking confused," I admit, sitting myself up again. "I can't tell if he's messing with my head or if any of it is genuine."

"What do you mean?" Lucia asks, eyeing me curiously.

I sigh. "Well, you both obviously saw us before that game. We've been doing a hell of a lot of flirting, both around people and when we're alone." I try to steady myself with a deep breath. "But then at the bar..."

"Did he end up following you when he said he was going to get more water?" Rory asks.

"Oh, he definitely did. And if you guys heard our conversation before that, you know how charged it was."

Lucia smirks. "You mean when you guys were not-so-subtly talking about his 'performance'?"

"Yeah... that." I start fidgeting with my hands, trying to calm myself. "I went to the restroom to try to collect myself, and when I came out, Knox was waiting for me. He asked me what I really thought of his 'performance,' and the innuendo was even more clear than before. He backed me against the wall, and when he told me that there shouldn't be anything left for me to learn, I said that I'm sure there were... things he could teach me."

"Holy shit, Lo!" Rory screams excitedly, repeatedly hitting my arm. "What happened then?"

"Then we almost kissed, and I could feel his dick against my leg... and then he said we should get back to you guys. Nothing actually happened."

"That's still a pretty big deal, Lo," Lucia says.

"Is it, though? I'm not sure he actually wants me. He was probably just caught up. Then he backed off so I don't get the wrong idea."

"Oh, you're so in denial, honey." Lucia gives me a soft smile. "He's not getting hard from being caught up."

"And like we both told you before," Rory chimes in, "Fake dating never works in the books. Feelings develop, and they always give in and sleep together."

Trying to get the heat off me, I say, "You know another popular trope, Ror? Single dad and the nanny." I wiggle my brows at her.

"Lane?!" she shouts. "No, that's definitely not happening!"

"Ooh, that's an extreme reaction, Ror," Lucia adds with a smile.

"I prefer men closer to my age."

"Lane is literally only thirty," I say.

"That's five years older than me. Besides that, though, Lane's not my type."

"Since when do you have a type, Rory?" Lucia asks with curiosity in her eyes.

"Oh, uh…" she stammers. "I guess it's not really a type…" she trails off. And it clicks for me.

"Oh my God!" I say excitedly. "You're already interested in someone, aren't you?"

"What?! No, definitely not. Nope, not interested in anyone."

"She totally is!" Lucia exclaims. "Who do we think it could be, Lo?"

"Well," I say. "I think we can safely eliminate Lane. She doesn't seem to want to play out her own romance book trope."

"I think I hate you both," Rory says, laying back on the couch and covering her face with a pillow.

Lucia and I both laugh while my mind starts to wander. Maybe Knox wasn't just caught up; maybe it really was something. But more importantly, who does Rory have her eye on?

❮❮❮❮❮❮❮❮❮❮❮❮❮❮❮❮❮❮❮❮❮❮❮❮❮❮❮

"We look fucking hot," I say, looking at myself in the mirror and then glancing at Lucia, Rory, and Ella.

"You might kill Knox with the top of that dress," Lucia chuckles.

I'm not sure she's wrong. The neckline comes halfway down my torso, but the structure of the top means my cleavage has never looked better. Not to mention the thigh-high slit on the side.

Rana was spot-on about the color as well. This shade of pale blue complements my complexion perfectly. My eyes look bluer than they ever have. With all that and the strappy silver heels I'm wearing, I'm not sure I've ever felt sexier.

"I really love that color on you, Rory," Lucia says. Her olive green dress has a V-neckline, small flowy sleeves, and a knee-high slit. The gown flounces around enough to hide all of Rory's insecurities, namely the shape of her body. Lucia, Ella, and I talk her up, but that only does so much.

"Yes," I say, agreeing with Lucia. "That dress was made for you, Ror."

"Thanks," she replies shyly. Rory is always so bubbly and boisterous that seeing her like this is a little jarring. So Lucia, Ella, and I will continue to do our part to make sure she believes us when we tell her how good she looks.

"Now, what do you ladies think of this?" Lucia asks, hands sliding down the cherry-red gown. It's strapless, with a corseted top and flowing skirt. "I think red is my color."

"Red is definitely your color," Rory says, handing her a tube of red lipstick. "You need this, too."

Lucia applies the shade of crimson to her lips, puckering them to ensure an even application. When she goes to return it, she calls back to me, "Lo, what color do you want for tonight?"

"Oh," I say, thinking it over. "I think a peachy pink would go well with the dress. It'll also tie in well with the rest of the makeup since I went for a softer look."

Lucia grabs the shade I requested and crosses the room to hand it to me. "I haven't said anything, Lo, because I didn't want to make a big deal out of it, but your makeup has been much softer lately."

"Uh, yeah. I guess it has been."

Rory walks over to join us with the dark nude lipstick she'll wear tonight. "I'm loving the new look, Lo. We missed your freckles."

"Speaking of freckles," Ella adds as she finishes pulling on her strapless light yellow satin dress. "Isn't that what Knox has been calling you for the past couple of months?"

I blush at the mention of the nickname. I didn't think I'd like it, but he has me starting to love my freckles again.

"Yes, he started calling me Freckles the night after we went public. When I read all those comments online, I had cried all my makeup off. He said that was the first time he even realized I had freckles since I always covered them up."

"So are you doing this for Knox then?" Rory asks. "Because it's not like you at all to do something like that for a man, minus that fuckface ex of yours."

"No, I'm not doing it for Knox," I reply honestly. "I'm doing it for me. But I wouldn't be as comfortable with them as I am now if he didn't make it a point to tell me how wrong Derek was about them—how wrong he was about everything."

They all smile at me. "I know we've spent some time teasing you, Lo," Lucia says, "but I really do like him for you."

"This is the happiest I've seen you in two years," Rory adds.

"I am happy, guys. I'm really happy."

And I am. Derek manipulated me, messed with my head, and tore me down until I was well and truly fractured. I'd never felt more broken. But I feel happy again. I feel like *me* again. And it's so good to be back.

There's a knock on Lucia's door, so we all head back to the living room. Knox wants to pick me up so we can arrive at the dinner together, so I'm not surprised when I see him walk through the door as Lucia lets him in. What is surprising, though, is how fucking *good* he looks right now.

I've never seen Knox in a suit, but this man is standing before me now in a deep navy blue suit, perfectly tailored to his body. He has a light blue button-down shirt underneath his jacket, with the top few buttons undone, no tie. His pants hit just above his ankle, and he's wearing a pair of camel-colored loafers without socks.

Dear God, no one has ever looked so perfect before.

He may have teased me about staring... if he wasn't doing some staring of his own. His eyes roam all over my body, slowly raking up from my ankle to the top of the slit in my dress until he lands on the bust. I can see his throat bob as he tries to compose himself.

"Harlow," Knox manages before clearing his throat. "You look incredible."

I cross the room to meet him. "Thank you," I say, giving him a soft smile. "You look great. I really like the suit."

He returns my smile with a gleam in his eyes. "Ready to get out of here, Freckles?"

"Lead the way, Slick."

Twenty-Seven

Harlow

The drive from Chelsea to the Flatiron District wasn't long since the neighborhoods border each other. We were quiet for the duration of the trip, just stealing glances when we thought the other wasn't paying attention. It seems safe to say that subtlety is neither of our specialties.

Knox pulls up to the valet in front of our destination for the night—a tall building with ample rooftop space. He exits and comes to my door, opening it before taking my hand and helping me out of the car and onto the sidewalk.

"Name?" the valet driver asks as he notes the license plate number.

"Knox Spencer," he replies.

"Enjoy your night then, Mr. Spencer." The valet driver nods at us, and Knox, hand in hand, leads me into the building. By some bit of fortune, we end up in the elevator alone as we ascend to the rooftop.

With no audience, he severs the distance he's been keeping between us, standing right behind me and running his fingers lightly up and down the exposed skin of my arms. "You're going to fucking kill me tonight, Pierce."

I lean back against him, surrendering myself to his touch. "Is that so?"

"You're a goddamn vision in that dress, Harlow."

I smirk. "Not so hard to picture me in a gown now, is it?"

"No, it isn't. And you look really fucking good." His breath on my ear causes my body to involuntarily shiver against him, and he softly chuckles. "You like that, do you?"

"I can't control how my body reacts when you're that close to me, Knox."

"But letting go of your control could be good, don't you think?"

Ohh, there's a whole other meaning to that, isn't there?

"I do think," I say breathily. "Maybe giving up control is exactly what I need to do."

The groan that escapes Knox's lips tells me everything I need to know. He wasn't caught up. He's been keeping some distance between us because he has the same thoughts I do—*sleeping together would be a really bad idea.* But he still wants it just as much as I do.

"No, I think that would be a very good thing for you, Harlow."

I turn to face him, and the fire in his eyes burns red hot. We may both think this is a bad idea, but holding back is arduous. I don't believe I have it in me to keep myself from him much longer, and if his rapid breathing is any indication, he doesn't have it in him, either.

Our saving grace right now is the ding of the elevator, alerting us to our arrival on the building's rooftop terrace. We break our eye contact as the doors open, and we step out to join the throngs of people meandering around.

I spot my brother over by the bar with Lane, which is perfect because I *really* need a glass of wine right now.

Actually, make that the whole bottle.

Things have been a bit awkward between Knox and me since we arrived. We're sitting at a table with our friends, and we've hardly joined in on any conversations, so lost in our own heads.

I've no doubt they noticed.

I'm two glasses of Riesling in, and Knox has already downed an entire beer. I know he doesn't drink much during the season; none of the players do. But between that and the way he keeps adjusting the collar of his shirt, he seems to feel as hot as I do right now.

Every look from Knox has me burning up. And he's hardly taken his eyes off me. Cole and Lane have been shooting each other glances but otherwise not addressing the obvious tension in the air.

But Lucia isn't one to refrain.

"What the hell is going on with you two?" she says loudly. "You've been quiet all through dinner."

"Because they're both being really fucking weird tonight," Cole replies.

"We're not being weird, dick," Knox states, annoyed.

"Well," Lane says, "you sure as hell aren't acting normal."

Rory sips her glass of wine from where she sits next to Cole. "You should've seen them when he came to pick her up from Luc's. You could've cut the tension with a knife."

"You're being dramatic," I reply weakly. "There was no tension."

Lucia stifles a laugh. "Babe, you were both eye-fucking each other the moment he walked into the room."

"Spare me, please," Cole groans.

"Your sister is dating Fort," Rory says, nudging him with her arm. "This all comes with the territory, Pierce."

"Hey, she doesn't want to hear about my sex life. I don't want to hear about hers."

"Do you even have a sex life, Cole?" Rory asks, eyeing him curiously.

"Why are we focusing on me right now?" Cole cries.

As our friends now turn their attention to Cole and Rory's bickering, Knox and I both breathe a sigh of relief at not being the focus of the conversation.

He takes a deep breath before leaning closer to me. "How is your salmon, Lo?" he asks.

"Not the best I've had," I reply, "but it's pretty good."

"Ah, good," he says back. "That's good. The weather's nice tonight, too, isn't it?"

I can't hold back a giggle. "Are you trying to make small talk, Knox?"

"If you have to ask, I'm doing a terrible job." He gives me a soft smile.

"Not terrible, I don't think... but why are you trying to make small talk with me?"

Knox sighs. "Things have seemed a little... awkward since we got off the elevator. I'm trying to get us past that."

"How sweet of you," I say with a smirk. "Such a thoughtful boyfriend I have." My hand rests gently on his thigh.

"You just love teasing, don't you?" Knox says as his lips lightly brush the outside of my ear. My shiver is involuntary and immediately creates a charge between us again.

No matter how hard we try, we always end up right back here. Same situation, same feelings, same internal monologue telling us this is a terrible idea. But I'm so tired of listening to that voice in my head.

That spark between us is never going to go away. So instead of running from it, maybe we should just give in. Maybe that's all we need to eliminate this awkward tension once and for all.

I turn my head to look Knox right in the eyes. "That's not teasing," I say before lowering my voice. "But I know how to tease if that's what you want."

He takes those words as an invitation to run his fingers gently up the exposed skin of my thigh without taking his eyes off me. "Bit of a dangerous game, that is, don't you think, Harlow?"

"What's life without a little danger?" I say, leaning in closer. Knox's throat bobs as he tries to maintain his composure.

"Harlow!" Lucia says as she claps a hand on my shoulder, and he all but jumps away from me. "Come with me to get another drink."

"Oh, uh… sure," I stammer out. "Let's go."

I stand up on shaky legs as Lucia leads me toward the bar. I glance back at Knox to find Lane leaning over, talking to him about something. Based on the vacant look on his face, I'm willing to bet I'm the subject of that conversation.

We get to the bar and stand while waiting for the bartender's attention. "So," Lucia says now that she has me alone. "What were you and Knox talking about?"

"Nothing!" I say too quickly. I know she won't believe me, but I've got to try. "We were just making small talk."

Lucia looks right at me. "Some small talk that must have been since he was ready to slip a hand under your dress."

"Lucia!" I whisper shout. "Be quiet, will you?"

"How interesting that you're not denying it," she smiles.

"Why didn't you bring Rory with you to get a drink?" I ask in an attempt to steer the conversation.

"Because," Lucia says, "she's been chatting up Cole all night, and he's hanging on to her every word."

"What's going on there?" I wonder curiously.

"Oh, *ojitos*," Lucia says, stepping up now to speak with the bartender. "You're so naive."

Twenty-Eight

Harlow

WHEN LUCIA HANDS ME my new glass of Riesling, I tell her I'm going to take a minute to collect myself. I've got quite a bit running through my head right now that I need to figure out.

I stand off to the side of the bar, leaning back on it, eyes closed, as I try to compose myself. To my right, I feel somebody join me before the silence is broken.

"I'm guessing you need to gather your composure, too," Knox says as I open my eyes and turn to face him.

"Something like that," I reply with a soft chuckle as I sip my wine. "Hoping this helps, too."

Knox leans his bottle of beer over. "Then a toast to us not looking like such fucking idiots." I toast my glass to his bottle as we both laugh. "So, uh..." he runs a hand through his hair, giving him that messy, tousled look I love. "How has tonight been for you?"

"Aside from a few awkward moments," I say with a small smile that he returns, "it's been kinda fun. I've never been to an event quite like this before."

"I guess you get used to it," he says. "But I hate things like this. I don't like having to talk to more people than necessary."

I place my palm on Knox's forearm. "Try not to overthink it. I know why you don't like talking to people, but try to remember that these people aren't looking to air out any of your dirty laundry. They're not writing gossip; they're not looking for a scoop. They're here to help Stars Charity raise money."

Knox lets out a deep breath. "Yeah, I'm trying. It's hard to just flip my mindset, but having you beside me…" he turns toward me and smiles. "That helps a lot."

I can feel the blush spreading across my cheeks. "I'm glad I can help, Knox."

He places a finger on my chin and brings my eyes to meet his. "You blushing, Freckles?"

"I might be…"

He chuckles. "Freckles and blushing, a lethal combination."

"So what you're saying is that I'm getting to you right now," I tease.

Knox wraps an arm around the front of my waist and leans closer. "You've been getting to me for a while, Harlow. You have no fucking idea."

My breath catches in my throat. Is this what tonight is going to be? Both of us flustering the other until we just can't take it anymore?

God help me.

"There you are, Spencer," we hear Paul Fisher bellow as he comes up to join us. Knox turns to face him and positions me right in front of him, pulling me close and resting his hand low on my hip.

"Hey, Skip," he says. "You've met Harlow, right?"

Paul and I both laugh. "Knox, you remember she's Cole's sister, and she's been working adjacent to the team for several years now, right?"

"Not to mention Rory being one of my best friends," I add. "Good to see you tonight, Paul."

"Paul?" Knox says, surprised.

"He's not my manager," I laugh. "He's Skipper to you. He's Paul to his daughter's friend."

"Harlow," Paul says. "I've got to ask something I think everyone is thinking." Knox's grip on my hip tightens. "How the hell did you end up with Fort Knox?"

I try to stifle my laugh as Knox groans. "Really, Skip?"

"It's a legitimate question, isn't it?" Paul laughs.

"Knox isn't like most people think," I answer. "I know he was famous for not sharing any part of his life before, but once you get to really know him, you realize he's an incredible person." I peer up at him with a soft smile. "He might be the best man I know." He gives me a bright but unbelieving smile before he presses a kiss to the top of my head.

"Another question then," Paul says. "Knox, what made you go for Cole's sister? That's kind of dangerous, don't you think?"

"Not really," he replies. "You know how Cole is. He's never been bothered by it. He's actually been incredibly supportive."

Sure, we can call my brother's constant teasing supportive.

"I don't know how he does that then. If one of my players went for my daughter, I'd lose my mind."

"Well, I'm grateful he's good with it. I know from the outside that she and I seem very different, but we're more alike than anyone realizes." I look up and catch the glint in Knox's bright, green eyes. "Honestly, I feel like I can actually be myself around her."

The next few seconds are silent, filled with unspoken words. If this is all supposed to be fake, why did that sound so genuine?

"Hell, you two make the same faces at each other as Garro and his fiancée." Knox and I laugh lightly as we both attempt to regain our composure... again. "But I'm happy about it. Knox has had such a change this season. You're good for him, Harlow."

"Yeah," Knox says, slowly letting his hand start drifting down my thigh. "I think she is, too."

"Make sure you both enjoy yourselves tonight, but also be sure to talk to the donors," Paul says before saying his goodbye and leaving us standing alone.

"Well, I guess we should get this part over with," Knox says.

"Happy to be your arm candy for the night then."

He laughs before taking my hand in his and leading me to the open floor.

<<<<<<<<<<<<<<<<<<<<<<<<<<<<<<<<<

After a couple hours of trying to subtly suck up to the donors, Knox and I find ourselves leaning against the glass railing to the rooftop terrace, looking out over the city. He seemed to do a great job of mingling tonight, but I can see that it's taken a lot out of him. He's open with me, but it's still hard for him to open up even a little bit with anyone else.

I turn my back to the railing and look at Knox. "Hey, the hard part's over now, at least."

He softly smiles. "Yeah. Thank fuck, too. I don't think I had any more of that in me."

"Well, I think you did great," I say, resting my hand on his arm. "You looked great, too."

He smirks before moving to stand in front of me, gripping his hands against the railing and trapping me in his arms. "You think it was my ass that looked great, don't you?"

I groan. "You drunkenly tell someone *one* time that they have a sexy ass, and they'll hold it close to their chest, just waiting for the right moment to bring it up." We both laugh. "If you must know, yes, your ass looks great tonight."

Knox leans in closer. "Well," he says, "your ass has been distracting me all goddamn night."

"Hmm…" I say. "I didn't think it would be my ass that did it for you." Our bodies are touching now, close enough for me to feel his racing heart and him to feel mine.

"No," he starts before leaning to my ear and whispering. "You thought it would be your tits, didn't you?"

"I had considered that," I reply coolly.

"Yeah, I considered that, too." I eye him knowingly. "You know how you look tonight, Harlow. It's hard not to stare at every inch of you."

"The way you're dressed tonight, I've been eyeing every inch of you." Knox cocks an eyebrow at me, and I reply in mock offense. "So dirty, Spencer." I lean closer and brush my lips against his. "What kind of woman do you take me for?"

"The kind of woman who goes for what she wants. The kind of woman that's tired of listening to the voice in her head telling her something is a bad idea."

My breath catches, and my body heats up. The honesty in this exchange is something we've both been fighting. But I think we're finally giving up.

"That does sound like me," I admit, lowering my tone to help reel him in.

We stare at each other momentarily, desire flowing between us. Knox presses his lips against mine, kissing me lightly. "Thought I saw someone walking by," he says with a smirk.

"There's no one around us," I reply. "If you want a kiss, you can just ask." he laughs before he captures my mouth again, roughly this time.

I drape my arms around Knox's neck as he rests his hands firmly on my lower back, very slowly letting them fall to my ass. He pulls me in closer as we continue our kiss, unable to fight his desire to have me all to himself. Everything becomes more heated when he grinds his hips into me, letting me *feel* how hot this all is for him.

Knox breaks our kiss. "Harlow..."

"Knox..." I say breathily.

He's fighting with himself right now; I can see the inner turmoil in his eyes. But when I place another kiss on his lips, he groans and kisses me back even harder than before.

When we part again, we both struggle to catch our breath. The air feels thick, deprived of oxygen. "Harlow..." he manages, pressing his forehead against mine. "Do you want to get out of here?"

All I can do is nod.

❮❮❮❮❮❮❮❮❮❮❮❮❮❮❮❮❮❮❮❮❮❮❮❮❮❮❮❮❮❮

As we leave the dinner, Knox and I don't say a single word to each other. He grabs his car from the valet as quickly as possible and breaks almost every traffic law to get us back to his place. The ride up the elevator to the top floor is excruciatingly long as we stand on opposite sides, knowing that's the only thing keeping us from each other right now.

When the elevator dings to let us know we've arrived, Knox grabs my hand and quickly leads me off the elevator and straight to the door of his penthouse. He hurries us both inside before using his foot to push it shut as he finally kisses me again. He walks me backward to his kitchen island, lifting me up to sit on the cold marble.

Once I'm seated, the kisses become more frantic, none of them enough to sate our desires. I push his suit jacket off his shoulders, and he lets it fall, pooling at his feet. As I drape my arms around his neck, he plants one hand on the counter beside me and lets the other tease the exposed skin of my leg.

He slowly moves around the hem before sliding his hand under the fabric. Knox strokes his tongue against mine as he lightly trails his fingers up the inside of my thigh. I break our kiss and throw my head back, unable to hold back the low moan that escapes.

He uses this opportunity to pepper light kisses down my neck. "Harlow..." he says, pressing a kiss to the hollow of my throat. "Tell me you want this." He kisses my jaw. "Tell me you want *me*." He nibbles my earlobe.

The culmination of all this pent-up desire is almost too much to take. We've fought this for months now, and we still ended up right where we are now—letting go of our worries and taking what we want. I have *never* desired somebody the way I desire Knox.

He said earlier that I'm a woman who goes for what she wants. Tonight, that's never been more true.

We part lips and press our foreheads together. I look into his eyes as the easiest words I've ever spoken flow out.

"I want you, Knox."

Twenty-Nine

Knox

I want you, Knox.

Any coherent thought I have leaves my body the moment Harlow says that. I'm done pretending I can hold back. I'm done listening to the part of my brain telling me this is a bad idea. Fuck all of the repercussions. We can deal with them tomorrow.

Harlow wraps her legs around my waist as I lift her from the counter, leading us directly to my bedroom, kissing her all the way. She removed her shoes, tossing them in the hall as we finally crossed the threshold to my room. Three long strides, and we hit the bed, her back hitting the mattress as I prop myself on top of her.

With her legs still wrapped around me, she makes quick work of the buttons on my shirt. "Eager to see me shirtless, huh?" I ask with a smirk.

"Eager to see you in a hell of a lot less than that," she replies breathily. It takes everything in me not to combust right now. Her confidence is so fucking sexy.

She pushes on my chest to stand me up. She smiles at me as I slowly let the shirt fall from my shoulders, leaving me in just my pants with my dick straining to break free. I reach out a hand and help her stand up, looking right into those deep blue eyes of hers. "You look beautiful tonight, Harlow," I say before pressing another kiss to her lips. "I love that dress on you." Now I lean my lips to her ear and whisper, "But I've been imagining taking it off you all fucking night."

"So take it off then," she says, challenging me to put my money where my mouth is. And where my mouth wants to be is kissing every bit of Harlow's perfect body.

I slowly drag my hand up her back until I reach the nape of her neck, untying the bow holding the dress up. With the knot undone, she watches as I shimmy the fabric down her body until it's just a pool at her feet. She now stands before me, bare save for the scrap of lace she calls underwear.

I take her breasts into my hands, squeezing them as she moans. "Fucking perfect," I assert as I press a kiss to her lips. "You are so goddamn sexy, Harlow." I place rough kisses down her neck before sucking her nipple into my mouth. "You have no idea how long I've wanted you."

"A couple of months, I'd guess," she says, voice wavering as she tries to control her breathing when I move to the other nipple.

I smile against her skin and kiss my way up to her ear. "Try three years, Lo." Her breath catches in her throat as I drop to my knees. I watch as I trail a finger teasingly up the inside of her thigh. "I may not have spoken to you much, but I've wanted you as long as I've known you." Her eyes meet mine from their position in front of her core. "You've wanted to fuck me just as long, haven't you?"

I pepper kisses along the waistband of the lace she's wearing as she struggles to keep her composure. "When I was... single..." she manages. "That's... about two of those... three years." She lets out a moan as my lips find the junction of her pelvis and thigh. *"Knox..."*

"Is that where you want my mouth, Harlow?" I kiss further down the same area. "You want me to keep teasing you like this?" She shakes her head, unable to speak right now. "Use your words, Lo."

"No..." she says just above a whisper.

"No what?" I ask. If she wants me, she'll need to be open about it. I'm in control here.

"No..." She lets out another moan as I kiss further in now. "That's not where I want your mouth."

"You want it right here, don't you?" I kiss directly on top of her lace-covered clit before nipping at the fabric.

"Yes!"

I stand up now, placing a bruising kiss on her lips as my hands rip the panties from her legs, letting them fall to her feet. *"Get on the bed, Harlow."*

I swear I could come from the desire in her eyes alone. She wants this *bad.*

We both position ourselves on the mattress, and she rests her head on a pillow as my lips meet her neck. I suck on the skin, and she arches, pressing her naked body against my bare chest.

With one hand on the mattress for support, I take the other and trace up her thigh, stopping when I reach her drenched pussy. "You're fucking dripping, Harlow." I slip a finger inside as she gasps. "That all for me?" I ask, lips brushing against hers.

"All for you," she says, moaning as I start to rhythmically move my finger. *"And all because of you, Knox."*

"Good answer," I say as I pull her bottom lip between my teeth. Harlow moans again, and my dick twitches, aching for some contact, some friction. Friction that she ends up providing when she cups me over my pants.

"You need some relief, Knox," she says, kissing my neck. "I can help with that."

"Not yet," I reply, looking into her eyes. "You come first, Harlow. Now..." I remove my finger from its place inside her and bring it up to her lips. "Open." She obeys, opening just wide enough for me to slip my finger inside. "Now taste yourself, Lo, and tell me how fucking good you are."

She licks my finger clean, and that has me wondering how good that tongue would feel running up and down my cock.

"How do you taste, Harlow?" I rasp.

"Delicious," she says with a malicious smile. I've never been with somebody as confident as her, and I'm fucking loving this.

"Good," I reply, pressing another kiss to her lips. "Now spread your legs so I can finally taste that perfect cunt." She quickly obeys. "Good fucking girl."

Harlow told me a few weeks ago that she's never been praised in bed. Oh, but she fucking *loves* it.

Her eyes go dark, and she slowly moves her hands to her chest, playing with her nipples while I sink back on the bed, leveling myself with her core.

Her eyes meet mine as I take my tongue and slowly stroke it up her slit. *"Fuuuck,"* I say before swiping at her again. "You taste so fucking sweet."

"Knox..." she moans. "Oh God..."

"Goddamn," I mutter, mouth pressed against her delicious pussy. "I could stay down here all fucking night, Lo."

My tongue circles her clit as I push a finger inside of her, sliding in easily through her slick heat. "Ohhh, just like that." Harlow places a hand on the back of my head, nails digging into my scalp as her grip tightens. "That's so good."

I replace my tongue on her clit with my thumb, slowly teasing it as I take slow, languid strokes of her pussy. I can't get enough of how she tastes. I need *more.*

Her hands are now both at her sides as she tightly grasps the sheets. She arches her hips into me, seeking what she so desperately desires. She's on the precipice and just needs a bit of help to fall over it.

I bring up my free hand and pinch her nipple while my other still teases her clit. "Oh fuck," Harlow moans loudly. "I'm almost there."

I pause just long enough to say, "Then be a good girl and come right on my tongue," before burying my head between her legs again. Her breathing is heavy, interspersed with deep moans, before she hits her peak, her orgasm ripping through her as she screams my name.

"Knox!"

She floods my mouth as I lick up every bit of her pleasure. When her breathing steadies, I kiss my way up her body, nibbling her nipple with my teeth as I pass over it. As I position myself over top of her once again, I kiss over the bruise forming on her neck from the attention I gave it before.

"You sound so fucking good when you come," I say, meeting her gaze. "Now I want to know how you feel when you clench around my cock." I nip at her neck. "Is that what you want, Harlow?"

"Mhmm."

I grab her chin and turn her to look at me again. "Words, Lo. Use your words when you're with me, and tell me what you want when I ask." She lets a low moan escape, signaling to me that she likes being told what to do as much as she likes being praised. God, she might just be the perfect woman.

"Knox," she rasps, still breathless from her orgasm. "I want that. I want to feel you inside me."

"Good girl."

I step off the bed to remove the pants I'm still wearing. They fall to the floor after I remove the belt and unbutton them, leaving me standing in a pair of black boxer briefs. Harlow doesn't take her eyes off me as I hook my thumbs under the waistband, pushing them down.

I'm now standing naked in front of the woman who's been consuming my mind lately.

I pump my cock a few times as I walk back over to the bed. She gasps as I climb on top of her. "Knox, is that…" she starts before trailing off and picking back up again. "That won't…"

I chuckle when I figure out where she's going. Smirking, I brush my lips against hers as I say, "Don't worry, baby…" I grind against her hip, pressing my hard dick between us. "We'll make it fit. Even if it takes all night, you're going to take everything I give you, Harlow."

She moans as I grind against her again, seeking out that friction I've been denying myself thus far. "Knox…," she moans as I tease my tongue over the hollow of her throat.

"Spread your legs, baby. Watch as I sink every fucking inch of my cock into that tight cunt." She spreads her legs wider, and I can see the arousal still glistening from her. "How long has your pussy been starved for pleasure? You just got off, and it still wants more."

"I haven't been with anyone in a year. But right now, I'm so wet because I just *need* to feel you inside of me."

"Beg me for it then."

"What?" she asks, wide-eyed.

"Beg." I nip at the skin across her chest, leaving marks in my wake as Harlow softly moans above me. I take my cock in my hand and stroke, spreading the precum at the tip down my shaft. "Beg me for it. I'm fucking dying to be inside you, baby, but I'll wait all night if I have to. *Beg.*"

Harlow writhes beneath me, breathing hard and heavy as I slowly and teasingly trail my tongue up the sensitive flesh of her neck. "Oh God…" she breathes. "Fuck me, Knox." I meet her eyes, full of desire and overflowing with need. *"Please."*

"Good girl," I smirk as I reach for a condom in my nightstand, rip the foil open, and slide it down my shaft. I capture her mouth with mine as I position myself, cock ready at her entrance. To let her adjust

to my length, I start to slowly push inside, pausing after the first couple of inches. "Jesus fucking Christ, Harlow."

"Oh God," she rasps before kissing me. "I need more."

"Can you handle more?" I ask as I slip another few inches inside. Halfway there.

Her moan is deep and needy. "Yes," she breathes. "You said we'd make it fit, *so make it fit.*"

In a quicker motion, I slide the remainder of my shaft into her, bottoming out as she screams underneath me. "Harlow... *fuck,*" is all I can manage to say. I can't even form a coherent fucking thought right now. All I can focus on is the sexy-as-sin woman beneath me and just how fucking good her pussy feels wrapped around my cock. "Fuck, baby. You're so goddamn tight."

"You're just so-" She moans as I start moving on her. "-big. Of course, I'll feel tight."

"You feel amazing," I admit, quickening my thrusts as I can already start to feel a slight ache in my balls. "You're gonna make me come way too fucking quick, Lo." I latch my mouth onto her throat, biting at the skin before kissing away the pain after. *"So. Fucking. Good."*

Harlow wraps her arms around my neck. "Then fuck me hard."

I smile against her lips. "That's the only way I know, baby." Before she can say another word, I slip myself out of her and flip her over. She lands on her stomach as she laughs. I lay down on top of her and brush my lips against her ear. "Hands and knees, Harlow. I'm going to fuck you so hard you'll never want another cock. You'll think of me anytime somebody is even near this dripping cunt."

She moans as I grab her hips and roughly pull her into position, on her hands and knees in front of me, pussy dripping and waiting for me. With my hands still planted firmly on her hips, I thrust myself inside in one fluid motion.

"Knox!" she screams.

I groan. "Keep screaming my name like that, Lo, and this won't last much longer." I drive into her harder, fucking her into the mattress as she moans.

"I can't help it," she manages between erratic breaths. "You feel... too fucking good."

Any sanity I had left is snapped as I'm so overcome with my need for Harlow, the woman who, to everyone else, is my fake girlfriend. And that's what she is still to me: my fake girlfriend.

...

Right?

We established no rules going into this tonight. Everything leading to Harlow naked in bed was carnal, both of us so overwhelmed with desire that nothing else mattered. We needed each other, and *nothing* was going to keep us apart anymore. I've been craving her for so goddamn long that I was going to lose my fucking mind if I had to hold back any longer.

But every moan I fuck out of Harlow makes this feel a little less fake. Every thrust of my hips into her makes this feel a little more... *real*.

Dangerous, that is. Getting so caught up in something that could unravel with the pull of a single thread. We're playing with fucking fire. Let's hope we don't end up burned.

She reaches one of her hands back and finds her clit, rubbing herself as we're both building to our orgasms. "Needy little thing you are," I rasp, leaning forward, my chest pressed against her back. "Your pussy can't get enough, can it? It needs me, doesn't it?"

"*Yes...*" she groans. "It needs you, Knox. Nothing else, *no one else* has ever made me feel so good."

Black.

That's all I can see as her words take everything out of me. I pump desperately until pleasure overtakes us both, Harlow screaming out my name in front of me as I reach my own peak.

We're both now moaning, writhing messes tangled together, gasping for breath. When she collapses down onto the mattress, removing herself from me as I fall down right next to her.

"That was…" she says, hand to her chest to calm her racing heart.

I bring my hand to my head and rub my eyes. "Really fucking good," I say as I finish out her thought as she looks at me and smiles.

But good doesn't even begin to describe what just happened. Mind-blowing, electrifying, best I've ever fucking had—those are much better descriptors.

There is another, though, that could fit.

Eye-opening.

Tonight has taught me just how much I fucking care for her. I'm in a situation I never thought I'd find myself in, but I wouldn't want to be doing this with anybody else.

That could be a problem because I *shouldn't* want her the way I do. We're so different, yet she's the only person I've ever truly felt I could be myself around.

Now I know how she tastes. How she sounds when she comes. How it feels to be inside of her.

Nothing else will ever come close to how I feel about what just happened with Harlow.

And I don't know if that's a good thing.

Thirty

Harlow

AFTER KNOX HELPED ME clean myself up, we settled back into his bed. I've only slept beside him once before—that first night in Pittsburgh—but there is no way in hell I'm leaving his bed tonight.

He doesn't even need to ask me to stay; I just know right here is exactly where he wants me. I take the spot next to him, intertwining my leg with his as we both drift off to sleep.

Well, he does, at least.

I try to fall asleep, but I'm wired right now. I feel like I just took a double shot of espresso. And since I can't see myself falling asleep anytime soon, I quietly slip out of bed once Knox is peacefully sleeping.

Since the only clothing I have with me tonight is my gown, and I don't want to walk around naked, I slide on his blue button-down when I find it on the floor. I roll up the sleeves so the shirt isn't as large on me, but it still falls to my knees.

It'll work, though.

Once I'm covered, I sneak out of Knox's room and make my way to the living room to look out his large front window. The city isn't peaceful to everyone, but it always calms me down. And with the way my thoughts are racing right now, I need some peace.

I lose track of how long I'm standing here, just enjoying the silence and the lights of the bustling city below. When I hear the floor lightly creak behind me, I realize I'm no longer alone.

"Did I fuck you into a daze?" Knox asks, wrapping his arms around my waist.

I laugh as I turn around to face him. "You think mighty highly of yourself, Slick," I say, trailing my finger teasingly up his chest.

He hooks his hands behind my back and pulls me against him. "Well, you did tell me nobody has ever made you feel so good. Seems to be a reasonable assumption."

I can't help but smile before standing on my tiptoes and leaning up to press a kiss to his lips. "I did mean that. That was…" I let out a breath. "Easily the best sex I've had. I'd tell you not to let that go to your head, but with your ego, I know it's already there."

He huffs out a laugh. "Think you got me all figured out, baby?"

"Don't I?" I ask, looking into his eyes, his gaze burning through me.

"Not even close, Lo." His lips brush against mine. "But I feel it's only fair to tell you that you are hands down the best sex I've had. *Goddamn*, Harlow. You drove me out of my fucking mind tonight."

My breath catches in my throat, lust washing over me. "Night's not over yet," I say, and I can feel every ounce of blood in his body rush into his dick as it presses against my stomach.

"No, it fucking isn't," he says before he crashes his mouth onto mine, parting my lips and slipping his tongue inside as he backs me up against the glass of the window. He quickly rips the shirt I'm wearing open, revealing nothing underneath. "You were just hoping I'd find you out here, naked and ready for me in my fucking shirt, weren't you?"

"The condom I slipped into the pocket before I came out here should answer that for you." I bite his bottom lip, and Knox hisses in satisfaction. "Maybe I wanted to be prepared if you found me out here. Maybe one time wasn't enough with you. *Maybe I need more*."

"Harlow, you know maybe isn't going to work with me. So do you *maybe* need more, or do you *definitely* need me on my knees with your greedy cunt dripping all over my face?"

"That one," I say, and his eyes darken. "I want you on your knees."

"Good girl," he murmurs against my ear before falling to his knees and looking at me above him. He already has me losing my goddamn mind. The sight of Knox on his knees between my legs is something I'll never forget.

I spread my legs for him, and he groans. "Your pussy is fucking perfect. And you're so wet for me already, baby. Were you out here thinking of how you screamed my name? How it felt when that tight cunt clenched around my cock?"

"Yes," I say, and he rewards me with a swipe of his tongue. *"Fuck."* I rest one hand on the glass behind me and tangle the other in his hair. "I'm going to get wet every time I remember tonight, Knox. Every goddamn time."

He takes another slow, languid stroke, lapping up the arousal that's dripping out of me. "And how often are you going to think about it, to remember it?"

"Every day," I moan. "Every day until you fuck a new memory into me."

"Fucking hell," he mumbles.

He lightly teases his tongue over my clit, and my grip on his head tightens. The blue fabric of my shirt—his shirt?—surrounds his hands from their place on my hips.

"Don't hold back on me," Knox mutters, mouth still buried in my pussy. "I don't want you to be gentle."

"But-" I start before a moan takes over as he laps at my clit. "But I'm trying not to suffocate you."

"Fuck that," he growls. "I want it all. Grind on my face. Smother me. Fucking drown me, baby. Just don't hold back and let me taste you again."

"Once wasn't enough?" I stammer, trying not to give in so easily.

Knox laughs, and I feel the vibration against my core. "No. I don't think one hundred times will be enough, either. Now, stop talking, push that cunt down on my face, and let me fucking *feast*, Harlow."

Goddamn. That's so fucking hot.

"Ohhh..." I moan, losing any thread of sanity I have remaining.

"There you go, baby," he mutters. "Just like that. Keep grinding on me. Make those perfect fucking tits bounce."

"Knox..." I whimper. "Oh God, I'm so close." His hands grip my ass as he dives his tongue in deeper, just waiting for me to flood his mouth with my climax.

I'm grinding my hips faster and harder, seeking out my release and finally just taking what I want. He's gazing at me like it's the hottest thing he's ever seen. When his teeth brush against my clit, the sensitivity pushes me over the edge.

"Knox! Oh fuck!"

I come hard, filling his mouth and more as my arousal drips down his chin. He uses his tongue to grab any bit left that he can coax out of me before finally standing himself up.

He presses an arm against the glass behind me, taking my chin in his hand and turning me to face him as I work on catching my breath. "Grinding on my face? Taking what you want?" My breathing is still heavy as he brushes his lips against mine, coating them in my own climax. "So fucking *sexy*." He presses his lips onto mine again as I moan into his mouth. "Need to fuck you again," he pants. "That what you want, baby?"

I moan as he grinds into my hip, his thick erection pressing into me. "Yes," I murmur. "Need you inside me again." I bring a hand to his face and guide my mouth back to his, my tongue sliding right in as he pulls out the condom I slid into the pocket of his shirt before he knocks it off my shoulders.

My hands slide down his chest, savoring the definition on my way to his waistband. I hook my thumbs underneath and slip them down past his thighs, letting them fall to the ground.

As I wrap a hand around his shaft, he audibly moans. I didn't touch him earlier before he sank into me, so I'm seizing this opportunity to grasp him, appreciating how thick and heavy he is in my hand. "You're so damn *big*," I say, trailing my tongue up his throat. "I don't know how you fit."

He thrusts into my hand, desperate for friction. "Because your pussy was fucking *made* for me, Harlow." I take the condom from him, ripping it open and sliding it down his length, readying him to sink into me again. "How flexible are you?" Knox asks, his lips grazing the skin of my collarbone.

"I'm flexible enough," I say, breathless.

"Good," he says, hooking my leg over his arm. "Because I'm fucking you right here."

I moan as he takes his cock into his hand and starts pushing inside. "Won't people see?" I manage between them.

"Penthouse, baby," he answers, slowly sliding in to the hilt. "No one can see you up here, getting fucked against the window as you beg me for more. Nobody will know you're here with me and coming all over my cock like a dirty fucking girl."

He slid out almost entirely before thrusting back in. "Ahhh... more, Knox. *I need more.*"

"Yeah?" he says, panting and breathless. "You know why you need more?" He buries himself inside me again as I moan. "Use your words, baby. I can't understand you when you're screaming."

"Fuck!" I throw my head back so he brings his mouth to my throat, sucking the skin between his teeth to leave a mark to accompany the first two. "Because..." I attempt to speak between moans, the words coming out strangled before I gather myself. "Because nobody will ever be able to fuck me the way you do."

"That's my fucking girl."

His girl.

I'm Knox's girl, and fuck, do I love the sound of that.

His thrusts become more frantic, desperate to feel me clench around him again. To hear my cries of pleasure as I come on his cock while he's still buried deep inside me.

"Ohhh, Knox. Yes!" I scream as I tighten around him, and he fucks me through my orgasm, now desperately seeking his own. When I come down from my high, I graze my lips against his ear. "Come for me, baby."

"Fuck, Harlow..." he yells, thrusting deeper than before, spilling into the latex as we both gasp for breath.

When we're both finally sated, he slowly pulls out of me and lets my leg fall to the ground. I pull him against me, mouth crashing into his.

All I know right now is that I've had Knox twice, and I don't think I want to let him go.

Hopefully, he's thinking the same thing.

I need everything he can give me.

Thirty-One

Knox

I WAKE UP THE next morning with Harlow still naked in my bed, the memory of last night flowing through my mind on repeat.

We slept together. I *actually* had sex with Harlow last night. The months of teasing, flirting, and denial reached their peak, and we both catapulted right over the edge.

We didn't talk about any of this beforehand, though. The desire overflowed, and we just tumbled right into my bed, not thinking of what any of this might mean for this fake relationship. For *us*.

Not that there is an us. We're just friends.

Friends who fuck, apparently, but still just friends.

It's not like I can give more than casual sex anyway.

I shake the sleep from me and slowly slip out of bed, not wanting to wake her since she's still sleeping so peacefully.

I sneak into the en-suite bathroom and make a beeline right to my shower, but this shower will be different from the others I've had lately.

This time, I won't have to jack myself off imagining what it would be like to be with Harlow because I already know. Hell, I won't need to jack off at all if she decides she wants to keep this new arrangement going.

And as I hear the bathroom door quietly open, I know that's exactly what she wants to do.

She carefully shuts the door behind her, no doubt trying to be sneaky.

"Morning, Freckles."

I hear Harlow grumble as she walks to the shower. "So much for sneaking up on you." She slides in now, wearing my favorite outfit of hers—absolutely nothing. "Would've been fun to scare the shit out of you."

I laugh as I look back over my shoulder, rinsing the shampoo from my hair and catching her eyes fixed directly on my backside. "Damn, you really do like my ass," I chuckle while I turn around.

"It's not like I was going to lie about that," she says, stepping closer to me as I reach out my arms to wrap around her waist. The feel of her water-soaked skin against me is already burning me up with need.

I press a kiss to the top of her head. "Didn't think you would. But it's a hell of a confidence boost to actually see you checking me out."

"You were just blind then, Slick," she says, turning her head up to face me, "because I've been checking you out for years now." Desire floods over me as I can feel my dick stiffen against her. "Really?" she asks, arching her brow.

"Baby, you're naked in my shower with your tits pressed against my chest. How the fuck am I *not* supposed to get hard right now?"

She stands on her tiptoes and kisses me before taking a step back. "Then you're in luck," she says, dropping to her knees. "I didn't get the chance to taste you last night."

"Been imagining what you'd look like on your knees for me. Been wondering how your lips would look wrapped around my cock."

"Want to find out?" Harlow says deviously, hand wrapped around my length as she starts pumping.

"More than you fucking know. Now, spit on it, Harlow. Make it messy." She does exactly as I ask before she takes her tongue and licks the bead of precum leaking out. "Shit," I say as she closes her lips around the head before sliding down my shaft and taking as much of my cock into her mouth as she can. "Fuck... look at you, Harlow. So pretty on your knees for me. You take me so fucking well."

I see the lust flash through her eyes at the praise as she takes me deeper, running her tongue along the vein on the underside. "God fucking *damn,*" I moan, my breathing rough. "That mouth feels almost as good as your pussy."

Her moan is stifled by my dick in her mouth, but I hear it all the same. "You like hearing that, Harlow? You like hearing how good your mouth feels?" Another light moan. "Dirty fucking girl," I say with a malicious smile. "Put one hand behind your back and bring the other to that tight cunt that I just know is already dripping for me. Fuck your fingers while I fuck your face. But don't come. *Save that for me.*"

She obeys, slipping one hand behind her back and trailing the other to her core, sliding two fingers into her slick pussy and moaning around my cock as I start thrusting into her mouth. I take no caution; I fuck into her with reckless abandon, desperately seeking my release. She starts teasing her clit with her thumb and cries out in pleasure.

"Don't come on those fingers, Harlow. You're only allowed to clench around mine." She lowly whines as she stops fingering herself so quickly. When she hollows out her cheeks for better suction, I lose it. "Fuck yes, just like that, baby. Not gonna last much longer if you keep that up."

Tears are streaming down her face as I keep thrusting, gagging her each time as I hit the back of her throat. Harlow drags her tongue along my shaft again and grazes her teeth lightly across the top of my length. "Yes, that's it, baby. I'm getting ready to come. I'm going to paint your throat, and you're going to swallow every fucking drop."

She moans again, and I can't hold back. I slap a hand against the tile on the wall and curse as I fill her mouth with my white-hot climax. So much that it's hard for her to swallow all at once, but she doesn't waste a single drop.

I finish riding out my high with a few more light thrusts. As I stop moving, I quickly stand Harlow up and push her against the wall with a bruising kiss. "Good girl," I murmur before stroking my tongue back against hers and quickly sliding two fingers into her pussy. "Such a good fucking girl."

"Knox, *oh God...*" I've barely started, and she's already a writhing mess, nearly falling apart around my fingers.

"Mmm," I mutter, lips brushing against the hollow of her throat. "You're already close. You almost made yourself come by choking on my cock, didn't you?"

"Yes...," she replies, breathless.

"Think you can take another finger, pretty girl?"

"Uh huh..." she mumbles while I grin devilishly. I slowly slip my ring finger inside her now, stretching her and filling her up. *"Fuck..."*

"So tight, Harlow." I thrust my fingers faster and harder. "You're so goddamn tight for me."

She moans as I hook my fingers inside of her. "I need to come..."

"You know what to do," I say, nipping at her earlobe.

She groans before gathering her composure. "Please, Knox," she murmurs. "Make me come."

I smile maliciously as I thrust my fingers harder than before and swipe at her clit with my thumb. She's already so close to exploding that that light motion shatters her completely.

She screams my name as I feel her pussy clench around my fingers, and she starts to come down from her orgasm.

"There you go, baby. I've got you," I say, kissing her forehead as I slide my fingers out of her. I then bring them up and lick every bit of my arousal from them. "Fucking delicious, Harlow."

Our mouths meet again, and she strokes her tongue against mine as our tastes mix together. Still skin to skin, I lead her to the water, positioning us directly under it.

This is a very different vibe now compared to what we just did. I almost had her blacking out, and now here I am, gently caressing her, planting kisses on her shoulder as I rinse her hair.

It's a side of myself I didn't know existed until Harlow.

And, strangely enough, I think I actually really like it.

Thirty-Two

Harlow

BEFORE RETURNING TO MY apartment today, I have to borrow some clothing from Knox. All I have with me is that damn dress, so I'm wearing clothing that is way too large for me to get back home and get ready for the day. Thankfully, he drops me off on his way to practice today, so I don't have to sit in a subway full of people staring at me with oversized clothing, wet hair, and red marks all over my goddamn neck.

All. Over.

If Knox's goal last night was to claim me, it's safe to say he succeeded. Anyone who even looks at me will see that I belong to somebody. Somebody so possessed with desire and need for me that he marked up so much of my neck and chest that I have to throw on a turtleneck to wear under my jersey.

A turtleneck.

In the middle of fucking *June*.

No amount of makeup is going to cover up those dark bruises, so a sleeveless turtleneck is my best bet. Combine that with the fact that I'm wearing leggings to a game due to Knox's penchant for sticking his scruffy face between my legs, and my friends will all know something is up. This is far from how I usually dress when I head to the stadium.

But I have to head into the stadium early today. Paul agreed to be my next interview, and I need to catch him in a short window after practice.

I knock on the door to Paul's office, a computer bag slung over my shoulder so I can take my notes. "Come in," I hear from the other side of the door.

I step into his office, still walking a bit funny from Knox and the raw skin he gave me between my thighs. I'm trying to play it off, but it's not going very well.

"You alright, Harlow?" Paul asks, glancing over the papers in front of him, glasses perched on the bridge of his nose.

"Oh, yep!" I say, trying to sound nonchalant. "Just pulled a muscle in my leg when I tripped in my apartment this morning."

"Well, if you live like Rory, you have things scattered everywhere. Easy to trip over."

"Haha, yeah. I'll have to get better about that." Oh God, this is not convincing at all.

Paul gives me a curious look before dropping the subject altogether.

Phew.

"You know," he says, sitting across the desk from where I sat. "You've been looking a lot happier lately, Harlow."

Paul doesn't know about everything that happened with Derek. He knows we dated and broke up, but that's the extent of his knowledge. It's not like my friend's dad needed all the intimate details, but that means he has no idea why I wasn't happy in the first place.

"I've been a lot happier," I admit, smiling brightly. "Life is really good right now."

"Knox has been looking a lot happier, too," Paul says with a knowing glance. "Not hard when he never gave anyone a damn smile before."

I laugh in earnest. His image has really been improving this season, but it'll take a while for him to shake the grumpy asshole persona entirely. "I like to think he's been happy, too," I reply as I feel a blush creeping across my cheeks.

Paul gives me a soft smile. "Team morale has been better, too. I never thought I'd want to delve into my players' dating lives, but considering you two are plastered on the front of every tabloid in the supermarket checkout line, it's hard to avoid. But you guys somehow work together. And I'm all for it if it means every goddamn reporter isn't asking me why the league's best pitcher never wants to talk to anyone."

We both laugh. "Okay, enough about my personal life, Paul. Let's get down to business, shall we?"

"Shoot," he says. "I've got about half an hour before I need to start preparing for the game."

"I can make that work. I'll start with my standard questions before we get to the deeper ones." I pull up a blank document on my laptop. "Favorite color?"

"Navy, of course," Paul says with a laugh. "Gotta be Stars navy."

"Favorite food?"

"A BLT. Simple and hits the spot every time."

"Favorite Taylor Swift song?"

"Why do you want that?" he asks incredulously.

I shrug. "It's just something for fun. My readers seem to really like it."

"Okay then. Well, what one did Rory pick?"

"She said, uh..." I'm absolutely *not* going to tell Rory's dad that she said her favorite song is *Dress*. A little white lie never hurt anyone, right? "She picked *Maroon*." She did technically say maroon but as her favorite color, not her favorite song.

"I don't think I know that one. What's that one about Romeo and Juliet? That one is fine."

I laugh heartily. "*Love Story*. Got it. Now let's get into the rest of this..."

❮❮❮❮❮❮❮❮❮❮❮❮❮❮❮❮❮❮❮❮❮❮❮❮❮❮❮❮

"Where's Sage?" I ask as Lucia and Rory walk into Lucia's office, where I've been taking refuge since I finished my interview with Paul. I've got time to kill before the game, so I've been hiding away from everyone and lying with my back on the floor.

"Lane wanted to keep her for a little longer today. He still struggles with leaving her sometimes." Rory and Lucia walk to where I'm lying on the floor and plop down on either side of me. "Lo," she says with a tone I can't quite place. "What are you wearing?"

Shit.

I knew they'd notice this wasn't my usual attire, but I completely forgot to spin a lie that would be believable.

Shit shit shit.

"What's wrong with my outfit?" I say in a dismal attempt to shirk this.

Lucia grabs my hand and helps me sit up, saying, "Lo, you're wearing a turtleneck. In *June*."

"I found it in the back of my closet and thought it would be cute for today."

"You're also in leggings," Rory adds.

"I desperately need to do some laundry," I say with a dismissive laugh that is far from convincing.

"Okay, okay," Rory says with a smirk as she shoots a look toward Lucia.

Lucia now squints her eyes at me, looking in closely. "What's that on your neck, Lo?"

"What?!" I yell, immediately bringing my hands to my neck to cover it up... but it's still covered by the turtleneck.

Fuck.

They caught me without even trying too hard.

Rory covers her mouth as she squeals, and Lucia yells, "Harlow Louise Pierce!"

"Show us your neck!"

"Do I have to?" I say as my face falls. They both just stare at me expectantly. I take a deep breath before pulling the turtleneck down, showcasing multiple dark marks across my fair skin. "I, uh... fell?"

"Fell onto Knox's dick, apparently," Lucia says with a giant smile.

I groan. "Fine, yes." I take another deep breath. "I had sex with Knox last night."

"Finally!" Rory shouts. "It was inevitable after the way you two were eye-fucking each other last night."

"What do I do, guys?" I say, sinking back down onto the floor.

"Well," Lucia starts, "I think that depends on how it was."

As much as I was trying to beat around the bush before is now how much I can't stop myself from spilling everything.

"Unbelievable. Insane. Incredible." I sit up again, discomfort washing away. "It was so good, guys. He has such a dirty mouth, and I evidently really like that. He was so commanding, and I can't stop thinking about it."

"How was he commanding?" Rory asks, a rapt look on her face.

"He, uh..." I have to hide my smile as I remember. Thinking about it already has me ready to jump back on him. "He made me *beg*. I had to beg him to fuck me, and I *loved* it. Who even am I now?"

"So the sex doesn't seem to be an issue," Lucia says with a smirk. "Sounds like you had fun after dinner last night."

"Yeah, he all but attacked me pretty much as soon as we got to his place. And then again when he saw me in his shirt overnight. And then I kinda attacked him in the shower this morning. And I have to wear leggings today because the man loves sticking his head between my legs, and his facial hair basically rubbed me raw."

"Fucking get it, girl!" Rory says with a whoop. "I'm not really seeing a problem here."

"The problem is that we aren't actually together, but I want to jump back on his dick and ride it off into the fucking sunset."

"Wow, Lo," Lucia laughs. "That's an image."

"I say you just go for it, Lo," Rory adds. "You had great sex—three times apparently—so I think you should just keep going for it. There's nothing wrong with some casual sex."

"I've never done casual sex before, though. Sex always involves feelings for me." Lucia and Rory both look at me with widened eyes, and I realize what I just said. That I *always* have feelings when I have sex. "No, uh... I didn't mean it like that."

"Harlow..." Lucia places her hand gently on my arm as a way to comfort me. "Do you have feelings for Knox?"

I just stare at them for a few moments before making a sound somewhere between a groan and a squeal. "I have no idea. But I love spending time with him. He's really sweet and caring. And the man gave me five orgasms in the span of like ten goddamn hours."

Rory says in a serious tone, "Lo, it really does sound like you have feelings for him."

"No," I say, vigorously shaking my head from side to side. "I couldn't possibly have feelings for him. I'm not living out a romance trope." My voice lowers now, wavering slightly. "I can't have feelings for him."

"Sweetie," Lucia says as she and Rory both lay their heads on my shoulders, "It's okay if you do."

"No, it isn't," I say, voice breaking. "This isn't real, and I wasn't supposed to actually start falling for him. Sex could make everything so much more complicated."

"So don't sleep with him again," Rory states.

I just stare at her in disbelief. "If he wants me again, I'm sleeping with him again. I know I will because I *want* to. I'll just have to learn how to keep things casual."

"If that's what you want, you know we're here for you," Lucia says, throwing her arms around my shoulders in a tight hug.

"Thanks, guys," I say. "But I'm not going to let it get to me. I had a great night *and* morning. I mean, I can barely fucking walk. I'm going to remember that and not focus on anything else."

"That's my girl," Rory says, joining Lucia's hug.

"I love you guys. Thank you for your support."

Things can only get more complicated from here. This is the first time I've acknowledged that I *might* actually have feelings for Knox. But I have Lucia and Rory with me to help navigate everything. I couldn't ask for anything more.

◄◄◄◄◄◄◄◄◄◄◄◄◄◄◄◄◄◄◄◄◄◄◄◄◄◄◄◄◄◄◄

"How are you feeling now?" Rory asks, taking a sip of her iced coffee as she sits across from me on the floor in the hallway outside the clubhouse. She and Lucia really helped me feel better about everything. It was nice to get everything off my chest, but accepting that I could have feelings for Knox is hard. That's something that would most likely end in me brokenhearted—not something I particularly want to go through.

"I'm doing better," I admit, snagging the cup from Rory's hand and taking a sip of it for myself. "I think I'm gonna be okay. I'm just going to have fun and try not to worry about anything else."

"Good," Rory replies with a reassuring smile. "We don't need another Derek situation."

"That would never happen with Knox." I smile shyly. "He's made it a point to lift me up. He's never put me down, and I can't see him ever doing that. He likes to tell me how wrong Derek was, especially about the freckles."

Lucia, Rory, and Ella have done so much over the past year to help me believe the things Derek would say aren't true. That he was just a small-dicked—Lucia's words—asshole who gets off on making himself feel better than women. But it wasn't until Knox that it all started to finally sink in.

It's not like I needed a man to tell me to actually accept it. I think it's more that he has no reason to say those things if he doesn't mean them. Lucia, Rory, and Ella are my best friends—they're supposed to say things to make me feel better. But Knox doesn't have that obligation since this isn't a real relationship. But he does it anyway, and I'm almost at the point where I've never felt better in my own skin.

"So you really did tell him everything about what happened, huh?" Rory says, snagging the coffee back from my hand.

"I did," I tell her. "It kind of just felt right to share it with him. He shared everything with me as well, and I think that's really brought us closer."

Rory raises her eyebrow questioningly. "What did Knox have to share?"

I take a deep breath. "It's not my story to tell. But I can say that he's not so withdrawn from everyone and everything for no reason. He's been through a lot."

"Fair enough," Rory relents. "I'd never want you to share something he doesn't want to be told. But whatever it was, you're definitely helping him get over it. Him being comfortable enough with you to say anything at all speaks volumes about what he thinks of you."

"Yeah, I guess so," I say, rubbing my neck. The clubhouse door opens then, and the team walks out and starts down the hallway while Knox, Cole, Lane, and Sage all make their way over to us.

Rory and I both stand up, and Rory reaches out to Lane. "Hey, Sagie! You ready to hang out with me again?" Sage smiles brightly and giggles as Rory starts to tickle her.

"Sometimes I can't get her to leave my side," Lane says to no one in particular. "And sometimes she can't get to Rory fast enough." He laughs and shakes his head as he leans down and kisses Sage on the top of her head.

"Hey, Lo," Knox says, turning his attention to me. I can see the hint of a smirk when he sees that I'm wearing a fucking turtleneck because he knows exactly why I'm in this damn thing. "Ready to watch the game tonight?"

"Ready to see how many runs you give up tonight, Slick," I reply with a mischievous tone. The urge to tease him is too strong.

"Such a fucking ball-buster, Harlow." Knox laughs and rubs his jaw. "I know I can count on you to always knock me down a few pegs."

Cole, who has been suspiciously quiet so far, chimes in now. "Lo, why the hell are you wearing that? It's like eighty degrees right now."

My eyes widen, and a worried look crosses Knox's face. Our silence right now is deafening.

Lane connects the dots faster than Cole, dropping his jaw in amusement as he chuckles.

"Why is Lane lau-" Cole cuts off sharply and groans, finally putting the pieces together. "Fucking hell. I don't want details, and I'm going to pretend to be blissfully unaware that my sister was in Knox's goddamn bed last night."

"Say it a little louder, won't you?" I say as I cross my arms. "I don't think the rest of the clubhouse heard you."

"Fuck me," Cole says, scrubbing a hand over his face.

Lane throws his arm around Cole's shoulder and slaps his other hand on Cole's chest. "Nope, no fucking for you. But I do believe that's what those two lovebirds got up to last night."

"Goddammit, Lane." Knox pinches his brow, probably wondering how neither of us could hide this for even a damn day. "We really don't need to get into my damn sex life right now."

Cole covers his ears like a child, and I can't help but laugh. I sure as hell don't want him to have details about what Knox and I did last night, but it's fun to torture him about it. He's been doing that to me my entire damn life.

"Fine," Lane says. "But if Knox pitches a good game tonight, Harlow, you know what to do before each start."

"I'm sure I can manage that," I say, batting my eyelashes right at Knox, who shakes his head and laughs.

"You're a goddamn menace, Freckles."

"You like it," I say, standing on my tiptoes to get closer to him.

"I don't mind it." He gives me a soft kiss, and Cole pretends to gag. So goddamn dramatic, that one.

I fall back on flat feet and look at Cole, throwing my hands in the air. "Okay, okay. I'm done torturing you now, Cole. You three go get to the field. Rory, Sage, and I will find our seats."

"Thank fuck," he says. "I want out of here." Cole runs down the hall to escape the situation we've put him in.

"Love you, Sagie." Lane plants a kiss on Sage's cheek as she smiles. "Daddy will see you after the game."

Knox throws an arm around Lane. "Come on then, *Daddy*. We've got to get on the field." They start off down the hallway before he looks back and gives me a soft smile.

And butterflies erupt in my stomach.

Butterflies?

Why am I getting butterflies again?

Knox just smiled at me. That's not a big deal.

Is it?

No, of course, it isn't. He's smiled at me too many times to count now.

But that smile was just for me. Even in a hall full of people, that smile was only for me. And the smile on my face afterward was only for him.

...

No.

No, no, no, no, no.

This wasn't supposed to happen. This isn't real. This is a show.

And yet, here I am, butterflies still fluttering around when Knox is nowhere in sight.

That means I did something I shouldn't have done.

I started falling for Knox Spencer...

Thirty-Three

Knox

Today has been a great fucking day.

Harlow slept naked in my bed and treated me to the best goddamn blow job I've ever had right after she woke up. I couldn't get enough of her last night or this morning. She seems to be just as damn insatiable.

Maybe I shouldn't enjoy the fact that she had to wear a turtleneck today, but I'm smug at the fact that I marked her so much that she couldn't easily cover it up.

Last night, I was a man possessed, and I wanted to claim every fucking inch of her body.

And as I'm out on the field throwing out practice pitches to Scholl, I see her in her seat by the first baseline with my name on her back, and a whole new wave of desire floods me. Josh has talked about how he feels seeing Ella in his jersey, but I've never paid much attention to it. But now that I've had Harlow, I fucking get it. She can keep that on tonight when I fuck her so hard she forgets her own damn name.

When Scholl and I finish our warmup, I jog over to Harlow, who is seated with Rory and Sage. "Media and tabloids seem to really like seeing me talk to my good luck charm before each start," I say as I come to stand right in front of her.

"Well then," she replies, "You certainly can't let them down."

"Lucia and Ella not joining you guys out here tonight?" I ask, noticing her absence.

"Not tonight," she says. "Lucia's hanging back tonight in case Ayala needs some assistance since he's just coming off the IL. And Ella usually hangs back anyway."

"Nos!" I hear, and I look down to see Sage standing right at the railing, smiling right up at me. She can't say Knox, so to her, I'm Nos. It's the cutest fucking thing.

"Sagie!" I say enthusiastically. "You gonna watch your daddy play baseball tonight?"

"No."

Rory sighs. "No is her new favorite word. Been a lot of fun lately when I'm trying to get her to do something."

"That's okay, Sagie." I kneel down to her level and whisper through the railing. "You'll have more fun watching Uncle Knox pitch tonight anyway." Sage giggles.

I stand up and catch a sweet look on Harlow's face as Cole walks over to join us. "Don't listen to him, Sagie. Uncle Cole is way more fun to watch."

"Uncle Cole is full of himself," Harlow chimes in. Now, she looks at Cole. "What's up? You never come over before a game."

"Can't I come say hi to my sister?"

"You can, but it's weird because you never do when you're on the field.

Cole rolls his eyes, and I snicker. When he eyes me, I lean over to him, whispering, "We both know your sister isn't why you're over here, man." My response is an elbow right to the ribs.

"Nice manbun, Cole," Rory says with a smirk.

He takes a hand and smooths back his hair. "You know you like it."

"I don't know. You could probably do with a haircut."

Cole's smile falters a bit. "Yeah, maybe," he says awkwardly. "It has been a while."

I have to whisper to him again. "Be a little less fucking obvious, will you?"

"Shut. Up." Cole says through gritted teeth.

"Nah, you know I'm fucking with you, Cole," Rory says, smiling. "If anyone can pull off a manbun, it's you."

Cole, in all his subtlety, blushes as red as a goddamn tomato. I need to save him from doing something stupid here.

"Well," I say as I throw an arm around Cole's shoulder. "Time for us to get back on the field, ladies."

"Good luck tonight, Knox," Harlow tells me in that flirty tone she loves to use.

I take my arm off Cole and wrap them both around her waist. "You are my good luck charm, so I should be fine." I brush my lips against her ear so only she can hear me now. "You're wearing that jersey again tonight, baby. *Just* the jersey."

"Whatever you want, boss."

She smiles as I kiss her lips, just like I do before every game.

But this feels a little... different.

Because I want to just pull her closer.

Because I don't want to stop.

Because I just want to get lost in her.

Thankfully, I have a game to pitch, so I don't have time to dwell on what any of that means.

Tonight is a good game for me. I pitch six innings, and the only run that comes during that time is based on a rare error on Lane, meaning it doesn't count against my ERA. Relievers give up four runs after I'm pulled, so we still get the loss, but it's a no-decision for me.

I spent some extra time in the shower tonight to try to get the hot water to loosen up my shoulder. Pitching can really take its toll over time, so it's good to try to keep things loose.

Since I'm the last one in the showers, I expect the clubhouse to be empty when I walk back in. But instead, I find Lane sitting on the sofa, hands behind his head as he leans against the back, waiting for me to walk in.

Goddammit.

"At least let me put on some fucking clothing before you start trying to interrogate me," I chide, crossing the room to my things. "I don't really want my dick hanging out while we're talking."

"Harlow wouldn't mind, though, would she?" He smirks.

Asshole.

I throw on a white T-shirt, black athletic shorts, and a black baseball cap before I take a seat next to Lane on the sofa and sigh. "What are you still doing here, Lane?"

"You know exactly why I'm here, man."

"Can't keep my sex life private, can I?"

"I'm not going to make you spill all the details. I don't need to know everything you did to Cole's sister." Lane turns to face me now. "But I am curious as to how that happened since you both seemed pretty adamant about not sleeping together at all."

"What happened is I am a weak man, and Harlow is sinfully hot."

"No arguments here," Lane says with a laugh.

I smack him with my hat. "That's my girlfriend, dick," I say before quickly correcting myself. "*Fake* girlfriend. She's my fake girlfriend. But I still don't need you sniffing around since I have to keep up appearances."

Lane cocks an eyebrow. "And part of keeping up appearances is sleeping together and leaving hickeys all over her goddamn neck?"

"I may be a tad bit possessive in the bedroom," I admit. "She definitely didn't mind that, though."

"So you had fun then?"

I sigh. "To put it mildly. Last night was... really fucking good. I, uh... fucked her against my living room window."

"Exhibitionism, huh? Kinky."

"Fuck off. It was after midnight—nobody could see us."

"So what happens from here?" Lane asks in a more serious tone. "I've known you since I came to the team five years ago, and I think I can count on one hand the number of hookups you've had in that time."

"Coming from the king of hookups."

Lane groans. "Yeah, yeah. We all know I used to fuck my way around every city we traveled to. But you also know that's not me anymore." He lets out a breath. "I don't regret Sage a bit, but she did come from one of those nights. I know what can happen, and I'd rather just focus on my daughter now."

I lean back against the sofa to join Lane and turn to face him. "Because you're a damn good dad, man."

"It's nice to have the reminder sometimes, so thank you. Anyway, my point is that while you've had hookups, those were all just one night. And you and Harlow are going to see each other every day until at least the end of the season. I care about both of you and don't want to see someone get hurt over this."

I take a deep breath. "I think we've got this. I'm not really worried," I admit.

"Knox," Lane says feebly. "It's not you that I'm really worried about. I think no matter what happens, you're going to be fine. Harlow I'm not so sure of. She's good and kind... and I've seen her hurt before. I just don't want to see that happen to her again."

"I get it," I say, scrubbing a hand over my face. "But I don't have any intention of hurting her. I really enjoy being around her. When this is all over, we're still going to be friends, I have no doubts about that."

"You enjoy having her around?" Lane shoots me an inquisitive look.

"Don't get any ideas, Brooks," I say. "She's fun to be around. And we sure as hell have fun together. But that's all it is."

"Mhmm."

I roll my eyes as a text from Harlow pops up on my phone.

Harlow

Hurry your ass up, Spencer

We've got a standing appointment with your bed

Or couch

Or kitchen counter

I'm not that picky

Knox

Dear God, you're going to fucking break me, woman

Harlow

And you'll enjoy every second of it, won't you?

Knox

I chuckle as I set my phone down and catch Lane with an interesting look on his face. "What's that for?"

"Nothing," he says with a dismissive laugh. "That was just a lot of happiness from you right there, so I know Harlow texted you."

"Yeah, it was her, but why does that mean anything?"

"I don't know," Lane says, standing up and crossing the room to the clubhouse door. "But I think you'll figure it out soon."

Then he's out the door. And I'm left to wonder what he was implying.

But I can worry about that later.

A gorgeous woman is waiting for me in the hall, and I need to get her home as soon as possible...

"Yes, there you go, baby. Fucking greedy for my cock, aren't you?"

"So greedy," Harlow says breathlessly as she rides me on the couch. We didn't make it far when we got back to my penthouse after the game. I almost just bent her over the kitchen counter until she said she wanted to be on top of me. There were too many steps to the bedroom when I wanted to be inside her *now*, so the couch sufficed.

"You and that greedy cunt look so good like this. My name on your back, and your tits in my face as you take every fucking inch of me. Fucking perfect, Harlow. *So fucking perfect.*"

I lean forward and bring my mouth to her neck, sucking and nibbling on the skin. One more mark to join the others she covered up today.

She throws her head back and moans. "You like that?" I kiss her before biting her bottom lip. "You like it when I mark you, don't you?"

"Mhmm."

I smack her ass. "Words, Harlow. Use your words, or I might need to do that again."

"Do it," she says, looking me dead in the eyes. "Do it again." I smack her again as she moans. *"Fuck, baby."*

"There you go. Keep moaning. You sound so fucking good when you moan, stretching around my cock like it was made for you."

She brushes her lips against mine. *"Maybe it was."*

I groan before grabbing her hips and helping her slide up and down. Harlow moans loud enough for the entire building to hear. I don't give a shit who hears, though. Let them know that the goddess always with me gets fucked just like she deserves.

"You're doing so well, Lo. Now, touch yourself. I want to feel you come on my cock." She plants one hand on my shoulder for stability as she slides the other down her body.

Slowly.

Teasingly.

When her finger finds her clit, she starts rubbing. "Mmm... it feels so good, Knox. I'm not going to last much longer."

"Good." I nip her ear. "Clench around me, and don't forget to scream my name when you do."

Harlow's breathing is heavy as I take over our movements, holding her steady as I start thrusting into her. The only sounds to be heard are the slapping of skin and her moaning, which grows increasingly louder the closer she gets to release.

When I lean forward and ghost my lips over her neck, she shatters. *"Knox! Oh God!"*

I slow my thrusts as I fuck her through her orgasm. "So good, Harlow. Screaming my name nice and loud while clenching around my cock. Such a good girl. Now get on your back—I'm coming all over those perfect tits tonight."

She slides off me and rests her head on the arm of the sofa, body lying out in front of her. Her jersey hangs open since we left it unbuttoned, displaying all of her for me.

I plant one leg on the floor, bend the other at the knee, and slide it on the other side of her so I'm standing over top of her. Now in position, I rip the condom off and take my cock into my hand as I start stroking. "So fucking pretty like that, Harlow." She bites one of her fingers, looking all innocent like she hasn't had my tongue buried in her cunt. "Displayed like that only for me to see. Desperate for me to come all over you."

"Yes," she rasps. "Give me your cum, Knox. I want it to cover me."

Fucking hell.

My breathing is heavy, and moans are slipping out as I'm pumping myself faster. Harlow whispers encouragements, begging me to come on her, and it's enough to push me over the edge.

"Harlow, fuck!" I scream as my white-hot climax erupts from me, covering her from tits to stomach.

I pump until there's nothing left, until everything is drained from me. As I catch my breath, she takes a finger, dragging it through the release coating her. With her finger now covered, she brings it to her mouth and licks it off, moaning softly when she does.

"Fucking Christ, baby. If I wasn't spent right now, that would make me so hard."

"I'll just have to keep that in my back pocket then." She laughs before I lean down to kiss her, bringing my body down on top of her. "Knox, I'm a sticky mess. Why did you lay on top of me?"

I just laugh. "Harlow, I've been taking care of myself for years. This is not the first time I've had my cum on me."

"When was the last time you took care of yourself then, huh?"

"Yesterday morning," I answer, unashamed. "Didn't think we'd end the night with you in my bed, so I had to get myself off to the thought of what it would be like."

"That's honest." She softly kisses me. "I like honest Knox."

I shift us now, rolling myself so I'm on my back with Harlow beside me, my arm wrapped around her. "I've always been honest with you," I say. "Hell, I told you about Emily. Aside from Simon and my lawyer, you're the only one who knows."

She looks at me in surprise. "I'm the only one who knows? Not even Cole, Lane, or Josh?"

"Nope. It's just you. You're the only one I've ever been... comfortable enough with to share that."

Her smile reaches her eyes. "I'm happy you were able to share that with me then. I'm so happy that you're comfortable with me."

Harlow rests her head on my arm as I gently run my fingers through her golden blonde hair. "In the name of honesty, I'll tell you this." She looks at me curiously. "I've never been as comfortable around anyone as I am with you."

"Really?" she asks shyly.

"Really. It's a little strange since we didn't know each other well before the season, but once I started getting to know you, I was just immediately comfortable. You have such a calming demeanor."

She doesn't say anything with words, but her expression tells me everything.

The sweet look tells me she feels honored to be the only one who knows something so monumental about me.

Her soft smile tells me she's happy to be where she is right now.

And the sparkle in her ocean eyes tells me that this woman is so fucking special.

This is the happiest I've been in seven years, possibly ever. I don't feel alone with my demons anymore because Harlow has made it clear that I have all of her support.

I've spent so damn long keeping those close to me at arm's length and everyone else out entirely. I've only ever been revered as Knox the baseball player. For years, I told myself that's all I actually wanted.

Then Harlow came along and changed everything. Because while she likes Knox the baseball player, she also celebrates Knox the *person*. To her, I'm more than just what I can do on the mound. I feel like I'm human again, which is something I didn't realize I was missing.

But the woman nuzzling herself into my chest right now came in when I least expected it and became everything I never knew I needed. I didn't think I needed somebody who was the epitome of sunshine, but now I can't imagine a day without her. I like the warmth she radiates and the comfort she brings.

And as I realize what all of that means, my stomach starts to sink. Because that's not what was supposed to happen. None of this is real.

But that doesn't change the fact that I understand what's happening. I recognize the way I feel around Harlow. It was the same way I felt seven years ago.

It's the start of falling for somebody... *and that fucking terrifies me.*

Thirty-Four

Harlow

"How the hell did we manage this, Rory?" I ask, applying another coat of mascara.

"Because Knox will give you anything you ask for, babe," she laughs. "You could probably tell him to get his dick pierced, and he'd do it."

"You're ridiculous." I shake my head. "I'm also certainly not asking him to get his fucking dick pierced."

"Not into that, huh?" Rory's smile is mischievous as she tries to rile me up.

"He can do whatever he wants. I won't care either way. But I can't picture him wanting one."

Rory thinks for a moment. "Yeah, he's too clean-cut, isn't he? Does he even have any tattoos?"

"Nope," I reply, rubbing my lips together to ensure an even application of my new favorite cherry-red lipstick. "No piercings, no tattoos."

"What a shame. Guys with tattoos are so hot."

"I've always liked them," I reply, leaning back against the wall as Rory finishes her makeup. "I love the sleeve Cole is working on. I just don't think I could ever actually get one myself."

"They aren't that bad."

"Didn't you tell me your foot went numb when you got your infinity sign?" I ask incredulously.

"Damn you and your good memory," Rory laughs. "Anyway, what are you wearing tonight?"

"Something that will torture Knox all night as he watches me dance."

Rory looks at me and crosses her arms. "Lo, you could wear a fucking potato sack, and that man wouldn't be able to take his eyes off you."

I can't help but blush as I smile. "Probably true. But mainly because he'd be thinking about how long until he could peel it off me."

"I'm not meaning to pry," Rory says, "but how has everything been going? It's been a few weeks, and you two are going at it like fucking rabbits."

"Really?" I roll my eyes. "It's going well. We're having fun."

"And what about how you feel?"

The question I was hoping to avoid. Telling Rory that I'm absolutely falling for Knox would only make it real.

But my God, I can't help myself.

He's so sweet. He's very attentive and selfless in bed, and then he'll pull me in, wrapping me up in his arms.

Those moments are so much more intimate than anything else we do. The sex is fucking amazing, but it can't compare to the way my heart swells anytime he just holds me, content to just have me there with him.

It's my absolute favorite thing.

And it's making it so much more difficult to pretend that I can keep my feelings to myself.

"I'm... okay," I manage. "I really care about him, though."

"Just..." Rory breathes. "Just don't get yourself hurt, Lo."

"Well, I'm certainly hoping I don't," I reply, walking over to the closet in Knox's guest bedroom, where Rory and I both have a few outfits hanging to choose from for tonight.

By some miracle, Knox and Cole decided they wanted to come out with us tonight. Rory and I want to go dancing, and Knox, my fake boyfriend who hates going out in public, practically invited himself to come with us, saying he wants to make sure nobody messes with us.

Cole also decided he wanted to come since the Stars are off today. He wants to help keep an eye on me and Rory, his sister and his friend. Cole's always been very protective of the people he cares about.

"What do you think?" I ask Rory, holding up a tight red mini dress. "I love the cut of this one."

"I bet you do," she smirks. "The top of that will put your entire chest on display."

"Well," I reply, "I did say I want to torture Knox."

"Then it's the perfect choice." Rory walks over to join me next to the closet, looking through her own options. "Do you think this black dress would be cute?"

"Hell yes, Rory. You'd look hot in that," I say, running my hand over the sequined black fabric.

"Really?" she asks. "You don't think it'll be too tight?"

"Ror, it's a loose, flared skirt. It won't be tight. Honestly, if I were you, I'd be more concerned about my tits popping out the top of it."

Rory chokes down a laugh as she sits down on the guest bed. "Fashion tape is my best friend on nights like these."

"I thought *I* was your best friend?!" I say in mock offense. "Rory Fisher, I'm heartbroken."

She playfully shoves my shoulder as I sit down next to her. "You're so fucking ridiculous, Lo."

"The ridiculousness is just a perk of my friendship." I pretend to bow, and Rory falls back onto the bed as she laughs.

"Girl, just get dressed. They have to be pissed that we're still not ready."

It's been so long since I've been to a club. They aren't nearly as packed on a weeknight, but there are still a good number of people here. Enough to make Knox and Cole get us into the VIP area so we're not surrounded by their fans all night.

There aren't many people back here with us, and the ones that are have largely left us alone, even if they do keep eyeing Knox and Cole as they try to figure out why they recognize them. And we have our own bar and dancefloor, meaning Rory and I don't need to join the throngs of sweaty people in the main part of the club.

And dancing back here means Knox and Cole have been able to keep an eye on us all night.

And *fuck*, has Knox kept an eye on me.

His eyes are roaming every part of my body.

He groans each time I throw my arms up.

He bites his lip every time I shake my hips.

I've never felt sexier.

"Damn," Rory says, walking back with another drink for me and breaking me out of my thoughts. "Knox has been eye-fucking you all night."

"He's just checking out his girlfriend in front of everyone else here," I shrug.

Rory stares at me in disbelief. "Yeah, I'm sure that's all it is." She leans closer to me. "Certainly couldn't have to do with him wanting to rip that dress off you."

"Rory Fisher!" I shout while a deep blush crosses my cheeks and chest.

As I try to compose myself, I feel two strong arms wrap around my waist. "That's definitely part of it," Knox says behind me.

"Fucking spare me, please," Cole groans, walking up to stand to the side of Rory and me.

"You complain too much," I chastise.

Rory elbows Cole in the side. "Get yourself laid, Pierce, and you won't be complaining anymore."

"Yeah..." he replies uneasily, rubbing the back of his head. "But I don't really want something casual."

"So get a girlfriend then," I say back, leaning against Knox's chest.

Cole pinches his brow and sighs. "I would love to *not* talk about my love life right now."

"Then dance with me instead," Rory says enthusiastically, shaking her hips as she does. Cole laughs before joining her, dancing terribly but with a smile on his face.

I turn around and wrap my arms around Knox's neck. "You gonna dance like that with me, Slick?"

"I don't dance, Lo. Pretty sure I actually have two left feet." He wraps an arm around my waist and pulls me back against his chest. Leaning his lips to my ear, he whispers, "But I'm more than happy to watch you shake your ass in that dress, baby."

I let out an involuntary moan. "I didn't realize you even noticed my ass since you haven't taken your eyes off my chest all night."

Knox laughs, a low rumble that vibrates down my spine. "How could I not stare? Your tits are perfect."

"Good to know. I'll have to add perfect tits to my résumé."

"Fuck that," he growls. "Nobody but me needs to know what you're hiding under that dress."

I can't help but laugh as he takes my hands in his, leading us back toward the booth. "Is Fort Knox *jealous* at the thought of somebody else seeing me?"

Knox sits down in the booth and pulls me onto his lap, lips now ghosting over the skin of my neck. "What if I am? I don't share, Harlow. Nobody gets to see what's mine."

"I thought this was fake." The words flow out of me thanks to the several vodka sodas I've had tonight. I hate even uttering those words because, every day, this feels more real.

"Makes no difference," he says, hand sliding under me and gripping my ass. "As long as I'm the one taking care of you, *you're mine*." Knox trails his fingers forward, running along the seam of my soaked panties. "And you're my dirty fucking girl, aren't you?"

"Yes," I breathe.

He slides the fabric to the side, running his finger along my slit. "Goddamn, you're drenched, baby."

"Drenched for you."

"The bar is full," Knox says maliciously. "So it's a good thing you're not shy, isn't it?"

He slips a finger inside, and I stifle a moan. "Knox..." His finger starts moving rhythmically in and out before he pushes a second finger inside. "Mmm..."

"Do you like this, Harlow?" he asks, lowering his voice and using a husky tone. "You like me fingering you in front of everyone here?"

"Yes," I manage. "I like it, and I want another."

I bite my lip and lowly groan as Knox presses a third finger inside. "Fuck, your pussy is just swallowing my fingers."

"Rather have your cock," I breathe before turning my face into his chest, groaning into his skin.

"I want you to come first, baby," he says, repositioning his hand smoothly so his thumb can brush against my clit. "I want you to get off in a room full of people that have no idea I'm knuckles-deep inside your tight cunt right now."

"Knox..." I moan, trying to keep my volume down. He keeps his pace, continually thrusting his fingers into me as his thumb teases circles over my clit.

I've never gotten off in public before.

I've never even wanted to.

But the possibility of us getting caught is turning me on far more than I thought it would.

There's still a small crowd on the dancefloor, and while our booth is tucked in the corner, we're still not more than five feet from someone else.

Anyone could see us right now. A stranger. Rory. *My brother.*

Knox hasn't been touching me long, and I'm already feeling the flutters of an impending orgasm.

As he asks me again to come and hooks his fingers inside me, I fall apart, stifling my moan with his shoulder.

"There you go, baby," he says, slowly sliding his fingers out of me and slipping his hand out from under my dress. He brings his fingers to his mouth, quickly licking them clean of the arousal dripping from them.

I bring my lips to his, tasting myself as I press my tongue against his. I trail my fingers down the fabric of his black T-shirt before settling them on his lap. His dick twitches as I drag my palm against it, Knox groaning as I do.

"Knox," I say, breaking our kiss. His eyes find mine, heat flaring behind them. "Take me back to your place. *Now.*"

Thirty-Five

Harlow

THE MOMENT WE STEP inside his penthouse after peeling away from Rory and Cole at the bar, everything is a frenzy. Our lips connect the second the door closes behind us.

I throw my heels in the kitchen.

Knox's sneakers are in the living room.

He slips my panties off somewhere in the hallway.

And as soon as he sits me on the bed, I quickly pull his shirt over his head.

Everything about tonight already feels different.

It's messy. It's sloppy. It's... intense.

More intense than how it usually feels when we fall into bed.

The air around us is different, and I'm so engrossed in the moment. *In Knox.*

I'm surrendering myself to him completely, letting him claim me as his own.

"Harlow," he rasps, severing the silence. "I love this dress, but it's got to go. *Take it off.*"

Without hesitation, I grab my dress by the hem of the skirt and slowly pull it over my body, tossing it to the floor in a pile of satiny, red fabric.

Now standing naked in front of him, I reach for his jeans, unzipping them and pushing them down his legs. Once he steps out of the denim, Knox hooks his thumbs under the waistband of his boxer briefs, sliding them down to the floor.

He picks me up now, and I wrap my legs around his waist as I find his lips again. He positions us in the center of the bed, laying my head on the pillows.

"God, you're fucking *beautiful.*"

"You're saying that because I'm naked for you right now," I tease lightly.

Knox chuckles. "You're beautiful in clothing, too, baby. Naked, though, you're a goddamn dream. *My dream.*"

The honesty catches me off guard. *I'm* his dream?

He told me before that he'd wanted me for years, but I didn't think he meant that in more than a physical, sexual way.

And maybe he didn't.

But maybe now that he knows me, he's thinking differently.

Maybe he's feeling the dynamic shifting between us, too.

I throw my arms around his shoulders and deepen our kiss, sliding my tongue into his mouth and swirling it with his. Knox groans as his dick presses into my hip.

"Fuck, I want you, Harlow," he says, peppering kisses down my neck and across my collarbone.

"So have me then," I breathe. "I just want you to fuck me, Knox. Please."

His smile is malicious as his lips meet mine again, taking me over in a searing kiss. "Begging without me even telling you. Good girl."

I sigh at the praise while mentally cursing myself for always being so affected by his words. This man turns me into something I've never been before.

Maybe it's ironic to say that Knox makes me feel empowered, but there's no other way to describe how I feel around him. He takes control in bed, but we both know I'm the one holding all the power.

I don't think I've ever felt more sure of myself in the bedroom than I do now.

"How do you want me, Knox?"

"Just like this," he replies, rubbing his thumb over my bottom lip. "Displayed like this, knowing I'm the only one who gets to appreciate you."

"You're the only one who's ever appreciated me," I admit. "No one else has ever cared enough."

Knox leans his lips to my ear, whispering, "Then all the other men you've been with were crazy because you deserve to be fuck-ing *worshipped*, Harlow."

"Is that what you do?" I ask, stifling a sigh as he lowers his head, sucking my nipple into his mouth. "Worship me?"

"Every goddamn time you're in my bed, baby." He takes his cock in his hand, giving himself a few tugs and swiping at the bead of precum leaking out the tip. "Now, enough talk. If I don't sink into you soon, I'm going to go out of my fucking mind."

His admission has my desire running rampant, wanting to get to know him even more intimately. So when he goes to reach into the nightstand, he looks at me in surprise as I grab him by the wrist.

"What are you doing, Lo?" he asks, curious.

"Um... stopping you."

"I need a condom if I'm going to fuck you."

I bury my face in his chest, hiding the fire burning across my cheeks. "What if we don't use one?"

I say it so softly that I'm not even sure he hears me until he places his finger under my chin and turns my face to meet his. "You want me to fuck you bare?" His tone is huskier than usual, making the heat just pool between my thighs. "You want me to fuck you like you're mine?"

"Yes," I say shyly. "I'm on birth control. I take it every day. And I got tested a couple months after I broke up with Derek, and I'm all clear. If you want it, too, I'd really like that."

"I want it," Knox says lowly. "I really fucking want it. I'm clear, too. I just got tested over the offseason. I haven't been with anyone else since before that."

I lean up and kiss him, regaining my confidence now that the awkward question is out of the way. "Then make me yours, Knox."

Our kiss is needier, *hungrier*, as he spreads my legs apart and settles himself in between them. He runs the head of his cock along my slit, coating the tip in my arousal.

When Knox breaks our kiss to look at me, silently asking if I'm sure this is what I want, I nod.

His forehead presses against mine as he slowly starts to push inside. I gasp at the feeling, reveling in the way he feels with nothing between us.

"*Fuck*," Knox curses as he slides in to the hilt. "Jesus fucking Christ."

"I don't think Jesus is involved in what we're doing right now."

He laughs with his lips brushing mine. "I'm not sure about that. I'm in Heaven every time I have you wrapped around my cock."

As he starts thrusting into me, I'm overwhelmed with how good it feels. *How full I feel*. He pulls his hips back and slams into me again, stretching me out perfectly around him.

"Knox," I moan.

"This won't last long, Lo." He's already breathless, sweat dripping from his brow. "You feel too fucking good. Slick and warm and fucking *mine*."

"I am yours," I say. "I'm yours, Knox."

He smiles before teasing his tongue over my bottom lip, waiting for me to open. And when I do, he slips right inside, tongues moving as frantically as Knox's hips.

I've never had sex like this.

Sure, Knox and I are always rough and needy with each other, but it feels different.

It feels more like I *am* his.

I feel like I belong to Knox Spencer.

The world already thinks that. Now, though, it's really starting to feel like it.

I've never been so consumed by someone, so filled with longing and need.

It's scary, being so enthralled with someone that might not see you the same way.

But I push that thought from my head. I'm just going to enjoy myself and worry about the rest another day.

"Goddammit," he swears as he increases his pace, slamming into me repeatedly. "So good, Harlow." He groans now, sinking his teeth into my shoulder. "Fuck, I can't hold back much longer."

"So don't," I murmur against his ear. "Come, Knox."

"Where-"

"Inside me," I plead, looking right into his eyes. "Come inside me. I want to feel you."

"*Fuck,*" he moans, thrusting his hips faster while snaking a hand between us and finding his way between my legs. "You come first. I need to feel your cunt clench around me. I need to know how good you feel when you come on my bare cock."

I moan as Knox teases my clit in time with his thrusts. "Don't stop then. I'm so close."

He bites on my neck, leaving me a new mark as I tangle my fingers in his hair. Every sensation right now is heightened, leaving me right on the edge of bliss, ready to tumble right over. And when he thrusts again, hitting a spot no one's ever been able to reach, I explode.

"Knox! Oh my God!"

"Fuck, fuck, *fuck!"* he shouts, pushing in one final time before his hips still. My pussy is still convulsing around him as he spills everything inside me, painting me with every drop of his cum.

Panting, Knox pulls out of me, and I already feel emptier.

"Goddamn, Harlow," he breathes. "Fucking incredible."

"It was," I reply before kissing him. "Really good."

He smiles before pushing himself off me and slowly moving his body down the bed.

"What are you doing?" I ask, looking at him curiously.

He kisses my knee and murmurs against my skin. "Want to see." Knox takes my knees in his hands and spreads them further apart, leaving me fully exposed. "Want to see how you look full of my cum."

"And?" I ask. "What do you think?"

He runs a finger up my slit before pressing it inside, coating it in his release. "Perfect," he replies, now trailing his finger down my thigh, leaving a white line in its wake. "Fucking perfect."

When he positions himself on top of me again, capturing my lips with wicked intentions, I finally realize where all of this is heading.

I'm falling heart-first for a man who hasn't had a relationship in seven years.

And I don't know if Knox will be waiting to catch me before I hit the ground...

Thirty-Six

Knox

"Good morning, baby," I say, wrapping Harlow in my arms as she wakes up.

"Good morning," she smiles. "You seem like you're in a good mood."

Hell yes, I'm in a good mood.

The way we fucked after we came back from the club last night was something else entirely.

Not that I thought I could get enough of her before, but I sure as hell won't be able to get enough of her now.

"I've been in a good mood quite a bit recently, I think," I say as I pull her closer, kissing her softly.

"Yeah?" Harlow teases, lips ghosting over mine. "And why is that?"

"Because I have you in my bed. That would put anyone in a good mood."

She smiles at me, bright and happy. "Sweet talker."

"Hey, I'm speaking from experience here, Lo." I kiss her deeply, leaving my lips brushing against hers after. "With the way I get to have you every night, I've got a good bit of personal experience to verify it."

"And what about the way you had me last night?" she asks, fingertips dancing up my bare chest.

I graze my hands down her back before tightly cupping her ass. "Nobody else gets to have you like that. Nobody is going to take you bare and fill up your tight cunt, leaving their cum dripping out of you, except for me."

"Is that so?" she taunts. Her hand ghosts my chest again, this time downward, as she slowly works her way to my half-hard cock. "You're getting turned on just thinking about it."

She starts lazily stroking my length, and in no time, I'm fully hard. "I get turned on just being around you, Harlow." I groan as she starts moving her hand faster.

"Damn, you know how to make a girl feel wanted."

"Baby," I grunt, barely able to focus right now, "I *always* want you. Fucking always."

"Mmm," she says, planting kisses down my neck. "So, what do you *want* me to do right now, Knox?"

"On your knees," I reply breathlessly. "Get on your fucking knees. I want you to choke on me."

Harlow's look is devious, *sinful*, as she crawls backward down the bed, sliding off and falling to her knees. "Come over here," she beckons, hooking her index finger to coax me down the bed. "I'm ready to choke."

God, she's perfect.

I crawl to the foot of the bed, sitting myself down on the edge with Harlow on her knees in front of me.

Such a pretty sight.

Without me saying anything, she leans forward, spitting on my shaft before taking her hand and spreading it down my length. With her fist around the base, she closes her mouth over the tip and starts sucking.

"Fuck," I moan. "Fucking love your mouth, Lo."

She works her mouth down halfway while running her tongue along the underside of my dick. I bring my hands to her head, grabbing a fistful of hair with each one, as I catch a glimpse of us in the mirror on the wall opposite my bed.

"Goddamn, I love watching your ass in the mirror." She smiles with her eyes as she places her hands on my thighs, slowly taking me further.

She stands now, bending over to keep the top half of her body parallel to the ground. And with this position, she can take me even deeper.

"Shit," I say softly as I watch Harlow take in all of me. Every goddamn inch. The head of my cock is buried in her fucking throat. "Didn't know... you could... deepthroat. *Fucking hell.*"

She keeps her eyes on me and brings a hand to cup my balls as she starts humming.

Humming.

Good fucking Lord Almighty.

The vibrations travel down my dick, and I'm about to explode.

I pull her off of me as quickly as I can. "Nope, not coming like that." I take her hands and move her closer. "Coming in your pussy. Turn around and sit on me."

"I like watching you lose control," she says, her back to my chest, as she slowly lowers herself on my cock. She moans loudly when I'm fully seated inside her.

I groan as I look across the room again. "Fuck, Harlow. Look." I turn her face and point it toward the mirror. "Open your eyes and look how fucking well we fit together."

"You fit perfectly," she replies, absolutely breathless, as I start moving her up and down my dick, my hands grasping her hips with force. She leans her head back on my shoulder, eyes fluttering closed.

"Watch, Harlow," I say roughly, and her eyes shoot open. "Watch how well you take me. There you go. That's my fucking girl."

Harlow sighs at the praise. "This feels so good."

"Yeah," is all I can manage in response. I'm so fucking close, but I'm not coming until she does.

I slip my hand between her thighs as she starts grinding on me, and I'm going to lose my fucking mind any second.

"Need to get you off first," I growl. "Come for me, baby."

"Uh... huh...," she moans as my thumb brushes her clit. One more flick, and her pussy is fluttering around me.

"Yes, that's it. Such a good girl for me, Harlow."

"Now you," she says as she's slowly coming down from her orgasm, still grinding her pussy all over my cock. "Be a good boy and fill me up, Knox."

Good boy.

Never in my life has someone called me a good boy in bed.

Apparently, though, I like that because before I know it, I'm coming harder than I ever have.

I'm screaming her name as I spill everything I have into her slick, warm pussy.

That feeling is unlike anything else. Absolutely *euphoric*.

And really fucking intimate.

Harlow's leaning back against me as I lean forward, placing my head on her shoulder. "Goddammit. I think you just killed me."

"I'll give the eulogy at your funeral," she lightly laughs. "Knox Spencer died doing what he loved best—giving incredible orgasms."

I howl with laughter before I find her mouth with mine, kissing her deeply as I slowly slide my dick out of her. I quickly lay her down beside me, positioning her on her back with her ass at the edge of the bed.

"What are you doing?" she says, amused as she watches me fall to my knees in between her legs, spreading them wide. "You want to see again, huh?"

"Yeah," I admit. "Love seeing my cum drip out of your sweet cunt." I place sloppy kisses up the inside of her thigh, inching closer to her core. "Want to clean you up, too."

"Wha-" Her words are cut off by a moan as I stroke my tongue up her pussy, tasting myself as my release seeps out of her. I press my face against her, driving my tongue deeper and lapping up both of our arousals. "Damn, that's hot."

I laugh against her core. "You're getting wetter, aren't you, pretty girl? You're getting wet from me eating my own cum out of your perfect, little pussy."

"Fuck, Knox... this is so good."

I push my tongue further in, sucking as much of my release out of her as I can. With my mouth full, I stand up and hover over Harlow, tapping her mouth with my finger. She opens, and I spit inside before kissing her, letting us both taste how fucking sweet we are together as our tongues battle for dominance.

As she moans into my mouth, I know there won't be an easy way to let this woman go when the season is over.

I think I'd keep her in my bed for the rest of my life if I could.

I just don't know if that will be enough for her.

Thirty-Seven

Harlow

AFTER AN AFTERNOON AWAY game win against the Chicago Wind-jammers on Sunday, Lane and Knox flew down to Miami for the All-Star Game while the rest of us and Sage flew back to NYC. Since most of the team wasn't selected for the game, only those who were attended. This means Rory and I stay behind as well since we're not even officially part of the team anyway.

Monday night is the Home Run Derby, which neither Lane nor Knox are competing in. But they are playing in the All-Star Game on Tuesday before they fly home right after. Lane considered not accepting the invitation at all because he didn't want to be away from Sage, but Rory assured him that Sage would be just fine.

Now, standing outside of Cole's apartment building in Tribeca on Monday morning, I run into Lucia. "Morning, Torres," I say as I stride over next to her.

"Oh, hey, Lo. This is the right building, isn't it? I've never been to Cole's before."

"Yeah, this is the one," I reply. "Rory said she and Sage got here a little bit ago, and Cole already had everything delivered for brunch."

"Smart man, that brother of yours." Lucia laughs. "But maybe not so much around Rory."

"What does that mean?" I ask as we cross the building lobby and step into the elevator.

"Lo, you can't possibly have missed the signs."

"Signs for what? Cole and Rory?"

"Babe, I honestly don't understand how you haven't figured it out."

"Figured what out?" I say, exasperated.

Lucia laughs lightly, softly smiling. "Are you unaware that your brother has his eye on Rory?"

"No, he doesn't," I say quickly. "Does he?"

"Harlow, Cole is not an awkward man... except around one person."

"Rory," I say, letting the puzzle pieces finally fall into place. "Holy shit."

"Indeed," Lucia replies as we step off the elevator and head down the hall toward Cole's apartment. "Rory remains oblivious as well, but I do have my suspicions that she feels the same way. She'll just never admit it or do a goddamn thing about it."

"Well, I'm sure as hell not meddling in that right now. I've got my own shit to worry about," I say with a laugh.

When we reach Cole's door, I knock. "Come on in," he says from the other side. Lucia and I walk inside to find Sage cuddled up on Rory's lap while she and Cole sit close to each other on the couch.

I have been really oblivious, haven't I?

"Good morning, guys," I say, throwing my bag on the floor and walking across the room to meet them. "Hey, Sagie!" I say, scooping her up into my arms as she giggles.

"What is Miss Sage having for breakfast this morning?" Lucia asks as she joins us.

"A bunch of bananas," Rory says with a light laugh. "Literally. I brought a literal bunch of bananas for her since it's her favorite food right now. Lane goes through a ridiculous amount of bananas."

"Nana!" Sage shouts.

"And that's our cue to head to the table," Cole says. "Come on, breakfast is already set up."

I sit Sage down in her portable high chair that Rory attached to the end of Cole's table. There are already two bananas split in half on a plate in front of her, and she immediately reaches over and takes one half of a banana in each hand.

I grab a cup of coffee before sitting in front of the plate of French toast, taking the spot across from Cole.

"So, what are your plans for the break, Cole?" Lucia asks from beside me. "Anything fun?"

"Still going to be spending some time in the gym," he replies, stuffing a piece of bacon into his mouth. "Gotta keep up if I want to keep playing well."

"I still can't believe you weren't invited to the All-Star Game," Rory says from beside Cole.

"I mean, it would've been nice," he says, "But I'm not one of the best shortstops. There are plenty of guys better than me."

"Don't be humble, Cole," I say. "I run a damn blog with player stats—you're not giving yourself enough credit. You say you're not one of the best when you're the number five shortstop for the entire league."

"Honestly," Lucia chimes in, "It's a crime you're not there with Lane and Knox."

Cole lets out a breath. "But I keep to myself, so I'm not a very popular player. I know that hurts me with things like this, but it's hard to give up my privacy. Maybe next year, though."

"Have you talked to Lane yet today, Rory?" Lucia asks.

She laughs. "Like three times already. He's been away from Sage for barely twelve hours now, and he's already missing her like crazy."

"Who wouldn't miss her?" I say. "Sage is the cutest fucking kid."

Cole laughs. "Lane's gonna be fucked in another year with all the swearing Sage hears."

"Most of what she hears is from Lane himself," Rory replies. "Mouth of a sailor on that one."

"I think that could describe literally every one of us," I say with a laugh. "Hell, we might just make some sailors blush."

"We're not *that* bad, Lo," Cole responds, slightly offended.

Lucia chuckles and says under her breath, "That's because you haven't heard Knox in bed."

"Lucia!" I shout.

Cole groans. "How the fuck do you even know what he sounds like in bed, Luc?"

"Because your sister tells me everything," Lucia replies with a smirk.

"And I'm regretting that right now, believe me."

"Speaking of Knox, though," Rory interjects. "Have you heard from him yet today, Lo?"

"Not yet," I say as I sip my coffee. "But he's got some things to do this morning to prepare for tomorrow's game, and then he'll be there to watch the Home Run Derby tonight. I probably won't talk to him until after that."

"How ever will you survive?" Cole says with a smug look.

"I'll be just fine, Cole."

"You sure about that?" he asks, eyeing me.

"Yes, I'm sure," I reply. "It's not like I've never been away from a boyfriend before."

"Harlow," Rory says, catching what I accidentally said. "You just called Knox your boyfriend."

"That was just a slip of the tongue."

"Is it that," Lucia asks with a serious look, "or is it because this isn't so fake to you anymore?"

"Umm..." I manage, trying to hold back... but it's futile. "It could be that..."

"Seriously?" Cole says, surprised.

I let out a deep breath. "Yeah... it's been feeling less and less fake. And I have no idea what to do about it."

"You should talk to him," Lucia says. "The way he looks at you makes it obvious that he's feeling it, too."

"I don't know. We both went into this with the expectation that the relationship wasn't real."

"Yeah," Cole says with an eye roll. "And then he started coming to talk to you before every game. He started happily talking to the media and going out publicly with you to be photographed for the tabloids. He started lighting up the moment someone even *mentioned* your name. Lo, that is not the man I've known for three years."

"Well, things can feel less fake without us wanting to actually be together. It's not like he has feelings for me or anything," I reply. But that last part comes out weakly, as if it hurts me to say it. Like it hurts me to think about the fact that my feelings might not be reciprocated. The feelings I've tried so fucking hard to deny, but it's so damn obvious to anyone that sees me with him that none of it is fake to me.

"I don't want to meddle at all, believe me," Cole says. "But I do think you're wrong. I've already been thinking that, but I didn't want to say anything. Whatever you do, though, just don't get yourself hurt." He reaches across the table and squeezes my hand. "We're all glad to have Happy Harlow back. You're finally back to the sister I always remembered."

"No matter what, I'm not letting myself go back down that road. There's the real possibility that nothing comes from this whole arrangement other than our pre-agreed terms and now sex. It all is what it is, and I'll handle it."

"You could talk to him when he flies home after tomorrow's game," Cole says before he takes a bite of his omelet.

Rory smirks. "I don't think talking is what they'll be doing then."

"It is not," I say, heat creeping across my cheeks. "Actually, Cole, I was thinking we could do a raincheck on our breakfast this week. I've, uh... got some other plans."

"Jesus fucking Christ," Cole mumbles.

The change of direction in the conversation was nice, but I know they're all right. I'm going to *have* to talk to Knox about all of this at some point. The longer this goes on without me saying anything, the more likely I am to get hurt.

But even the thought of having that conversation makes me nauseous.

All of this would have been so much easier if Knox wasn't so fucking perfect.

Thirty-Eight

Harlow

AFTER BREAKFAST THIS MORNING, I went back to my apartment and spent the rest of the day working on *Starred and Fast*. Things are going really well, and I want it to maintain the momentum it's gaining.

I work on some more articles to post over the coming days, and when that's finished, I finally allow myself to relax. I read a smutty romance book, use a shower steamer since my apartment doesn't have a bathtub, and enjoy half a bottle of Riesling. Now, at eleven PM, I'm wine drunk, dancing around my kitchen while singing Taylor Swift very off-key.

"I'm the one on the phone as you whisper, 'Do you know how much I miss you?'"

My song time is interrupted by my phone ringing, cutting off the music. I grab my phone from the counter, still swaying my hips to the song that's no longer playing, and look at the screen. And I smile. Knox is calling.

"Hey, Slick," I say, answering the phone and bringing it to my ear. "You're interrupting my drunken singing."

"Oh God," Knox says from the other line, stifling a laugh. "Can you even sing?"

"Not well," I say as I chuckle. "But after half a bottle of wine, I'm up for anything."

"Then I'll be sure to grab some wine for my place."

"You're terrible," I reply, shaking my head but still smiling. "How was the Home Run Derby tonight?"

"It was fun to watch," he admits. "It's entertaining to see players from other teams hit home runs when you're not the one pitching them."

"Like you give up a lot of home runs, Fort. Nobody can hit your damn knuckleballs."

"I wouldn't say nobody," he replies with a light laugh. "I've given up my share of home runs and all."

"So modest," I say. "What are you up to?"

"Got back to my room a little bit ago and thought it would be nice to talk to you."

"Aww," I say in a singsong tone. "You miss me."

"I wouldn't go that far," he scoffs. "I think it's more just noticing your absence."

"Call it whatever you want. I know what you mean."

"Are you at your place right now, Lo? Or are you with Lucia, Rory, or Ella?"

"I'm in my apartment. My little shoebox," I say with a laugh. "Why?"

"Hang on," Knox says before I hear the call disconnect and a Face-Time call comes through.

I cross the room and settle onto my bed, leaning back against the pillows before I answer the call.

And I'm greeted with a shirtless Knox leaning back against the headboard of his hotel bed.

"Well, hello there," I say, involuntarily running my tongue over my bottom lip.

"Damn," he says with a smile. "You're already checking me out."

"You called me when you weren't wearing a shirt. What did you expect from me?"

"Baby, I'm not judging you. If you didn't realize, you're in a fucking sports bra right now. I can barely think straight seeing you in that."

"Mmm," I say, settling down into my pillows. "You just wish you were here to take it off me, don't you?"

Knox groans. "You definitely wouldn't be wearing that if I was with you. I'd have taken it off hours ago."

"Well," I say, a mischievous smile pulling at the corners of my mouth as I move my phone to my nightstand, prop it up against a book, and sit myself on the side of my bed. "Let's just pretend you are here." I grab the sports bra by the hem and slowly pull it off in full view of the camera, letting my breasts fall free.

"Fuck, baby."

"You like that?" I say, teasing him by pushing my tits together.

"I fucking love that." His tone is guttural, so full of desire and need. "I'd like it even more if the rest came off with it."

"Naughty, Knox. Trying to get me naked on the phone."

"I'd much prefer you were naked in my bed beside me," he says huskily. "But if all I can get is the phone screen right now, that will have to do."

Phone sex isn't something I've done before. But the lust in Knox's eyes right now has me so emboldened that that doesn't even faze me.

"Take off your shorts first," I say, meeting his eyes. "You need to take something off before I do anything else."

His smile is devious as he props his phone on his own nightstand, positioning himself in front of it. "I called it that first night we were together. You're a dirty fucking girl." He hooks his thumbs under the waistband of his shorts and slides them down, leaving him in only a pair of black boxer briefs that leave *nothing* to the imagination.

I hum my approval as I take all of him in. The tight fabric clings to the muscles of his thighs, muscles earned from years of running around the baseball field. The waistband dips just below the V in his abdomen. And the dick that's already hard as stone is straining to break free. "So turned on just from me taking off my top," I tease.

"Yeah," he says, a smirk pulling at his lips. "And what would you do about it if you were here, Lo?"

"Mmm... I'd sink to my knees and take your cock into my mouth. Maybe even have you fuck my face."

"Fucking hell," Knox mutters as I see his hand slip under his waistband.

"Baby," I say, lowering my voice. "If you're going to touch yourself, take the boxers off. I want to watch you."

"I'll take off mine if you take off yours."

He and I are both breathing heavily as we slide off the remainder of our clothing, leaving us both bare in front of our phone screens.

"Goddess, Harlow," he says, grabbing his phone from the nightstand and bringing it with him as he sits back against the headboard again. "You're a fucking *goddess.*" His hand finds his dick, and he tightly grasps it, slowly pumping his shaft a few times.

"What do you want me to do, Knox?" I ask, already breathless with how hot I feel right now.

"Spread your legs. Let me see that perfect cunt." I do as he asks, and he groans from the other end. "Goddamn, Lo. You're already dripping, aren't you?"

I slowly take a finger and drag it against my folds. "So wet. I've been thinking about you all day."

"Me too, baby. I haven't been able to stop thinking about you and the way you moan when I sink my cock into you. I can't be there, so let me hear you instead. Show me how you fuck yourself when I'm not around."

Knox's filthy words only make me feel hotter. The only way to cool down will be to find my release first. So I ask, "How then? With just my hand? Or should I use a toy?"

"Toy," he pants. "Let me watch you get off as you fuck yourself with a toy, imagining it's me."

"You think I'll be imagining it's you?" I say as I reach over the phone to get to my nightstand drawer, leaving the only view be my tits hanging in front of the camera. I can hear him groan as I return to the screen with my favorite dildo and bullet vibrator in hand.

"*Fuck...* you just grabbed a dildo. You better be imagining it's me."

"I don't know," I tease. "Maybe I'll think about Lane tonight."

"The fuck you will," Knox says, amusement falling from his face. "You're mine, remember? You should only be thinking about your boyfriend."

"Fake boyfriend," I reply with a smirk.

"Doesn't matter," he says, smirking back slightly. "Real or fake, my cock is the only one you should imagine fucking you."

I involuntarily moan at the possessiveness. "Don't worry, baby. *I always imagine it's you.*"

"Then show me what you do. But keep it down. I don't need the entire hotel to hear what you sound like. That's only for me."

"I make no promises," I say with a smile as I slide the dildo up my thigh, positioning it right between my legs. "If I'm imagining it's you, being quiet may be impossible."

I can see the pride wash over his face. "Slide that into your pussy, Harlow. I'm dying over here waiting for you."

"So impatient," I say, laughing lightly. I start to slide the dildo in, and I throw my head back and moan. "Fuck, Knox. I really wish this was you."

"So do I. I really fucking wish it was me."

He still has a tight grip on his dick and starts slowly pumping his shaft as I push the dildo in to the hilt. "I think I'm going to need a larger one now. You're so much bigger."

"Did that one used to be big for you?"

"Used to be… until a few weeks ago." I start pumping the dildo with my hand while my other flicks on the bullet vibrator. "Now, what to do with this one."

Knox is stroking faster now. "I don't care where you start with it as long as it ends between your legs."

I start by teasing the vibrator over my nipples, enjoying the sensation before I slowly slide it down my stomach, inching it closer and closer to the desired spot. When I finally reach my clit, I can't help but moan. *"Fuck…"*

"There you go, baby." My eyes are closed now, but I can hear him stroking himself faster. "Just like that."

"Knox," I moan. "This feels so good."

"Better than me?" he asks breathlessly.

"Never." I can already feel my orgasm closing in. I had myself so worked up that I should've known I wouldn't last long. "Nothing is better than you."

"Fuck, Harlow." Knox softly moans. "You gonna come all over those toys?"

"Mhmm," I manage between breaths. "Already… so close."

"Because you're addicted to me, baby."

I don't even argue. Partially because I can't even speak right now I'm so close to the edge. Mainly because he's right. I'm fucking addicted to Knox. Every side of him. The hot and heavy side. The sweet and caring side. The playful and flirty side.

I'm freefalling without a parachute. Nothing can slow me down. Nothing can stop me. I'm falling so goddamn hard, and all I want is Knox. To be with him. *Really* be with him.

My breathing is so heavy now that I'm practically panting. I just need a little more to tip over the edge. Knox saying, "There you go, baby. You're doing such a good job," is all it takes to fall apart.

"Knox... oh God!" I scream, pussy clenching around the toy inside me. I turn off the vibrator and toss it on the bed as I slowly slip the dildo out. All I hear from his end of the phone is the slapping of skin, rough and needy.

I open my eyes and look at the screen just in time to see him release himself all over his chest. *"Fuck, Harlow!"* He pumps himself until he's empty, trying to catch his breath while he does.

"Such a waste," I say. "You could've had that inside me instead."

He smiles and laughs. "Wednesday, baby. I'll give you everything inside me when I get back home."

"I can't wait," I reply, grabbing my phone and lying down on my bed, nestling my head against a pillow.

Knox grabs a few tissues to clean himself off before tossing them in the wastebasket. After he does, he sinks back into his pillows. "I can't wait either."

We're silent as I smile sweetly at him. I can't believe I ever thought I could resist falling for him. Knox is everything I never knew I wanted.

"What's that look for?" he asks.

"Nothing," I say, not wanting to give myself away. "I'm just happy right now."

"Yeah," he says with a smile. "I'm happy, too." We're silent again as he seems to be trying to decide whether or not to say something. "Harlow, I, uh..." He takes a deep breath. "I miss you."

"I miss you, too, Knox."

He smiles softly, but I can also see the worry on his face. I don't know what that means for this, for us, but I'm not ready to find out. I want to enjoy him a bit longer before I talk to him.

Let me just live in bliss for at least a few more days.

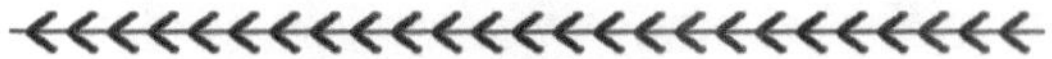

Knox and Lane both have great appearances during tonight's All-Star Game. Knox pitches two innings, and Lane bats in two runs, leading the American League to beat the National League five to two. I know the plan is for them to fly back to NYC immediately after the game, so that'll put them in the city sometime after two a.m. Because of that, I'm heading to Knox's first thing in the morning.

But then I'm awakened around three a.m. to a loud knock at my door. What the hell? Who is pounding on my door in the middle of the night?

I pad across the room in nothing but the Huntington Devils shirt I snagged from Knox that first night I stayed in his penthouse. I have a baseball bat by the door that I grab, just in case. Normal people don't bang on people's doors overnight, so I need to be prepared.

With the baseball bat over my shoulder, I swing the door open... and find Knox drenched from head to toe from the rain outside. "Knox?" I say softly, setting the bat back down. "What are you doing here?"

He charges into my room, setting his bag down and closing the door behind him. "I couldn't wait any longer to see you, Lo."

Once he closes the distance between us, his mouth crashes into mine as he leads us backward across the small room and over to my bed. We fall down on top of it, Knox on top of me, as his hands gently caress the skin of my thighs. "I thought I wasn't seeing you until morning," I manage between frantic kisses.

"Too long," he says. "I told you I missed you; I meant that. I wanted to see you now."

Knox starts moving us up the bed, positioning my head on top of a pillow before he grabs his soaked T-shirt by the back of his collar and pulls it over his head. Once he's shirtless, his lips find mine again.

Now fully awake, I throw myself into this. My hands run down his back and slide over the slick fabric of his athletic shorts to grip his ass and pull him in closer. And I'm not surprised at all to feel how hard he is when he presses his hips against my leg.

"Are you wearing anything under my shirt, Harlow?"

"No," I admit. "There's nothing under this."

"Take it off then. I want to see you."

His voice is husky and needy, so full of the desire that had him barge into my apartment in the middle of the night. He slips off his shorts and boxers as I pull the oversized T-shirt over my head, leaving us both bare.

Naked and ready, Knox settles between my legs, the head of his cock rubbing against the wetness pooling between them. He doesn't say another word before he slowly slips himself inside, bottoming out and filling me so completely.

Every thrust of his hips now tells me how I'll never be able to get enough.

Every kiss on my lips tells me how much I need him, and I need him like I need oxygen.

And every point of contact between our skin tells me how this will never be enough for me.

I want more, *need* more. I want all of Knox.

I don't just want the parts he's sharing with me now.

I want him wholly and fully.

I want him to fall for me just as I've fallen for him.

And I don't want to talk to him about this because I'm scared of what he'll say, but I need to do it anyway.

No matter what happens, I have to talk to him.

Soon.

Thirty-Nine

Knox

Harlow is naked and cuddled up against me, hand splayed across my bare chest as she's nuzzled into my side with my arm around her. It's been just over a week since I came back from the All-Star Game.

Just over a week since I so desperately needed to see her that I went to her place in the middle of the goddamn night.

Just over a week since I broke my own rule—I had sex with Harlow at her place, not mine. I haven't trusted anyone enough to do that in seven years.

So, how fake is this anymore?

When was the last time it even *felt* fake?

I honestly can't remember.

She quickly worked her way into my life, and she's already become such an integral part of it. We've been faking this relationship for three and a half months now, and I don't want to ever go a single day without her.

It's been seven years since I felt like this, and that's causing all the memories I've repressed in that time to resurface.

I know Harlow isn't Emily, but that doesn't make this easier. I didn't think Emily would be Emily either.

All this getting closer is bringing up the hurt from the past. I'm so out of my fucking element right now. I've been able to stay strong for seven years.

But then Harlow came along, and she tore out any remaining thread of sanity I had left.

I'm internally panicking. I know we'll have to talk about this, but I'm not prepared to have that conversation because if it were to happen right now, I have no clue what I'd say or if either of us would be happy when it's over.

"You okay, Knox?" she asks, looking at me with concern.

I give her a soft smile. "I'm okay, Lo. No need to worry."

"What time do you need to leave for practice today?"

I check my phone. "About five minutes ago."

"Paul's going to be pissed if you're late, Slick," she says with a playful smile. "You better get your ass going."

"I know," I sigh. "But I'm pretty damn comfortable right here."

"And you'll see me again after practice."

"Fine," I grumble, finally sitting up and stepping out of the bed. "Why don't you stay here while I'm gone?" I say as I walk into my closet, coming out with a white tee and black shorts. "Practice ends at two today, so I can bring a late lunch back with me."

"Okay." Harlow smiles brightly. "I brought my laptop last night, so I'll just work on the blog while you're gone."

"Perfect." I slip into my boxers and clothing before coming to meet her again. I tilt her chin up and press my lips to hers, setting off a storm in my heart. "I'll see you when I get back, Freckles."

Since I know my weakness—Harlow—I turn around immediately and head toward the door. If I linger any longer, I'll miss practice and make sure we don't even leave my bed. I have to move along so Skip doesn't chew me out and I don't let the team down.

Her gravity is just too damn strong, and it's so hard to find it in myself to even want to escape.

Practice is brutal today. I can't pitch a strike to save my damn life, and our pitching coach, Joe Pemberly, is on me the entire time.

He makes sure I stay late to practice more with Scholl so I can try to be ready for my next start in a few days. And that is just as bad.

My mind is so clouded with how I feel around Harlow that I can't focus on anything else. That's why I ask Lane to wait for me. If I don't talk to someone soon, I'm going to lose my fucking mind.

When I find Lane in the clubhouse, he demands I shower before we talk because, according to him, I "smell like ass."

Now towel-dried and back into the clothing I came in, I sit next to Lane on the sofa. "Thanks for staying, man," I say. "I know Rory needs to stay longer with Sage because of this."

"Rory, my daughter's favorite person in the entire world?" Lane laughs. "I don't think either of them are suffering right now." His face turns more serious now. "What's going on with you, Spence?"

I rest my head back against the sofa. "I'm so fucking confused."

"About Harlow?"

"Yeah," I sigh. "It feels like everything is changing, and it's scaring the hell out of me."

"Are you going to finally admit you've got feelings for her?"

I take a deep breath and let it out. "I know I do," I say softly. "But that's exactly the problem. None of that was supposed to happen. This isn't real. None of it was supposed to *become* real. I don't know if I can handle that right now."

Lane turns to face me, raising his brow. "Why is that a bad thing? You have a great time with Harlow, and I've never seen you happier than this. Why is this a problem?"

"Because..." I groan. I don't want to open up and be honest with someone else, but I don't think I have much of a choice. If I want to figure out what the hell to do about her, I've got to talk. "Because the last time I fell for somebody, it ended badly. I don't want to go through anything like that again."

"What happened that was so traumatic, Knox? You're not overly emotional, so it must've been pretty bad if it's still affecting you."

So, I open up.

I tell Lane everything that happened with Emily. I tell him about being drafted, the videos, the lawyers, and Simon. I tell him I wouldn't even have a career right now if it weren't for Simon. And I tell him how everything that happened left me gutted.

"Fuck, man." Lane rubs a hand over his face. "I don't even know what to say to that."

"There isn't much to say. But it's the kind of thing that stays with you. That makes you distrust people, even the ones you know you can trust."

"Like Harlow."

"Exactly like Harlow. I really trust her; I do. I told her about everything with Emily a couple of months ago, and she's been nothing but supportive and understanding. I know she has a heart of gold."

"So, I'm still not really seeing your problem with Lo. You're happy; you trust her. That seems like a good thing."

I sigh. "That's all good, sure. But everything I'm feeling right now, everything I feel for Harlow... that's how I felt for Emily. I trusted Emily, too, and she betrayed me in the worst fucking way. In my head, I know Harlow would never do that. But I can't seem to get my heart on board."

"Man, Mushy Knox isn't something I had on my bingo card for this year," Lane laughs.

"Dick," I say, smacking him lightly with my hat. "You're supposed to be helping me."

"I'm not sure what I'm supposed to help with when you already know the damn answer." I eye him curiously, and he sighs. "Stop being afraid of getting hurt like that again. That's not Harlow, and it never will be. She'd never betray you like that."

"It's not that easy," I sigh, head in my hands.

"Look," Lane says, putting a hand on my shoulder. "I know we've all joked about this and teased you both through the season. But you also know that we're here to support you at the end of it all. *Both* of you. Knox, you're actually fucking happy. And she's happier than she was before she met Derek. That's not nothing, and I think it's something worth exploring."

"Maybe," I say uneasily. "I just hope I don't fuck this up before we even get to that point."

◄◄◄◄◄◄◄◄◄◄◄◄◄◄◄◄◄◄◄◄◄◄◄◄◄◄◄◄

"I was wondering if you were coming back," Harlow jokes as I walk into the penthouse, a bag of Thai food in hand.

"Sorry," I say as I set the bag on the kitchen island. She joins me here and slides on top of one of the barstools. "I had to practice a little extra today."

I decide not to mention my talk with Lane.

"Why did you have to practice extra?" she asks, taking the food containers out of the bag and setting them on the counter in front of her.

I grab us both a bottle of water from the fridge before I sit next to her on the adjacent barstool. "Because I pitched like shit today."

"Why?" she asks, wrinkling her brow and opening up her pad see ew. "You never pitch like shit."

"Not sure," I reply. "Happens, though."

"Are we back to short answers now, Spencer?" she asks, smiling, but I can tell she's nervous. "I thought we'd gotten past all of that."

"Sorry," I sigh. "Just been a long day, I guess." I place my hand on top of hers, and instead of providing comfort, it just gives me more unease. That talk with Lane doesn't seem to have helped a goddamn bit. If anything, it just made this more complicated.

"Okay. Well, we don't need to talk unless you want to. We can just eat."

I want to tell her that I don't want silence.

I want to talk.

I want to hear her voice because it's become my favorite sound.

But I don't say a word.

Instead, we eat to the sound of our forks hitting off Styrofoam containers and Harlow nervously tapping her feet against the island.

When we finish eating, Harlow jumps up to sit on the counter in front of me. "Okay, I can't take the silence anymore. What's going on, Knox? This morning, you didn't want to leave me and asked me to wait here for you while you were gone. But since you came back, you've barely even spoken to me. Is everything okay?"

She softly presses her hand against my chest in concern. "Honestly, Lo..." I take a deep breath. "I have no fucking idea."

"This has to do with us, doesn't it?" she asks, voice breaking.

"Yeah," I say, unable to meet her eyes.

"Because things feel different..."

"Things shouldn't feel different, though, Lo. This is a fake relationship."

In the silence that follows, I hear what I can only imagine are the pieces of Harlow's heart shattering to the floor.

"Fake," she manages with a derisive tone, tears welling in her eyes. "What about this feels fake, Knox? Does this honestly feel fucking fake to you?"

No! I want to scream. *No, this all feels real, and it scares the fuck out of me, Harlow. I know I can trust you, but I don't know if I can give you my heart.*

But what I actually say is, "Yes," my voice so weak it's almost a whisper.

"Bull fucking shit." She slides off the counter now, tears actually streaming down her face. "You've been fucking me for a month, and you still have the audacity to lie and say it feels fake to you?"

"I'm not lying." I slide off my stool and turn to face her. "We both know this isn't real. None of this was meant to be real, Lo."

"Harlow."

Now, I feel my own heart shattering. In less than five minutes, I've done enough damage to have the right to call her Lo taken away. The right to call her a *friend*.

"We just got too caught up in this, Harlow. We're both playing parts, and we're playing them well." I reach out an arm to comfort her, but she shrugs me off.

"Don't touch me."

"I'm sorry, Harlow." My own voice is breaking, barely even audible.

"I'm sure you are, Knox. I'm sure you are." She wipes the tears from her eyes. "In all honesty, this is on me. We set the expectations for this at the beginning." Her words come out more choked now. "You never asked me to fall for you."

The words all but rip the shattered pieces of my heart right out of my chest.

Harlow... fell for me?

I sure as hell don't deserve that.

She takes a deep breath and musters some composure. "Fake. That's what this will continue to be. We agreed at the beginning that I'd be *playing the part-*" Her words come out like venom. "-of the doting girlfriend, so I'll keep doing that. We said we would take a walk around

The Battery tomorrow morning, and that's exactly what we'll do. I'll meet you here at nine. In the meantime, I'm going to go. There's no reason for me to be here right now."

She turns on her heel and stalks out the door, sniffling as she goes.

And I know I just let the one true chance I had at finding real, unconditional happiness just walk out the door.

Forty

Harlow

Please tell me neither of you are busy right now

Yeah, I'm not doing anything

Me either

Is everything okay, Lo?

No

I'm hurting, and I'm sad, and I just really need my best friends right now

Should we grab Ella, too?

No, she's happy with planning her wedding

Let her be happy

And she has no idea about anything that's going on right now since I never told her

Rory

So this must involve Knox

Lucia

I'll bring a bottle of wine then

Rory

And I'll bring the Ben & Jerry's

Keep your chin up, Lo

Luc and I will help you with whatever's got you down

Lucia

We'll see you shortly, ojitos

I tell Lucia and Rory everything as soon as they walk in my door. We're now all cuddled together, sitting on the floor in front of my sofa, open containers of ice cream in front of us.

"He's fucking joking, right?" Lucia says.

"Oh, I wish," I say with a sigh. "But he made it clear that it's all fake to him, that we're only playing our parts."

"He can say whatever the fuck he wants," Rory says, clearly pissed, "but he's lying through his goddamn teeth."

"He's not lying. He explicitly told me he wasn't lying."

"Because someone who's lying about their feelings certainly wouldn't lie about lying about them," Lucia chides.

"Not helping, Luc." I go to wipe a tear from my eye, but the tears are gone. There aren't any left in me right now. "Even if he is lying, it makes no difference. It's abundantly clear after tonight that he wants nothing more than what we already had going. I'm just the stupid girl who fell for a man who was never going to want her in return."

Lucia cups my cheek with her hand. "Harlow Pierce, I will not sit here and let you talk about yourself like this. There are only two possibilities I see here: Knox is a great liar who can deny his feelings for somebody to her face out of fear, or he's the biggest dumbass in history to let a catch like you walk away."

"Both can be true," Rory adds. "He's stupid for letting you walk away if he doesn't have feelings because he *should* have feelings for you—you're fucking amazing. But he's even more stupid if he lets you walk away when he *does* have feelings."

"Well, men are idiots," Lucia says.

"Says the woman who's had no luck with online dating," I mutter.

"I'm ignoring that because you're hurting, Lo." She and Rory pull me in tighter. "But no matter what he meant or didn't mean tonight, you still got yourself back through all of this. Harlow is back to her normal, bubbly, pre-Derek self, and Knox is a large part of why."

I let out a breath. "Yeah, he is. Hearing the things you, Rory, and Ella have been telling me hit different when they came from someone who had no obligation to say them. That was the push I needed to finally disregard everything Derek ever put into my head."

"We're beyond grateful for that aspect of this," Rory says. "We really missed this Harlow."

"I missed me, too."

"Are you going to be okay, Lo?" Lucia asks, looking at me in concern.

I nod my head. "I'll be okay. I'm strong, and he's not the first man to hurt me like this. It's painful, but it's not the end of the world. I'll be able to move on eventually."

"So, I gotta know," Rory says with some pep, clearly trying to lighten the mood. "Did you walk off in a blaze of glory? Did you tell him to kiss your ass and that he can find another fake girlfriend because you deserve more than that?"

For the first time since Knox got back after practice today, I laugh. "It would've been so much cooler if I had, wouldn't it? Alas, I did no such thing. I told him I'd keep playing my part until the season ends."

"Is that really a good idea?" Lucia asks. "You could get hurt all over again."

"Call me a masochist then," I say with a shrug. "We made an agreement, and I'm not one to break my word. I told him he'd have me through the season, so through the season he shall have me. We won't be close like we were, but we can make it believable in public."

"You're tough, Pierce," Rory says, playfully punching my shoulder. "I'll give you that. I don't think I could do that if I were in your shoes."

It's not like I *want* to do it, but I feel like I *have* to.

Knox and I set up this fake dating arrangement well before we really got to know each other. I'm going to keep the promise I made then because nothing that happened after should impact an agreement already made.

I might hate this, and it might really fucking hurt to see him again, but I've got to do this.

For my pride, if nothing else.

Once Lucia and Rory leave, I slip into one of my favorite oversized T-shirts and settle on the couch, hoping to just fall asleep while watching some TV so I can forget everything about this horrible fucking day.

But as soon as my back hits the cushions, my phone rings. I sigh and grab it, finding Cole's name on the screen.

"Hey, Cole," I say softly when I answer, bringing the phone up to my ear.

"Lo, you okay?" he asks, concerned. "You seem upset."

"I, uh... I'm fine."

Cole sighs. "Don't lie to me, Harlow. I'm your brother; I know when you're upset."

"Goddamn you," I breathe, trying to prevent myself from becoming emotional again. "It's Knox," I admit. "We talked after practice today, and, uh..."

"Lo, did he hurt you?"

"Physically? No. Emotionally? Yeah... I told him this didn't feel fake to me anymore, and he lied to my face, telling me that none of this was real."

"What the fuck?" Cole yells. "I'll kick his ass."

"You will do no such thing, Cole," I say in exasperation. "I don't want you to do that."

"You're hurting, Lo."

"I am," I say, sighing. "But I'll be okay. It stings right now, but I'm resilient. I'm still going to fake the relationship for our agreement, though."

Cole takes a deep breath, and I can all but hear him pinching his brow, trying to control himself. "I'm pissed at him right now."

"Please stop," I reply, hand to my head. "Nothing that happened between Knox and me should impact your friendship. I don't want it to."

I hear him sigh. "I know. But you're my sister."

"I'm also a grown woman," I chide. "I made this decision myself, knowing that our arrangement wasn't real. I want what happened tonight to stay between Knox and me, no one else. I don't want this to fracture our friend group. We're both going to be okay once we process this."

"Fair enough," Cole breathes. "To change the topic, do you have anything planned for the blog right now?"

"I'm still looking for my next interview. I haven't found one yet, though."

"Don't make me regret this," Cole replies while I imagine he's shaking his head. "I'll do it. Interview me before the game tomorrow."

"I'd ask if you're sure, but at the risk of you changing your mind, I'm running with it and saying I'll see you tomorrow."

"Yeah, that's the sister I always remembered," he chuckles before we say our goodbyes and hang up.

Tonight still sucks, but at least I'll be able to distract myself now as I prepare for Cole's interview.

Maybe I can spend a couple hours not thinking about Knox.

Forty-One

Harlow

AFTER THE SHITTIEST NIGHT of sleep I've had in ages, I wake up Friday morning ready to just go back to bed. But seeing as I have to be with Knox and walk around The Battery, I have to get my ass up and plaster a fake ass smile on my face.

I decided to get ready for the day before I go meet him, so I don my favorite jeans and my *Pierce* Stars jersey because Knox isn't getting the pleasure of seeing me in his, and I pull my hair up into a high pony. After applying a light bit of makeup to make it seem like my eyes aren't all puffy from crying, I take the subway into Battery Park City to get this over with.

I only have to knock on Knox's door once before he swings it open, looking far more disheveled than I expected. The bags under his eyes tell me he didn't get much sleep, either.

"Harlow..." he says softly. "It's good to see you."

I roll that off. "Let's just go, Knox. This doesn't need to last longer than necessary."

His shoulders slump at the words. Was he expecting me to just move on from everything he said yesterday? Or was he expecting my feelings to be enough for me to welcome him back with open arms?

Either way, seeing him is already a stab in the chest. I can't be around him too long, or the last fragile pieces of my heart will shatter entirely.

Knox and I are silent as we leave his building and walk to The Battery. We've been here multiple times since we first came all those months ago. That was the day that started me on this journey, falling heart-first for somebody who claims he doesn't see me the same way.

The Battery always felt so warm and inviting. Now, it's just cold and unappealing. The overcast sky doesn't help, but I don't think it has much impact on how I'm feeling right now.

As we walk through the entrance to the park, he severs the silence between us. "So, uh... how was your night, Harlow?"

"Shitty," I scoff. "Thanks for asking."

He sighs. "I'm sorry about how yesterday went down, Lo... Harlow."

"I know you are, Knox," I admit. "But I'm going to need time to get through all of this on my own."

"I just don't think I can take the thought of you hating me..." he says softly.

I close my eyes and let out a deep breath. "I don't hate you. I don't think I could ever hate you. But I'm hurt, and it's going to take time to get past everything. It'll take time before I can call you a friend again."

He just nods his head in understanding, staring at the sidewalk under his feet.

We continue walking through the park, slowly traipsing along in the silence that consumes us again. For a Friday morning, the park is full of more people milling about than usual.

As we approach a group gathered around the base of a tree, I reach out and take Knox's hand in mine. He gives me a look that's a mix of surprise, understanding, and gratitude.

"I did say I'd play the part," I say, my voice low. "This is all just part of the act."

"Right..."

For someone who was adamant yesterday that this entire arrangement is fake, he sure seems downtrodden over the whole ordeal. Even before Knox regularly smiled, he never looked like *this*.

He just seems so... sad.

And I hate that.

But I'm sad, too.

He can hate the situation we're in now, but he should also realize we're here because of the lies he's telling himself, no matter how much he's hurting from it, too.

As we continued our stroll, I noticed someone with a camera on the trail ahead of us.

And I take a deep breath.

"Knox, there's someone with a camera."

"Oh," he says. "Just smile as we walk by then."

"No," I say, stopping and facing him. "We're selling this, re-member?"

And before I have time to tell myself this is a terrible idea, I stand on my tiptoes, bringing my lips to his and kissing him.

It's not a long kiss, just a tiny peck.

But all the hurt from yesterday bubbles up again when all I feel are the butterflies taking flight.

No matter what, I won't be able to move on while we're keep-ing up this charade.

The rest of this season is going to be hell...

"Yeah," Cole says from the clubhouse sofa. The guys went out to the field early, so Cole snuck me in to do our interview here. "Getting to play for the Stars has been a dream. Having grown up in Brooklyn, I grew up a Stars fan, and I always said I'd play for the Stars one day. This is a lifelong dream realized."

"You did always say that," I reply with a laugh. "How often did you tell Mom and Dad that you only wanted to play on the Stars?"

"Hey, I meant that. Those three years I spent between the Kansas Huskers and their farm system just solidified it."

"Didn't enjoy the cornfields, huh?" I tease, finally smiling today. I spent some time with Rory and Sage to try to recuperate after seeing Knox before I met up with Cole. It helped a bit but didn't cheer me up as much as I'd hoped.

"You know damn well how much I hated that," Cole says, crossing his arms. "I'm pretty sure I called you every fucking day to ask you to find a way to get me out of there."

"Yes, your sister—with absolutely no pull in the MLB—was definitely going to be the one to get you out of Kansas."

"Thankfully, Kansas eventually wanted me out of Kansas, and now here I am where I always wanted to be." He laughs and smiles. "It's all I ever dreamed of."

"I do enjoy having you here as well, Cole. I missed you when you were in Kansas."

"Because I'm the best big brother anybody could ever ask for," he says with pride and a smirk.

"Such a fucking ego," I say, pushing Cole's shoulder. "You're the only brother I know, so I have nothing to compare it to."

The clubhouse door swings open, and Knox walks in. When he spots us, he quickly turns around and leaves. I can't hide the hurt on my face.

"You okay, Lo?" Cole asks seriously.

"Yeah," I say, dusting myself off, though there's nothing there. "I'm fine."

"It's okay if you aren't, you know." He smiles at me reassuringly.

"I know," I reply. "Lucia and Rory came over last night, and I got all of that out of my system with them. Today still sucks, but it's not nearly as shitty as yesterday." I take a deep breath. "Okay, back to the interview. I need to finish before you decide to tell me you changed your mind."

Cole laughs heartily. "Better be quick then."

I roll my eyes before looking through my list of questions and topics. "What's your favorite part of getting to play for the Stars? You said it was always your dream, so what do you love most about seeing that dream unfold?"

"Familiarity and family mostly," Cole replies. "I know the city well since I spent my life here. And getting to stay around you, Mom, and Dad is awesome. I've always been family-oriented, so I didn't like being away from you all. Aside from those, the Stars are an incredible organization with love for their players. You feel cared for and know they aren't just looking for a buck off of you. That's always nice."

"Fun questions now!" I chime. "My favorite part."

"Lay 'em on me, Lo."

"What's your favorite color?"

"Blue. Just a standard blue."

"Favorite food?"

"Chicken wings. Only really eat them during the offseason, but I still love them."

"Last but not least, favorite Taylor Swift song?"

"Hmm..." Cole rubs his chin, thinking. "What has everyone else said to that?"

"Lane said *The Very First Night*." I decide to tease him a little bit. "But Rory said her favorite is *Dress.*"

"Oh," is all he can say before an unmistakable blush flushes across his cheeks. "Interesting." He coughs now, trying to regain his composure. "My favorite would be... *Shake It Off,* I guess. That one's fun."

"So stereotypical," I say as I laugh. "Going for one of her biggest singles."

"I don't know her entire discography front to back like you do, Lo."

Cole and I dissolve into conversation now, enjoying a bit of downtime before he needs to warm up for the game. And it actually gets my mind off Knox for at least a bit.

This hurts, and it's going to hurt for a while.

But I'm strong.

I'm going to be okay.

I know I am.

Forty-Two

Knox

THE PAST THREE NIGHTS, I've slept like absolute fucking shit.

I know Harlow and I are in this situation right now because of me, but that doesn't change the fact that I'm completely torn up over it. The last thing I wanted to do was hurt her.

But that's exactly what I did.

I hurt her so much that the only times I've seen her since were Friday morning when we walked around The Battery and right now as we're grabbing coffee on Sunday.

This is another prearranged outing that Harlow said we shouldn't cancel. That we still need to "keep up appearances."

Fuck appearances.

I just want to go back to the way things were.

I just fucking *miss her*.

I don't care about the sex. I don't care about the goddamn fake dating arrangement.

I just want her to really talk to me again.

The closest I can get to that right now is her making small talk during our public outings. She's not speaking to me outside of that.

I hate this so fucking much, but I have no one to blame but myself for this situation.

"So," Harlow says, grabbing my attention. "Ready for your start tonight?"

"Not at all," I admit. My pitching has only looked *worse* since Thursday's practice. The game tonight is going to be a shitshow with me on the mound. "But I'll get through it."

"I'm sure you'll do great." She smiles at me, but it's forced. "You always do."

"Yeah," I say, letting out a breath. "I guess we'll see."

She seems somewhat reassured by my words. Like she wants to believe that, no matter what's going on between us, this won't affect my performance on the field.

But the words are meaningless. I don't believe them.

With everything running through my head, I don't have any chance of pitching a good game tonight. My only hope is that the team bats well enough tonight to make sure that doesn't matter.

"Have you, uh... been okay, Knox?" Harlow asks, voice wavering.

"Not really," I admit. "This whole situation just fucking sucks."

"Yeah," she says so softly it's almost a whisper.

Every thread of sanity I have left snaps with how broken she seems. How did I go from this uncaring, grumpy asshole at the beginning of this season to where I am now?

I'm sitting across from the only woman in seven years that I've felt a connection with, caring about how this is all affecting her.

And hating myself for being the one to make her feel this way.

I sigh. "Harlow," I say lowly. "Do you think we'll ever get back to what we were?"

She looks down at the coffee in front of her. "I don't know," she whispers. "I hope so. But I'll need time away from you to do that, so as far as for the rest of this season, I can't see it happening."

"Right," I say back, the word almost getting caught in my throat.

The only way to get us back to what we were eventually is to give her space from me. Space she can't get when the world believes she's dating me.

To get what I want, the only thing I can do is let her go.

"Harlow," I mutter before she stops me.

"People are walking down the street. Pretend you're happy to be around me." She leans her head on her hand, elbow propped on the table, smiling softly as she tries to be convincing. I mirror what she does.

"I am happy to be around you, Harlow."

"Oh."

"What I wanted to say, though, is that you can't move on from everything as long as you're around me." I take a deep breath. "Let's just end this thing. I want you to be happy, and if that will get you there, I think that's what we should do."

"Knox," she sighs. "I'm not trying to end this. I gave you my word, and I don't break my word."

"You're miserable right now."

"I'm not miserable," she says. "I'm hurting, yes, but I'm not miserable. I told you I don't hate you. I genuinely enjoy your company, and I hope once we have some time apart when the season ends, we can really be friends again."

"We can get back to that sooner if you walk away now."

"Do you want me to walk away?" Harlow's lip quivers as she asks.

"*God*, not at all." The absolute *last* thing I want is for her to walk away. It's even more clear now that I lied to her when I said none of this was real because I still want her around. I *always* want her around. And I don't know what the fuck I'm going to do about it. "But I want to be fair to you, and I know how shitty it must feel to be around me right now."

"And what about your Axis contract?" she asks. "That's still on the line. That's the whole damn reason we started this."

"Fuck the contract." I scrub a hand over my face. "It doesn't matter anymore."

"It does matter," she says, reaching out to touch me before she decides against it. "We wouldn't be here if it weren't for that. You deserve to get that contract."

"I'm not sure I'm deserving of anything," I admit.

"Knox, don't let this get to you too much. I'm okay, I promise. Stop worrying about how I'm feeling and keep performing on the field. I'll keep up my part of the deal, and you're getting that contract."

I gave her an out, and she's still staying with me to do this. I can see the hurt on her face every time she sees me, yet she still shows up, determined to play the part she said she would.

I knew she'd do that. She's strong and capable. There was no chance she wouldn't continue our arrangement because she's not a quitter.

So did I give Harlow an out for her sake... *or mine?*

Coffee with Harlow could have been better.

Could've been worse, too, but still could've been better.

I hate that talking to her in public is all I can get right now, but I'm grateful to get *something*. As difficult as this is, I'm thankful I still have her in my life.

Skip has us do our usual warmup routine around two before our Sunday night game. I might feel stretched and loose right now, but I don't know how that will actually translate into the game tonight. I'm hoping for a better outing than I've been anticipating.

I'm walking through the hall on my way back to the clubhouse to relax before we need to get ready for the game. But I find Simon leaning against the wall, waiting for me.

"Simon," I say as I walk up to him, a little less than gracious at the unexpected visit.

"I see we're back to grumpy," Simon says.

Pinching my brow, I say, "The last few days have been shit. Excuse me for not rolling out the red carpet for you."

"Everything is going well. The media is still thrilled about all the pictures of you and Harlow together, which means Axis is very happy. That contract is all but a done deal at this point."

"Fuck the contract," I snap. "I don't know if it's worth my goddamn sanity."

Simon crosses his arms. "What's going on? When you emailed me last week, you said everything was still going very well."

"It was until a few days ago. Now things have all but fallen apart."

"You were just photographed getting coffee together this morning."

"We're still going through with what we agreed upon. But it's all so fake now."

Simon eyes me suspiciously. "It was always fake, Knox. This whole arrangement is fake."

"Yeah," I say with a derisive laugh. "Then you picked somebody who *actually* makes me happy. I haven't been faking that. All the smiles, the laughs you see in the tabloids? That's all real, Simon."

"That's great, then. Maybe my client will stop being so difficult to work with."

I roll my eyes. "It's not fucking great. Hence the past few days being utter shit." I lower my voice now. "I wasn't supposed to start actually feeling something for her."

"Jesus Christ," Simon mutters, rubbing a hand over his forehead. "Look, I don't care what you do with your personal life as long as it doesn't impact your career. So we need to get this situated as soon as possible. Why is this an issue for you?"

"You, of all people, should know that. The entire situation with Emily was traumatic. Now, the first time I let myself get close to someone since that happened, the same feelings came. Harlow has barely spoken to me in days now because all the hurt that's bubbling up is making me pull away."

"So stop pulling away then," he says dismissively, like it's easy.

"Ah, thank you," I say sarcastically. "Hadn't thought of that."

"Look, Knox. There's nothing I can really tell you other than get your shit together and get that damn contract. If you start slipping now, everything you've been working toward disappears."

"Great pep talk, Helbin."

"I don't do pep. I do blunt. So, to put it bluntly: get your head out of your ass and figure out your damn problem. Postseason starts in two and a half months, and you need to keep up the image you've created this season."

With that, Simon adjusts his perfectly tailored suit jacket. He walks down the hall, leaving me with the reminder that, at the end of it all, this is just a business transaction to him.

Harlow and I both have our hearts on the line, and it's up to us to protect them.

Forty-Three

Knox

Well, I was right.

I fucking suck tonight.

I throw twenty-eight pitches in the first inning and give up two runs. The second inning isn't faring much better since I've already thrown another twenty pitches. There are two outs right now, but there are runners on second and third.

Tonight might be better if I could see Harlow... but she's not here. This is the first game of the entire season that she's missed. Seeing me on the mound and not just in the dugout must've been too much for her right now.

God, I fucked up.

I rear up for another pitch, throwing a fastball to the Phoenix Sandstorms' right fielder. To my dismay, he hits the ball just out of Josh's reach, flying right over his glove and bouncing into the outfield. Ayala nabs it and tosses it to Pena on second, who is then able to tag him out. But the damage was already done since both of the baserunners ran home, meaning the score now sits at 4-0.

The atmosphere is bleak when we get back into the dugout. I take a spot on the bench in the back and pull my baseball cap over my face. We're losing this game, and it's all because I can't get my head in it.

I feel someone take the spot next to me on the bench. "You look like shit tonight, Fort."

"Surprised you're even talking to me, Cole."

He takes a deep breath. "Harlow specifically told me not to let what happened affect anything. Spent the past several days reminding myself not to hate you."

"Not sure I deserve that."

Cole sighs. "She's okay, Knox. She's resilient. Stop worrying so much." He lowers his tone now. "It's okay if you didn't have the same ideas about what was happening between you two."

I stay silent, unsure if I can get myself to tell Cole that I do actually have feelings for his sister. It doesn't seem like I need to, though.

"Knox..." Cole starts. "You do feel something for her, don't you?"

I let out a breath. "Yeah... It's just... complicated."

"Define complicated."

"We'll talk after the game. This isn't the place for it."

Cole nods understandingly before Skip shouts, "Pierce, you're on deck!"

"Gotta run." Cole stands before turning around with a serious look. "You're going to be okay, too, you know."

As soon as Cole leaves the dugout, Josh makes his way back in after striking out.

And just like Cole, he comes to sit directly beside me.

"Man, you're not looking too hot tonight."

"Does everyone need to point that out?" I sigh. "I get it; I'm pitching like shit today."

"Not trying to rag on you, man," Josh says. "Just making an observation. You okay?"

All my frustrations come rushing to the surface, boiling over until I'm ready to spill it all. Fuck keeping this from Josh any longer. Maybe he can give me some outside insight.

"I'm very much not okay." I look down the dugout to make sure Josh and I are alone over here. I don't need everyone's prying ears listening in. "So, Harlow and I aren't actually dating."

"What?" he shouts before lowering his voice. "What do you mean you're not dating? You two are on the front of every fucking tabloid. Ella and I have seen you two getting cozy with each other for months."

"It's fake," I admit. "My agent, Simon, set it up. I'm up for a contract with Axis and need a better image. Dating Harlow has helped me with that."

"Fuck, man." Josh rubs a hand over his face. "I had no idea. You seemed to be head over heels for her." He thinks for a moment. "That's why you weren't sleeping together."

"Well..." I sigh, rubbing the back of my neck.

"Oh my God," he says with a laugh. "You did end up sleeping with her, didn't you?"

"Yeah... then things started feeling real, and I panicked."

"Why would you panic over that?"

"Because I have a... history. I don't want to get into the details, not here. But because of that, I pulled away, and now Harlow will barely speak to me."

"She's not faking it, is she?" Josh asks.

I sigh. "No, she told me she wasn't anymore. Now, we're back to putting on a fucking show, and I fucking hate it. I can't sleep. I'm pitching like shit because I can't get it together. I can't get her out of my goddamn mind."

"Oh man," Josh says with a knowing chuckle. "You aren't faking it either."

"Not according to what I told her," I say, my head falling back to hit the wall of the dugout.

"You're an absolute dumbass," he says, shaking his head. "No wonder she won't talk to you."

"Yeah, I fucked up. I know that." I take a deep breath. "I'm in so fucking deep, too, because I... I miss her. I really just fucking miss her."

"Shit, it's not just not fake to you. You sound like you're in love with her."

"Love? No. I don't know exactly what it is, but it isn't love."

"Of course, it isn't," Josh says with a smirk. "Get your ass up, though. Lane and Cole just struck out, so you're back on the mound."

"Fuck me," I groan.

We all jog back onto the field, and I'm hoping I can pull myself together for the third inning.

My hopes are dashed when my first two pitches of the inning end with two runners on base.

I'm beyond pissed at myself for letting this affect me so much. My career rides on me taking charge on the mound. A poor outing like this happens to every pitcher at one point or another, but it always stings when you can't help your team during a game.

But the game can't get any worse from here, right?

So, for my next pitch, I give it my all. My knuckleballs are all over the place tonight, so I settle on another fastball. I get into position and bring my arm back to toss the pitch.

But my form must have been off.

I must have moved too suddenly.

As soon as that pitch is out of my hand, I feel a pop in my left thigh. And I'm down.

The play continues since it's still a live ball, but it ends soon when Phoenix's catcher hits a three-run home run off the fastball that just took me to the ground. Cole and Martin are at my side as soon as the play ends.

"Knox, what happened?" Cole asks, bending down to reach me on the ground.

I groan in pain. "I felt a, uh... pop in my thigh. Hamstring, probably."

"Fuck, that's not good," Martin says before signaling to Skip that we need help.

"Yeah," I say through gritted teeth. "Hurts like a motherfucker right now. *Fuck*."

"Knox, what's going on?" I hear a female voice running toward me. Lucia.

One of Harlow's best friends.

Just perfect.

"Hamstring," Cole tells her.

"Shit," she mutters as Dr. Coltrain, our team physician, leans down beside her. I see Lane and Josh standing behind him, worried expressions on their faces.

"How is it feeling now, Knox?" Dr. Coltrain asks.

"Like... shit," I manage.

"Okay," he says. "Just nod or shake your head to answer my questions. Did you feel a popping or tearing sensation before you went down?"

I nod.

"Do you feel any swelling starting?"

I nod again.

"Are you able to fully extend your leg?"

I try to do so, fighting through the pain, but I can only extend it so far. So, I shake my head.

"It certainly sounds like a hamstring strain. The medics are coming over now with the cart. You need to get to the hospital."

When the cart arrives, Lucia and Dr. Coltrain help the medic load me, and then I'm heading off the field. I do a slight wave to let the fans know I'm okay, but I don't think they'll really be missing me on the mound tonight. I've already given up seven runs.

Now I'm off to the hospital. Depending on the severity of the injury, there's a potential need for surgery.

A surgery would take me out for the rest of the season.

I really fucking hope that doesn't happen.

If I'm recovering from surgery, I won't be making any media appearances or going out in public.

If I'm not going to be seen anywhere, there's no reason for a fake relationship since I'll be out of the public eye.

And if there's no fake relationship, there's no reason for Harlow to stick around.

And that might actually break me.

Forty-Four

Harlow

I try watching the game tonight.

I really do.

I can't watch beyond two innings, though. Knox doesn't have outings like this, giving up four runs on fifty-nine pitches. The only thing that changed recently for him to perform like this is what happened between us.

The change over the past few days has him so distracted he can't focus on pitching.

I need space to think for myself, but doing that clearly has a negative impact on him.

So, can I make it through the season without pulling so far away? Can I do that without falling apart in the process?

I don't know, but I think I've got to try for the sake of the team.

After I turn the game off, I put in my earbuds to drown out my thoughts to some upbeat pop music.

It's not working.

It's almost nine, and I'm still stuck on how poorly Knox performed tonight. No matter what's happening between us, I don't want it to distract him from his own game. He's built a career on performing well under pressure and stress, and tonight's performance is so out of character for him.

And almost no one really knows why it's happening.

But I do.

I know.

It's because of *me*.

The song I'm listening to is cut off by an incoming call.

Lucia's calling.

Why is Lucia calling? She's at the game, and she's technically working.

I answer the call, and Lucia's voice now rings through my earbuds.

"Harlow! Were you not watching the game?" she shouts from the other end. I don't know where she is right now, but it sure as hell doesn't sound like the baseball field.

"I turned it off after the second inning," I admit. "Knox looked like shit, and it was hard to watch because I know that's my fault."

"Well, that tells me why you weren't blowing up my phone a little while ago."

"What do you mean, Luc? What happened?"

"Knox went down on one of his pitches in the third. I'm at the hospital with him right now so I could fill his providers in on what happened."

"What?!" I yell. "Knox was injured tonight?"

"Yeah. It was a non-contact injury, though. He thinks it's his hamstring, so he's getting imaging done to determine the severity. Then they'll figure out if he needs surgery. Dr. Coltrain said he will be out for a bit regardless, though."

"Fuck," I say, standing up from my tiny couch. Fatigue is a perfect way to end up with a hamstring strain as a pitcher. And the way Knox has looked like shit the past few days, I've no doubt he hasn't been sleeping. "What hospital?"

"Bellevue," Lucia says.

"You're in Kips Bay," I say back as I slip on my shoes. "I'll be there in ten minutes."

The emergency room is overrun with fans trying to garner any information they can about Knox Spencer's injury. He's been here about an hour, and everyone already figured out where he was, completely flooding the waiting room.

I'll never understand those fans. The ones who show up after an injury or medical emergency, trying to get a glimpse of their favorite athlete in one of their worst moments. Compassion should be shown, and privacy should be given. Unfortunately, that's not what happens when you're in the public eye.

Because of that, there's security posted at the doors leading into the hospital from the waiting room.

"Hi," I say, somewhat intimidated by the large man in front of me with a stoic expression on his face. "I'm here for Knox Spencer."

The security guard scoffs. "You and everyone else. You have no reason to be here. Unless you're staff or have a medical emergency, you're not getting through."

"Excuse me," I say, slightly offended. "I'm not just a random fan. I'm Harlow Pierce."

"And?" he says, giving me a dismissive look.

"And I'm-" I start before the doors behind the security guard open, and Lucia walks through.

"There you are, Harlow! Come with me—I'll take you back." Lucia grabs my hand to lead me through before the security guard stops her.

"You can't just take her back there," he says. "Fans aren't allowed back."

"She's not just a fan," Lucia says, clearly annoyed. "This is Harlow Pierce, Knox Spencer's girlfriend."

"I was trying to tell you that," I add softly.

"I need to verify that first," he says gruffly.

"Fine," Lucia replies as she takes out her phone. "Watch me as I Google 'Knox Spencer and girlfriend' so you can see all the articles about them."

Lucia hits search, and article after article about us appears on her screen, showing my face on every one of them. The security guard finally relents. "Alright, go on then."

"Thank you," I say quickly as Lucia leads me through the doors.

Lucia walks me through the halls of the emergency room until we stop right outside room eighteen. There's another security guard posted by the doors.

"Hi," Lucia says to the man. "This is Harlow, Knox's girlfriend. Your colleague has already verified that."

"Very well," he says, stepping aside to let us through.

We walk into the room, and I see him lying on the bed in a hospital gown. "Hey, Knox," I say weakly, but it's enough to grab his attention. "How's your leg doing?"

"Freckles!" he says loudly with a bright smile. "I was hoping you'd come!"

"Um, yeah... here I am," I say warily before turning to Lucia. "Is he okay?"

She laughs. "He's hopped up on Morphine. He's a bit loopy right now."

"Morphine?" I say questioningly. "Morphine is a banned substance."

"Babe, he's not playing for at least a few weeks. Based on the on-field evaluation, he's got either a grade two or grade three strain. He's going to need time to recover. They're already talking about moving him to the 15-day IL. That Morphine won't even be in his system by the time he's back."

"Oh."

Shit. He's actually going to miss time from this. An injury he sustained likely because his focus wasn't on the game but on *me*.

"Lo," Lucia says, putting an arm around my shoulder and leaning closer. "Don't blame yourself for this. I know you, and I know how you're going to internalize this. Sure, this could have happened because he was distracted, but that's on him, not you. He's a professional; he needs to be able to separate his personal life from his professional one."

I take a deep breath. I know she's right. It'll be easier said than done, but I can at least help him in the meantime.

I walk over and sit on the edge of Knox's bed, and he smiles at me softly. "How are you feeling, Slick?"

"I don't feel much right now," he says. "They gave me some of the good medicine." That pulls a laugh from me, and he smiles brighter now. "Hey, I got you to laugh again."

I smile softly. "Yeah, I guess you did."

"Maybe I didn't fuck everything up completely." He reaches his hand down and places it on top of mine. "I've missed you, Harlow. The past few days have been awful."

"So awful you forgot how to throw a good pitch?"

He smiles and laughs. "You giving me shit must be a good sign."

"Yeah," I admit. As painful as it is to be near him right now, it hurts worse to be away. "I've missed you, too."

His smile is soft and sweet, tender and caring. A smile so captivating that I forget we have an audience until Lucia clears her throat behind me.

"Well," I say, quickly shooting up from where I'm sitting. "I'm glad you're doing okay. Seems like it could have been worse."

"We don't know the severity yet, though," Lucia says. "We're still waiting on the imaging results."

"Right," I reply. "I guess we don't actually know how he's doing yet."

"You're here," Knox chimes. "I'm already doing better." A blush creeps across my cheeks as Lucia covers her mouth to hide her smile.

The door opens behind us, and one of the ER physicians walks in. "Hi, I'm Dr. Agarwal." He walks over beside Knox. "I have your imaging results, but I'd like to talk to you alone first."

"We'll be in the hall," Lucia says.

We walk into the hall and close the door behind us as Dr. Agarwal pulls the curtain shut. I lean back against the glass as Lucia stands in front of me with a smile on her face.

"What's with the smile, Luc?" I ask.

"Lo, that man can say whatever he wants, but he's down so fucking bad for you."

"No, he isn't," I say quietly, barely above a whisper. "Knox all but told me he isn't."

Lucia's look is more reassuring now. "I know what he said. But a man that doesn't actually feel anything won't sit there and tell you he misses you, even if he is hopped up on Morphine."

"He said he missed me before, though. That didn't seem to matter."

"When was that?" she asks.

"When he was away for the All-Star Game. He told me on the phone Monday night, and I also kinda just let everyone believe I didn't see him until Wednesday morning. That's not completely true." Lucia raises her eyebrow in curiosity. "It's technically true but a bit misleading. Knox actually came directly to my apartment when he got off the plane. It was three A.M., and he was pounding on my door. He told me he couldn't wait any longer to see me."

"Interesting," Lucia replies with a smirk. "Those aren't the actions of a man who says everything is fake, Lo."

"Please don't, Luc," I plead. "Please don't give me hope where there isn't any."

"I won't keep going on about it," she says. "But I think there's more to the situation than what Knox has led everyone to believe. Like maybe something happened, and it's making him freak out about everything."

And it clicks.

Emily.

It's Emily.

He and I have talked about her at length over the past few months, and I know he hasn't gotten close to any woman since her. He hasn't let anyone in.

Until me.

He let me in. I'm the first person he's let in since he went through everything with Emily, almost ending his career before it even began.

I can't believe I didn't see it before.

Of course, he's panicking.

I'll still be cautious, and I won't hold out too much hope, but there may be a chance for something.

A chance for *us*.

The door to Knox's room opens again, and Dr. Agarwal walks out. "Mr. Spencer says you're both welcome to return now."

We follow Dr. Agarwal into the room, and Lucia and I take the seats to the side of his bed. He looks stressed now, so I'm guessing the imaging wasn't great.

"So," Dr. Agarwal says, grabbing our attention. "Just like everyone suspected, it's indeed a hamstring injury—a grade two hamstring strain, more specifically. Because the hamstring didn't tear completely, surgery won't be necessary. It did tear significantly, though—more than half of it has torn. Because of that, he needs to take it easy for a while. I want him on crutches for at least a few days, and then he'll start physical therapy."

Dr. Agarwal takes a seat on the edge of the bed. "Even with all of that treatment, he will need to stay off of his leg as much as possible. The RICE method is the recommended treatment—rest, ice, compression, and elevation." He turns his attention to Knox now. "Now, Mr. Spencer, do you live alone?"

"I do," Knox replies, voice strained.

"Then I recommend having somebody stay with you for the next few weeks. You're going to need help if you're to stay off your leg so you can recover."

"I doubt anyone will want to stay and care for me, Doc."

"I will," I say softly before I can think better of it. "I mean, I am your girlfriend, after all. I'm happy to help you out."

Knox gives me a sweet smile as Lucia eyes me curiously. Dr. Agarwal says, "Well, there you go. It seems like you already have that worked out. We'll set you up with a pair of crutches and a referral for physical therapy. In the meantime, I'll get your discharge paperwork started. We'll send you home with instructions that your girlfriend can help you go over in the morning once the Morphine wears off."

Dr. Agarwal wishes Knox well and leaves the room. And the weight of what I just did falls on my shoulders.

I just agreed to stay with Knox to help him recover.

I'm going to be *living* with him for at least the next couple of weeks.

Living with the man who sent my heart into a freefall.

What could possibly go wrong?

Forty-Five

Knox

THE MORPHINE MUST HAVE worn off overnight because I wake up in a lot of pain Monday morning.

I've had some grade one hamstring strains, which have always healed in a few days. Grade two is significantly more painful.

"Fuck," I say more loudly than intended as I sit myself up in the bed. I desperately want pain medication right now, and I need to go find some. I need my crutches, though, because I want to follow the doctor's orders to get back on the field as soon as possible.

My crutches must have fallen overnight because they aren't leaning against my nightstand anymore—they're lying on the floor about three feet away from my bed. "Goddammit," I mutter, figuring out how I'm going to hobble over to them without hurting myself more.

But then I hear footsteps in the hallway leading to my bedroom door.

Harlow.

In my haze this morning, I completely forgot she agreed to stay with me and help me while I recover.

The woman that has me going out of my fucking mind is going to be living with me for at least the next couple of weeks.

I can't decide if that's going to be good or bad. But I don't have time to consider that now when Harlow lightly knocks on the door a few times before slowly pushing it open. "I thought I heard you," she says, walking into the room with a glass of water and what looks to be a bottle of over-the-counter medication. "How are you feeling?"

"I'm in a lot of pain, honestly," I admit. "I've had hamstring injuries before, but this is the worst one."

"Yeah, your MRI showed a pretty bad tear." She sets the water and pill bottle on my nightstand. "Take some of the Aleve; it'll help with your pain and swelling."

She bends down to pick up my crutches as I ask, "Where did you get the medicine? I usually only have Advil lying around."

"I ran to the pharmacy before you woke up," Harlow says, leaning my crutches against my bed as I take two pills from the bottle. "Naproxen lasts longer and always provides me better pain relief. Figured it would work well for you, too. I also grabbed a shower chair while I was out because you need to stay off your leg, and, no offense, I'm not bathing you."

I laugh heartily. "Fair enough," I say with a smile. "Thank you, Harlow. I appreciate you helping."

"It's no problem, Knox." She smiles, and it seems less forced than it's been lately. "I don't mind helping you out."

"I know, but..." I sigh. "I know how hard it is for you to be around me right now, so I just want you to know it means a lot that you're still willing to help."

"You're welcome," she replies softly. "Here, let's get you up. You can do whatever you need to do for your morning routine, and then you can come out to the kitchen. I grabbed some coffee and bagels for breakfast."

I wince as she helps me up and hands me my crutches. "Thanks. I'll be out to the kitchen shortly."

"Oh, uh... no problem," she says awkwardly. "I'll just, uh... see you out there."

"Why are you being weird right now?" I ask before looking down and realizing I'm literally just in a pair of boxer briefs. Ah, that'll do it. "Sorry," I mutter quickly. "I, uh... didn't think about that. Don't worry, I'll throw some clothing on before I come out."

"Right, of course," Harlow quickly replies. "I'll see you in a few minutes."

She starts walking to the door, so I use my crutches to propel me to my bathroom to brush my teeth and clean my face. When I get to the bathroom doorway, I can feel eyes on me. I peer back over my shoulder as Harlow quickly turns her head and walks out of the room.

Was she just checking me out?

I guess she could've been assessing the giant fucking bruise on the back of my left thigh, but I don't like that option as much.

I'm choosing to believe she was checking me out. That she was staring at my ass covered in black fabric, just like she used to do.

And even if only in my mind, it feels good to have her looking at me again.

<<<<<<<<<<<<<<<<<<<<<<<<<<<<<<<<<<<

"So," Cole says as he walks into the living room to join me where I'm sitting with my leg elevated on the couch. "How awkward has this morning been so far?"

I sigh. "It could be worse," I admit. "She's still not talking to me a lot. Breakfast was pretty quiet."

"She'll come around again," Cole says, sitting on the chair.

"I'm not going to rush her or make her uncomfortable. If not talking to me helps her, then so be it. It'd be selfish of me to want her to just ignore everything that happened."

"Damn," Cole laughs. "I told you Harlow would brighten you up. Now you're here making sure you do everything possible to keep her comfortable when she's here to do that for *you*."

"I know. But I'm half-expecting her to not come back from her apartment at all. That she'll get there and be like, 'Fuck this, and fuck him.' I wouldn't really blame her."

Cole shakes his head. "You're great at some self-loathing. God-damn, man. Lighten up."

"I'll try," I say before taking a deep breath.

"To change the subject, how do you feel about being put on the IL?"

"Don't love it, that's for fucking sure. But I don't need surgery, so thankfully, I can just go on the 15-day IL. I'm going to be antsy tonight, though. It'll be weird watching the game from home and not the dugout."

"Knowing Harlow," Cole says, "she'll try to keep your mind off missing the game. I don't know what she'll do for that, but I can confidently say it won't be sex with you being in the doghouse and all."

"Dick," I say, tossing my hat at him. "I'm in a fuck ton of pain. Sex is the furthest thing from my mind right now." He throws my hat back. "Also, don't be so fucking weird. That's still your sister."

"Yeah, I regretted it as soon as I said it," he replies with an uneasy laugh. "I'm still used to being able to tease you, Lane, and Josh about this shit. I keep forgetting that it's my sister you're... involved with now."

I wince. "I don't think you can really say we're involved now."

"You're both still playing it up for the tabloids, right?" I nod. "Then you're involved in some way."

"I guess," I sigh. "I just wish she would talk to me normally again. I just..." I trail off.

Cole smiles. "You miss her."

"I think that's pretty fucking obvious," I groan.

"Man, you gotta figure your shit out," Cole says. "You're in fucking deep, and you don't even realize it, do you?"

"Oh, I realize it," I admit. "Why do you think I've been such a mess the past few days?"

"I get that," he says with a sigh.

"You actually do, don't you?"

"Don't be coy, Knox. I already know you figured it out."

"In my defense, I think everyone but Rory has figured it out."

Cole groans. "I fucking know."

"It's not like you could do anything about it anyway," I tell him. "She's Skip's daughter. He'd probably bench you just for looking at her."

"Yeah," he sighs. "Probably for the best that she hasn't figured it out then."

"Keep ogling her, and I'm sure she will figure it out," I smirk.

"Fuck off," Cole replies, tossing a throw pillow at me.

I toss the pillow back at him. "Don't you have a game tonight, Pierce?"

"Yes, but my sister asked me to stay with you until she gets back with her things. You're a fall risk, you know."

I want to hate that Harlow had Cole come over to watch me like a child while she was gone. But I don't hate it all.

Honestly, it's really sweet that she's so concerned she's calling in reinforcements to keep me from being left alone.

In fact, I think I feel my heart fall a little bit further.

The past few days have driven me stir-crazy.

I've always been a homebody, but I want the option to easily get out. These goddamn crutches make getting around tricky as it is, so I'm sure as hell not trying to navigate Manhattan when I can't fucking walk.

Harlow and I have been watching the Stars' games, more so just in the background. She needs to see what's going on for *Starred and Fast*. She's doing a lot of writing while she's here, but just like Cole said, she's distracting me when the games are on.

We talk. We play mindless games on our phones. We even play "Guess the name of this celebrity." She is evidently very into pop culture, so she already knows them all. Me? I think I get two correct.

But all of that is precisely what I need. I'm able to rest and elevate my leg, and Harlow makes sure I ice it periodically as well. The pain is starting to get a bit better now. It's easy to forget that I can't easily move from my spot on the couch or that I'm missing another game with my team when I have her beside me to take my mind off things.

We spent days barely speaking before I was injured. Monday was still somewhat awkward as we both adjusted to being around each other after everything that had happened. Now, we're falling back into a more familiar rhythm.

Harlow is talking to me again. And it doesn't feel forced now. It seems like once she got past the unease, she was able to enjoy being around me again.

That's all I could ever ask for right now.

"Alright, Slick," she says from the other end of the couch, turning my attention away from the game playing on the TV. "You're on a desert island and can only have three things with you. What are you picking?"

"Why would I be on a desert island?" I ask incredulously.

"Maybe you were on a plane that went down, and the only safety you could find was an uninhabited island in the middle of the ocean."

"Does the volleyball already come as my best friend, or do I need to include that as an item?"

Harlow laughs heartily. "We'll say he's already there, washed up with you from the plane's wreckage."

I can't help but smile. This might be one of her most random attempts to take my mind off the game, but I'm enjoying the spontaneity. "What would I take?" I ask myself aloud. "Baseball cap. I definitely want a baseball cap."

"Of course you do, Mr. Baseball Star." Her smile is bright and teasing.

"Mr. Baseball Star," I say with a smirk. "I like that. I might have to formally request you start using that from now on."

"Not a fucking chance," she laughs. "Come on. You still need two items to join you, your volleyball best friend, and your baseball cap."

"A pocketknife. That would probably be really useful. Now for item number three..." I think for a moment. "Can I take a person?"

"I don't see why not."

"Perfect. I'm taking you with me then."

Harlow blushes as she sweetly smiles at me. "Why do you want to take me with you?"

"Because," I say, "I don't think a volleyball will be enough company to keep me sane, so I need a person with me. I think you're the only person I could ever tolerate enough to take with me."

"I'm tolerable?" she says, hand on her chest. "Knox Spencer, that might be the nicest thing you've ever said to *anyone*."

"You think you're funny, don't you?" I laugh. "That's the exact same thing you said to me when we started this whole fake dating thing."

"It is," she says. "Nice memory, Spencer."

"Harlow..." I start before trailing off.

"Yes?" she asks.

I let out a breath. "You know you're more than tolerable to me now, right?"

She smiles at me. "I know, Knox. I never questioned that."

"Good," I say, smiling back at her. "I don't want you to question how important you are to me."

Her smile falls a little bit. I can see that she wants to believe me, but my telling her last week that this is all fake to me makes it hard. I can understand that. It sucks, but I understand.

I'll just have to help her see that I mean it.

To change the subject back, I ask her, "You gotta tell me what you're bringing to a desert island with you, Freckles."

"Ooh, okay," she says, finger tapping her chin as she thinks. "I'm gonna take a page from your book and say a pocketknife. I want a water purifier thing since you can't drink ocean water; I'll need something to take the salt out. And if I'm bringing a person like you did, I'm definitely bringing a man. I'm a woman; I have needs." I have to choke down a laugh. "Cole's my brother, and Josh is engaged, so I'm nixing both of them. So I'd probably have to go with Lane. He'll do."

"Lane, huh?" I ask, cocking an eyebrow.

"Why not? He's fun to be around. We'd probably have some interesting conversations."

"You know," I say, "I'm glad you're still more than willing to tease me."

"You'd probably be concerned if I didn't."

"I'd *definitely* be concerned if you didn't."

We both smile and laugh, and things start to feel more like they did—the times when we just genuinely enjoyed each other's company without the expectation of anything more.

Taking me by surprise, Harlow slides her foot down the couch cushions, bringing it just in front of the pillows propping up my left leg. Her foot falls down to the side, brushing her skin against mine where it rests.

"Knox..." she says softly.

"Yeah?"

Her gaze meets mine, those ocean eyes drawing me in and taking me prisoner. "Why do you like my freckles so much?"

"Where is that coming from?" I ask.

"I'm just curious. You know about Derek and how he felt about them. Why do you feel differently than he did?"

"Are you still uncomfortable with them, Lo?" That slips, but I don't correct myself this time. Harlow's sweet smile tells me I don't need to.

"I'm not, actually," she admits. "I loved them before Derek, and now I'm finally loving them again after Derek. And that's because of you. Well, sort of, at least. You helped me see that I didn't need to hide them from anyone."

"I'm happy to hear that. I really am." Her smile is so bright it's almost blinding, but I just take it all in. I've missed being the one to put a smile on her face. "To answer your question, though, I think the freckles are very pretty. They just make you... you."

"Thank you. That's very sweet."

"I do mean that, Harlow."

"I know."

God, I was such a fucking idiot last week.

I can't believe I ever claimed this to be fake when I'm falling so goddamn hard for this woman right here.

Now, we're back on the path that might enable me to do something about it.

Forty-Six

Knox

In the two weeks after my injury, I was released from my crutches and started physical therapy. I'm able to tolerate more and more activity again, but Harlow is still making sure I rest and elevate my leg as well.

Harlow is the greatest blessing during this. It would be easy for me to slip back into my self-loathing tendencies, but she's with me, brightening everything up. It's hard not to be optimistic when the poster child for happiness is prancing around your penthouse.

Any awkwardness and tension between us has all but dissipated. We talk frequently now, both deep conversations and completely meaningless ones. They're all just as interesting because I hang on to every word she says.

Am I in deep?

Yeah, deeper than I ever fucking realized.

I knew before that I loved spending time with Harlow, but having her around twenty-four/seven for the past two weeks has shown me how much.

My recovery is going really well so far, and I may be able to return to the baseball field in another week or two. And since she's only staying with me while I recover, I'm not as thrilled about that as I should be. I can't wait to return to the field, but I also don't want Harlow to leave.

Bit of a catch-22, honestly.

I finally convinced her that I was well enough to be alone for a few hours so she could grab dinner with the girls. The Stars had an early afternoon game today, so they're free, and she should be seeing people other than just me and my physical therapist right now.

I spend the time while she's away relaxing and elevating my leg.

Okay, that's partially true.

I am elevating my leg, but there is no relaxation. I'm currently just sitting here, wondering what Harlow's talking about with Lucia, Rory, and Ella. Is she talking about me? If she is, is she saying good things?

I guess that's where I am now, so consumed by someone that I had a temporarily fraught relationship with that I can't focus on anything other than what she might be saying about me.

God, I sound pathetic.

But the strangest part is that I don't even hate it.

I can't remember ever being this fucking *happy* before. I'll take the pathetic feelings if it means I'm actually enjoying my life, not just getting by.

The sound of my door opening grabs my attention, and my eyes remain fixed on that spot as Harlow walks inside.

"Hey, Knox," she says sweetly. "I brought something back for you."

"Consider my curiosity piqued," I say, slowly getting off of the couch. "What do you have there, Harlow?"

I limp my way into the kitchen to find a white box on the marble countertop. "Open up the box and see," she says brightly.

I pull the lid of the box back and peer at the dessert sitting inside. "Chocolate cheesecake?" I ask.

"Mhmm. I stopped by your favorite diner on my way back and grabbed it. Thought you might enjoy something sweet since the past couple of weeks have been pretty shitty to you."

"It's probably not been as shitty as you think," I say with a soft smile. "I've had some pretty good company."

Her blush is unmistakable. Even after everything, my words still mean enough for her to believe them.

"It's not been too bad from my end either," she says.

I slide myself carefully onto the counter as Harlow grabs two forks and joins me. Taking one fork from her, I say, "Thank you for this, Lo."

"I know how much you want to get back on the field, so I just wanted to help you find a bright spot in this shitty situation." Her words are so genuine, laced with sincerity.

"Harlow," I say, catching her eyes with mine. "*You* are the bright spot in all of this. I'll take the cheesecake, but it doesn't hold a candle to you."

"Oh," she says softly, blushing again. "I'm glad I can brighten things up for you then."

The air is charged, coursing with the electricity flowing between us. All I want right now is to kiss her, but I shouldn't. We're just getting back to normal. I can't take us backward again.

In an effort to prevent myself from doing something foolish, I shove my fork into the cheesecake and bring a bite to her lips.

"*Mmmm...*" she moans.

This may not have been my wisest decision because now I'm thinking of the times she made similar sounds.

Okay, think of something disgusting to take your mind off Harlow's moaning.

Moldy sandwiches.

Dirty diapers.

Naked grandmas.

I wince. That did the trick.

"You alright, Knox?" Harlow asks, eyeing me curiously.

"Oh... yeah," I reply uneasily, not wanting to divulge both the sinful and the disgusting thoughts running through my head right now. "I'm totally good."

"Whatever you say, Slick," she smirks.

"What's that face for, Freckles? You don't believe me, do you?"

"Not at all," she laughs. "You were staring off into space when you suddenly looked repulsed. You were thinking about something."

"Believe me," I say. "You don't want to know."

"Fine," she relents. "What did you get up to while I was out?"

"I sat on the couch and elevated my leg," I say. "I live a fascinating life, you see."

"Thrilling," she replies with a smile. "But your leg is doing so much better. How's the bruising?"

"It's fading. Still there, but my thigh is finally no longer black and blue, so I'm considering it a win."

She laughs, the sweet sound echoing off the walls of my kitchen. "A win is a win."

A win is definitely a win, and Harlow enjoying my presence again is the biggest win of all. "Definitely," I say as I finally stick my fork in the cheesecake and take a bite for myself. "Fuck, this is good."

"It's chocolate cheesecake," she says in a 'no shit' tone. "Of course, it's good."

"So, you like chocolate cheesecake in addition to French toast, onion rings, and pad see ew. I'll add it to my mental list."

Harlow looks at me in surprise. "You're keeping track of the foods I enjoy?"

"I keep track of everything you do, Lo," I admit. "You're very captivating, you know."

"No, I didn't know that." The look on her face is so sweet and sincere. "I appreciate that."

"You really like sweet words, don't you?"

"Words of Affirmation is my love language," she shrugs. "Words go a long way for me. That's why I would take everything Derek said to heart."

I look at her, confused. "What do you mean that's your love language?"

"Of course, you don't know the love languages," she says, shaking her head. "There are five love languages—Words of Affirmation, Acts of Service, Quality Time, Receiving Gifts, and Physical Touch. Words build me up, so my love language is Words of Affirmation."

I never thought I'd find myself interested in something like this. I previously would have said this was pointless. But it seems to bring her joy, and that brings me joy.

I grab my phone and pull up the list Harlow is referencing. After reviewing the different types, I say, "I'm definitely Acts of Service then. Someone doing something small has always meant a lot to me."

"Like bringing home a chocolate cheesecake."

"*Especially* if they bring home a chocolate cheesecake."

"Lucky me then."

"Not as lucky as me, Harlow."

My response is involuntary, but I mean it all the same. I feel so damn lucky to have her sitting beside me right now. She knows everything about me, and here she still is.

I've already let her in. What harm would there be in letting her get even closer?

One step at a time, though.

"So," I say, severing the silence. "Any recent articles on your ?"

"Just stats and game recaps right now," she replies. "I posted my interview with Cole a couple weeks ago, and I haven't had a chance to interview anyone else since I've been helping you."

"Who do you want to interview?"

"I don't know," she says. "I haven't given it much thought since I've been busy."

Before I can really think about it, I say, "Interview me then."

Harlow looks at me incredulously. "You want me to interview you, the man notorious for sharing *nothing* with any form of media?"

"Why not?" I say, shrugging my shoulders. "I trust you."

"Thank you for trusting me then, Knox."

She looks at me now with endless affection, and I can feel my heart swell.

I'm falling headfirst without a safety net, but I've never felt more at ease in my life.

"You know," she says, "when this season started, I told Lucia my goal was to get you to do an interview for my blog by the end of the season."

"Seriously?" I say with a chuckle.

"Scout's honor," Harlow replies. "That's why I came up to talk to you after the season opener. I wanted to be friendlier with you so you'd know you could trust me. I didn't want you to think I was just another tabloid."

"That's what set off this whole chain of events, Lo."

"What do you mean?"

"Simon saw you talking to me after that game, and that was right after he told me I need a better image to get the Axis contract. He saw us together, so he devised this whole scheme. That conversation is how you became my fake girlfriend."

She throws her head back and laughs. "Really? One of the only times I talked to you, and Simon already started scheming."

"I'm glad he was there to see it," I say.

"Because now that Axis contract is all but certain, huh?" She looks at me with certainty.

"I keep forgetting about the damn contract," I laugh. "I'm glad he was there because *now I know you*. You're way better than a contract, Harlow."

"But the whole reason we did this is for your contract, Knox," she says, surprised.

"Fuck the contract. If I ever had to choose, I'd pick you every time, Harlow. *Every damn time.*"

She stares at me, breathless, with her signature blush crossing her cheeks. "I'm really glad I know you, too."

The light in her eyes helps me forget about everything that's happened.

There's no Emily in the back of my mind.

There's no fear or uncertainty about what could be.

There's no lying to myself, saying this is fake when it's the most *real* thing I've ever felt.

Harlow is my reality.

And reality seems much brighter now.

"So, Freckles. What questions you got for me?"

Forty-Seven

Knox

Harlow sits across from me on the couch, computer perched on her lap. "How do you handle the fame? You have the lowest ERA of any starting pitcher in the league, bringing you a lot of notoriety."

"I'm pretty sure I can't handle the fame at all," I reply with a low laugh. "I'm pretty well-known for trying to *avoid* any of the fame that comes with this. I've never been one to seek out the limelight, so being thrust into it was never something I dreamed of. Honestly, it's more of a nightmare, but I think I'm finally getting a better handle on approaching it."

"What's changed in your approach then? You've been known as Fort Knox for years—why the sudden change?"

"As if you don't know," I smile.

Harlow sighs. "Of course, I know, but I don't think I can put 'I'm faking a relationship thanks to my agent, and because of that, I have to pretend to be happy.' That won't be well-received."

I laugh heartily. "No, I suppose it wouldn't. But just so you know, I'm not pretending to be happy, Lo." She meets my gaze. "None of that is fake."

She takes a deep breath. "But you said-"

"I know what I said," I sigh. "I'd love to forget I ever said it, but I can't. But let's not focus on that right now. I want to finish this interview for you."

"Right," she says warily. "So, why the sudden change?"

"The change is thanks to something I don't think anyone expected before this season—my girlfriend, who just so happens to be *you*. You made me this way."

"You're talking to my readers, not to me. Tell *them* how you ended up where you are now."

"Okay then, my girlfriend, Harlow, is the brightest and happiest person I've ever known. Even the most stoic and grumpy of people—yes, I do mean myself—can't help but soak that all in. Her optimism is contagious, and that's already having an impact on the field this season. Her brother is my teammate, Cole, so she's somewhat familiar with what our lives look like. Because of that, she's been able to help me navigate the increased fame. I couldn't do any of this without her."

She looks at me nervously. "That should help sell it. The man who never spoke before has quite a way with words."

"I would hope that sells it," I say, leaning back against the sofa. "It's all true." I face her now. "I couldn't do this without you. You have no idea how grateful I am for you."

"I think I'm starting to," she says with a soft and sincere smile. "Thank you, Knox."

"You don't need to thank me, Lo. I know how much words mean to you."

"It's not an act of service," Harlow says, "but I'm pretty good with words, too." She reaches her hand out and rests it on my arm. "You're very special to me, Knox. I hope you know that."

"I do."

There's tension in the air. That itself isn't unusual, but for the longest time, that tension was sexual. It was us trying to deny our physical desires.

This feels different.

This is starting to feel like... something I don't think I'm ready to say, even in my own head.

But I'm not afraid.

And I think that means that this is *right*.

"Anyway," she says quickly. "There are just a few more questions, the fun ones I ask everyone. What's your favorite color?"

"I've always liked green," I say.

"Like your eyes," she replies with a smile, and I smile in return.

"Yeah, I guess so. Maybe I should say blue."

"You flirting with me, Slick?"

I smile even brighter. We're back to our usual banter. God, I missed this. "I flirt with you every chance I get, Freckles."

"Lucky I like that then. What's your favorite food?"

"Burnt pizza."

Harlow picks up the throw pillow beside her and tosses it at me. "You're an ass. I told you my oven is shitty."

"You're violent, Pierce." I laugh as I put the pillow beside me. "Honestly, though, I do love any type of Thai food."

"And the last question—what's your favorite Taylor Swift song?"

"The Way I Loved You."

"You didn't even know any Taylor Swift songs a few months ago. How do you know that one?" Harlow looks at me, curious and skeptical.

"You played it for me on the plane the day after we launched the relationship. When you asked what I was listening to, I told you to put on Taylor Swift because you mentioned she was your favorite artist. You played your favorite album. I've listened to the rest of her discography now, but that album is played heavily in my rotation."

"You listen... because of me? Because I like that album?"

"Yeah," I shrug. "Is that so hard to believe?"

"Yeah, a little bit. But it's also really sweet, Knox."

"I figured out your favorite song that day, too."

"How?" she asks. "I didn't tell you my favorite song."

"No, you didn't," I reply. "But I think it's a safe bet to say that your favorite song is probably on your favorite album. And there was one song you played a bit more often than the others." She looks at me curiously now. "You played *Fearless* multiple times during that flight, Lo."

"Uh, yeah…" she blushes. "That's my favorite song."

"It makes sense," I reply, gently pulling Harlow into my lap. "It's a bright and happy song—perfect for you."

She leans her head against my chest. "You've done nothing but surprise me this season."

"In a good way, I hope."

"In the best way."

"I really enjoy you talking to me again, Harlow. I missed this."

"Yeah," she says. "I did, too. I just wanted to protect myself. Turns out, though, it hurts more to stay away from you."

"So don't stay away then."

"As long as you promise you don't try to pull away again."

I smile. "That seems fair."

She does her best to stifle a yawn, but it's unsuccessful. "It's getting late. I think I might head to bed."

"Yeah, good idea," I say before adding, "If you want, you can, uh… sleep beside me. Just sleep. You don't have to, but like I said, I've missed you."

"Oh," she says softly as she slides off of me. "I'm not sure that's a great idea."

"Right, of course," I say, a bit disappointed. "That's more than fair."

I stand from the couch and place a kiss on the top of her head before I walk out of the living room and toward my bedroom.

When I reach my door, I hear Harlow call out, "Good night, Knox."

"Night, Lo. I'll see you in the morning."

Sleep eludes me.

Wow, that sounds dramatic.

But still. I can't sleep.

Thoughts of Harlow have taken up permanent residence in my brain, and they're swirling even stronger tonight.

I've been trying to give her the space she needs, but that's hell for me. Now, she doesn't seem to want any distance between us again.

That's all I've wanted since we went back to "playing our parts," but if I was playing a part after our argument, I did a fucking terrible job. I'm not getting nominated for an Academy Award anytime soon, that's for fucking sure.

All that matters, though, is that Harlow wants to be around me again. And her bringing back an entire cheesecake tonight helps me realize it.

She didn't need to do that. She could have come back without it, and I wouldn't have been any the wiser.

But she didn't.

She brought back that damn cheesecake, and we ate it together before I did that interview for her.

All of this tonight makes things feel like they were before. Before I told her this was fake because I thought opening myself up completely would come back to bite me in the ass like it did with Emily.

But Harlow is not and never will be anyone but Harlow.

She's going to be the sweet, kind, bright soul that she is no matter the circumstance.

Asking her to sleep beside me tonight was probably a leap too far, though. Hopefully, that doesn't push her away again. But once the words were out, it's not like I could take them back.

She only slept beside me for a few weeks, but my bed has felt empty without her ever since. I don't know how she got to me so quickly, but she did. She did, and I actually enjoy every part of it. I miss having her here beside me.

I look at the clock on my nightstand—it's a quarter 'til one, and I still haven't gotten a goddamn wink of sleep tonight.

I rub my eyes out of frustration, hoping to find a way to fall asleep. Nothing is coming to mind.

Then, across the room, I hear my door knob slowly turn before the door opens. I can't help but smile.

"I'm hoping that's you, Freckles, and not somebody coming to murder me in my sleep."

"What makes you so sure I'm not here to do just that?" Harlow asks, gently climbing into the bed beside me as I turn on my side to face her.

"If you're here to kill me, at least the last thing I see will be you."

"Oh my God," she laughs. "When did you become so fucking cheesy?"

"I have no clue," I reply, chuckling. "Wasn't expecting you to come in, though."

I hear her sigh. "I told myself I shouldn't, that it was a bad idea."

"Yet here you are."

"Yet here I am." I can hear the smile in her voice. "I guess I can't really stay away from you."

"You won't hear me complaining about that, Lo. I haven't slept well without you beside me."

"Me too," she admits. "I guess I got used to having somebody next to me."

"Somebody next to you," I ask, "or *me* next to you?"

"I could tease you about it, but we both know it'll end with me saying the same thing: not just somebody, *you.* I only want it to be you beside me."

"I like that answer," I admit. "I really fucking like that answer."

"I had a feeling you would."

My hand finds hers under the covers, and I rest it on hers. "Good night, Harlow."

"Good night, Knox."

For the first time in weeks, I'm going to get a good night's rest.

Forty-Eight

Harlow

Wʜᴀᴛ ᴀ ᴡʜɪʀʟᴡɪɴᴅ ᴛʜᴇ past month has been.

Knox is now four weeks post-injury and should be cleared to return to the field soon—hopefully at his appointment today.

I spent a few days trying to put distance between us, but there was no point in it. None of that mattered when I came here to help him recover. We were together all day, so I couldn't have stayed away if I wanted to.

And the thing is, I *didn't* want to.

I was hurting those few days before Knox's injury, but I missed being with him. It didn't take long for things to return to normal.

We're flirting and having fun together, nothing more than that.

I'm also sleeping in the bed beside him again. I tried to tell myself I shouldn't, but in the battle between my brain and my heart, my heart always wins.

Could that come back and hurt me all over again?

Possibly.

I'm just trying to remain optimistic and enjoy my time with him.

Currently, that means we're still lying in bed, legs tangled together with Knox's arm draped over me.

"We should really get up, you know," I say.

"I'd rather just stay right here," he replies. "I like this view."

"The view of me with sleep hair and teeth that definitely need to be brushed?"

Knox smiles softly and pushes my hair behind my ear. "Yes, that view."

I shake my head. "I look like a mess right now."

"You don't see yourself the way I do then," he assures me. "You're just as beautiful when you wake up as you are after you get ready for the day—maybe even more beautiful, honestly. Your guard is down, and you shine even brighter. You're confident in your skin, and it's sexy as hell, Harlow. Own it."

All I can do is melt. His words sound genuine and sincere. How could I not listen to them?

"Thank you, Knox. That's very sweet."

"Ooh, don't tell the guys then," he says with a smirk. "I have a reputation to uphold here, Lo."

"Can't have that," I laugh. "It would be tragic for everyone to discover that Fort Knox is such a simp."

"A simp?" he asks, trying to decide between laughing or being offended. "I think I'm just being nice."

"Call it whatever you want, Slick. I know the truth."

He rolls on top of me, pinning me beneath him. "You think you know me, Freckles?"

My heart is racing. We last found ourselves in this position a month ago. It's giving me thoughts I've been trying to suppress, but they're all rearing back to the surface. "I do know you."

He leans down closer, almost pressing our bodies together. "What makes you so sure?"

"Because I do," I say, lowering my voice and molding my body against his. He groans when I press his hard length between us. "Knew it."

"Harlow," he says, no humor in his tone. "I might not be fucking you now, but I sure as hell still think about it. I remember the way you feel, the sounds you make." Knox brushes his lips against the outside of my ear. "I'll never forget that."

My breath catches in my throat. What did I think was going to happen here? That I'd press his dick between us, and he would just let it go?

Not a fucking chance.

Now it's eight in the morning, and my fake boyfriend is pressed on top of me. I got myself all fired up, and we can't do a fucking thing about it. I couldn't handle another rejection down the line. It's clear I can't do sex without feelings.

"We, uh..." I stammer. "We should get ready. Your appointment is in a couple hours, and there's going to be traffic."

"Right," Knox replies, peeling his body off mine. "We should, uh... do that. I'll go make some coffee so you can shower."

He and I both pull away from each other and set about our morning routine.

But the air is still charged with the electricity flowing between us and coursing through us.

I'll never be able to fight this off entirely.

I was doomed before I even tried.

I think I'm going to go insane if I have to watch the same damn looping set of videos one more time.

I'm sitting in the waiting room of Dr. Coltrain's office, the Stars' sports medicine physician, waiting for Knox to finish his visit. It's been a month since his injury, and he's itching to return to the field. He's been healing well, so we're hoping he gets released today.

Well, sort of.

I want him to be healthy again, but I won't lie and say that I won't miss all our time together. When he gets back on the field, he won't need me around to help out. I'm dreading that.

To distract myself from those thoughts, I keep watching the goddamn videos that are playing on the TV in this waiting room. I'm going to be an expert on sports medicine by the time he's finished.

The vibration of my phone turns my attention away from the TV. My mom is calling.

I accept the call and bring the phone to my ear. "Hey, Mom. What's up?"

"Just wanted to see how you're doing right now, sweetie," my mom says from the other end of the phone. "You've been so busy helping Knox with his injury over the past month, and you didn't reply to my text this morning."

"Oh," I reply, "I must have forgotten, but I did read it, so thank you, Mom. I appreciate it. I'm doing well, though. Just busy, like you said. I'm in the waiting room right now while Knox is at his visit. He's hopefully getting released to return to the field today."

"Oh, that's wonderful!" she chimes. "You must've been a good nurse to him."

I chuckle. "I mainly had to just make sure he stayed off his leg, Mom. It didn't take a lot of skill."

"And I'm sure he appreciates it all the same." I smile softly because I know she's right. He's made it clear how much he appreciates the help I've given him over the past month. "What are your plans for tonight?"

"Um," I say, "I'm not sure, honestly. That kind of depends on how this appointment goes. He might suit up for the game tonight if he's cleared. I'm not sure if we have anything planned otherwise."

"Ah, I see. Well, your dad wants to video call you when he gets home from work."

"Of course he does," I laugh. "Dad would never forget to call today, would he?"

"Absolutely not," my mom chuckles. "I'll let you go for now. I know you're busy, but hopefully, you'll not be too busy to video chat later. Love you, Harlow."

"I love you, too, Mom. Bye."

As soon as I disconnect the call, Knox struts into the waiting room, looking on top of the world.

"Well, that's a happy look," I say, standing up and walking to him. "Good news, I'm guessing?"

He smiles. "I'm cleared to return tomorrow. Dr. Coltrain wants me to take one more day to get myself ready. He suggested I walk around to loosen my leg up so I'll be ready to pitch tomorrow."

"That's great, Knox!" I wrap my arms around him, and he pulls me in tighter. "I'm happy for you."

I may still have another night before he doesn't need me around anymore. I can make the most of today.

"What do you think about traipsing around midtown right now?" He looks at me, and his eyes meet mine. "We can grab some lunch. Celebrate a little bit."

"Celebrating your release?" I ask curiously.

Knox removes himself from my hug and starts walking toward the door. "Of course," he says with a mischievous look as he peers back at me. "We don't have anything else to celebrate today, do we?"

He walks out of Dr. Coltrain's office now, leaving me wondering.

Does he know?

I don't know how he would, but he's acting a little suspicious right now.

Guess I'll find out.

Forty-Nine

Harlow

"Even with a hamstring injury, I can't keep up with you and your long ass legs," I grumble as I try to catch up with Knox on the crowded Manhattan sidewalks.

"Technically, I'm no longer injured," he smirks as he waits for me to catch up. "My hamstring is good to go again."

"Good. Now don't fuck it up again tomorrow, and try to avoid another damn loss."

"I'll just blame you if I do." His smile is teasing. I kinda want to just wipe it off his face.

"Dick," I say, playfully shoving his shoulder when I finally reach him. "Now, are you finally going to tell me where we're going?"

"Like I've said the past dozen times you've asked, you'll see when we get there."

"I have not asked a dozen times," I huff.

Knox laughs. "Are you saying I'm being dramatic, Harlow? I'm offended."

I want to be annoyed, but I can't find it in me. Knox is happy, smiling, and having fun. Even if we are traversing half of fucking Manhattan, I've never seen him this... joyful.

"Fine," I say as he comes to a stop in front of me. "Are we almost there then?"

He just smirks. "Considering we're here now, we are indeed almost there."

"Oh, thank God. I don't think my legs can take anymore."

"You're out of shape then, Freckles." Knox starts leading me toward the entrance.

"Not all of us are professional athletes, you know."

He places his arm low on my back, steering me through the doors. "I know, Lo. I don't need you to be a professional athlete, though." He leans closer now. "You've always had more than enough energy for me."

"Knox!" I chastise. "Don't be dirty!"

"Who says I'm being dirty?" I give him an unbelieving look as he laughs. "Come on, Lo. I need you to turn around."

"Why?" I ask as I start turning. My question is quickly answered as I see all of my favorite people waiting for us—my parents, Cole, Lucia, Rory, and Ella. "Oh my God!"

His lips brush my ear. "Happy birthday, Harlow." He stands up straighter now. "I'm glad you could all make it. I'm looking forward to getting to know you, Vivian and James."

I turn back around, throwing my arms around his shoulders and standing on my tiptoes. "Thank you, Knox," I say before softly kissing him.

That's, uh... totally just playing the part.

Nothing more.

Once I regain my bearings, I whisper, "I didn't tell you when my birthday was."

"You didn't," Knox smiles. "I had to ask Cole. I knew it was this month but didn't know the day. I asked your brother a couple weeks ago so I could plan this."

"You're full of surprises, Spencer." I look at him in reverence, my heart bursting with his gesture. He didn't know my birthday, so he made it a point to find the day and ask my family and friends out to lunch to celebrate.

I've been wondering what I feel around Knox. It feels somewhat familiar but also foreign.

And I think I just figured out why.

That feeling I've been trying to place?

Love.

It's familiar because I've been in love before.

It's foreign because it's never felt this *strong* before.

I was left heartbroken because those strong feelings I had weren't reciprocated.

At least, that's what he said.

Now, I'm not so sure.

We're getting closer again, back to how we were a couple months ago. This time, though, he knows about my feelings for him. He knows how hurt I was last month when he told me nothing between us was real.

And I know Knox.

I *know* he wouldn't find his way back into my good graces just to turn around and hurt me again.

So, Knox allowing us to get back to where we were tells me that nothing is one-sided. He just needs to process all of that at his own pace.

Me, though?

Seems like I already have it figured out because *I'm desperately in love with Knox Spencer.*

Lunch is perfect.

Fort Knox is nowhere in sight today. He's relaxed and conversational, engaging my parents in chats on the most mundane topics. And Cole does what Cole does best—endlessly tease us when we can't say a damn thing about it. My parents don't know about our arrangement, and with how much they like him today, I don't really want them to find out.

He's completely endearing himself to them. They'll be heartbroken if they find out what's really going on.

Knox wants to keep walking after lunch since Dr. Coltrain recommended he walk today to loosen up before tomorrow's game. The breeze lessens the mid-August heat as we walk along the Hudson River Greenway.

"So," I say. "You haven't pulled another hammy, have you? Star pitcher needs to be ready to go tomorrow."

He howls with laughter. "No, the hammy is still fine. I'm ready to get back on the mound tomorrow."

"I'm excited to watch you tomorrow," I say shyly.

"You know," he says, "Dr. Coltrain *technically* hasn't released me yet. I think I'm going to need a helper for at least another night."

I smile. "You just trying to get me to stay again, Knox?"

"Did it work?" he asks, lips curling into a mischievous smile.

"Yes," I admit. "It did work."

"Good. I still need to give you shit for not telling me when your birthday was. Your boyfriend should not have to find out from your brother."

We stop now, and I turn to face him. "*Fake* boyfriend," I say, wrinkling my nose.

"Semantics," Knox replies, leaning in closer. "I still wish you had told me."

"I wasn't purposefully keeping it from you. It just didn't cross my mind since we were so busy with your recovery. Hell, I forgot until this morning, and I didn't want to tell you the day of."

"Thank God for Cole, then," he smirks. "I wouldn't have been able to get you a gift if I only found out today."

That catches me by surprise. "Why did you get me a gift? You really didn't need to do that."

"Yeah, he told me you'd say that," he laughs. "Lo, I got you a gift because I *wanted* to. Here." Knox reaches into the back pocket of his chino shorts and returns with a small jewelry box that he hands to me.

I flip the lid of the black velvet to find a dainty gold chain with a small gold baseball charm hanging from it. "Knox, this is beautiful."

"If there's one thing I know about you, it's that you love baseball. So much so that you write an entire blog about it."

"You know me well," I smile. I take the necklace out of its box, and he helps me clasp it around my neck, where it hangs just below my collarbone. "How does it look?"

"Perfect." He wraps his arms around the small of my back, hooking his hands together and pulling me against him. *"You* are perfect, Harlow."

In a quick movement, I'm on my tiptoes again, draping my arms around Knox's neck and pressing my mouth against his. I tease my tongue over his bottom lip before he opens it, now stroking his tongue against mine.

My body is on fire, so consumed with need. I can't help but be captivated by everything that he is. Every second spent together just makes me crave him even more.

One more kiss, and we part, now resting our foreheads together.

"Thank you, Knox. I love the necklace."

He smiles at me sweetly. "Happy birthday, Lo."

The outside world ceases to exist. Right now, it's just us in this moment.

Knox and I are the only people around on the busy greenway. I'm sure there are fans milling about snapping pictures that will be plastered all over the internet later, but I pay no mind, so engrossed in us in our own little bubble.

A bubble that pops when a man walks up behind me.

"Knox, I wasn't expecting to see you here."

"Simon," Knox says as I turn around now, leaning my back against his chest as he places his hands on my hips. "I didn't think I'd run into you here."

"Out for a walk with my wife," Simon says, gesturing to the woman beside him. "Knox, this is Helen."

Knox reaches out to shake her hand. "It's nice to meet you, Helen." He gestures to me now. "This is my girlfriend, Harlow. We're out for her birthday today."

"Ah, well, happy birthday then, Harlow."

"Thank you," I say softly. "We just grabbed lunch with my family after his appointment this morning."

"Yes," Simon says more enthusiastically, "How did the appointment go? Axis is looking forward to seeing you back on the field."

"They'll catch me tomorrow then," Knox says with a smile. "Dr. Coltrain cleared me as of Wednesday. I talked to Skip earlier, and I'm starting tomorrow night's game."

"Wonderful, wonderful. I look forward to it. This season has seen such a change for you." Simon shoots us both a knowing look.

Knox wraps his arms around my waist now. "I guess all I needed was a reason to be happy." I blush as he kisses the top of my head.

"You two are just so sweet together," Helen pipes in. "I've probably said that to Simon too often this season."

"Thank you," I reply sweetly. "I've really enjoyed our time together so far." I glance up at Knox now. "He's my favorite person."

The look on his face is disbelief.

Disbelief that I could say something like that and mean it after everything that's happened.

But it's true.

No matter how hard I try to pull away, he always manages to pull me right back in. Even though we constantly see each other, I can't spend enough time with him.

Because he truly is my favorite person.

"Well," Simon says, "we'll let you go about your day. Good to see you, Harlow. I'll catch you before the game tomorrow, Knox."

Once we say our goodbyes, Simon and Helen continue down the greenway, leaving Knox and me alone.

"That was unexpected," I say as I turn around before looking at him in surprise.

Knox stands before me now with the most genuine smile.

It's the kind of smile that hurts your cheeks.

It crinkles the skin around your eyes.

It lights you up in a way only pure, unadulterated happiness can.

He's happy right now in a way I've never seen him.

"What are you so happy about, Slick?" I ask, unable to contain my curiosity.

"Nothing," he says, shaking his head while keeping the smile plastered on his face. "Nothing at all, Harlow. Come on. Let's walk a little longer and then find a birthday cake for you. Sound good?"

I nod as I match his stride, and we take off down the greenway again.

I don't believe that joy was for nothing.

No, that look matches my own recently.

That was a look of love.

Fifty

Knox

Yesterday was eye-opening for me.

I learned that not only do I care about Harlow, but that I care about her more than I've ever cared about *anyone*.

That helped me realize why I panicked when she asked if I thought this was still fake.

It's because I wasn't ready to face the truth; doing that meant allowing myself to be completely open. I wouldn't have been able to hide anymore, and that scared the shit out of me.

Spending the past month with her reminded me of why I fell for her in the first place.

Past tense because I've fallen so fucking hard for her.

I don't want anyone else.

I just want *her*.

Yesterday, I finally realized what word describes how I'm feeling, and I smiled like a goddamn fool.

I didn't tell her then, but the word is still on the tip of my tongue, waiting to escape at the right moment.

All this means that I'm done denying everything. I'm done pretending this isn't the most real thing I've ever felt with somebody.

I've already let Harlow go once. I won't make the same mistake twice.

"Good morning, baby," I say, walking up behind her and wrapping my arms around her waist. "How'd you sleep?"

She leans into my touch, molding her body against mine. "Great. Your bed is so much more comfortable than mine."

"Are you sure it's the bed? I thought maybe it was me."

She repositions herself, turning around with her body still pressed against mine as she leans back against the kitchen counter. "Maybe it was you."

"What have I told you before about maybe, Harlow?" My voice comes out husky and needy.

I catch her gaze and see a fire burning red hot in her eyes. "That I need to use my words, right?" Her voice is dripping with desire.

It's taking all of my damn willpower to not just bend her over the counter and fuck her again. To hear those moans I've been craving for the past month.

Thank fuck now is when Cole knocks on the door.

"Who's here?" she asks, snapping her attention to the door as I walk over it.

"Cole," I reply. "It's Wednesday morning, Lo."

I open the door, and Cole bursts inside. "Good morning to my two favorite people."

I cock an eyebrow. "I'm one of your two favorite people? I thought your two favorite people would be Lo and Ro-"

"Be quiet, will you?" Cole groans. "Don't finish that sentence."

"You know I know already, right?" She tries to hide her smile. "I'm well aware that you're in love with my best friend."

Cole's eyes go wide. "What?! No, I'm definitely not." He crosses the room to set a bag of food down on the counter, coming to stand by Harlow.

"Oh, please," she says derisively. "You're not that subtle, Cole."

"Goddammit," he mutters, scrubbing his hand over his face. "How did you figure that out, Lo?"

"I'll admit I was oblivious until the All-Star Break. That's when Lucia pointed it out to me, and I finally put the pieces together."

"Fuck." Cole groans before trying to compose himself. "So, Lucia knows, too. Fucking perfect."

"No one is saying anything to her, man," I say as I join them at the counter. "That wouldn't serve a point since Rory's off-limits anyway."

"Which is why my place will be permanently in the friend zone."

"Friends make the best lovers, though," Harlow teases.

"Not if I want to keep my fucking job." Cole sighs. "Enough of this, please. I'd rather not think about that."

"Alright," I say, stepping away from the counter. "I'll let you two be. I'll be in my room if you need anything."

"You're not joining us?" she asks.

"This is a thing between you and your brother. I'm not going to intrude on that. You guys eat, and I'll join you after that."

Harlow flashes me a sweet smile as I walk away.

And *that word* gets a little bit closer to escaping.

"I'll find you before the game," I say as I wrap Harlow in a hug. I hear Cole snickering beside me, but I'm ignoring that for now. "On the field, though. I'm going to do some extra stretches before the game so I can make sure my leg is loosened up."

"Alright." She snuggles her head up against my chest. "I'll talk to you then, Slick."

I press a kiss on her forehead. "See you later, Freckles."

Harlow says her goodbyes to Cole before she walks out the door. She wants to work on her blog before she gets ready for the day, and Cole and I need to get to the field soon anyway.

As I shut the door behind her, I turn around to see Cole with a big ass smirk on his face. "What's that face for, Pierce?"

"Like you don't fucking know." He laughs, and I groan. "Come on, man. When are you going to stop lying to yourself?"

I sigh. "Soon."

"How soon is soon?" Cole asks, eyeing me. "Because I think it's obvious to everyone that you're in lo-"

"I know," I reply, cutting him off. "I know," I say again, smiling this time. "I know I am."

"Damn," Cole remarks. "You actually are."

"Yeah. I finally realized that yesterday. We walked on the greenway after lunch and ran into Simon. Everything just clicked into place then."

"I can confidently say that this isn't how I expected this season to go," he admits. "I did think you'd become friends, but I don't think I ever truly thought you'd be something more."

"Neither did I," I reply honestly. "But I'm glad everything happened the way it did. This is the first time I've actually felt happy in seven damn years."

"And you finally realize that my sister isn't Emily?"

After my injury, I talked to both Cole and Josh about Emily, adding them to the list of Harlow and Lane who know the story. That helped them better understand why things happened the way they did. They could see why I was freaking out.

I didn't open up about that time until Harlow, but now that she and the guys know, it's like a weight was lifted off me. I've kept my feelings about the situation with Emily to myself. Now, I have friends in my corner. I don't have to shoulder all of this alone.

"Yes," I say emphatically. "I know she isn't Emily. I think my head finally got on board with that."

"So, you're going to talk to her when? This whole 'will they, won't they' shit is exhausting."

"Fuck off," I laugh. "But I'm over it, too. I'm going to talk to her tonight."

<<<<<<<<<<<<<<<<<<<<<<<<<<<<<<

Some extra stretching today after practice does wonders. I meet up with Lucia and work to make sure I'm ready to start tonight. It's my first start in a month and the first since I've been injured. The last thing I want is a showing like last time.

Once I suit up for the game, I throw on my Stars baseball cap and head toward the field with the team. As soon as I'm out of the tunnel, I make a beeline straight to the seats I secured for Harlow and her parents tonight, right by the dugout. Cole, Lane, and Josh seem to take note of that, but I pay them no mind.

"Hey there," I say, walking up to the railing she's now standing behind. I smile at her before turning to her parents. "Good to see you again, Vivian and James. Hopefully, I won't disappoint tonight."

"We're just happy to be here, Knox," Vivian says.

"As long as you don't pitch like your last game," James adds, "you shouldn't be a disappointment."

"Dad!" Harlow shouts, turning to him as James and I both laugh. "Please ignore him, Knox," she says in exasperation. "My dad has no filter."

"I see where Cole gets it from," I laugh.

"How's your leg feeling?" she asks, genuine concern in her tone.

"Great," I answer. "The stretches helped today, and I feel good as new. I hope I can pitch a game worth watching today."

"I'm sure you will. You're a fantastic pitcher."

I wrap my arms around her lower back. "With the perfect good luck charm."

Harlow blushes as Cole, Lane, and Josh walk up, unbeknownst to me.

"Ah, there are the lovebirds!" Cole says as he and Lane take spots on either side of me, Josh sliding in beside Cole.

"Here we are," I say with a smile.

"You two are my favorite couple," Lane says, sliding an arm around my shoulder.

"You're both ridiculous," she replies, rolling her eyes while chuckling.

"Honestly," Josh says, "I think you're both lucky Cole is so great about this." Now that Josh knows about the whole fake relationship thing, he's jumping in to torment us, too.

"Yes," I tease. "He sure has been great with my girlfriend being his sister and all."

"I take back what I said," Harlow chimes in. "You're *all* ridiculous."

"And you love it," I whisper.

She smiles brightly. "Maybe I do."

"Maybe?" I ask, cocking my eyebrow.

"Maybe." She bites her bottom lip. She's about to get me all riled up right before my first game back.

"Scholl's waiting for me, so I need to get out there."

"Good luck, Knox. You're going to do great."

I lean in and press a kiss to her lips. There's probably a camera around somewhere, but that's the furthest thing from my mind right now.

Fuck the cameras; I'm doing this for *me*.

"Find me after the game, Lo." I smile at her and push her hair behind her ear. "I need to talk to you."

"Okay." Harlow smiles before softly kissing me again. "Nice base-ball pants, by the way," she whispers against my ear.

"Don't stare too much when I'm walking away," I laugh.

"No promises," she teases. "Now go, your team needs you."

"I'll see you after the game, Lo."

I finally leave the stands and make my way over to Scholl to throw out some practice pitches with the biggest damn smile on my face.

‹‹‹‹‹‹‹‹‹‹‹‹‹‹‹‹‹‹‹‹‹‹‹‹‹‹‹‹‹‹‹

After the game tonight, Skip wants me in the media room, so here I am, sitting in front of numerous reporters with that damn smile still on my face. Josh is also here with us since he hit tonight's walk-off home run.

"Spencer," a female reporter in the second row says. "How are you feeling after your first game since your injury?"

"I feel good," I reply honestly. "My recovery went well, and I felt great on the mound tonight."

"Garro," says a male reporter from the back of the room. "How does it feel being the one to break the Stars' four-game losing streak?"

Josh smiles. "It's nice, I won't lie. It's good to help us get the win, but I would've been just as happy if any of the other guys won the game for us. I always want us to get the W, and I'm happy with whoever can help us get it."

"Spencer again," says a female reporter in the front. "We've seen such a personality shift in you through the season. Can you attribute your stellar numbers this year to that shift?"

"Yeah, I think I can," I reply. "It's obviously not a surprise that I was very closed off before, and I do think some of that showed up on the mound as well. My numbers were still good, but not what they are now. Apparently, happiness can go a long way."

The room laughs. When was the last time I got a room of people to laugh? It feels nice.

Josh pipes in. "We've been trying to tell you that for years, Fort. At least you'll listen to Harlow." That earns another laugh from the room.

"Another one for Spencer," says the same female reporter. "We know Josh is engaged. Any future plans for you and your girlfriend?"

"Let's stick to baseball, please," Skipper says, trying to steer the conversation back.

"It's alright, Skip. I don't mind." I turn back to the reporters. "It's way too early to answer that question. We haven't been together long enough for either of us to have considered that. But never say never, I suppose."

Josh shoots me a disbelieving smile as Skip closes out the questioning and releases us from the media room. As soon as we're in the hall, I take off toward the clubhouse to find Harlow.

I turn the corner and find her in the hall with Lucia, Rory, Cole, Lane, and a sleeping Sage. She's mid-conversation when I come up and grab her from behind, spinning her around as she shrieks before setting her back down.

"What the hell was that?" she says, laughing. The other four are giving me very curious looks.

"Seemed like it would be fun," I say, leaning back against the wall. "I did get you to scream, though, so I'm calling it a win."

"From what I've heard," Rory says maliciously, "you're *great* at getting her to scream."

"Fuck, Rory," Cole moans. "I don't want to hear about that."

"Maybe you just need to make someone scream, Pierce," Rory fires back. "Maybe then you'll be less cranky about it."

God, these two just need to fuck and get it over with. Just don't let Skip find out.

"Yeah, I'm not getting involved in that," Harlow says, turning around to face me. "Good game tonight, Knox. Five innings and no runs. Much better than your last outing."

"I didn't have my good luck charm at my last outing," I say, wrapping my arms around her waist and pulling her in closer, ignoring our friends surrounding us.

"And who's fault was that?" she replies with a smirk.

I smile back. "Don't worry. That won't happen again."

"That so?" She eyes me curiously.

"You're going to be at every game from now on, Lo."

"Big talk, Slick." Harlow leans closer now, standing on her tiptoes to bring her face closer to mine. "Don't forget that you only have me through the season, though."

I chuckle. "Baby, we both know that isn't true."

Her eyes go wide. "What does that mean, Knox?" Unease washes over her. I can see she's trying not to get her hopes up after the last time.

I press my forehead against hers. "That means I'm not letting you go again, Harlow. I'm keeping you."

"How do you plan on keeping me?" she asks, breath hitching in her throat. "What- what are you saying here?"

"I'm going to start by saying I hope you don't have plans for tomorrow night." I push her hair behind her ears, now getting a better view of those ocean eyes that have etched a permanent place in my heart.

"You guys don't have a game, so I'm free."

"Perfect," I say, smiling wide. "I'm taking you on a date tomorrow night, then. A *real* date. Just us, Harlow. No cameras, no show."

Her smile is blinding. "You want to take me on a date?"

"As long as you say yes."

She quickly presses her lips against mine, kissing me softly and tenderly. Pulling back, she says, "I would love that, Knox. *Yes,* I'll go on a date with you."

I kiss her again as I hear Lucia speak. "About fucking time!"

We both laugh. "Seems like our friends are eavesdropping."

"In their defense, we're standing right beside them."

"Alright, Knox," Rory says, grabbing Harlow by the shoulders. "Lucia and I are stealing your girlfriend. I think it's time for a girl's night."

"Yes!" Lucia shouts. "Perfect idea, Ror."

Harlow laughs. "I guess I have plans for tonight now."

"Go have fun, Lo." I kiss her one more time. "I'll see you tomorrow night."

The girls say their goodbyes before they all but usher Harlow out of the hallway, eager for their impromptu girl's night. I have a feeling I'm going to be the main topic of discussion tonight.

"Only took him four and a half months," Lane pipes in, "but he finally made his fucking move."

"I don't think four and a half months is fair," I state. "This wasn't real in the beginning."

Cole claps a hand on my shoulder. "But it's real now."

"Very real." I smile again. I went from a man who never smiled to one who can't stop smiling. But how could I not smile when I think of Harlow, the epitome of sunshine and happiness?

"Just don't hurt her again. We may be friends, but I will kick your ass if I need to."

"I've got four inches and thirty pounds on you, Pierce. You couldn't kick my ass if you tried."

The clubhouse door opens now, and Josh strides out after his shower. "Did I miss the meeting memo?" he asks, gesturing at us crowding around each other. "Is this an intervention or something? Knox's smile is kinda freaking me out."

"Dick," I mutter, shaking my head.

"What's got you all happy right now, Fort?"

I mull it over momentarily, thinking about how to phrase it before I go all in.

"I have a date with my girlfriend tomorrow night."

Fifty-One

Harlow

"So wait," Ella says, glass sloshing as she moves her hand to the side. "You're telling me that this was fake? That you've been keeping it from me *all fucking season?!*"

I'm sitting with the girls in a circle on Rory's floor. She has the biggest apartment of the four of us—having a Hall of Fame baseball player for a dad has its perks—so we're sipping wine in our pajamas as my mind reels.

"Um, yes?" I answer warily. "But it wasn't to exclude you. You're planning a damn wedding, so you were busy, and I didn't want to take you away from that. I also needed to tell as few people as possible to keep this realistic."

"Well, I'm not happy about that, but I'm letting it slide because *ohmygodyouhaveadatetomorrow!*"

I can't help but laugh. "It's so hard to believe this is real."

"Oh, it's real, sweetie," Lucia replies. "I told you from the start that Knox would fall in love with you by the end of the season."

"We don't know that he's in love with me. We just know that he actually asked me on a date."

Rory smirks. "Babe, I've known him for years. I have *never* seen him the way he is around you. He's got it bad for you."

"That makes two of us, then," I say lowly.

"Lo," Lucia asks, an excited look in her eyes. "Are you subtly telling us that *you* are in love with Knox?"

I take a deep breath before saying it for the first time out loud. "Yes," I reply softly. "I'm in love with Knox."

"I fucking knew it!" Rory shouts. "You were so bad at trying to hide it."

"I was even worse with that internally," I laugh. "The past month has been hell in my head."

"So everything is okay between you two now?" Ella asks. "Not that I ever knew anything was wrong in the first place."

"Damn, you're laying it on thick, Ell," I laugh. "Yeah, we're all good. I actually, uh... started sleeping next to him again." Rory cocks an eyebrow at me. "Not like that, Ror. It was just sleeping. But he said he missed having me next to him. I tried to tell myself that was a bad idea, but I wound up next to him anyway."

"Love makes you do crazy things," Rory smiles.

"I hate you guys." I take a sip of my wine. "I can't believe I just admitted it. That's the first time I've said it out loud."

"Are you going to tell Knox?" Ella asks.

"I have no idea," I admit. "He's only just now acknowledging that this isn't fake anymore. I'm not trying to freak him out by telling him I'm in love with him before he's ready for that."

Lucia smiles. "I don't think you'll have to worry about that, Lo." I eye her curiously. "I'm telling you, that man is in love with you. I'd bet my left arm he tells you that."

"Let's not be rash here, Luc. Let's leave all of our appendages attached." She smirks. "I guess we'll just have to see. We need to get through the date before any love confessions come out."

"Speaking of the date," Rory says. "Do you know what you're wearing yet?"

"I have no idea," I admit. "I don't even know what we're doing."

"Girl, text him then!" Ella says excitedly. "How are we supposed to help you plan your outfit if we don't know what you're doing?"

I lift my brow at her. "Why are you helping me plan my outfit?"

"Because," Rory replies, "this is going to be the best damn date of your life, and you need to look stunning. Take Knox's breath away."

"I don't think that's ever really been a problem." I smile. "He's always been very upfront about how he thinks I look."

"God, I just love him for you, Lo." Lucia leans over and hugs me. "I'm glad you started fake dating him. I mean, look where you are now."

Rory leans on my other side and joins the hug. "Happier than I've ever seen you."

"Because Knox is the most amazing man I've ever met," I admit, grinning widely. "It was impossible *not* to fall in love with him."

"So," Lucia says, "text this amazing man and ask him what the hell you two are doing tomorrow."

I laugh as I pull out my phone and send off a text to Knox.

Knox

Well, I think I'm going to keep our plans a surprise

Harlow

Slick

Don't do this to me

Knox

What are you gonna do about it?

Harlow

Beg

Knox

Fuck...

Save the begging for now

I don't want to get all worked up again before I can take you on a proper date

Harlow

Look at you being a gentleman

Knox

Can't promise that's what I'll be tomorrow night

Harlow

Good

Now, can you at least tell me what to wear tomorrow?

Knox

Whatever you want

Harlow

That isn't helpful, Knox

I need specifics

Knox

Dressy casual?

Is that a thing?

Harlow

Yes, that's a thing

And that helps, so thank you

Knox

Glad we have that settled, then

I can't wait to see you tomorrow, Lo

Harlow

I can't wait to see you either

<<<<<<<<<<<<<<<<<<<<<<<<<<<<<<<<<<

I'm not sure I slept a wink last night.

I'm a bundle of nerves and anticipation.

I've spent so much time around Knox that I shouldn't be apprehensive, but I still can't shake the jitters.

What if the date doesn't go well? I've already acknowledged that I'm in love with him—if this goes poorly, my heart will shatter all over again.

Lucia, Rory, and Ella have done what they can to make sure I'm staying optimistic, but for the first time in my life, it's hard. I *really* want tonight to go well, and I'm so afraid I'm going to screw something up.

"What about this dress, Lo?" Lucia asks me, showing me a sundress she pulled from the rack when I wasn't paying attention.

"Luc," I say, trying not to laugh. "When have I ever picked out something bright orange?"

"Hey, I'm just throwing out ideas."

"What about this one then?" Rory asks from behind me.

I turn around to see her holding up an off-white lace dress with a fitted bodice and flowy skirt. "Oh, I love that!"

"That's perfect, Rory!" Ella turns to me now. "Go try it on, Lo!"

I take the dress from Rory and head into the fitting rooms. I slide off what I'm currently wearing and slip into the dress, bringing it up my legs and over my torso. I fan the skirt out so it's hanging correctly before I turn around to look in the mirror... only to find a bare spot on the wall where it used to be.

I slide open the curtain to the fitting room and say, "There's no mirror, so I have no idea how this looks," as I step outside. "Does it look okay?"

"Okay?" Rory scoffs. "You're fucking gorgeous, Lo!"

"Absolutely!" Lucia adds. "Look at the mirror out here."

I step beside them and turn to the side, finally finding my reflection. "Wow," I say softly. "I love this."

This dress is perfect. The off-white color doesn't wash me out, and the cut of the bodice and the thin straps show off all of the freckles that are usually hidden by my T-shirts.

I feel *beautiful*.

"That necklace looks really nice with it, too," Ella says.

"Where did you get the necklace, Lo?" Lucia asks. "I don't remember seeing that before."

"Oh," I smile. "This was my birthday present from Knox. He surprised me with it."

"That's so sweet of him," Ella swoons.

"He's a sweetheart, honestly," I admit. "He's probably the sweetest man I've ever met."

Lucia comes up beside me and throws her arms around my shoulders. "I never, in a million years, would have guessed that Fort Knox is such a nice guy. I assumed he'd be nice in bed, sure, but I didn't know if he would be nice outside of that."

"Well, he's very nice in bed, too," I laugh. "Very, *very* nice."

Rory sighs. "I need to find someone like that. Every man I find is shit in bed."

"What about the man you're totally not crushing on?" Lucia smirks. "How do you think he would be?"

"W-what are you talking about?" A dark blush spreads across Rory's cheeks. "I'm not crushing on anyone."

I walk over and wrap my arms around her. "I'm sure you're not, Ror. But if you were..." I look her in the eyes. "You should probably just go for it, don't you think?"

Lucia stifles a laugh. "I agree with Lo. Nothing should hold you back, right?"

"Hang on," Ell says, holding up her hand. "Rory likes somebody, and I don't know about that *either*? Do you guys tell me anything anymore?!"

"I don't like anyone," Rory says softly. "They're, uh... reading into things."

"So," I say, changing the topic to ease Rory's discomfort. "Do we think this dress will sweep Knox off his feet?"

"Off his feet and right into his bed," Lucia says.

"Let me get through the date before I start trying to get him into bed, Luc," I laugh.

"Fine," she replies. "Now go change. I've got another stop we need to make for you."

Fifty-Two

Harlow

Lucia's other stop?

The lingerie store.

She said I need something hot to surprise Knox for when he decides to ravish me tonight. Her words, not mine.

But I did pick out a cute set: a matching light green mesh bra and thong. Lucia and Rory both tried to talk me into something a bit more risqué, but if tonight goes well, I'll have plenty of time for things like that. Starting off small is the better way to do this.

When I get back to my apartment after we finish shopping, I'm still riddled with anxiety over tonight. I should just be happy, but I can't shake all of my worry. So, to clear my head, I decide to go for a jog.

A jog.

Me, jogging.

Me, someone whose physical activity doesn't exist outside of walking around the stadium.

I circle the neighborhood a few times before giving up. It's not working, and I'm practically out of energy already. I'm dying for a bubble bath to soak in right now and mentally cursing myself for choosing an apartment with only a shower.

During my shower, though, my head finally seems to stop racing. It's like I'm finally realizing that even after everything last month,

Knox still *chose* to ask me on a date. Why am I so worried when it's clear he doesn't honestly believe any of this is fake anymore?

With a calm mind, I get ready for our date. I dry my hair so it settles into my signature waves before fixing my makeup—eyes neutral with a bit of blush pink and that cherry red lipstick Lucia had me wear out for her birthday.

I slip into the off-white lace dress I bought this morning and pair it with nude strappy heels and the baseball necklace I'm still wearing.

I give myself a once-over in my floor-length mirror, and I can't help but smile. I look good. I *feel* good.

And I finally have a good feeling about tonight.

Right as the clock hits seven, I hear a knock at my door. Knox is here precisely when he said he would be.

I pad over to the door and take a deep breath to calm any remaining nerves before swinging it open.

Knox stands before me with an arm behind his back, looking absolutely flawless. His beard is trimmed and even. He's wearing a white short-sleeve linen shirt with the top buttons undone, tucked into a pair of above-the-ankle navy slacks, and finished off with a pair of white sneakers.

God, he looks so *handsome*.

"H-hi," I manage, breathless.

"Harlow," he stammers, stepping into my apartment. "You look… beautiful."

I blush. "Thank you, Knox. You look great, too." He smiles at me as I take notice of his still-hidden arm. "What are you hiding behind your back?"

"Oh," he says in surprise, apparently forgetting he was carrying anything. "I brought something for you."

Here is where, on every first date I've been on, I'm presented with a bouquet of flowers, colorful and fragrant. I always smile and graciously accept even though they're something I'd never want. But when Knox pulls out a bouquet of red roses, I'm left in awe.

They're fake.

He remembered.

"You-" I pause momentarily, trying to collect myself so I don't cry. "You brought me fake flowers, Knox." My voice comes out barely above a whisper.

"I remember what you said, Lo. You don't like flowers, and if you ever get any, you prefer fake ones." He gives me a soft, sweet smile that I just want to kiss off his face.

I clap my hands over the lower half of my face, still trying but failing to keep it together. "I only told you that once."

He looks at me sheepishly. "I remember everything you tell me, Harlow. I took a mental note of that when you told me and kept it in my back pocket. Right now, I'm happy I did."

The tears welling in my eyes finally spill over. For so long, I dated men who wouldn't put in much effort. I told myself that was normal. But here Knox is remembering something I told him once months ago.

He put in the effort I told myself no one ever would.

He cared.

I leap forward and wrap my arms around his neck, bringing his mouth to mine and kissing him between sobs.

"Thank you," I say when we part, pressing my forehead against his. "These are absolutely perfect."

"If this is how the date is starting, I'm ready to see how the rest of the night will go," Knox says.

I smile at him, happy and content. "So am I."

He reaches out and takes my hand. "Shall we then?"

When we leave my apartment, Knox walks me down to his car before opening the door and helping me inside. He's done that before, but it feels so different, so much *better* knowing that it isn't for the cameras this time.

He holds my hand the entire drive back to his penthouse in Battery Park City, shooting me sweet smiles amid some light conversation.

Knox is so relaxed tonight. I was so anxious about this date earlier, but he isn't nervous at all. He's getting what he finally acknowledged he wants—*me*.

I tease him a bit when we pull into his parking garage. "Little soon to be taking me back to your place, don't you think?" I say with a sly smile.

"Ah, you think you're funny," Knox grins in return. "Our date is not at my place, but it is in this building."

I look at him, confused. "Your building is nothing but apartments, though. How could we have a date here?"

"Don't worry, Lo." He takes my hand, still entwined with his, and kisses it. "I've got it all planned out."

He exits the car then and walks around to open my door, grabbing my hand again as I step out. Now, hand in hand, he leads me inside, and we head to the building lobby.

"Hi, Stephen," Knox says as we approach the concierge desk. An apartment building with concierge service. My budget could never afford something like that.

"Mr. Spencer!" Stephen drawls. "I have the key card ready for you right here."

Knox reaches out and takes a card from Stephen's hand. "Thank you, Stephen. I appreciate this."

Stephen waves us off as Knox and I walk over to the elevator. We step inside, and instead of pressing the button for the top floor, he hits the button for the roof and scans the key card.

"I guess it's not much of a surprise now," he says, rubbing the back of his neck, "but we're heading up to the roof. I want tonight to be just us—no cameras, no fans. This was the only way I could think of to make that happen on such short notice."

I lean back against him as we continue our ascent. "This is perfect. I honestly love this idea."

"Thank God," he says, letting out a breath as I turn around to face him. "I've been worried about this all damn day. Cole told me to stop overthinking it, but I really want tonight to be nice."

I wrap my arms around his waist. "You talked to my brother about your plans?"

Knox runs a hand through his hair—his nervous tic—and sighs. "Yeah, I didn't want to do something you wouldn't like."

"Have you not learned how easy it is to please me, Slick?" I chuckle.

His smile turns mischievous as he says, "I like to think I learned that well."

I instinctively blush. "Uh... yeah... but that's not what I meant."

Knox kisses the top of my head as the elevator dings and the doors slide open. Across the way from us, there's a red-checked picnic blanket with a bottle of champagne, two glasses, and what appears to be an assortment of sushi.

"This looks lovely," I say as we step off the elevator and walk over to the picnic blanket.

"I picked the spot and set the blanket up before I came to get you. Stephen procured the sushi and champagne and brought them up right before we arrived."

"Procured?" I shoot him a curious look.

He rolls his eyes. "Come on, I'm trying here."

Knox and I both laugh as we sit on the blanket, him directly across from me, our knees brushing. "For someone who didn't get close to anyone, you sure know how to plan something romantic."

"Romantic, huh?" he asks, popping the champagne and filling our glasses.

I take my glass from him. "Very romantic. We're fifty stories up, and only we know we're here. We have privacy, champagne, and quite a bit of sushi. This is absolutely perfect."

His smile brightens his face. "Well then, I've learned today that I can be romantic."

"Lucky me," I say lightly before sipping my champagne.

And I've truly never felt luckier.

I'm sitting here on a rooftop in lower Manhattan with the man I love.

My life is perfect right now.

Fifty-Three

Knox

"If I have another piece of sushi, I might actually explode," Harlow laughs.

I prop myself up on my elbow from where I'm lying while working off a food coma. "So, you don't have room for dessert, Lo?"

"I can always find room for dessert." She smiles, and I lightly chuckle.

"Thought so," I say as I grab the white box tied up in gold string and set it between us.

I've learned over the past several months that she has a bit of a sweet tooth, so when she immediately leans over and unties the string, I can't help but smile. It's a small thing, but I love it when I can make her happy. Her joy is genuine, and it's so damn contagious.

"Ooh," she says, flipping the box open. "Chocolate-covered strawberries. Why'd you pick those?"

"So I can do this." I grab one of the strawberries and bring it to her lips. Harlow opens her mouth and takes a bite.

"Mmm," she moans. "That's delicious chocolate."

"I spared no expense tonight, baby."

"Is that why we're on the roof, then?" she asks, teasingly looking at me.

"You think you're funny, don't you?" I smile.

"Fucking hilarious," she laughs. "And you know you love it."

Yes, I certainly do *love* it.

"In case you missed it then, Harlow…" I say, dragging out her name with a look of faux offense. "I want to be alone with you tonight."

She leans closer to me, and I can smell the scent of her perfume. Heady with notes of citrus. *Intoxicating.* "Why'd you want me alone?"

God, that flirty tone always gets me. I'm an absolute sucker for her seduction. But I'm not sure I've earned that back yet.

"Because," I say, gently tilting her chin so she's looking into my eyes, "I don't want to share you. *You're mine*, remember?"

"I remember," she replies softly. "I'm yours, Knox. I've been yours."

"I'm yours, too, you know," I admit. "I don't want you to doubt that. I'm all fucking yours, Harlow."

Her smile is disbelieving, but not in a negative way. In a way that seems more like she can't believe that I *mean* that.

I sit up and bring her in closer, leaning her head on my shoulder as we sit and soak in the sounds of the city below us. The sun is already setting, and we have a great view of the sunset from this vantage point. The amber light shines off Harlow's perfectly blonde hair, casting her in an ethereal glow.

She's breathtaking.

Sitting with her like this is something I didn't think I'd get the opportunity to do again a month ago.

I nuzzle my face against her neck. "Thank you," I whisper.

"Why are you thanking me?"

"Because," I say, voice muffled by her hair, "I hurt you last month. You didn't have to forgive me, but you did anyway."

Harlow twists her head, now looking right at me and pressing her forehead against mine. "I know you didn't want to hurt me. You're a good man, Knox. I truly believe that. I couldn't for one second believe that you said any of that out of malice."

"Why do you think I said that then?"

"Fear," she answers assuredly. "I'm the first woman you've gotten close to since Emily. It must have scared the hell out of you when I told you this didn't feel fake to me anymore."

I let out a breath. "I'm an open book to you, aren't I?" She just smiles at me. "Lo, I know what I said last month, and I still regret it. Because it was a lie."

"Was it?" She rests her hand on my thigh as I start tracing lines up her arm.

"Yes," I admit. "I can't remember the last time this felt fake. What I have with you feels more real than anything I've felt before. It terrified me, and I panicked. But as soon as you walked out my door, I knew it would be the biggest mistake of my fucking life letting you go. All I wanted was for you to talk to me again so I could prove that to you."

"You didn't have to tear your hamstring just to get me to talk to you again." Her tone is playful, so I can't help but laugh.

"It was partially torn," I state. "And I sure as hell didn't do that on purpose. I missed a month of the season. My mind was a mess, and my game suffered. But I wouldn't do it differently even if I could. Having you around me again was everything I wanted."

"It would've taken a bit more time if you weren't injured, but I always would have forgiven you. I was hurt, but I still understood that you didn't have the same feelings, and that was okay. I didn't want to lose you forever. Maybe offering to stay with you full-time wasn't the greatest idea, but go big or go home, right?"

We both chuckle before I press a soft kiss to her lips.

And another.

And then another.

I could kiss Harlow every minute for the rest of my life, and it would still never be enough.

"You know what I think we need right now?" I say, murmuring with my lips still brushing hers.

"What's that?"

"Music. I may or may not have created a playlist specifically for tonight. It also may or may not be a bunch of... love songs."

Harlow smiles brightly as the darkness grows deeper, the sun falling beyond the horizon. "You're such a fucking romantic."

I tickle her side as she squirms. "And you love it, don't you?"

"Very much."

I grab the portable speaker Stephen brought up from my penthouse, connect my phone, and bring up the playlist. Once I hit shuffle, Christina Perri's soothing vocals start playing.

"I love this song," she says happily. "I've always wanted to dance to this at my wedding one day."

"Well, this isn't your wedding, but we can still dance."

I stand up and reach out my hand to help her. "You want to dance?" she asks incredulously.

"Having you pressed against me while I get to look into your eyes? Oh, I'm going to just hate that, Harlow." She laughs as she stands up and wraps her arms around my neck.

I position my arms around her lower back and pull her close as we sway to the music.

"I know I've said it before," she says, "but you're not at all what I expected you to be, Knox. You're so sweet and kind. I'm so happy I've gotten to know you."

"Knowing you has been the greatest pleasure of my life, Harlow."

I slowly spin her around as we dance, and my mind starts to wander.

To imagine things.

Things like doing this in the future with Harlow in a long, white dress.

A veil flowing behind her as she twirls with all our family and friends watching.

I've never envisioned anything like this with anybody else, and I never really considered myself marriage material.

But with Harlow? Well, maybe one day I actually could be.

And just like the first time I realized what all this means, I smile like a goddamn fool.

"What's that smile for, Knox?" she asks, curiosity in her eyes.

"Just thinking," I say, spinning her around again.

"Thinking of anything good then?"

"Well," I reply, bringing her back in close, "I'm thinking of you, so I'd say it's good."

"So charming," she says softly, looking up at me with an unmistakable look in her eyes.

Love.

I lean down to kiss her before we stop swaying, and I pull her against me with my arms wrapped low around her back.

"Harlow," I say, "do you know how much you mean to me?"

"Yeah," she replies with a soft smile. "I think I do."

Just then, a breeze blows by, unobstructed by anything when we're so high up. She shivers against me.

"Do you want to head inside, Lo?" I ask.

Harlow nods in response, and we walk off toward the elevator.

The descent on the elevator is quick since my penthouse is just one floor below. We could have taken the stairs, but I didn't want her to trip in her heels.

When the elevator doors open, we take a few steps to my penthouse door and walk inside, closing the door behind us. As soon as it clicks, Harlow leans back against the wall, grabbing my shirt by the collar and bringing my mouth down to meet hers.

I return the kiss as she moves to drape her arms over my shoulders, and mine grab her low on her hips. I feel her tease her tongue lightly across my bottom lip, so I open it, and she slides inside. When she softly moans against my lips, any semblance of restraint I had snaps.

I kiss her harder, hands slowly roaming her body. She slides her hands down and begins to untuck my shirt, pulling it free from my slacks. Before she can start working the buttons at the front of my shirt, I grab her wrist, stopping her.

"Harlow," I rasp.

She looks at me, mortified. "Oh my God! I'm so sorry! I just assumed-"

I cut her off. "Don't you dare start thinking this is because I don't want you, Lo." Her expression eases. "I *really* fucking want you. But..." I take a deep breath. "But I don't know if I really deserve to have you."

"Are you still hung up on last month?" she asks. "Obviously, you don't think everything is fake anymore, or we wouldn't be where we are now. I'm not worrying about what you said then because all that matters is right now. And right now, I just want to be with you, Knox."

I softly smile. "That's all I want, Harlow. To be with you. *Actually* be with you."

Her smile is so bright that even the sun can't compare. "You want to be with me?"

"Yes," I reply, brushing her hair out of her face. "More than anything. I want to be able to call you my girlfriend and for it to actually mean something. I want you to be mine."

"I am yours, Knox," she says before pressing her soft lips against mine again. "I've been yours. And if you're asking me to be your real girlfriend, not just your fake one, that's a very easy yes."

This time, I kiss *her*, letting my emotions take control and convey everything I'm feeling. But even if actions speak louder than words, sometimes you need those words of affirmation to truly get the point across.

"Harlow," I say, resting my forehead against hers and staring into the blue abyss of my girlfriend's eyes. "You are everything I want, everything I've ever wanted. I'm sorry that it took me a bit to see that. But there's no mistaking it now. How I feel about you is unlike anything I've felt before."

"And how do you feel then?" she asks, her smile lighting up her face with understanding.

I press one more kiss to her lips.

"I love you, Harlow."

Fifty-Four

Harlow

ALL THE AIR HAS been stolen from my lungs.

He said it.

He actually said it.

Knox loves me.

Knox Spencer loves *me*.

I barely knew Knox when this whole charade started at the beginning of April. I never expected that we'd fall in love with each other by the end of summer. In fact, I explicitly told Lucia I *didn't* want him to fall in love with me.

But he did anyway. He fell in love with me just as I've fallen in love with him.

Knox continues looking at me as I gaze into his emerald eyes. "I finally put it together the other day. I thought before that I was in love with Emily, but I realized everything I feel for you is different. I think you're the only person I've ever really loved."

"Knox," I say, smiling and trying not to let the tears welling up spill over. "I love you, too. I expected to become your friend when this started, but I never expected to get to know the man who could very well be my person."

"Your person?" he asks, raising an eyebrow and wearing the brightest smile. "You think I'm your person, Lo?"

I lean up and kiss him softly and tenderly. "Yes," I whisper, lips brushing against his. "I think you are. I think you're special and incredible and so fucking lovable. I think that makes you my perfect person."

"You know what I think, then?" Knox kisses me before looking into my eyes again. "I think you're everything I never knew I wanted. You came into my life right when I needed you, and I think I might just want to spend the rest of my life falling more in love with you. Harlow Pierce, I *know* you're my person. Nobody else will ever compare to you and everything you are."

My God, this man knows how to get me to swoon.

"Knox," I say before my lips find him again. "I love you, and I promise you *do* deserve to have me. *So take me to bed and show me how much you love me.*"

Without another word, he scoops me up, hands positioned under my thighs as I wrap my legs around his waist. With his tall legs and long strides, we're quickly in his bedroom. Knox carries me over to the bed, sitting me down on the edge.

He places his hands on either side of me, and his mouth meets mine. His kiss is full of longing, need, and affection. I can feel his love for me with every press of his lips and every glide of his tongue against mine.

He leans me back and bears his body on top of me, enveloping my body within his. Even in such a vulnerable position, I've never felt so secure, so *safe*.

Being wrapped up in Knox feels like *home*.

I gently push him off of me so he's propped up on only his arms. Then I trail my hands up his chest before starting at the buttons of his shirt.

When his shirt is fully unbuttoned, Knox breaks our kiss and lets it fall to the floor. I seize that moment to savor the definition of his chest as he hums his approval at my touch.

"Harlow," he says before leaning down, pressing his lips to mine again. "I want to savor this. I want to go slow and enjoy you, but I don't know if I can."

I smile against his lips. "I don't want slow. I just want you. So, stop overthinking and just fuck me already."

"You're already begging," he smirks. Knox starts peppering kisses down my neck and chest, pausing when he reaches the swells of my breasts. He murmurs against my skin, "I love you in lace, Harlow. You're so fucking beautiful."

He stands up and grabs my hands to bring me with him. Now, standing in front of him, he takes me in, spending time looking me over as if trying to make sure he can always remember this moment. His smile as he does is soft, sweet, and so full of love.

With one hand on my hip, he takes the other and slowly slides down the zipper at the back of my dress. I let the thin straps fall from my shoulders before Knox fists the fabric, sending it to the floor in a rough push.

His look is different now as he takes in the sight of what's underneath the dress. His eyes darken, and he bites his bottom lip.

Knox is now looking at me like a predator looks at its prey. It's so animalistic, like it's taking everything in him not to tear me apart.

The heat of his gaze sends fire coursing through my body, and a whole new wave of desire floods me. "Like what you see, Slick?" My tone is teasing as I try to mask how hot I feel from his eyes alone.

He pushes me back on the bed and leans over me, our bodies almost touching but not quite. "Fucking love what I see, baby. You look like a goddamn dream here right now, wearing my favorite color for me."

I lean up closer to him, lightly teasing my finger up his chest. "Thought you might like this set. Thought you might lose your damn mind when you saw me in it."

Knox places his finger under my chin, tilting my face. "Baby," he says, voice husky and low. "I lost my mind with you months ago." He brushes his lips against mine. "Now, where do I begin?" He palms my breast, and I softly moan. "Maybe I should start with your nipples, hard and desperately trying to break free of the fabric."

His hand slides down my body slowly now until it rests between my legs. "Or I could start with your pussy. I just know you're already dripping. My cock would probably slide right in." My breathing is heavy in anticipation. "Or," he says, lightly brushing his thumb over the front. "Maybe I get on my knees, head between your legs while I unravel you with only my tongue."

"Knox," I rasp, just needing him to do *something* right now.

"What's it going to be, Harlow? Tell me what you want."

"All three," I reply with confidence. "I want everything tonight. I want your mouth all over me and your cock inside me. But first..." I place my hand on the back of his head and pull him closer, the tips of our noses brushing together. "First, I want you to stick your head between my legs and taste just how *wet you make me.*"

His smile is devious as he stands up and removes his slacks. I prop myself up on my elbows for a better view of his long, thick erection straining against the black fabric of his boxer briefs. "You missed my dick, didn't you?" he smirks.

"Well," I say, "my vibrators just don't do it for me anymore."

"I'm counting ruining vibrators an achievement." Knox falls to the ground and taps on my knee. "Open up." I let him nudge my legs apart, spreading me wide open. "Fuck, Lo," he says, voice strained. "You're soaked for me. Your panties are drenched."

"Take them off then," I say, breathing heavily.

"Patience, baby," he replies, nipping at the inside of my thigh. "I'm just getting started."

Knox begins his ascent slowly.

Leisurely.

Torturously.

He kisses, licks, and nips at my skin, leaving marks in his wake and leaving me softly moaning while I wait for him to reach his resting place.

When he kisses the junction of my pelvis, I think I'm about to have him right where I want him.

But I don't…

Instead, he switches to my other thigh, now repeating what he did to the first.

I groan. "Fucking torture, Knox."

He laughs against my skin before sending me a wicked smile. "Not into teasing tonight?"

"You realize you haven't fucked me in a month, right?" I retort. "I don't know how much teasing I can handle before I come without you."

I barely finish my statement before he nips at the fabric directly over my clit. "You're not coming until I get a taste."

I smile at him maliciously. "Big talk from a man that's taking his time," I prod. "I'll have to make myself come if you don't do it for me soon."

I go to slide my hand between my legs before Knox catches my wrist. "The fuck you will. When you're here with me, that cunt is mine. It doesn't come without me."

I moan as he slides my thong to the side, tongue running up my slit. "God, I love your tongue."

With his lips grazing my clit, he says, "And I love tasting your delicious pussy." He takes his hands and slips them into my waistband, quickly sliding them down my legs. "I love how wet I make you." He takes another swipe as I moan. "I love the sounds you make when you lose control." He slips his tongue inside. "God, I love every fucking thing about you, Harlow."

He brings his hands to my thighs and spreads my legs further apart while he feasts on me, alternating between rough flicks of his tongue and light nips at my clit. His hands ghost my skin as he moves them to my breasts, pulling my bra down and rolling my nipples between his fingers.

I'm in goddamn heaven right now. Bliss like I've never experienced. It's too much and not enough all at once. Like I want more, but I'm not sure I could actually take more.

But more comes anyway as Knox stops what he's doing, now taking his tongue and slowly working his way down... and down... until I feel him at my backside. "Oh!" I shout in a half moan. "Oh, that's... that feels... good." I breathe out another moan.

"My dirty fucking girl," he says, amusement and lust in his voice. His mouth moves back to my clit, stroking it with his tongue and sucking it into his mouth as my hips arch off the bed.

When Knox moves his hand and slides two fingers inside of me without warning, I cry out. "Fuck, Knox!" My hands are tangled in his hair as I push him in closer. "I'm so close."

His fingers pump faster, and his tongue moves quicker as my orgasm closes in. As he takes his other hand and slides it further down, teasing the new spot his tongue explored before, I explode.

"Yes, fuck!" I come hard, pussy contracting around his fingers as he works me through my orgasm.

When I finally come down, Knox slides his fingers out and peppers kiss up my stomach and chest before brushing his lips over mine. "Goddamn. You sound so fucking good when you scream for me."

I run my finger lightly up the column of his throat, catching his chin and tilting his face. "You're just so good at making me scream."

I press our lips together, and Knox deepens our kiss, thrusting his tongue into my mouth and letting me taste myself. He lowers his body, fully embracing me as I drape my arms around him. "Fuck, I missed tasting you, Lo," he pants.

"Mmm," I reply. "I missed how enthusiastic you are with your head between my legs."

Knox chuckles. "I'd like to think I'm enthusiastic in all aspects with you." He presses a kiss to the hollow of my throat before ghosting his lips over my neck. "But if I'm not enthusiastic enough with my dick, I'll have to step up my game tonight."

The moan I try to stifle slips out anyway. "I don't think there's any room for you to improve, but do whatever you want to me tonight. I just want you to fuck me."

He smirks against my lips. "Where?" I give him a curious look. "Here..." he says, rubbing his thumb over my bottom lip. "Here..." Knox takes his other hand and slides it between my legs. "Or here..." he slips the tip of his finger inside me to coat it before he then slides it down further, slowly teasing it around the other hole.

"Oh..." I say, a gasp mixing with a moan.

Knox buries his face in the crook of my neck, lips grazing my skin. "Dirty girl. You'd like that, wouldn't you?"

"I'm not sure," I admit. "Never even considered it until now."

"But you'd let me take you there, wouldn't you?"

"I'd let you take me wherever you want, Knox. My body is yours to play with."

He groans into my skin before picking me up and lightly tossing me up the bed, my back landing on the pillows. I'm laughing as he descends on me again, roughly capturing my lips. "We'll work you up to that then, baby. I know your pussy misses me."

"It does," I whisper against his lips. "You make me feel so good. No one has ever fucked me the way you do."

He groans again before sliding his hand behind my back, unhooking my bra, and tossing it across the room. I might never find that thing again, and I don't even care.

Knox arches his hips off of me so I can slide his boxers off. I push them down, and he kicks them to the side. My hands explore him more earnestly than before, sliding down his muscular back before tightly gripping his ass.

He laughs against my lips. "You always did like my ass."

"Always have." I peck his lips. "Always will."

I slowly slip my hands toward his front, taking hold of his cock in one hand and his balls in the other. "Fuck," Knox hisses. "You can't even fit your hand around me, baby."

"And now you know why you've ruined vibrators for me." I kiss him again. "But I prefer you anyway."

"Good answer. Now spread your legs for me, baby. I need to sink into you so I can feel that perfect pussy wrapped around my cock again."

I quickly let my hips fall open as Knox positions himself between my legs. He teases the head of his cock through my wetness, coating the tip, readying it to plunge inside me. I lean up and capture his mouth with mine as he starts slipping inside.

As he slides in to the hilt, I throw back my head and moan. "Knox, oh my God..."

"Goddamn." He starts moving on me, thrusting his hips roughly and desperately. "You take me so fucking well." He latches onto my throat, sucking the skin into his mouth, leaving his signature mark behind. "Fucking made for me."

"Yes," I breathe. "Made for you, Knox." I wrap my arms around him, bringing him closer to me as he moves. "And you were made for me, too."

With his lips brushing my ear, he whispers, "I am. Made for you and only you, Harlow. I'm so fucking yours."

Without warning, Knox pulls out and rolls me onto my side before repositioning himself behind me, wrapping me up in his arms. "This is new," I say, turning my face to look at him.

"I just want to hold you," he replies, rubbing his thumb over my bottom lip.

"Hold me and fuck me," I tease.

"I thought that went without saying." He places his hand under my thigh and lifts it up, draping it over the leg he now slides in between mine so he has a better angle.

Knox grasps his cock and starts pushing inside. "Ohhh..." I moan. "You feel so damn good, Knox."

"So do you, baby," he rasps, breathless. "I can't ever last once I'm inside your tight pussy. You make me lose all control."

"Good. I don't want you to control yourself with me." He slides further inside, and I gasp—this angle hits so much deeper. "Oh God. I don't think I can take anymore."

"You can take it," he replies, trailing kisses up my neck and behind my ear. "You're going to take all of me, baby. You know why? Because every fucking inch is yours."

With my nails digging into the skin of his thigh, he presses further inside, sliding in to the hilt as I scream. "Oh fuck..."

"Just like that, baby." Knox starts thrusting while murmuring in my ear. "You always take everything I give you. Such a good fucking girl, Harlow."

His praise, combined with how deep he's hitting, already has me feeling the first flutters of an impending orgasm. "Knox," I moan as he starts moving faster, breathing strangled. "This is too good, too much. Oh God..."

He snakes his hand up, grasps my breast, and plants kisses along my jaw. The intimacy of all of this is more than I've ever experienced. I've never felt closer to someone—figuratively and literally—as Knox holds me and moves inside me. The feel of his muscular chest pressed against my back heightens all of the sensations.

When he slams into me again, I moan his name as I feel myself edging closer. "You gonna come again, baby?" he asks, voice strained.

"Ye- ohhh fuck, baby."

Knox nips my neck. "Answer me."

"Yes," I manage in a ragged breath. "I'm so close."

"Me too," he says before he removes his hand from my breast and moves it to my head, turning it so I can face him. "Come with me."

Knox captures my mouth, stroking his tongue against mine as he moves his hips faster, slamming into me as he desperately seeks his release. When he moves a hand between my legs and brushes his thumb against my clit, I fall apart, moaning into his mouth as I clench around his length. He gives two more hard thrusts before he stills, spilling into me as he comes without breaking our kiss.

We're a moaning, writhing mess, entwined together as we both start to come down from our highs. Knox still has his arms wrapped around me, keeping me pressed against his chest, with his hands now resting on my stomach and forehead leaning on mine.

After a minute, he finds my lips again as he slowly trails one of his hands from my stomach back down between my legs. "Knox..." I pant. "I can't."

"One more, baby," he whispers against my lips. "You can give me one more, can't you?"

With my body still pressed against him, he works his thumb over my clit and slides a finger inside. But that's not what pushes me to another release.

No, that comes after Knox whispers a string of sweet nothings into my ear. Pulling me closer and telling me how beautiful I am. How much he missed me. *How much he loves me.*

I can't believe I ever thought I could resist falling in love with this man. Never in my life have I known someone so kind and caring, so in tune with both my emotions and my body.

This is the feeling I've been chasing. This feeling of love and passion and security.

Laying here with him now feels like I'm finally right where I was always meant to be.

Knox is my forever.

Fifty-Five

Knox

THE SUN STARTS PEEKING out from behind the blackout curtains in my bedroom. I rub my eyes and glance down to see Harlow's blonde hair splayed across my chest, a stark reminder that last night really did happen.

I didn't dream it up—we made things official, and I confessed that I love her.

And she loves me, too.

I'm the happiest damn motherfucker on the planet right now. I'm sitting on cloud nine, holding my girlfriend and, for once, believing that I deserve good things.

And Harlow is the best thing of all.

She stirs now, lifting her head as she blinks the sleep from her eyes. And when they open, she flashes me the sweetest smile. "Good morning, Knox."

"Good morning, beautiful," I say as I place a finger under her chin and gently bring her lips up to meet mine. "Did you sleep well?"

"Best night of sleep I've ever had," she smiles.

"Every night I have you beside me is my best night."

Instead of smiling, Harlow laughs. "Oh my God, Fort Knox really is a simp."

I chuckle in return. "Yeah, maybe I am." I brush my thumb across the freckles on her cheek. "But I don't fucking care. I've got you, Harlow. Nothing else matters."

Her smile back is genuine, lighting her face up in pure warmth. She is the most beautiful thing I've ever seen. I just want to live in this moment forever.

"I still can't believe last night actually happened," she says. "That I didn't dream it up."

I lean in closer, brushing my forehead against hers. "It happened, Lo. And I meant every word I said. I'm so fucking in love with you."

Harlow melts into me, sighing in contentment. "I love you, too. So much more than I ever thought I could love anybody."

"And all that because you decided to come talk to me after the home opener."

"Best decision I ever made." She smiles. "What are our plans for the day?"

"Well, I've got a game tonight, and I assume you'll be there to cheer for your boyfriend."

"My boyfriend, who will be sitting on the bench tonight?" she smirks.

"Meaning I'll have all the time in the world to sit and just look at you." I wrap my arms around her and pull her closer, leaning my lips to her ear. "My other plans for today involve you and this bed."

"Knox!" she shouts, lifting her head and looking into my eyes. "How do you go from sweet to horny just like that?"

"Because you are laying on top of me completely naked, and nothing is going to stop me from worshiping that body the way it deserves."

I take hold of her hips and sit her on top of me as Harlow lightly moans. "I was trying to be sweet and romantic this morning."

I pepper light kisses up her neck and stroke my hands up and down her sides. "Come sit on my face, baby, and tell me you don't want to be horny, too."

"I won't say no to that," she replies, breathing already heavy. "I daydream about the things you can do with your tongue."

"Good," I say roughly. "Now get that pussy up here and let me eat, Lo. I'm fucking starving."

<<<<<<<<<<<<<<<<<<<<<<<<<<<<<<<<<<<<

An orgasm for Harlow turns into her riding me until I make a complete mess of her. And a shower to clean her up turns into me pinning her against the wall, creating even more of a mess. But goddamn, I'm even more ravenous for her now than I was before.

Her sounds, her taste, her feel have only become even more addicting now that we're finally together.

Once we eventually clean ourselves off, she throws on one of my old T-shirts and joins me on the sofa, climbing onto my lap and snuggling into my chest.

If I could live the rest of my life like this, with Harlow wrapped up in my arms, everything else would be inconsequential.

All I need is this.

All I need is *her*.

We were both content to relax in the silence until our phones start vibrating. "I'm just ignoring that," I say, moving my phone to the coffee table.

"Works for me," she replies, nuzzling her face into my neck.

We settle back into silence, trying to enjoy each other before I head to the field in a few hours.

And then our phones start vibrating again.

"Goddammit," I mumble. "Who the fuck is bothering us?"

Harlow grabs her phone and takes a look. "Literally everybody. There's a whole new text chain with all of our friends."

"Fucking hell," I reply, grabbing my own phone and opening it up.

Lane

I think I speak for everyone when I say we're dying to know what happened last night

Cole

Nope, I don't want to know everything they did

Rory

Don't be a prude, Cole

Cole

Am I really a prude if I don't want to hear about my sister's sex life?

Lucia

Better get used to it, Pierce

Harlow

Hi, can we not discuss my sex life in a damn group chat?

Ella

It's not like I was ever given the opportunity to talk about it before, to be fair

Josh

I think that's all I've heard about for the past day and a half

Lane

We could always just talk about Knox's sex life instead

Knox

And those just happen to be one and the same

Rory

I'm going to take it the date went well

Ella

Oh, I bet it did

Cole

You're all purposefully torturing me

Knox

Torture Cole on your own

I'm a little busy right now

Harlow

Super subtle, Knox

Knox

Like they weren't already guessing

Cole

Guessing and confirming are different things

Knox

Well, I could tell you about this one thing she does…

Cole

NO

Harlow

KNOX!

I'm going to kick you

Knox

Your legs are in my lap

You won't have to reach very far

Lucia

Anybody else finding this really cute?

Rory

Super fucking cute

Lane

I'm living for this

Harlow

Why are all of our friends so fucking weird?

Knox

We can always find new ones

Lane

Dick

We're just invested in your relationship

Harlow

Which is really fucking weird

Cole

I, for one, think it's just adorable that Fort Knox is finally dating my sister

Ella

According to the rest of the world, they've been together for months now

Wait, what counts as the day you got together then?

Knox

Don't know, don't care

Harlow

The date doesn't really matter to me

I'm just happy we're together

Knox

Me too, baby

Josh

You know, it has been nice to see Fort smiling finally

Rory

Right?

His smile is so cute

Cole

You think his smile is cute?

Rory

Jealous, Pierce?

Cole

You wish, Fisher

Knox

Okay, I've had enough of all this

I'm going to enjoy some time with my girlfriend before I need to head to the field

Harlow

And we'll probably be a bit too busy to respond to anything else

Cole

Gahhh

I'm out of here

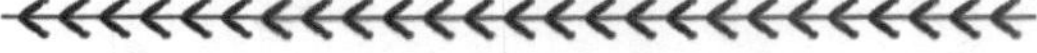

The bat cracks as Josh connects with the ball, hitting a solo home run past center field. We're in the bottom of the eighth, and while Damian Anderson gave up three runs before he was pulled in the seventh, the Stars are still in the lead, currently winning 5-3.

Ayala pops out after Josh's home run, ending the eighth inning. Chris Rockman takes the mound now, looking to get the save against the Kansas Huskers.

And he starts off strong, striking out the first two batters. Batter number three hits a line drive into center field and makes it safely to second base when Lane bobbles the ball as he goes to scoop it up.

Batter number four then connects on a fastball right down the middle, sending the ball flying into the right field wall. The runner on second speeds home, bringing the score up to 5-4.

Rockman looks a bit rattled now, but he still hasn't blown the save. So, he gears up for a curveball, which he throws at the edge of the strike zone.

But it wasn't enough. The batter sent the ball over the wall in right field, and with a two-run home run, the Huskers now lead 6-5.

Rockman does strike out the final batter he faces, but the atmosphere in the dugout after is bleak. The home team never wants to play in the bottom of the ninth because that means you aren't in the lead. Now, the pressure is on to tie the game or pull ahead.

And when we go three up, three down, the win goes to the Huskers.

I'm not as upset as you'd expect, though.

I don't think anything can dash my happiness right now.

And that's all because of the blonde-haired, blue-eyed bombshell sinking into her seat after our loss. As the guys start to make their way out of the dugout to the clubhouse, I jog over to Harlow instead.

Now, standing in front of her, I say, "Prettiest fan here."

Harlow opens her eyes now, and she smiles at me. "You guys just lost, and you're over here to tell me I'm pretty?"

"Get used to it," I reply, leaning closer and wrapping my arms around her waist. "We're only just getting started. I'm going to remind you every day how goddamn stunning you are."

She blushes as she grasps my jersey, bringing her face to my chest. "You're way too happy right now, Knox."

"Funny how things change, isn't it?" I press a kiss to her temple. "But you can't win them all anyway."

"Shouldn't you want to win more, though?"

"I've got you, Harlow. *I've already won.*"

She quickly turns to face me, her lips pressing into mine with so much affection—enough for me to drown out everyone around us, soaking her in as if it were just us.

This season has been so unexpected for me.

I started out as Fort Knox, the man with a poor reputation who refused to let anybody in.

And now, as we approach the end of the regular season, I'm just Knox, the man who can't stop smiling and has found the most incredible woman.

Once again, I owe everything to Simon. My future would be dark and lonely without him setting up this arrangement with Harlow.

Now, I want things I never thought I would.

I want love.

I want marriage.

And truthfully, I think I want kids, too.

And I want all of that with Harlow.

It happened so fast, but I know she's it for me. I'll never feel like this for anybody else. I don't *want* to feel like this again if it's not with her.

"I love you, Freckles."

"I love you, too, Slick."

Epilogue

Two months later...

"Yes, just like that, Knox!"

Knox leans over me now, pressing his chest against my back and bringing his lips to my ear. "Does that feel good for you, baby?"

I moan as he thrusts harder. "So... good... *oh my God*."

"I'm no deity, but you can pray to me anytime."

He bites at my neck, sucking on the skin as he starts moving faster. "*Knox...*"

"Do you want to come, Harlow?"

"Please," I pant. "Please make me come."

He wraps his hand around my body and slips it between my legs, thumb teasing my clit. I moan the moment he touches me. "There you go, baby. You're doing so well. Taking my cock nice and deep into your wet pussy. Fucking perfect, Lo."

"*Ohhh*," I moan as he presses down on my clit in time with his next thrust. My breathing is labored as he brings me to the edge of bliss.

Knox nibbles on my ear as he starts breathing heavier. "I need you to come, baby. I need you to come before I paint your cunt with mine."

When he presses on my clit one last time, I fall apart, clenching around him and loudly moaning as he fucks me through my orgasm.

"Such a good girl, Harlow." He's thrusting faster now, closing in on his own release.

"So."

Thrust.

"Fucking."

Thrust.

"Good."

Thrust.

And he shatters, groaning into my neck as his hips still, and he fills me up, spilling every last drop of cum inside me.

We both collapse onto the bed, Knox falling down beside me as we catch our breath.

"There's no way you don't win tonight now," I say, turning to face him. "Not after sex like that."

"Because you have a magic pussy," he chuckles. "I fuck you, and I can do anything."

"Like pitch a win in game seven of the World Series?" I smile.

Knox leans over and kisses me. "I really fucking hope so."

"You're going to do incredible tonight," I reassure him. "And I can't wait to watch my boyfriend become a World Series champion."

"Meaning your brother would also become a World Series champion, Lo."

I groan. "Knox, you just fucked me into delirium, and we're both still naked. Can we please not talk about my brother right now?"

"Of course, Lo," he smiles before pressing a soft kiss to my lips. "I'm not ready to leave you soon."

"You need to be with your team," I say, laying my hand on his cheek. "You all need to make sure you're ready for the game. Someone is winning the World Series tonight, and we all hope it isn't the Thunderbirds."

"I know," he sighs. "But I would also like to just spend all day in bed with you."

"Offseason starts tomorrow. We'll have plenty of days where we won't have to leave the bed at all."

"Can't fucking wait," he says as he kisses me again before helping me sit up.

"I should probably go to my apartment for a bit. You have to leave soon anyway."

"Why do you even need your apartment anymore?" Knox asks, wrapping his arms around me and putting the back of my head on his shoulder.

"Because that's where I live."

He eyes me. "When did you last spend the night there, Lo?"

"It's, uh... been a while," I admit sheepishly.

"It's been since before I tore my hamstring if you want to be specific."

"Because you keep me up all night," I say, poking his side, "and you won't let me take the subway when it's late."

He laughs heartily. "Or because I just don't want you to leave. I love having you here with me, Lo."

I turn my head to face him. "Are you getting at something, Knox?"

"I can't keep anything from you." He grins widely before softly kissing the tip of my nose. "Why don't you just move in with me?"

I look at him in surprise. "You want me to move in?"

Knox repositions me now, bringing me to sit on his lap as I face him. "Why not? You stay here every night anyway. You're practically living with me now, just without having your things here."

"Yeah, but if I move in, I'll always be here."

"Good." He gently kisses my forehead.

I study him now to see how serious he is. He looks completely relaxed. This isn't a stressor. This is a genuine want from him, to have me around all the time.

"You really want me to move in?"

Knox smiles at me. "I wouldn't ask if I didn't mean it, Lo."

"The offseason is getting ready to start. You'll never be away from me."

"Perfect," he says, brushing his thumb over my bottom lip.

I blush as I turn my face, burying it in his chest. "Alright then."

"Yeah?" His smile is wide, lighting him up in genuine happiness. "You'll move in?"

"I'll move in."

Knox is on me in a flash, knocking me backward as he descends on me with his mouth on mine. He parts my lips and slides his tongue inside as his hand starts roaming my body.

When he teases his fingers up my thigh, I stop him. "Slow down, buddy. You need to get to the field."

"You don't think we have time for one more?" He cocks an eyebrow at me with an ornery smile on his face.

"Jesus, where do you get your stamina from?" I say in exasperation. "You've fucked me twice this morning already."

"I'm a professional athlete, baby. I've got stamina for days."

I roll my eyes as I laugh. "Well, this professional athlete needs to get his ass to the field. You're starting tonight."

He groans before moving off me. "Fine. I know you're right, but that doesn't mean I like it."

"You're insatiable." I shake my head.

"Only for you."

"Well," I say, sliding my hand up his chest, "if you get the win tonight, we'll have to celebrate after, won't we?"

"Yeah? What do you have in mind?"

"I think we can try something new. Something you've been wanting."

Knox licks his bottom lip as he catches on to my meaning. "Think you're ready for more than my fingers, baby?"

"Guess we'll find out if you win."

Knox moves quickly, pinning me to the bed as he brushes his lips against mine. "I've got all the motivation I need."

There should be a handbook on how to handle the stress of watching your boyfriend pitch in a World Series game. Sure, it wouldn't sell many copies since that's a pretty niche market, but goddamn, do I need one right now.

I've been watching the game from the suite Knox and Cole got for us. , Sage, my parents, Simon, his wife, and some executives from Axis are all here with me, watching from the comfort of a box.

And I've been so fucking nervous that I've bitten my nails down to the quick and all but put a hole in the floor with all of my pacing.

They're not even playing poorly, though. Sure, the game is tied -2 as they prepare for the bottom of the eighth, but they're playing well.

Especially Knox.

He's so in control tonight. He may have given up two runs, but he gave them both up in the first inning. The Thunderbirds have had seven scoreless innings thanks to Knox not losing his composure after the first. Hell, in the eighth inning, he was still pitching. His pitch count is just over one hundred, and there's a chance that Paul will keep him in for the complete game.

But I can only see that happening if we pull ahead in the bottom of the inning now.

The home-field advantage the Stars earned will hopefully help. The stadium is packed to the brim, with thousands more fans surrounding the outside, listening in to hear how the team is playing.

Rory has spent basically the entire game trying to keep me calm. I'd ask my parents to help if they weren't just as anxious as I am right now. This is the Stars' first World Series appearance since Cole joined the team—their first appearance in more than a decade, at that.

We're all stressed and hoping to see New York bring home that pennant.

One of the Thunderbirds' relief pitchers takes his spot on the mound as the Stars get ready to bat. Our designated hitter, Andrew Pelton, leads this half of the inning.

The crowd stands as we hear the crack of the bat and see the ball soaring into the outfield... and we all deflate as the center fielder makes the catch.

Lane is next up. The first few pitches end in foul balls, but pitch four ends as a ground ball hit toward third base. Lane speeds off toward first as the third baseman fields the ball and tosses it. The play is close, and we all hold out hope until the umpire reviews the footage to find that Lane was tagged before he hit the base.

And just like that, we've got two outs.

Cole now strides over to the batter's box, taking a few practice swings to loosen up.

"Oh God," I say, covering my eyes. "I don't know if I can watch."

Rory peels my hands from my face. "Watch your brother, Lo. He'll be pissed if he gets a hit, and you didn't see it."

I groan and agree. Even though I'm unbelievably nervous, I keep my eyes on the game for Cole.

And when he knocks that first pitch right into the stands of left field, I'm so fucking glad I did.

"Cole!" I shout as Rory jumps and yells beside me.

"We're fucking winning!" she yells as she runs over to hug my parents.

I grab Sage, who has no idea what's going on but is excited by all the dancing, and spin her around as we all carry on our excitement after Josh strikes out, ending the eighth inning.

When the Stars take their places for the top of the ninth, I'm elated to see Knox return to the mound.

"I see he's going for the complete game," a man beside me says before turning to me. "I don't believe I introduced myself yet. I'm Matt Trelon, VP of Marketing for Axis."

"Oh, it's so nice to meet you!" I say, extending my hand to him.

"You as well, Harlow," he replies, taking my hand and shaking it. "I've been talking with Simon a lot recently. We both agree that you seem to be very good for Knox."

"Oh," I blush. "I think I've just helped him become more open."

"Well, whatever it is you've done," Matt says, "you've completely changed how people see him. His attitude has progressed so much through the season."

"Like he said to me a couple months ago," Simon chimes in, walking up to stand on my other side and shooting me a soft smile. "He just needed a reason to be happy."

My blush is deeper now as I feel it creeping down my neck and across my chest. "That's all I want for him."

We fall into silence as we all watch Knox rear back for his first pitch of the inning, a foul ball the Thunderbirds' second baseman hits to the left. He connects on pitch number two, sending the ball shallow in the outfield. The Stars' right fielder, Neil Mansfield, is quick and catches it on a dive.

Out number one.

The next batter is the Thunderbirds first baseman, Ari Morgan, one of their strongest batters. And when Knox sends him back to the dugout with a three-pitch strikeout, the crowd is reaching insanity.

Out number two.

The Stars are one out away from the World Series title.

Rory slides in beside me with Sage on her hip. "I don't think I've ever been this nervous," she says.

"Fucking tell me about it. My brother and my boyfriend are one out away from winning the damn World Series."

"Cole's played such a great game," she says aloud, but not to me, more as though she's just stating a fact. With her bright smile and slight flush to her cheeks, it's obvious why she's focusing on my brother to anyone paying close enough attention.

"He has," I respond, grabbing her hand to ground myself so I don't start pacing again.

The silence that falls over the crowd is deafening as Knox gets into position for his pitch to the Thunderbirds' left fielder.

He rears back with the pitch he's most well-known for and sends a knuckleball down the middle. The bat connects, but the hit is shallow, soaring up high but not traveling far.

The cheers start early as Cole gets in position, glove up under the ball falling toward him. And when his glove closes around it, the crowd erupts.

My dad runs up behind me and scoops me up as we all start screaming. We're jumping and yelling and celebrating almost as much as the guys on the field.

The Stars just *won* the damn World Series!

I glance down at them in time to see the traditional cooler of Gatorade poured over Cole's head—Knox, Lane, and Josh doing the honors.

"Can we go down?" I ask Rory excitedly.

"Hell yes, we can!"

I hug my parents quickly before Rory, Sage, and I dash from the box. The team passes we have on us allow us to get there easily.

Two minutes after leaving the box, we step onto the field and run alongside the other family members doing the same.

Knox sees me before I'm halfway there and sprints to me, picking me up and spinning me around, kissing me the moment my feet are back on the ground.

"You won!" I shout. "You fucking won the World Series, Knox!"

"Couldn't have done it without you, Harlow. God, I fucking love you."

He lifts me again, this time taking me over to the rest of the team to join in on the celebration.

Once the on-field celebrations end and Cole is named World Series MVP, the festivities move inside. The clubhouse is usually reserved for athletes only, but the team is making an exception, allowing family and friends to join the team.

When we're all crowded inside, the bottles are brought out, ready to be popped for the classic champagne shower.

As several of the guys start working on the corks, Lane holds Sage to his chest. "Keep that alcohol off my fucking daughter, please."

"We'll just get you instead," Knox says deviously, popping the cork from the bottle he's holding and spraying it all over Lane's legs.

"This Fort is a hell of a lot more fun than the old one," chimes Josh, joining us with Ella under his arm and taking a swig from his own champagne.

Lucia finds us now. "Congratulations, guys! World Series fucking champions!"

"Duck," Sage says in her adorable little toddler voice.

"Oh, I'm fucked," Lane groans. "Kids who run around swearing are cute, right?"

"The fucking cutest!" Ella replies, leaning over and pinching Sage's cheek.

Josh starts looking around curiously. "Where the hell is Cole?"

I try to find him when I notice something else. "Rory's missing, too."

"That's interesting," Lucia smirks.

"What do you think is happening?" I whisper to Knox.

Knox picks me up again. "Don't fucking know. Don't fucking care. We won the World Series, and I have the most beautiful woman in my arms right now. I don't care about anything else."

I just smile and nuzzle into the crook of his neck. "I'm so happy for you."

He leans down and kisses my temple as Simon fights his way through the crowd to us. "Knox," he says, flagging him down. "I need you to come with me."

Without setting me down, Knox follows Simon out of the clubhouse and into the hallway, where we find Matt, the man from Axis I met during the game, waiting for him.

He puts me on my feet and looks to his agent. "What's this about, Simon?"

"Knox," he says, gesturing to the man beside him, "this is Matt Trelon. He's the VP of Marketing at Axis."

"Oh!" Knox grabs his hand and shakes it heartily. "It's a pleasure to meet you, sir."

Matt laughs. "Please call me Matt. Sir makes me feel old." His tone turns more professional. "But the other Axis executives and I thought now would be a great time to give you some good news."

"I'm not sure there's any news that can surpass what just happened," Knox replies, pulling me closer. "But I'm all ears."

"Well," he starts, "we've kept a close eye on you through the season. You're known now for being more than just this unbreakable pitcher; it's been a great change for you. You're happier and have more love from the fans than ever before."

"Yeah, I think this season has been great for me. This has been the best year of my career."

"We agree. And now I'd like to formally tell you that Axis is looking forward to moving forward with your endorsement deal."

Knox stares at him in disbelief with a bright smile. "Seriously?"

Matt chuckles as he places a hand on Knox's shoulder. "Very serious. We'll work out the logistics with Simon here, but expect to hear from us soon." He adjusts his suit jacket now. "Congratulations on your win, Knox. We're excited to work with you."

Simon gives his congratulations—both on the World Series win and on successfully getting the Axis contract—before he and Matt turn on their heels and head down the hall in the opposite direction. Once they're out of sight, Knox has me pinned against the wall, mouth on mine.

"Knox," I manage between frenzied kisses. "You did it."

"All because of you, Harlow. You're the best fucking thing that's ever happened to me."

I smile wide and press my forehead against his.

"God, I'm so fucking proud of you. You're talented and incredible and deserving."

"Wouldn't be here without you, baby."

I never imagined myself like this, wrapped in the arms of Knox Spencer, *my boyfriend*, before this season, but I'm so happy I know him. *Really* know him.

Life is great at throwing curveballs, though. You live, and you learn, and you're better for it after all the pain wears off.

When you get through that, it all feels a bit easier, and you can take everything in stride when life throws you a little off pitch.

Glossary

1-2-3 Inning – an inning where the pitcher faces three batters and none make it safely to a base

6-4-3 Double Play – a specific double play involving the shortstop (6), second baseman (4), and first baseman (3)—the shortstops grabs the ball and tosses it to the second baseman to force out the runner that's advancing; the second baseman then tosses it to the first baseman to force out the batter

ACL – anterior cruciate ligament; the ACL stabilizes the knee and connects the upper leg to the lower leg by connecting to the femur and tibia

At-Bat – a completed plate appearance by a batter

Ball – a pitch that does not land inside the strike zone

Baseline – the line that runs between two bases on the baseball field

Baserunner – a player on the offensive team (the one currently batting) that has safely made it to base

Bases Loaded – runners on all three bases

Bat Bunny – a woman that wants to get with a baseball player; also known as a Baseball Annie

Batter's Box – the rectanglular boxes on either side of home plate where the batter must be standing for fair play to resume

Batting Average – average number of hits a player has per at-bat

Batting Practice — a period usually before a game where players work on their batting technique

Blown Save — a charge a relief pitcher receives after they enter the game in a save situation and give up either the tying or winning run

Bottom of the Inning — the second half of an inning in which the home team bats

Bullpen — area used by pitchers and catchers to warm up and practice before taking the mound when play has already begun; usually off to the side of either the left or right side base line, or behind an outfield fence

Catch — when a fielder catches a batted ball in their glove or hand before it hits the ground and keeps possession of it until they release it

Catcher — the player that crouches behind home plate while the opposing team is at-bat; receives the pitches from the pitcher

Center Field — central part of the outfield, behind second base

Center Fielder — the outfielder that plays defense in the area of center field

Changeup — a pitch meant to look like a fastball but with less speed

Closer — relief pitcher that is used most often to close out the game by getting the final outs

Clubhouse — a team's locker room

Complete Game — when a pitcher pitches the entire game himself without using a relief pitcher

Curveball — a pitch that curves from a straight path toward home plate

Designated Hitter — player who permanently bats in place of the pitcher

Double — a two-base hit

Double Play — a defensive play where two offensive players are forced out during continuous play, resulting in two outs

Dugout – where a team's bench is located on the field; a depressed area slightly below field level

ERA – earned run average; the mean (average) of earned runs given up by a pitcher over nine innings

Error – a fielder's misplay that allows a batter or baserunner to advance to one or more additional bases when that advance could have been avoided with ordinary effort

Fair Territory – the area of the playing field between the two foul lines

Farm System – affiliation of farm teams for each team; there are three levels in the farm system: A, AA, and AAA

Farm Team – a team affiliated with a specific professional team that provides experience and training for younger players with the expectation that successful players will move to the Major League at some point

Fastball – a pitch thrown more for speed than for movement; the most common type of pitch

Field Manager – the "head coach" of the team; controls the team strategy on the field

First Base – the base to the right of the pitcher when looking from home plate; the first base a baserunner needs to touch to score a run

First Baseman – the defensive player who fields the area closest to first base

Force Out – an out where a runner that is forced to advance is tagged out

Foul Ball – a ball that is batted into foul territory

Foul Lines – two straight lines drawn from home plate to the outfield separating fair territory and foul territory

Grand Slam – a home run hit with bases loaded; earns four runs

Ground Ball – a ball that bounces in the infield; also known as a grounder

Hit – the act of safely reaching base after hitting the ball into fair territory

Hit By Pitch – when a pitch hits the batter in the batter's box; automatically advances to first base

Home Plate – where the batter stands, and the final base a runner must touch to score a run

Home Run – homer; a base hit where a batter is able to circle all the bases, usually done by hitting the ball into the stands or beyond

Infield – the square area within all 4 baselines

Infielder – a player stationed at one of the defensive infield positions between first and third base

Injured List – a way for teams to temporarily remove players from their active roster due to injury; another player is able to be called up to take their spot on the active roster; formerly called the Disabled List

IL – see Injured List

Inning – a unit of play consisting of two halves; there is the top of the inning (away team bats) and the bottom of the inning (home team bats); there are nine innings in a regular length baseball game

Knuckleball – a pitch thrown with no spin, usually with the knuckles; flutters and moves suddenly and erratically on its way to the plate

Leadoff Batter – leadoff hitter; the first batter in a team's lineup

Left Field – part of outfield on the left of center field if looking from home plate

Left Fielder – the outfielder who plays defense in the area of left field

Line Drive – liner; a batted ball that is hit hard in the air and doesn't have much arc

Mound – pitcher's mound; raised section in the middle of the diamond used by the pitcher; area the pitcher stands to throw the pitch

MVP – Most Valuable Player; player that was instrumental to the team during the season, playoffs, or World Series

Netting – a large net separating the field from the stands, behind home plate and up the baselines, to prevent injury to spectators

No-Decision – when a starting pitcher doesn't get either the win or the loss for the game

No-Hitter – a game where one team does not give up any hits; a player may still reach base by walk or error to earn a no-hitter; a no-hitter without any walks, hits, or errors is called a perfect game

Opening Day – the first day of the regular season

Outfield – the area of the field beyond the infield and between the foul lines

Outfielder – a player in one of three defensive positions in the outfield – left fielder, center fielder, and right fielder

Pitch Count – how many pitches a pitcher has thrown so far during a game

Pitching Coach – coach who works with pitchers on how to pitch, what pitch to throw, and how to throw them

Pop Out – when a player catches a pop up to get the player out

Pop Up – a fly ball that doesn't travel far but does go high

Postgame – after the game has finished

Postseason – the playoffs

Relief Pitcher – reliever; a pitcher brought in to relieve another pitcher during a game

Right Field – part of outfield on the right of center field if looking from home plate

Right Fielder – the outfielder who plays defense in the area of right field

Run – a score in baseball when a player runs through all of the bases and makes it safely back to home plate; baseball scores are counted by runs

Save – when a relief pitcher, usually the closer, maintains the lead successfully until the end of the game; certain criteria must be met before a save is credited

Second Base – the base behind the pitcher; the second base a baserunner needs to touch to score a run

Second Baseman – the defensive player who fields the area closest to second base

Series – a set of games between two teams, typically three or four games in a row

Shortstop – the fielding position between second and third base; considered the most demanding defensive position

Single – a one-base hit

Skipper – Skip; field manager

Slider – fast pitch with a slight curve opposite to the direction of the throwing arm

Starting Pitcher – the first pitcher in the game for each team; starting pitchers are expected to pitch for a large part of each game, so they usually rest for three to five days between starts

Strength Training – weightlifting to increase strength and power and improve speed, agility, and coordination

Strike – when a batter doesn't hit the ball when swinging; when a batter doesn't swing at a pitch that lands in the strike zone; when a foul ball is hit with a strike count of less than two

Strike Zone – volume of space above home plate and between the batter's knees and the middle of their torso; pitches that land here without the batter swinging count as a strike

Strikeout – three strikes in one plate appearance; qualifies as an out

Sweep – winning all the games in a series

Tag — when a fielder reaches to touch the baserunner either with a live ball or the glove holding a live ball; called a tag out when the fielder tags the baserunner before they reach the base

Third Base — the base to the left of the pitcher when looking from home plate; the third base a baserunner needs to touch to score a run

Third Baseman — the defensive player who fields the area closest to third base

Three Up, Three Down — when only three batters face a pitcher during an inning, meaning the three outs are obtained on the first three batters

Top of the Inning — the first half of an inning in which the away team bats

Triple — a three-base hit

Triple A — the highest level of play in Minor League Baseball; each team has an affiliated A, AA, and AAA team

Umpire — ump; in charge of the game; makes the calls on strikes, balls, fouls, catches, and when a batter safely makes it to base

WAG — abbreviation for wives and girlfriends; wives and girlfriends of the players

Walk — when a player advances to base after a pitcher throws four balls

Walk-Off — when the home team immediately wins the game when they score a run in the bottom of the final inning

World Series — the championship in major league baseball; a best of seven series to determine the best of the United States and Canada

About the Author

Ashley Bow is an indie author based out of the suburbs of Pittsburgh. A 2013 graduate of West Liberty University, Ashley earned a Bachelor of Science in Business Administration with a specialization in Marketing. In her personal life, she is a stay-at-home mom to two boys and has been married to her high school sweetheart since 2015. She enjoys both reading and writing romance novels and is now affording herself the opportunity to share her works with others.